The Devil's Luck

THE DEVIL'S DUE

JAYCE CARTER

The Devil's Due
ISBN # 978-1-80250-556-6
©Copyright Jayce Carter 2023
Cover Art by Kelly Martin ©Copyright August 2023
Interior text design by Claire Siemaszkiewicz
Totally Bound Publishing

Published in 2023 by Totally Bound Publishing, United Kingdom.

Totally Bound Publishing is an imprint of Totally Entwined Group Limited.

Totally Bound Publishing books by Jayce Carter

The Omega's Alphas
Owned by the Alphas
Shared by the Alphas
Saved by the Alphas
Protected by Her Alphas
Caught by Her Alphas
Tamed by the Alphas
Claimed by the Alphas
Exposed by Her Alphas
Trained by the Alphas
Reclaimed by Her Alphas

Ready or Not
Fake It 'til You Make It
Opposites Attract
Third Time Lucky
Enemies Closer

Grave Concerns
Grave Robbing and Other Hobbies
Hell Raising and Other Pastimes
Saving the World and Other Bad Ideas

Dark Sanctuary
Bound by Fear
Trapped by Doubt
Buried by Despair

Nemesis
The Corpse Princess
The Resurrected Queen

Larkwood Academy
Silenced
Whispers
Screaming

The Devil's Luck
A Devil of a Time
Devil May Care
Run Like the Devil
The Devil's Due

Collections
Sun, Sea and Sinful Delights
Secret Santa: To Catch a Fox
Cupid's Academy: Stolen
Hot Bite: Summer Trips and Other Reasons to Get Naked

THE DEVIL'S DUE

Dedication

To my dear, wonderfully supportive friend, E.
You may send me to horny jail,
but you never judge me
<3

Chapter One

"Huh, heaven is a lot nicer than I would have figured." I closed my eyes and tipped my head back, savoring the feeling of the sun on my skin.

Or, rather, whatever light source they had here. Given I was in the Plains, it wasn't the sun.

Which sure was the one place I'd never figured I'd get to.

With the life I'd lived, hell hadn't been a shock to me, but heaven? Good people ended up here, and I hadn't ever fool myself into thinking I belonged in such a place.

"I miss the Chasm," Yazmor said from beside me. "When you breathe in there, ash sort of coats your throat and tongue."

"And you think that's a good thing?"

He shrugged, tucking his hands into the pocket at the front of his hoodie sweater. "It makes me feel like I'm back home."

For Yazmor—a remnant from an old version of the world—home meant a place that didn't exist anymore.

I recalled what I'd seen of his world, the universe that had come and gone so long ago that no one else remembered it. Smoke, ash and fire had filled the landscape, so I could understand how that might make him nostalgic.

"Well, I'm planning to enjoy this sun and fresh air. Who knows if I'll get a chance again."

"Are you planning on dying or something?"

"I didn't plan to die the first time, but that didn't stop it from happening. I've learned that no one really plans to die—it just happens."

Yazmor bumped his shoulder against mine, making me trip slightly from the impact. "Yeah, well, I don't plan on letting that happen."

From anyone else, that would have seemed like some empty boast. Coming from Yazmor, though? If anyone had the ability to keep death at bay, it'd be him.

I glanced at him and fought my smile. He was back to himself, and it was hard to believe just how awkward things had been so recently.

Our trip through the Path—the only way to get from the Chasm to the Plains—had twisted all five of us. None had reacted as bad as Yazmor. He'd lost himself to his other form, unable to keep his human one. Worse, he'd pulled away, putting distance between himself and the rest of us.

He hadn't been the only one to struggle. I'd been so quick to doubt myself, afraid to make any choices in case they were the wrong ones, in case someone else suffered because of it. Gorrin had turned even more over-protective than usual. I was lucky we were stuck there, because if he'd been on Earth, he'd have surrounded me in bubble wrap and never let me out of his sight. Tyrus had let his paranoia run wild, causing him to hoard goods and watch us all as though we were planning to fuck him over. And Hale?

He walked ahead of me, his jacket off, which showed his tattoos in the sunlight. He had been terrified that I'd betray him, had looked at everything I'd done or said, looking for proof that I would hurt him.

I could understand each of their behaviors, their fears, which the Path had played upon until they could hardly recall the uneasy trust we'd found.

When we'd finally gotten here, to the Plains, that heavy feeling had let up. Still, it was a lot harder to move past the things that had happened, the things we'd all admitted, the sides of ourselves and one another that we didn't love or want to examine.

Worse, we all looked like hell. Gorrin had warned us *not* to use our powers unless we had no other choice. Angels and Hubis could feel if we did, and while a little could get overlooked, using our powers too much would get us caught.

"So, this is heaven," I said for what had to be the hundredth time already. I just couldn't fully believe it.

"Were you expecting clouds and cherubs?" Yazmor asked.

"I mean, I wouldn't mind any of that. This just seems too normal, like we could be in any little town. Why does this place look like that? Doesn't it pre-date this sort of place on Earth?"

"Well, some of the Plains changes, just like the Chasm does. Areas can look different based on the people there. Also, since angels do a lot of work on Earth, they influence human trends."

"You're saying Hubis wastes angels' time by making them decide whether adobe or brick are going to be on trend? They've got nothing better to do than that?"

"Of course not—that would be crazy! Angels care more about style trends. Remember those super baggy pants with the tall platform sneakers that were popular in the nineties? Yeah, those were *all* Azael."

That was before my time, but I recalled seeing pictures of teens wearing them. "Well, now I'm even more glad he's gone."

"Right? If you have that sort of power, you should use it better. That's why I made those little keychain pet video games big."

I would have laughed him off—most people did—but I'd gotten to know Yazmor well enough to guess he was telling the truth. The more outlandish something sounded, the more likely it had actually happened.

We'd only been in the Plains for about an hour, according to Tyrus' watch. Despite turning my phone off in the Path, it had still ended up drained. *Leave it to the Path to still be fucking me over.*

Gorrin had taken the lead as soon as we'd arrived, his comfort here reminding me that this was his home, that he knew this place better than any of us.

Fuck, he knew this place better than any other place.

It made me glance his way, to see his wings out and pure and almost sparkling in the light. They'd appeared as soon as we'd arrived.

Were they harder to hide here? I didn't dare ask, because Gorrin had one hell of a *do not cross* on that subject.

Gorrin had been rather strange about his angel form in general, as though it made him uncomfortable. I had a feeling that being here, in the Plains, was the worst time to question him.

Something moved to the side of us, making the brush rustle. It was the sort of slight shifting that came when a person was trying hard *not* to get noticed.

After dealing with Guardian and his overly enthusiastic tentacles, my nerves were shot. It meant I reached out and grabbed for the person, then hauled them from the bush they hid in.

Instead of the weird shit I'd dealt with in the Path, however, I didn't at all expect to find a child in front of me, my hand wrapped around their thin arm.

It was a young girl, her eyes wide as she stared up at me. "I'm sorry," she rushed out, not bothering to pull away as if she knew it would prove useless.

And a glance around told me why she might just react that way. The Lords and I looked rough when we were at our best, and after barely surviving the Path?

We were *far* from our best.

Our clothing was tattered and dirty. Dirt and blood streaked our faces. Enough time had passed that our injuries had healed, but that didn't remove the stains from our fight with Guardian.

If *I* saw us somewhere, I'd have run in the other direction, too.

And that didn't even go into Hale and his tattoos and piercings or the tattoos on my face, along with my green hair.

Basically?

We were one hell of a hot mess.

I smiled, pretending that'd soften my appearance and our whole vibe. "What's your name?"

The girl swallowed hard, then answered in a small voice, "Emma."

She appeared to be seven, perhaps, and rather slim. She had long dark hair and matching dark eyes. In fact, she looked a lot like Tyrus. However, the most notable feature was the way her lip on the left was tucked up, toward her nostrils. I was pretty sure it was called a cleft lip, though I'd never really seen it before in real life.

I didn't take much to not react to her appearance. I might have been surprised if I'd still been alive, but after five years in the Chasm, with damned who were twisted into almost unrecognizable forms, nothing really threw me anymore. "Emma is such a pretty name. I'm Loch."

Emma glanced at Yazmor, her gaze suspicious and unsure. At least that told me she had some smarts.

"My name is Yazmor." He crouched in front of Emma, giving her one of those smiles that unnerved normal people.

Except she seemed taken by it. Maybe it was similar to how children liked cartoon characters with exaggerated features — that sure described Yazmor, after all.

"Why were you hiding from us?"

"I thought you might get mad at me."

"I'm never mad," Yazmor lied. "But you've been following us for the last ten minutes."

I turned my gaze on him, frowning because I'd totally missed that. In fact, I'd stupidly thought I'd done so well, that I'd managed to spot her when no one else had. *Turns out I'm a step behind, like always.*

"Not a lot of people live this far out, so I was curious who you were."

"I don't like a lot of people." Yazmor balanced on the balls of his feet, not wavering in the least despite the awkward position. "So I prefer quiet places. You look like the type of person who'd understand that. I bet you always have your nose in a book or your head in the clouds."

Some of the shadows fell from Emma's expression, a sure sign that Yazmor had won her over. It seemed he could charm anyone if he really wanted to.

Well, he sure charmed me, didn't he?

Emma nodded quickly, then reached for a book I hadn't noticed before, one clutched in her other hand. "I was reading this one when I heard you pass by. It's about a dragon and a princess."

"Does a knight come and save her?" Tyrus asked as he walked over, his tone somehow softer than I was used to. In fact, despite the way he could intimidate the hardest of people, he seemed almost kind as he spoke to Emma.

Emma shook her head, pulling the book against her chest. "Of course not! She saves the dragon from the knight, and her and the dragon live happily ever after."

A sharp bark of laughter escaped me before I could even think about it. I wiped my fingers under my eyes when the laughing fit made my eyes water, then leaned forward a bit as I caught my breath. "Sorry, but that is so my kind of story. Who wants the knight when they can have the monster, huh?"

I peered to the side for a moment to see Yazmor and Tyrus with similar grins on their faces, as though they understood exactly what I meant. If my men weren't considered monsters, then nothing deserved that title.

I stood back up, then winced when my stomach decided that was the right moment to growl, the sound loud, even above the chirping of birds and general relaxing atmosphere that sounded like a sound machine used for meditation.

Emma stared at my stomach in surprise, then looked up at my face again. "If you're hungry, why don't you come eat at our house?"

"Our?" Tyrus asked. "Who is 'our'?"

"Obviously it's her and her family," I said.

Tyrus lifted an eyebrow, as if telling me to think it through. Only when he did, did his point hit me.

This was the Plains—basically heaven. It meant people didn't grow up and live together and have kids like I was used to.

It also meant that Emma, despite appearing like a child, might very well have been impossibly old.

Emma didn't seem fazed by Tyrus' question or my stupid guess, which thrilled me. The last thing I wanted was to show up in heaven and make the first child I ran across cry.

"I live in a house with a few others. It isn't very far from here, and we have plenty of food there." She paused, then frowned. "Are you new? Most new souls appear in the center of the palace."

"Yes, we're new," Tyrus acknowledged.

"Did you get here together?"

"The five of us met out here," he said, the lie slipping from him so easily that it reminded me not to ever trust Tyrus. Even I couldn't catch it when he lied.

"Five?" Emma twisted, staring at Hale as if she hadn't noticed him before. Maybe watching me had so distracted her that she hadn't seen us all.

She showed no real reaction to Hale, despite how he looked. That wasn't even close to the case when she finally spotted Gorrin coming back, since he'd walked ahead quite a while.

Emma stumbled backward, her feet tangling into the brush that lined the walkway, so she ended up on her ass. "I'm sorry," she rushed out, her voice thin and terrified. "I didn't realize you had an angel with you. I would never have spied on you if I had, would never have done something so disrespectful."

Her words rushed from her so fast that I struggled to understand them.

Not that Gorrin appeared all that surprised when he finally reached us, where Emma still scooted away in the dirt without taking her eyes off him.

"Be at ease," he assured her. "I am not angry."

She went to speak, but nothing came out at first, as if her throat had tightened to the point where even words couldn't escape. She pressed her lips together then swallowed before trying again. "I'm sure you don't want to come to my place. It isn't what you're used to, and it isn't nice enough for someone like yourself to step into it." She didn't look at him, her gaze down, her voice trembling.

Gorrin sighed, his wings shifting to show how much he didn't care for this reaction. Of course, he also didn't seem surprised by it, which made no sense to me.

On Earth, people viewed angels as saviors, as holy creatures meant to protect and watch over us. Sure, I'd been dead long enough to know that was total bullshit. Angels were like every other type of being — some were good and some were absolute shit. Still, I'd figured that of all places, in the Plains, they'd be loved.

Instead, the terror in Emma's face told the truth.

Gorrin reached his hand out, bending down to offer it to Emma. "I would appreciate any food you could spare and some clothing if you have it."

Emma stared at his hand but didn't move to take it. "We don't have anything you would find worthy."

Gorrin let out a sigh then retracted his hand. He must have realized Emma wouldn't accept his help. "I assure you, whatever you have will be most appreciated."

Emma scrambled to her feet but kept Gorrin in her line of sight. His final words had given her no way out, no way to refuse. Even if it was clear she wanted him nowhere near her home, to deny him now would be to go against an angel, and even if I didn't know much about the Plains, I had a strong feeling that *that* just wasn't done.

"Okay," she said softly, moving around us, giving herself a large swath of space. "It's just up this way a little farther. Come on." She walked quickly, looking tiny and fragile compared to the five of us, especially with the way her shoulders trembled.

Yazmor, Hale and Tyrus followed her, leaving Gorrin and I a few steps behind.

"What was that about?" I asked him, keeping my voice low so it didn't carry to Emma.

Gorrin closed his hands into fists, and somehow, he seemed just as bothered as Emma was. While it was fear from her, he held on to frustration. "I told you before that the Plains are not the heaven people believe this place to be. That includes angels."

"She's terrified of you. Why?"

"Because she is smart. Anyone who wishes to survive in the Plains should avoid angels. If you believe Azael to be alone in his cruelty, you are sadly mistaken. The most dangerous things here are the beings who appear just like me."

He didn't wait for a response before he walked off, following Emma and the others, leaving me to stare at his back and his wings, which still fluttered as if to display his unease.

All the time I'd spent wanting to get here, and it suddenly didn't feel like the reward I'd hoped for.

Maybe heaven really wasn't all it was cracked up to be...

* * * *

Hale

The way Emma had carried on about her place not being good enough for Gorrin had made me think she'd undersold herself.

As it turned out, she'd oversold it.

The place could barely be called a house. The roof had holes in it, and the windows were all boarded up. If I'd seen a kid living in a place like this on Earth, I'd have immediately kicked the shit out of whoever should have been taking care of them.

Yet here we were, in fucking *heaven*, and they had a kid living in this?

"It's not that bad," Emma whispered, shame filling her words.

I tried to clear the look from my face. The last fucking thing she needed was for me to make her feel bad. How often had idiots offered me pity like that while not doing shit to help. "I've lived in worse places—trust me. All a person really needs is a place that keeps the rain and wind out."

Emma shrugged as she moved deeper into the single large room, with beds set up in areas along the outside edges of the space, almost like small camping areas. "We fix the holes when we can, and we've got lots of blankets. Before I found this place and the other people who live here, I mostly slept outside, so this is a big step up."

"And that was safe?" Tyrus asked, slipping into his, 'I'm going to fix this,' mode he usually was in.

"There aren't a lot of people this far out. Most people stay in the city, close to the palace."

I sure as fuck heard that evasion. She hadn't answered about it being safe, not really, which meant it wasn't safe, but she'd done it anyway.

I cut a glance Gorrin's way, wanting to strangle that asshole. This was *his* world, and from what little I'd seen, it fucking sucked. Might as well blame him for that.

Tension lined Loch's eyes, a sure sign the girl didn't like this shit any more than I did. Then again, Loch and I understood each other in a way the others didn't, had a shared background unlike the others.

Tyrus had been used to being in charge for a long time, had grown up with rich and doting parents. Yazmor wasn't even from this world, and Gorrin hadn't really grown up at all since Hubis had created him as the first angel.

Loch and I had been raised dirt-fucking poor, amongst the filth of the Earth, forced to cheat and steal and struggle just to survive. We understood one another — and Emma, it seemed — in a way the others never would.

The back door of the place opened, and a woman walked in, brushing her hands on the front of her pants, leaving dirty prints behind. "You're back early, Emma." She spoke as she moved, without looking up, as if it never occurred to her that it might not be Emma there.

Which really sold the fact that not many people were out here.

She sucked in a sharp breath when she finally did look up, when her gaze settled on Gorrin — or more specifically, his wings — first. She didn't run the way Emma had tried to, and I liked the woman immediately when her first reaction was to grab Emma and yank the young girl behind her.

"What are you doing here?" the woman asked, her voice careful but strong.

"My stomach," Loch said, and right on cue, it grumbled as if to make the point for her.

"I said they could eat here. I met them out on the road," Emma said from behind the woman's back.

The woman tried to look at each of us, but her gaze kept returning to Gorrin as if he were the only one who could hold her attention. Then again, to her, she had one angel and three souls. We were chump change in her eyes. "I can't believe that an angel doesn't have better places to go than here…"

Her words made me snort, a balancing between respectful and rude as fuck. I could hear the battle, the desire to tell Gorrin to get the fuck out of her place, but her fear of what he might do if she didn't treat him with the utmost reverence.

"I told him that," Emma whispered. "He still said he wanted to come here."

The woman twisted and crouched, staring straight into Emma's eyes. She lowered her voice, but it wasn't nearly quiet enough for me to not hear what she said. The benefits of being a Demon Lord included fantastic hearing.

"That isn't just any angel, Emma. That is *Gorrin*, the first."

"I didn't recognize him," Emma said.

"He's been gone since before you came here, but he's the strongest of them. You should know better than to invite strangers here, especially angels." The woman grasped Emma's hand, holding it tightly as if she wanted to pull her away from all of us immediately.

She seemed smart enough to know that she couldn't outrun us, though. In fact, I could almost see in her eyes the plan forming as she worked out what to do.

If I had to guess, I'd say she'd feed us, give us what we wanted and needed, play nice until we turned our backs just long enough for her to grab Emma and bolt.

"I am not planning on harming any of you," Gorrin said, his voice the same flat one he used when talking at underlings. It might have seemed mean, but fuck knew I understood.

People as terrified as Emma and that woman wouldn't listen to reason. They saw Gorrin as an enemy, as a threat, and him reassuring them wouldn't change shit.

It was like a man-eating tiger swearing up and down that it wouldn't eat someone. History showed the tiger's true nature, and only an idiot would believe what came out of their mouth.

The woman rose and kept Emma behind her and out of sight. "Of course — our home is yours. I'm afraid we don't have much, but what little we have you are welcome to."

"We don't need much," Loch said. "And we aren't freeloaders, either. I can help cook."

"We need some clothing as well," Tyrus added. "We're strong, though, so please allow us to complete some chores to repay you."

The woman pressed her lips together, all the refusal bright and clear in her expression. Still, she couldn't outright say no, so she nodded. "We don't need any help but thank you. I'll have Emma go and see what clothing might fit you while I get food from the garden and pantry. I'll have something cooked up and ready in the next hour or so, so please rest until then." She leaned in to talk to Emma, whispering something that I couldn't catch.

I didn't really need to hear it to know it was a warning, though. Emma nodded in response then headed out through the back door. Only once she'd left did the woman take her first real, deep breath, as though without Emma in the crosshairs she could finally relax.

"Please, take the time to rest here," she said, then turned and left through that same door.

Loch took off after her, but Gorrin caught her arm. "Where are you going?"

"To help."

"She said not to."

"So? She said that because she's terrified of you. What better way to prove we aren't as bad as she thinks than by making ourselves useful?" Loch peered around the large falling-apart building. "I mean, obviously they could use some help."

Gorrin released her. "Okay but be cautious. Angels are rarely out this far, but that doesn't mean it can't happen."

Loch nodded before following the woman out of the back door, leaving the four of us in the place alone.

"Aren't they worried we'll steal something?" Tyrus asked.

"Nah," I answered. "They know there isn't anything here worth stealing. If they've got shit worth anything, it'll be hidden somewhere else."

My words took me back to my own childhood. I'd lived in group homes as far back as I could recall, and we'd all learned early that anything of value needed to be fiercely guarded. I still recalled a hollowed-out area of a wall in an abandoned building where I'd stashed my valuables.

Of course, being only six at the time, those *valuables* were less than twenty bucks in cash, some non-perishable foods and an extra set of clothing. Still, that was important in that world. A little bit of food could mean the difference between life and death back then.

I'd stored them away like a squirrel, making damn sure no one knew about them in case I had to take off for some reason.

Tyrus turned toward Gorrin, his expression severe. "Should we expect similar reactions to you while we're here?"

"Most likely."

"Can't you just hide those fucking wings of yours like you do in the Chasm?" I asked.

"No. Being here makes it almost impossible to hide them. Besides, even without seeing them, the spirits here can sense my powers. They can spot me as an angel even if I could hide my wings."

"So fucking much for being able to sneak around," I muttered. "You didn't think to mention before that we'd be that fucking obvious with you here?"

"I had been considering that," Gorrin answered. "The thing is, in the Plains, what you just saw is common. The spirits avoid angels whenever possible. They are likely to spot me and take little notice of anything else. That may work in our favor. Terrified people ask fewer questions."

"And you don't think anyone will gossip about Gorrin strolling around with four others? That they will not think that is rather strange?" Tyrus asked, crossing his arms and cocking up one eyebrow.

"Why would they? You could walk through the Chasm, and no one found that strange. Seeing an angel in the Plains is normal."

"What if they see *us*?" I gestured at myself. "I don't isn't exactly have a normal, blend into the background look. You don't think anyone's going to recognize me?"

Gorrin shook his head. "The spirits here have never been to the Chasm, so they will have no idea who or what exists there. Most will not even know that there are Demon Lords let alone who they are or what they look like."

"What about angels?"

"Azael handled trips to the Chasm prior to his death, and since then, it has only been a single angel who has done so. That limits the people who have seen any of you to only Hubis himself and that single angel, and since that angel took over Azael's position, he will stay in the palace. Until we reach the city, we should be safe. I would suggest you remove your piercings, at least."

I grumbled, even if I knew he was right. Since I'd died with the piercings, the holes wouldn't close up, but fuck did I dislike the idea of not wearing them. Those bits of metal felt like a part of me, an armor I really enjoyed having, but that didn't matter. They'd call attention to me.

Instead of arguing, I went about taking them out.

"And when we get to the palace?" Tyrus asked. "What then?"

"I cannot give you specifics yet, but I do have a plan in the works." Gorrin's expression was so flat that it would have given nothing away to any other person. I'd known him for a long damn time, though, so I could read him better than most people.

That is a lot of uncertainty there. Doesn't seem like he's too confident in whatever plan he's got.

I peered up to try to release the anxiety inside me, the part of me that wanted to know the plan so I could do *something*. A ray of light poured in, making me flinch against the brightness.

Gorrin headed toward the front door.

"Where are you going?" I asked.

"As if you planned to allow them to continue living in this state. We should fix the roof first." He didn't wait to see if I agreed, and that annoyed me more.

I didn't love that he felt as if he knew me, even if he had been right.

Tyrus didn't move, so I paused to look at him. "Not planning on helping?"

He undid the buttons at his cuffs, then rolled up his sleeves. "I don't care for heights. You two handle the roof. I'll see what I can do about the windows. Yazmor can..." Tyrus looked around as if realizing for the first time Yazmor had disappeared on us.

The sound of a pissed-off bull from outside made me sigh. *Sounds like Yazmor is once again petting an animal that isn't all that into it.*

Of course, as annoying as he was, I had little doubt that after getting himself gored, he'd do some chores out there.

Who would have figured Demon Lords would end up as handymen? Part of me wondered what Emma and that woman would think if they knew the truth, if they realized that the demons who ran the Chasm were here fixing up their place? I even found myself craving that credit, wanting to see Emma smile when she saw it, wanting to see that woman let down her guard and see me as...

I shook away the idea as soon as it occurred to me. I knew my place, had accepted it. I was a scary-looking delinquent, and it didn't matter what I did — the world would never see me as anything else.

Chapter Two

Loch

"I said you don't need to help," the woman said, her nerves obviously frayed by my appearance out back.

"Please," I pressed. "I don't like to take advantage of people and I don't like needing to owe anyone anything. Just let me help."

She let out a big sigh, the sort I recognized easily. People did that a lot when they were around me, as if my antics were always frustrating to the point of near disbelief. "But you're here with *Gorrin*. I can't ask you to do anything. It wouldn't be right."

"Yeah, well, trust me—being around Gorrin isn't the honor you seem to think it is." I muttered the words softly, trying to be careful not to admit to too much.

"He is a holy being here. Any angel deserves the most respect possible, and he was the *first*. He is second only to Hubis himself."

"*Holy being?*" I couldn't keep the disbelief out of my voice when I tried to picture Gorrin as she did. What

I'd wanted to say was that Gorrin had a terrible sense of humor, was far too over-protective, and I'd once seen him pick his nose when he thought no one was looking.

If he was holy, he was a shit example of it.

Then I considered what I'd done with Gorrin, and those things were a fucking long ways from anything holy.

My cheeks burned, and I coughed into my hand to cover my reaction.

The woman stared at me, and the way she did made me think she was a lot smarter than she liked to let on.

My kind of woman.

"My name is Mae." She peered over my shoulder, toward the house. "Is Gorrin forcing you to be with him?"

"What? No." Her question surprised me so much that I nearly shouted the denial. Even the thought of Gorrin forcing himself on me was unthinkable. He was, if anything, *far* too careful around me.

Mae didn't seem to take my word, nodding toward the back of the property before walking that way. "Let's talk more when we're farther away from the house."

I followed her in silence, taking in the surroundings. While the house was rundown, the actual property was quiet and relaxing. Fuck, I'd almost call it picturesque. A soft breeze blew through the grass and trees, and the small path we followed wound through the nature. The path was narrow and kept clear only due to people walking along it.

It took a few minutes before we reached a large shed, one that was better kept than the main house. The roof was solid, and it lacked any holes for wind to blow into.

"You're wondering why we fix this and not the house, right?" At my look, Mae smiled, the expression softer than it had been when around the men. "You have an expressive face. We keep our canned goods and other foods here. Those are more important than where we sleep. We can't die from exposure here, but we can from a lack of goods."

Food mattered more than a dry place to sleep? Given that it didn't get very cold, I guessed that made sense.

Shelving covered each wall and more sat in lines in the center, filling the entire shed. Glass jars full of all sorts of ingredients were on the shelves, all nicely organized and none showing signs of dust or dirt. I had no idea if that was because Mae cleaned often or if the Plains just didn't have an issue with dust.

"Why do you have so much? If you don't have bad weather, why do you need to stock up so much?"

"We don't have winter here, but we get snow and rain sometimes."

"Snow in heaven? That just seems mean."

"This *isn't* heaven." Mae's words came out tinged in bitterness. It lacked the joking that the men and I used when we said that, and it reminded me of the fear Mae had when meeting us—especially Gorrin. She sighed, then kept speaking. "We don't have regular weather cycles, but the weather is connected to Hubis and his moods. So when he wishes it or when he is feeling overly upset, snow or rain happens. It is unpredictable, and it can kill our crops."

"So does everyone here just grow their own food?"

She shook her head. "The cities have stores, supplied mostly by angels and sometimes by other farms. Only those who live outside the city have to fend for ourselves."

"So why live out here?"

Mae turned, staring as if she could see the city rather than just the wall of the shed. "There are a few reasons people live out here. Some of us decide we don't care for living there, in the center of all that, under the thumbs of someone else. Others are cast out as undesirable."

"Undesirable?"

"The angels value order above all else, and anything that falls outside of that order is seen as unsightly."

My thoughts went to Emma. The sight of her, her lip tucked up, made me frown.

Mae nodded. "Emma was driven from the city. The angels found the sight of her to be unwelcome."

"Do they always drive out anyone who isn't perfect?"

"No. Sometimes they simply kill them, sometimes they require they cover the imperfection. It's why hoods are so common in the city. Lots of spirits leave there but give up when forced to live out here. Life in the city can be stifling, but life out here is hard in a different way. It feels like getting cast out, like being thrown away. Some souls just can't tolerate getting thrown out of paradise."

I recalled the way I'd stared at the gateway in the meeting house, the stone arch through which Hubis and Azael had traveled. I'd wanted nothing more than to cross through that, to get into heaven. I'd dreamed about it, felt a pull so difficult to resist.

That had happened before I'd ever seen the Plains, so I could imagine just how difficult it would be to endure being cast out after spending time there.

"So you left the city? You weren't thrown out?"

Mae smiled, sadness coloring the expression before she turned her back on me and ran her fingers along the glass jars. "I wouldn't say that. I was given a choice — run or die. I chose to run."

"Why?"

"I asked if Gorrin had you against your will." She didn't continue, but did she really need to? Her previous question, her fear, it all made more sense.

"Do the angels..."

"They believe in complete obedience — in *all* things. Most take what they want and ignore the feelings of others. Most people opt to give in, assuming they even get that option. Sometimes angels simply use Euphoria to get what they want."

"What's that?"

She shook her head. "It doesn't matter. The angel who wanted me didn't use it, and I wasn't about to become a plaything for anyone."

"What happened?"

She turned back toward me, two jars in her hands, the shed too dark for me to easily tell what they were. "I bid my time until she was sated, then grabbed a knife from the table and drove it into her wing." A chilling smile spread across Mae's lips, as if she couldn't stop herself from recalling it fondly. "You see, angels scar, because they have bodies. I buried the knife into the hinge of her wing, and from what I hear, even to this day, no feathers will grow in that spot."

I swallowed hard as I pictured the anger that would inspire in something as vain as angels seemed to be. "And they just let you go after that?"

Mae let out a laugh that held more pain than humor. "She was more concerned with getting to a healer to see if it could be fixed than in punishing me. I was brought before Hubis, and I expected him to destroy me on the spot. I had harmed one of his holy beings on purpose — that doesn't usually go unpunished."

I recalled Hubis' lesson for me, when he'd forced me to live through the memory of a horrific attack after Azael's death, and I shuddered. He certainly had a lack of mercy. "But since you're here, I'm guessing he didn't do that?"

"No. I don't know why, but he told me that if I left, as long as I fled from the city and never returned, I could keep my life. If I ever came back, however, I'd forfeit it."

I narrowed my eyes as though that could make me understand him, could help me to figure out what he meant or why he'd do such a thing. He'd proven to me that he had no issue with punishing others, and that he treasured order above anything else.

So why would he let Mae live? Why cast her out instead of destroying her? I'd bet the angel had screamed for her head, had wanted to destroy her, yet Mae still lived. It meant not only had Hubis not killed Mae, but he must have told the angel not to touch her either, at least so long as she didn't return to the city.

Why?

"I don't know," Mae said, making me realize I'd zoned out. "You're wondering why he let me go, but I can't answer. It doesn't make sense, and even now, after so long out here, I don't know. However, when I came out here, when I saw so many others who had gotten thrown out, who had nowhere to go, I created this place. I can't ever return to the city, but the longer I live in the outskirts, the less I care. Sometimes..."

When she didn't continue, I prodded her. "Sometimes what?"

"Sometimes I wonder if the Plains is really the good place people think it is. How would we ever know the difference, right? I wonder if the city is really hell, and maybe the closest any of us can get to true paradise is out here?"

I thought back to the Chasm, her words reminding me that I *knew* more than most people here. The spirits

30

in the Plains came here without seeing the Chasm, without seeing demons or damned or anything of that sort. Only a few had witnessed as much as I had, had seen both heaven and hell and the darkness that spanned between the two.

And yet, despite all I had seen, despite everything I'd experienced, I wasn't sure I really understood more than anyone else.

The only thing I knew for absolute certainty was that however this system worked, whatever the rules, it fucking sucked and I wouldn't put up with it anymore.

This shit needed to end — *now*.

* * * *

Yazmor

"You know, getting gored isn't much fun."

A smile tugged at my lips when I heard Loch's voice, and I saw no good reason to fight it. Instead, I scratched the large bull under his chin. "Paul here would never gore me — would you, Paul?"

"You never think an animal will hurt you — then they always do." Even as she chastised me, Loch came up just beside me. The fact she still did this, that she treated me normally despite all she'd seen, helped melt any defense I might have built up against her.

Paul snorted in her direction, then stomped his hoof. He swung his head toward her, but no matter how much I liked the bull, I liked Loch far more.

I caught one of his huge horns and held him still with ease. "Bad bull. No hurting Loch. She is much too important to me."

Paul let out another huff, stamped his foot once more then backed away when I released him.

"Is he going to pout? He's like a two-thousand-pound beast and he's going to pout in the corner like a child?"

I wrapped an arm around Loch's waist, pulling her closer in case Paul decided to go for round two. "The larger something is, the easier it is to hurt their feelings."

"Why doesn't he like me? What did I ever do to him?"

"I think he likes me a little much and doesn't care for you because he's jealous."

"Figures. No one is ever jealous over me except a fucking bull." She paused, then glanced up at me, drawing me in with her bright blue eyes. "Is that your type?"

"No. It would never work with him and me."

"I've heard of donkey shows, but I don't even want to think about how something like that would mess a person up…" She shuddered, and yet again, her humor pleased me. Loch was easily as random and chaotic as I was, which was likely why I adored her as I did.

"Oh, that's not it. It's more that he is a horrible conversationalist. Plus, given the nice fence I just fixed up, he can't go very far, and I suspect I'd get lonely fast if I were all alone."

Loch elbowed me playfully, then snuggled closer to my side. It was the first time we'd been together alone since the Path, since she saw the real me in all its horror, since I lost myself to my old form, to the predator I was at my core.

"How are you all right with being here with me?" I whispered.

"Well, I mean, I'm not really an outdoorsy type, and I'm sure as fuck no country girl, but I can manage to be at least this close to livestock." She not-so-subtly gave me an out, an ability to play along with her words and let my question go.

But I couldn't. I'd done that my entire existence, had played off everything as unimportant, had floated through each world without caring about any of it. I cared about *this*, about her, about whatever we had between us.

"You saw what I really am. I didn't think you'd be comfortable around me again, especially alone."

She pulled away, and for a moment I thought she'd leave. A sudden bottomless fear struck me that I'd pushed too far, that by asking her this, I might have made her reconsider.

Except, she didn't go. She turned and looked into my face, her expression having that strength that ran through her, the unexpected toughness that filled her. Despite how small she appeared, how fragile she seemed at times, she was one of the strongest creatures I'd ever known.

I had an amazing amount of power, due both to the souls bound to me and the fact I had existed for so long, had gained knowledge and power through the endless years.

Despite that, when I looked at her, I knew she had an edge inside of her I lacked, that she could outlive me due to sheer stubbornness. Loch *refused* to give in. Even when things appeared hopeless, even when any sane person could see no path forward, even when life crushed her until she could no longer stand, she dug her fingers into the dirt beneath her and crawled.

"I'm not afraid of you," she said without an ounce of hesitation. She reached out and caught my hand in hers, squeezing it as if to prove the point that she planned to go nowhere. "I know who and what you are, and now that I've seen you without that mask, now that

I've seen everything you've tried to hide, can't you believe me?"

I refused to look away from her eyes even when I wanted to hide, when I wanted to turn my face from hers. "Why? Just tell me that and I'll drop it and never bring it up again. Explain to me why you're still here, why you trust me, and I will accept it."

Loch tilted her head, the action reminding me of a dog who heard a sound that made no sense. It was an adorable reaction, though a comparison I had a feeling she wouldn't like so much.

Finally, she smiled, the expression causing a crease that changed the shape of the tattoos on her cheeks. Her smile was lopsided, causing more distortion to the devil wing than the angel wing. "Do you remember when Cain drugged us?"

A vicious sound escaped me at that memory, at the way my body had turned heavy and unwieldy. I disliked having my control taken from me, and that was exactly what he had done.

Loch continued to speak. "You didn't give up. You crawled toward me, even when it was clear you couldn't move much. You could have tried to escape, but you didn't. You wanted to get to me, no matter what it cost you." I went to respond, but she lifted her hand to silence me. "You did that over and over again. Even in your other form, even when you said you were a monster, you *always* put me first. You were the first one to find me when Guardian dragged me off, you found me again and again. That all showed me that even when you're at your most basic, even when you are entirely your original form, you still care about me." She smiled up at me, then set a hand on my cheek. "How could that *not* charm a girl?"

"But my true form —"

"Look, I want you in whatever form you're in. If you think being a tree-fucker bothers me, you don't know me that well."

Her words took a moment to filter through my brain, and when they did? I felt even more for her, the strange new feelings inside me not as bothersome as they were.

Confusing? Sure. I didn't understand the needs inside me, the things I wanted, but they didn't worry me as they had.

I'd told her that if she could explain why to me, I would accept it. I'd promised that and I wouldn't break it now. Loch was the only person I never wanted to lie to, who I never wanted to give a reason to doubt me.

I moved without thinking, tugging her closer, then bending down the short distance to her soft lips. I was sure I wasn't doing this right, but I didn't worry about it. I tried to connect with my human form, with the instincts buried deep inside it, as my lips moved against hers.

Her breath came out in a rush of surprise, but she hesitated for only a moment. It seemed her brain had to catch up, and as soon as it did, she slid her hands up my chest, then wrapped her arms around my neck, holding me closer.

I felt every inch of her body pressed tight against my own, the softness of hers against the hardness of mine, the differences so stark and interesting.

I still lacked the same drive that she had, that the others had, but even I could admit that this was nice. Her lips were warm, and a pleasant tingle ran through my body each place we touched.

Something wet slid along the seam of my lips, and after a moment, I realized it was her tongue. I parted for her, willing to give her access to anything she wanted. She teased the inside of my mouth, her motions soft and slow, giving me a chance to decide how I felt about it.

And my reaction showed that my human body enjoyed it all. An unfamiliar aching in my cock, a fullness there — it was new and different but not nearly as unsettling as I had feared.

Had it been anyone else, I doubted I would have reacted in such a way. Feeling as though someone else controlled my body would have sent me reeling.

Somehow, with Loch the source of this, I didn't struggle in such a way. I entrusted myself to her, believing that anything that occurred with her was worth the risk.

I rocked my hips forward, the touch testing and unsure, but the friction as I ground against her soft stomach drew a moan from Loch.

She broke the kiss and pressed her forehead against my chest, her breath fast and uneven. "Maybe this is enough."

"I thought you said you didn't mind being a tree-fucker." I kept the playfulness in my voice despite the vulgar words. Even though I was hard, even though I wanted to feel more, I found each interaction with her unbearably fun.

"I don't, but I have a feeling if we go any further here, Paul is going to decide he's had enough."

Her words made me peer back toward where the bull stomped his feet. Had I really failed to notice that? Had she distracted me so fully that even a two-thousand-pound bull no longer mattered to me?

I let out a laugh at my own stupidity, at the fun of doing something so reckless and chaotic and *new*.

"Fair enough." I pressed one last kiss to the top of her head.

After a moment, she looked up at me. "That was okay? You liked it?" That uncertainty in her made me smile, the sweetness there unexpected. Even at a time like this, she worried for me.

"You're the one with experience. I would have figured you'd notice my reaction and know what it meant." I allowed myself to roll my hips forward again to prove my point.

She hit my arm playfully, that uncertainty disappearing. "So we'll try again later? When we don't have an audience?"

"Absolutely." The quickness with which I responded surprised even me. In fact, I felt almost excited about it. "Then we can put the whole tree-fucking thing to the test."

Loch laughed and pulled away from me, straightening her clothing as if that put her on solid ground again. "I'm up for about anything—just be careful. I don't need splinters in any delicate areas." She winked once before turning and walking out of the barn, leaving me there with Paul.

I stared after her, my brain stuttering like she'd just moved the needle off a record, like it wasn't tracking properly anymore and now skipping around. Was this desire?

I ran my finger along my bottom lip, feeling the dampness left behind from our kiss, then laughed. "She's going to be the death of me, but what a way to go."

Chapter Three

Loch

Wearing clean clothes felt amazing. How was it that I could take for granted something so simple?

When we left for the Path, we hadn't brought much in the way of extra clothing. That which we did have ended up just layered for warmth. I didn't sweat as much as I did when alive, so I didn't get dirty as fast, but after all we had been through, I was glad to have something else to wear. Even the *new* clothing that I'd gotten from Cain had ended up thrashed in our fight with Guardian.

The items Mae had gathered were all nice enough, even if they didn't fit perfectly.

"How do you get these if you can't go to the city?" Gorrin took a seat at the last spot at the table, Mae placing food at the center.

She froze in place, as if time stopped, the way she reacted each time she had to talk directly to Gorrin. She seemed to try her hardest to ignore him the rest of the time, but when she heard his voice, she had to acknowledge his existence.

After a loud gulp, she spoke softly, with little feeling to her voice. "There are still a few people who come out of the city proper to trade. I keep extra clothing in lots of sizes on hand since I never know who might end up here." Her gaze darted toward Gorrin, but as quickly danced away.

I could almost hear her thinking aloud that *he* was the last person she'd expected.

"I have no intention to turn you in to anyone for trading with those from the city," Gorrin said.

He used a tone that implied he didn't appreciate *having* to say that.

"Believe it or not, I'm not worried about myself." Mae's words came out clipped, but their meaning was loud and clear.

Gorrin must have heard it as well, because his response came with a far softer tone. "I do not plan to turn in someone willing to trade with outcasts, either. I would gain nothing from such an action."

"In my experience, angels like to hold up their precious order no matter what. People don't need to do much wrong for angels to jump on the chance to punish them." Mae brought the last plate over, then took a seat on the other side of Emma, so the young girl sat between the two of us.

Emma had been absent the whole time we'd been here, and I had no doubt that had been intentional. Despite Mae acting at least somewhat polite in front of the men, she made it obvious that she didn't trust them.

"Where is everyone else?" Tyrus asked.

"It's just Emma and me," Mae said, the lie standing out.

Tyrus gestured around with his fork. "There are ten beds in this room, all with bedding and belongings. It would make no sense to keep up such space if others were not actively using them."

Mae narrowed her eyes, the expression telling me she was taking Tyrus far more seriously than she had before. Of course, without a suit, Tyrus lacked some of the initial impact he normally had.

He wore a pair of slacks and a polo shirt now, the clothes still more *him* than jeans and a T-shirt would have been, but a far cry from his suit. Fuck, he almost looked normal.

It was strange, even for me, but it seemed to have camouflaged the power he held. Now, though, Mae seemed to understand just how sharp that man really was, and I got the sense she didn't care for it at all.

"They decided it'd be best not to come back until this place was less crowded."

"By which you mean they saw us and ran the other way?" Yazmor added in just as he shoveled more food into his mouth, his words cheerful.

And just like that, Mae stared at Yazmor, then the rest of us, as if she just realized we might be completely nuts.

Yazmor has that effect on people.

"Can't say I'm sorry about that. I don't like new people." Hale gulped down the water in his glass, a soft clink when his lip ring hit the rim of the cup.

"You don't like anyone," Tyrus reminded him.

Hale shrugged as he set his glass down. "Yeah, well, most people aren't worth liking."

The conversation went on like that, with the men holding up most of it. They bickered, as they usually did, allowing Mae a glimpse of them all. Her expressions said that while she took in all of it, she struggled to accept it.

No doubt, after her experience with angels, she didn't think they had much of a personality. She probably assumed they were like Hubis—just anger and cruelty wrapped up in a body.

I'd thought that about the Demon Lords when I'd first arrived in the Chasm, and it had taken five years for me to feel as if I really understood them, before I peered beneath their jagged exterior.

Not to say that what was underneath was all that pretty, either.

"Why are his eyes that color?" Emma whispered the question to me, leaning in to keep her voice low as she gestured subtly at Yazmor.

I looked across the table at Yazmor. A crease in his cheek said he'd heard despite her trying to keep her voice down, but he didn't interrupt, didn't answer.

Of course this is the one time he keeps his mouth shut…

"His name is Yazmor," I whispered back to her, leaning close so it felt like a conversation just between the two of us. "He's just a little different."

And boy, do I mean more than just his eyes.

"I've never seen eyes that color before. They match his hair. Does he dye his hair?"

"You know what? I don't know."

Yazmor leaned in, flashing a smile with less edge than usual, as if he calmed it for Emma. "I don't dye it. It's naturally this color. Don't worry, though, I might look a little weird, but I won't hurt you."

A line appeared between Emma's eyebrows before she shook her head. "I'm not afraid of you."

"No? But you asked about my eyes."

"I think they're pretty," Emma admitted, her voice soft. "Here, there isn't a lot of stuff that's different. It's nice to see something different." As Emma spoke, she lifted her fingers to touch her upper lip, at the imperfection there, the reason she'd been cast out of the city. The action seemed mindless, and I got the idea that she probably did it a lot when stressed.

"Pretty?" Yazmor repeated the word back as though he had to test it, like he had to roll it around in his mouth to decide what he thought about it.

I cast Emma a conspiratorial grin. "Yeah, I think they're pretty, too."

And just like that, a flush appeared on Yazmor's cheeks, the sight so unexpected as to be fucking adorable.

Mae moved her gaze between Emma and Yazmor, a tension inside her. No doubt she wanted Emma to form no additional connections between herself and these clearly dangerous men. Mae didn't need to know exactly who they were to recognize just how lethal they could be.

"Emma," Mae said, "can you go out to the shed and pick a dessert?"

"Really?" Emma's bright eyes sparkled. "But you said we couldn't have those often."

"I think today is a good day, since we've got company."

"What should I get?"

"Whatever looks the best to you. The strawberries were extra sweet, so those might do well with one of the canned cakes."

"*Both*?" Emma's disbelief drew a smile from me, and when I glanced around, I almost laughed at the similar expressions from the men.

Funny that given what hard-asses they could be, they could so easily be swayed by one sweet kid.

Mae chuckled and nodded. "Yeah, both. How often do we have company? We should splurge."

Emma didn't wait, as if she thought Mae might change her mind if she hesitated too long. Instead, she took off at a run.

Tyrus' gaze followed Emma. "Is it safe for her to go in the dark?"

"She'll be fine. As I said, there aren't many out here, and Emma is smart enough to stay out of sight." Mae paused, then shook her head. "At least, she *usually* is."

I almost opened my mouth to defend the young girl, to explain that I was a Demon Lord, so I probably had a better sense of those around me than normal spirits. That wasn't likely to make her feel any better, though, so I caught myself before I made that mistake.

"You wanted to talk?" Gorrin said, his eyebrow lifted. "You sent Emma away like that to speak to us without her present, right?"

Mae pressed her lips together for a moment, then sighed. "Every time I think I have a handle on you five, you prove yourselves to be more dangerous than I thought. You're right, though. Because I gave her the choice to pick something, it'll take her longer, giving us time to talk."

"What do you want to talk about?" I asked.

"I want to know the truth."

No one responded at first. There were so many things she could mean by that, which meant I didn't want to out us by talking first. It seemed the men felt the same.

Or at least, I thought that before Yazmor opened his trap. "What truth is that?"

"You're not here for no reason. I might live out here in the middle of nowhere, and people might not think much of me, but don't think I'm stupid. Angels don't come out here, and angels don't stroll around with four other people for fun." Mae cut a sharp look at Gorrin. "You hardly act like an angel at all, let alone the Gorrin I've heard about."

"If you are as smart as you claim," Gorrin said, "you should know better than to ask that question. The answer would be rather dangerous, wouldn't it?"

"Ignorance is *always* more dangerous than knowledge. You're already here, which means we're already involved in whatever you're doing. Don't you think someone else might come looking for you? Do you think they'll just believe that we had no idea what was going on?"

"That sounds a fucking lot like a threat," Hale said. "But you wouldn't be stupid enough to threaten us, would ya?"

I had to respect Mae, because most people folded under Hale's harsh gaze. They gave in because when a man who looked like Hale glared, it frightened anyone with a brain.

Somehow, Mae just pulled her shoulders back, reminding me of a mama bear ready to take on any threat to her cubs—and I had a feeling that meant all those who lived here, not just Emma. "I wouldn't turn you in."

"And you expect us to just believe that?" Tyrus asked.

"Not really. I'm not saying it because I'm some great person, but I *am* an outcast, just like the others out here. Even if I wanted to turn you in, I'd be slaughtered before I could tell an angel anything. Assuming I lived long enough to get out what I wanted, no one would believe me, especially against an angel. So, no, I won't turn you in because it wouldn't do any good."

Her words hit me hard, a reminder that the Plains wasn't the place I'd imagined it to be. In fact, a part of me wondered if I'd lucked out by getting sent to the Chasm.

The Chasm was harsh, sure, but they accepted people even when they didn't fit some mold. They respected strength and power, and those were things a person could *earn*. The Plains crushed those traits. If I'd come to the Plains, I'd probably be in this house if I were lucky enough not to get myself killed almost immediately.

Also, from what I'd seen, I probably wouldn't find nearly as many angels that I wanted to fuck.

Gorrin exchanged looks with me, as if leaving the choice to me. I let out a sigh, but the reality was that Mae already knew more than she should. We'd already dragged her into this enough to become a target if things went badly. Plus, I'd found that a little information was far more dangerous than a lot.

The least she deserved was the truth, right? She should know why she might pay for this later.

"You're right—we're more than we let on." I took a deep breath, then repeated our story, at least the highlights of it.

Our positions as Demon Lords, the fact we came from the Chasm, and our plan to overthrow Hubis, the fact I'd slept with them all.

That last one wasn't for any reason other than I was sort of proud of it.

Mae didn't interrupt through any of it, letting me pour out the story. Her expression didn't change, which made me wonder if she believed any of it. Maybe she stayed quiet because she thought it was all bullshit and didn't want to set off the crazies.

"And that's why we're here," I said at the end, shrugging as if that put a period at the end of the wild tale.

Mae remained silent, her gaze shifting to her plate. No doubt she was poring over the details I'd given her, sorting through them to find any spark of truth that she could verify. If I were in her position, I'd want proof, after all.

"I know it is hard to believe," Gorrin said, "but it is all true."

"Oh, I believe you," Mae answered.

"You believe us without any proof? Foolish." Tyrus sat back in his chair, his expression tight.

Mae shook her head. "I believe you because the story makes sense. It explains why you would appear out here rather than in the center of the city, why you don't know much about the Plains and why you're traveling with an angel. It's the only thing that fits with the evidence I've seen from you all. Besides, the story is too dangerous to offer up if false. Just uttering such a plan — to attack Hubis — would be a death-sentence. No one would do so unless they planned to follow through."

Her words reminded me of the fact that, should we fail, should we get caught, she might very well pay the price for us. "We should probably get going. There's no reason to put you at risk any more than we already have." I pushed my chair back, ready to go before Emma came back.

I didn't know if I could handle saying goodbye to Emma, if I could stand the idea of leaving when I wasn't sure she'd be safe.

A hand on my forearm stopped me, and I turned to find Mae had leaned over to grab me. "Don't go."

"I don't want you or Emma suffering because of us."

"We're *already* suffering here. We all are. You've shown up as the first new thing in so long, the first thing that might change things. I can't just ignore that."

"But you could get caught up in this all."

"You aren't even from here. This is *my* world, and if I can't be brave enough to help change it, I can't expect anyone else to, right?" She turned to stare at the back door, where Emma had gone. "Every day I worry about her. I worry that she'll cross paths with an angel, that she'll get caught. I want her to have a better life—I want everyone out here to have a better life. I can be brave enough for her, for them all."

The door opened and Emma came in, jars clutched in her arms in a haphazard way that made me think she'd lose them. A closer look showed dirt on a few, suggesting she'd already dropped them on her way back.

I looked back at Mae and nodded. "Okay. Let's talk tonight after Emma goes to sleep."

Mae squeezed my forearm then released me, and I found myself humbled by her expression. She had a bravery in her eyes, a strength there, a willingness to do whatever it takes to protect those that she loves.

The world might just end up saved by people like her, by those brave enough to risk it all for those they love.

I glanced at the four men who had followed me here, who had risked so much for me.

Who the fuck would have thought love would end up saving the world?

* * * *

Gorrin

"Is she sleeping?" I asked.

"She fell asleep fast. It was a long day for Emma." Mae nodded as she approached me. Despite us seeming to have come to an understanding, she still showed signs of tension when she interacted with me. I couldn't blame her for that, of course.

I had always known the cruelty of angels, but for a long time it hadn't bothered me. I'd heard Hubis' voice in my head, explaining how maintaining order mattered more than anything else. He had said that some must suffer for the greater good. I'd followed that, been willing to do things I hated, because I believed it was for the greater good.

Looking back, I had been foolish.

Of course, I'd never done as Loch had said had happened to Mae. I'd heard stories of such things, back before I'd left the Plains, but since I spent all my time in the palace, I hadn't known the truth of it. Even if I had known, I wasn't sure I would have done anything. Back then, I had been too far beneath Hubis' thumb, too devoted to him and his vision.

So I remained seated on the log as Mae approached, trying to make her as comfortable as I could despite the way her gaze constantly returned to my wings. Loch sat beside me, like a signal to Mae that I was safe.

Yazmor had wandered off — as he often did — and Tyrus and Hale were doing a few more chores before we headed off. They were gathering firewood, from what I understood, having built a shelter to help keep the wood dry for when Mae would require it.

"The trip to the palace normally would only take a day or two, but you can't take the normal route. Once you get closer to the city, the roads will have angels that patrol them," Mae said.

"How many angels are there?" Loch asked, looking at me.

"I can't answer that. Hubis creates them as he wants and has need. There are the upper angels, the old ones, but he makes few of those. You can think of them sort of like the Demon Lords in the Chasm — they stay mostly in the palace or travel to Earth. The others, the lesser angels, spend their time in the city keeping order, or venturing just outside the walls."

"I haven't seen many upper angels," Mae explained. "Even when I lived in the city, they don't leave the palace much. It's the lesser angels that you have to worry about. They'll take one look at Gorrin and recognize him. You can't possibly think you can sneak into the palace with him."

"When we get closer, I'll put distance between us," Gorrin said. "I can even go back to the palace to wait for them there."

"I have a different idea." Mae pulled a scrap of paper from her pocket and handed it to me, trembling as I reached for it. I ensured our fingers did not so much as brush when I took it. "That's a map of the area, and the best path toward the city."

"You think we should enter through the west side?" I asked.

"Maybe it's less about where you enter than it is about *how*. Here" — she pointed at the map — "a friend of mine works as a merchant. He trades to outcasts."

"He is a fool, then." The words slipped from me before I could consider them, before I thought about how negatively they could be taken. I rushed out more words, hoping to smooth things over. "I mean that is a very dangerous business to be in. Should he be caught, he risks expulsion from the city at best and death at worst."

"He knows the risks, but he does it anyway. If it wasn't for him and others like him, then those of us out here would be even worse off."

"Why would he help us, though?" Loch leaned forward, placing her elbows on her knees. It was strange how often she could appear a formidable enemy yet also like a lost little kid. "He doesn't know us, so why risk it?"

Mae reached to her hair, removing a clip from it. She held it out to me, then dropped it into my palm. The piece had a diamond at the center and silver details that wrapped around the gem like vines. A single long silver stick at the back would secure it to the hair.

It was a lovely piece, and it showed a surprising amount of age on it. "This is from Earth?"

"Yes. It was given to me by a friend, by the wife of the merchant. If you give him that, he'll know I sent you. If he knows that, he'll help you." She sighed and wrapped her arms around herself. "I wish I could go with you."

Loch responded so fast her words came out almost a shout. "You can't do that. It's too dangerous, and you have Emma to think about."

"I know. I know I'd only make everything riskier for you, that I can't leave Emma on her own. I just... I hate the idea of sitting behind and not being able to do anything."

I tucked the hair clip into my pocket along with the map. "You have done more than you realize. You have given us information and access to help that I would have never found on my own."

Mae's shrug implied she didn't agree. "The merchant's name is Noah. He will also have something else that can help you. There's an amulet that can hide the true nature of a person. If he still has it, it will hide your angel nature. Anyone who recognized you by sight would still see you, but you would read as just another spirit here. It would let you hide and stay with the others."

She ran her tongue along her bottom lip, then stared off in the direction of the city. "You should all stay together as much as you can. I've seen a lot of people come and go, and what I've learned is that it's only together that any of us have a chance. When left alone, all people become twisted and fall to their worst natures. It's only together that we can ever really succeed."

I thought about Hubis, about how he'd always looked so set apart from others. He never spoke to anyone beyond what he needed to, never relied on anyone. I had lived the same for so long, but when had it all really changed?

Loch. It wasn't until I had found a connection with others that things mattered that the world hadn't felt quite so dark or hopeless.

"I'm going to go inside and check on Emma." Mae took a step backward. "I wish you all the best, and when you succeed? You'd better come back and visit Emma, or I'll never hear the end of it." She didn't wait for a response before rushing inside, leaving Loch and I alone.

"She's tougher than I would have figured," Loch said.

"She is." I struggled to make sense of my fragmented thoughts, of the unease in my chest.

Loch leaned against my side and rested her head on my shoulder. "You look bothered."

If she'd have demanded answers, I didn't think I'd have been able to supply them. Instead, she just pointed out the fact and waited for me to decide if I wanted to share or not. That patience of hers, that understanding, got my lips moving.

"She mentioned being alone. I have grown so used to being alone that I struggle to think about what life with others means."

"You say this after our time in the Path? Because you haven't been all that alone for a while." The smirk on her pink lips said she meant far more than just walking.

"That was a necessary evil. It was a temporary alliance for a shared goal. We will either fail in that goal—at which point such an alliance will be a moot point—or we will succeed and no longer require it."

"You weren't alone even before we left for the Path."

"How can you say that?"

"I've been in the Chasm for five years, and we rarely went more than a day or two without seeing each other. Maybe you *wish* you were more alone, but the fact is, you weren't. Fuck, even before I was there, can you really say you didn't have others? I did your job for just a month but I sure as hell didn't get much time alone when Myers wasn't up my ass. Then there's the other Lords, and you sure know them well enough to tell me you spent time around them."

I went to tell her she was wrong, but the words stuck in my throat. I recalled how often I would see Tyrus, when we would sit across from one another while trying to get the upper hand. We weren't the type to yell, to show any outward aggression, but that didn't lessen the way we had circled, trying to one-up each other. Then there was Hale, who was far more outwardly violent. He yelled and I stared, for the most part, but we had had more than our fair share of exchanges over the years.

Even Yazmor spent time around me, as one of the few who didn't mind showing up in my territory for no good reason. Even when I'd had no desire to see him—which had been most of the time—he'd never failed to appear and refuse to leave, making jokes I hardly understood, as if he'd wanted to keep me company.

It forced me to acknowledge that Loch wasn't entirely wrong. I *had* had other people in my life, those who I passed time with, who made it feel as if I were not quite so alone. They paled in comparison to the changes Loch brought, but they were still there, still important, still a strange foundation.

"You see?" Loch asked and nuzzled her cheek against my shoulder. "But I think Mae's right about something. When I think of all the worst people I know, the ones who really lose themselves, who turn into things I don't recognize, they're always alone. Hubis, Azael, Gunnar. Maybe, at the end of the day, hell is just loneliness. It's isolation."

"You shouldn't be so quick to blame evil on an outside force. People choose to do as they wish—they are not forced into it. I can say that with certainty because I attempted to force you into a great many things, yet you never allowed that."

"That's just because I'm really stubborn."

"Perhaps. Still, make no mistake. Others are not just victims." I dropped my voice and ground out the next part. "*Especially* not Gunnar."

She let out a sigh, her breath warming my skin even through the sweater I wore. "I wonder how Gunnar is. Not just him, but Myers and the entire Chasm. I never figured I'd miss them."

"You can talk to them."

Loch lifted her head from my shoulder. "Really? I thought we couldn't go back, not without having to go through the Path again, and I sure as hell don't want to let Guardian get his tentacles on me a second time."

"You can't return, but you *can* communicate with them. Give me one moment." I didn't wait for her response before transporting myself to my room in the Palace. Using my powers usually was risky, but transporting wouldn't raise eyebrows. I fished the needed item from my desk, then returned to Loch.

She smacked my arm. "I thought you said we couldn't do stuff like that! If we can just use our powers, why didn't we get some clothes that fit a bit better?"

I let my gaze travel down her body, ashamed by how quickly I heated at the sight. She wore a pair of slacks that were slightly too snug, the fit showing off her ass, and a basic blouse. "I find no fault with what you're wearing."

"Flattery doesn't work on me."

I ran my thumb along her bottom lip, pressing into the tempting fullness there. My own need surprised me, the way I wanted to pull her in and kiss her until we focused on nothing but each other.

Except I knew that wasn't possible, so I dropped my hand and ignored her disappointment. Instead, I held my hand out flat, the silver ring about the size of my palm that I'd retrieved from my room there.

She didn't take it, suspicion written all over her features. It made me laugh.

Loch would not so much as flinch when sleeping with Tyrus and me, yet she would hesitate at accepting a simple silver ring? I caught her hand and pressed the item into it.

"It is a communication device, connected to the well in my office." I paused at my own words, then let out a soft laugh. "In *your* office, I suppose. If you summon Myers, he will go to the well and you can communicate through this."

"Then we'll know everything is okay there?"

"That is correct. I used such items to speak to Hubis and others while I was in the Chasm. It also can reach out to Earth, but to do that, it requires the person to have the other ring."

"And you can transport to Earth?"

"Yes." I frowned slightly, a surprising amount of jealousy striking me. I found it to be an ugly feeling, something I didn't care for. "Who is it you would wish to contact on Earth?"

"Jay."

Oh.

The name of the girl who had started so much, who had truly pushed us to where we were today. If I had never sent Loch to make a deal for Jay's soul, if she had never met her, I had to wonder where we would be. Would Loch and I have remained as we were before? Would we have just been a Demon Lord and the demon whose soul I owned?

So much had happened since then, where we had both suffered terribly, and yet I couldn't bring myself to regret any of it. It had brought us to this place, to a relationship and closeness with Loch I never would have thought possible before.

"You keep in contact with her, then?"

Loch nodded. "We visit when we can, and we write letters back and forth. She's doing pretty good. I think she's going to end up taking over for her father."

"She is far better suited for that than her brother." I left it at that, unsure what else to say. I couldn't bring myself to apologize for what had happened, not again, not when it had brought us here. Instead, I took her hand in mine and showed her how to use the ring. "Run your finger along this edge, and it will connect to the well. If you want to connect to another ring, simply tap here while you think about who you are trying to connect to."

"That easy?"

"That easy. Are you going to use it now?"

She stared at the ring, then shook her head. "I think I'll wait until tomorrow."

I nodded and drew my hand from her. "I will take an additional ring to Jay tomorrow as well."

"Not sure she'll be happy to see you."

"Oh, I am sure she won't be. However, with so much unknown, so much risk, I don't know how long we have. You wish to speak to her, right? I would not suggest waiting, because our future is very uncertain here." I hated having to tell her that, but I forced myself to.

Loch deserved to know just how much danger we were all in, and I owed it to her to tell her the truth.

Chapter Four

Loch

I let out a long, drawn-out sigh that any teenager would have been proud of.

"I'd have figured you'd be happier to be walking here after dealing with the Path," Hale said.

"As it turns out, I don't like walking here any more than I did there."

"But look at the sky!" Yazmor tipped his head back, basking in the light. "I wouldn't say the Plains is better, but at least it has night and day cycles. You have to enjoy this part of it."

I held my arm out. "Do you see this skin? I burn, so no, I think I prefer the Chasm." *And fuck did I never expect to say that.*

I still recalled when I'd first arrived in the Chasm, when the darkness had seemed depressing. When had that changed? Sure, a few minutes in the sun could cheer me up, but it quickly got old, and I'd find myself missing even that thin layer of ash that covered everything in the Chasm.

And if I'm agreeing with Yazmor now, I know that I really am screwed.

The small ring in my pocket seemed heavier than before, as if reminding me that I could reach out to the Chasm.

I'll do that when we get to the next stop.

I wouldn't have thought myself to actually care about how things were going there, but maybe it was some weird Stockholm syndrome — maybe the Chasm had kept me locked up long enough that I now found myself drawn to it, now I ignored all the many ways it had hurt me and mixed up obsession with love.

A figure burst from the side, through the picturesque tree line, and into our path. It was a man, his clothing torn, his skin flushed and his breathing rapid and uneasy. No wings, so at least he wasn't an angel.

He turned toward us, his eyes wide, and stumbled in our direction.

Before he got close, however, Tyrus caught him with a hand around his throat, stopping him short.

Instead of the fear he should have shown, however, the crazy bastard *moaned.*

"Please tell me we aren't dealing with another kinky masochist," I said.

Yazmor smiled, standing taller. "I enjoyed playing with the last one."

"You *stabbed* the last one."

"Exactly!" Yazmor moved forward until he could look right at the man. He inhaled, breathing in deeply then scrunching his nose as if he'd caught a whiff of something bad. "Ah, I see."

"Please," the man begged, writhing in Tyrus' grip in a way that was way more sensual than frantic.

"What the fuck is wrong with him?" Hale lifted his lip in a snarl and stared at the man like a person would look at a racoon who might have rabies. "He looks like he's whacked out on ecstasy or something."

"Euphoria," Yazmor offered, then shifted to meet the man's gaze directly. "That's it, right?"

The man nodded, another moan leaving him. Tyrus still had a good grip, so I came forward until I could see him clearly.

The more I saw, the more my temper rose. I recalled the little that Mae had said about the drug, about the way it was used to turn people into willing slaves. This man had that look. Bite marks and small red bruises covered his body, everywhere I could see.

Sure, the guy looked fucking crazy, but understanding it had come from some drug, that others had taken advantage of him, softened me.

"Will he be okay?" I asked.

Yazmor caught the man's chin, holding his face still so he could study it. "I think so. You can tell it's Euphoria because of the smell, and he has purple in his eyes. So long as the eyes don't turn entirely purple, the person usually can come back to themselves when the drug wears off."

I pressed in close beside Yazmor, seeing the blue that still rested in the man's eyes. They reminded me of Hale's eyes, and that threw me, made me think about Hale's past.

A glance to the side revealed a sharp expression on Hale's face, and when he met my gaze, it told me not to ask.

So I focused back on the man in front of me. "Are you being chased?"

"Please," the man begged again.

"Please what? What do you need?"

The man reached out, fast but clumsy, and wrapped his fingers in my shirt. He yanked me forward until he pressed fully against me, the hardness of his cock not even close to being hidden by his scraps of clothing. "Please touch me. It *hurts*. It hurts so much."

"Whoa, buddy. Thanks, but I just want to be friends." I tried to move away, but the man's grip was incredibly strong.

Hale caught the man's wrist and undid his grasp, peeling one finger off at time off. "Not a fucking chance. She's taken."

As soon as Hale got the man to release me, however, the man shifted his attention to Hale. He switched so fast that I found myself a bit insulted. Sure, I didn't want the crazy drugged-out man focused only on me, but I would have liked if he didn't toss me aside *quite* so fast!

"Then you. I'll be good for you, I swear. Use me, however you want, anyway you want." The man tried to get closer to Hale, his roving hands worse than the darkest, most packed club I'd ever been in.

"Yeah, no, sorry. Not into that." Hale turned his attention to Yazmor. "How long does this shit last?"

"I don't know—depends on the dosage, the tolerance, the purity. Euphoria is only available in the Plains, so I don't know a lot about it. Not really my kind of thing."

"You seem like the type to enjoy this weird shit."

Yazmor released the man and pressed a hand to his own chest as though insulted by Hale's words. "How *dare* you! Life is more than interesting enough to not need any pharmaceuticals to enhance it. Gorrin would know more about it, but since he's putting in face time at the Palace, I think we're on our own."

"Well, I don't think this trip is going to be made any easier by dragging some horny, drugged-out man with us," I said. "So what do we do with him?"

As soon as I asked, I realized my mistake.

"We are *not* killing him."

"The fact that you always reject the easiest and smartest plan is probably why you end up in trouble so often," Tyrus muttered. "So if we can't kill him, what now?"

"Well, people like to sleep post-orgasm..." Even saying that made me shudder.

"Not on Euphoria," Yazmor argued. "The drug keeps them awake. That's why he has bags under his eyes, because he's probably been up for a few days."

"Please." The man trembled, tears running down his cheeks, straining for us, for anything. He repeated the plea over and over again in a mindless whisper, as though some chant to the gods for mercy.

Except he didn't have gods here. He had four Demon Lords and that was it.

Yet I couldn't stop myself from wanting to help. From what Mae said, Euphoria was sometimes taken willingly but often forced on people, to make them malleable and easy to control.

Before I thought about it, I set my hands on his cheeks and stared into his eyes, the blue obscured by purple ribbons. I used my power, whispering to him to sleep, rewarded when he fell limp against Tyrus' grasp.

"I thought Gorrin warned us not to use our powers," Tyrus said, his voice tight to show his displeasure.

"Well, it was the best of bad options. If he kept that up, he'd have drawn attention to us, and we didn't need that. Gorrin said using it in an emergency was okay, but not to do it much."

"And this was an emergency?" Hale asked. "We could have just killed him."

"No killing." At that, I let out a soft laugh and shook my head. "Well, no more killing than absolutely needed."

Tyrus shook his head and easily lifted the man, more gently than I would have expected. He moved the man off the path, laying him down in the grass to the left of the road.

Except, after he did that, he remained crouched. "I don't like this."

"You sell a lot of nasty things in your bar," I reminded him.

Tyrus didn't look at me, his gaze locked on the man's still form. "Yeah, but none of it does *this* to a person. None of it forces people against their will. We've never had Euphoria in the Chasm, but we've had a few similar drugs that have shown up, and anything that does this to a person I ensured did *not* continue."

I peered at Tyrus' profile, at the tightness of his expression, the severity of his gaze. It was strange to think he had his own moral code after everything I'd seen him do, after all the horrible things I knew he'd done. "I'm surprised this bothers you so much."

"A person should always have their mind. They should never lose that, should never have to give that up. I will kill others, I will use whatever is at my disposal to manipulate and force their compliance, but in the end, it is always their choice. I find drugs like this reprehensible, and those who use them do not deserve the power or advantage they gain."

He pulled at the man's clothes, righting them best he could given their state. It was strange to see him give a damn about that, about someone's modesty, but I'd learned that Tyrus was deeper than he appeared at first glance.

Then again, we all were. We all wanted things that we didn't ever admit to, all craved to be more, all had hidden pain and desires that we kept close to our hearts.

It was true of me and true of every other person in the world—every part of the world and afterlife.

People were *far* more complicated than they appeared at first.

"So that's Euphoria," I said, unease creeping into me. Sure, I had no idea who the man had been, what he was like normally, but the idea of losing myself like that terrified me.

I wasn't the best person on my own, of course, but I was *me*. For better or worse, I was who I was. I knew it, understood myself, but what if I ended up like that? What if some stupid chemical changed the very person I was?

It reminded me of that pain in my head when Gorrin had given me commands, when despite wanting to fight it, I found myself doing things I'd never wanted to. I never wanted to go back to that, to feel that helplessness again.

A hand came to rest on my shoulder, and I jerked my gaze up to find Hale there. He squeezed gently, his gaze hard as if to tell me he wouldn't let that happen.

And if anyone understood just how horrible that would be, Hale would. His history, the fact he'd sold himself to some pervert to protect others, the indignities he'd suffered, it all meant he got this in a way Tyrus and Yazmor didn't.

So I set my hand on his and squeezed back. It was both a thank you and a promise in return that I wouldn't allow him to suffer that, either.

"Come on, we'd better get going." Tyrus rose and turned his back on the man as though writing that off as no longer important. I'd guess it was more about trying to put it out of his mind so he could focus on what was important, on what he had to do rather than something he could do nothing about now. "We should find the merchant within the hour, and Gorrin will meet us there."

It would be far easier for us to talk the merchant into helping us without an angel there. At least I'd guess that, given Mae and Emma's reaction to Gorrin.

I nodded and stepped away from the man, trying to put it out of my mind as Tyrus had.

However, even as we walked, as we put distance between that man and us, I couldn't stop thinking about it. It plagued me, this nagging feeling in my head that we weren't finished with it yet, that it would end up being a bigger problem.

That man, that drug — I had no doubt that it would come back and bite us in the ass. That seemed as sure a law of the universe as anything else.

If it *could* fuck me over, then I could just about guarantee it would.

* * * *

"Well he looks shifty as fuck." I crossed my arms and stared at the man who had to be the merchant. He had long braided black hair, the end falling to the middle of his back. His green eyes were made more compelling framed by his dark eyebrows, and his cheekbones were high and sharp. We'd found him at the location Mae had sent us to.

On top of all of that, he had that *I really care* vibe that women tended to go crazy for. Talk about a far cry from my guys.

My men weren't the sweet and caring type. They gave off more of a *I might sell your organs for beer money* vibe.

"I know you're there, so you might as well just come out already." The merchant didn't turn toward us as he spoke, but his words left no room to mistake the comment for anything but a warning to us.

And given that, I figured, why hide?

I walked forward, into the clearing where he stood in front of an unassuming cave, the entrance small enough a person would need to crouch to enter.

The merchant turned toward us, his hands at his belt but not reaching for any weapons.

That set my nerves on edge. People tended to go for weapons when startled, and only a few types didn't. Either those who had no hopes of defending themselves or those who didn't need weapons to keep themselves safe. They were both dangerous in their own ways.

"Who are you?"

"My name is Loch," I offered.

"And what do you want from me?" When I frowned, the merchant let out a soft laugh and shook his head. "This place is out of the way. No one comes here unless they come looking for me."

"Mae told us where to find you."

He lifted one of those dark eyebrows, then crossed his arms over his wide chest. "She isn't the type to sell people out. Why would I believe you?"

I reached into my pocket and pulled out the hair clip that Mae had given Gorrin. I held it out to him, holding my hand flat so it rested in my palm.

The merchant narrowed his eyes, then came closer. Hale and Yazmor crowded me, pressing tight to my sides as a warning for him not to try anything stupid. Tyrus stood a few steps behind, keeping watch in case someone tried to ambush us.

The merchant seemed to notice, but he didn't comment. Instead, he took the piece and turned it over, studying it. "You really did get this from Mae, huh? How do I know you didn't just take it from her body after you killed her?"

"No blood." At his stern look, I sighed. *No one appreciates my humor.* "She said that someone important to her gave that to her, and that you would know about it. If we just took it, how would we know that it would mean anything to you?"

The merchant nodded, staring down at the jeweled piece before sliding it into his pocket. "If Mae sent you, then she must have good reason. What do you need?"

"She said you have an amulet to hide the true nature of a person." I didn't offer more details than needed. If he knew it was for Gorrin, for an angel, he might not agree to help. We'd won Mae over, but that didn't ensure we'd win this guy over.

Noah narrowed his eyes, and it gave me the sense that he was a lot sharper than I might have first guessed. Maybe that was because I'd gotten used to dealing with men like the Lords, men whose intelligence was wrapped up with their violence. It seemed almost crazy to think about someone who was both smart *and* kind.

People like that weren't a part of my world, after all.

"So you need the amulet that hides an angel? And to think I thought today might be boring."

"An angel?" I laughed, but fuck knew it was thin and about the worst example of acting that anyone had ever tried. "That's crazy. Who would spend time with an angel? I mean, really, who do you take me for?"

Hale groaned. "Yeah, right, because *that* really sold it. Damn it, Loch, I know you're a better liar than that."

Noah moved his gaze between Hale and me then chuckled. "I can see why Mae sent you. She likes to help others, but she's also suspicious."

"What? She likes terrible liars?" Yazmor asked.

"No. She just likes impossible causes, and whatever you all are up to, it reeks of the impossible. That seems like something Mae couldn't just ignore."

"Are you telling us you have that amulet?"

"They aren't easy to come by, but yeah, I've got one. I don't keep it here with these goods, though. It's a special item, after all, so I keep it close."

"And what are you planning on charging for it?" Tyrus, ever the pragmatist, asked from behind us.

The merchant smiled wider, as though amused by our conversation, before waving for us to follow him into the cave.

Sure, let's go into the creepy cave with some weird black market merchant. If he tries to sell our organs, I'm out of here.

Of course…with how well we healed, I wondered if our organs would regrow…

"They do," Yazmor said.

I turned a surprised look on him. "Okay, that was *too* good. How the fuck did you know what I was thinking?"

Yazmor flung his arm around me as he pulled me toward the cave, following the merchant. "I just know you that well. I must be getting better at reading you. You see, if the injury doesn't kill you, you'll regrow anything. Lose your heart and you're dead before you can regrow it, but lose a kidney? You're probably fine."

"Probably?"

"Probably fine is the best most people can hope for."

The darkness of the cave closed in around us, and it reminded me of the Forgotten Caves. It took me back to walking into those with Yazmor by my side, when we'd gone through the pitch-black cave system.

And it also reminded me of how he'd distracted me then, making me suspect he'd done the same thing again. I moved closer to him, as a thank you.

We didn't walk nearly as far as we had in the Forgotten Caves, and within a minute, I found myself in a rather large and open space, with a tall ceiling and soft sand beneath my feet. Flickering orange bathed the walls, more light joining the first as the merchant lit candles around the large space.

My eyes adjusted as I took in the shelves and chests that filled the cave. Was this where he kept most of his goods? Given what Mae had said, he probably had to keep it hidden so he didn't get caught trading with outcasts.

"No security?" Tyrus asked.

"Fucking stupid. Can't believe you ain't been robbed blind yet," Hale added on.

The merchant shrugged as he lit the last candle. "There aren't a lot of people out here, and even fewer who would want to steal what I have here. None of it is worth that much, and they could get it in the city easily."

"What about outcasts?" I asked. "Wouldn't they want this since they can't go into the city anymore?"

"Sure, but I trade with them already, so pissing me off wouldn't help them much."

I thought about the Chasm, about how tight security had to be there.

Or, rather, how tight *my* security had to be. No one stole from the others.

Hale didn't keep things worth stealing for the most part, so I doubted he had to deal with that. Tyrus was far too scary for anyone but the dumbest asshole to risk stealing from him. People might want to take something from Yazmor, but even if they tried, whatever they could get wouldn't make any sense. I could almost see some thief breaking into Yazmor's place only to find themselves faced with a crocodile named Smiley and a hundred books on animal trivia.

"You were going to tell us the cost," Tyrus pressed.

Noah turned away from us, searching a chest, heavy items inside it banging around. He moved them as though they weren't that important.

Finally, he brought out a handful of glass vials.

"I'd like to keep my organs," I shouted, unable to help it after what I'd thought about before.

He snorted, then set the vials on a large table at the center of the cave. "Well, feel free to keep them. There's not much I can do with a Demon Lord's liver."

His words made the temperature of the cave drop.

Sure, I hadn't kept things too close to my chest, but I knew I hadn't said shit about what we really were.

So how the hell did he know that?

Before Hale and Tyrus could start threatening — and it was an easy guess that they planned to do exactly that — Noah spoke again.

"I'm not going to turn you in."

"Why not?" Tyrus asked. "I imagine you could make some friends and gain favors if you did so."

"The sort of people I could sell you out to wouldn't make good friends, so no thanks."

"How did you even know?" I asked.

"It wasn't that hard. I deal with a few people who are well connected, and they've had plenty to say about the Demon Lords of the Chasm. Lots of people in the Plains don't believe such stories, they don't think the Chasm even exists. I know better, though."

"How?" Tyrus asked. "How is it you know the truth when so many others do not?"

"Let's just say that I've heard stories from others, and the stories are all too similar for me to not believe it. You four show up here, just after Gorrin returns after his long absence, looking as you do? It was an easy guess, and your reaction told me I was right."

He leaned against the table, crossing his feet at the ankle. "The amulet you want is for Gorrin, I'm guessing. It'll work for what you want, will hide his wings and his power so he can move through the Plains without people sensing what he is. Anyone who knows him can still recognize him, but even if someone knows him, they're likely to brush it off and think they're wrong. It's a rare item though, and that makes it pricey."

"And now you'll tell me what exactly you're expecting in return, I'm guessing?"

He nodded. "That's right. I want blood samples from each of you, and one from Gorrin."

"Blood samples? What for?" Yazmor asked, his tone surprisingly serious. At my look, Yazmor went on. "Blood speaks to blood, so you should always be careful who you leave any with."

"You've heard of Euphoria?"

I recalled the man we'd run into earlier, to the way he'd been so out of his mind. I shuddered at the memory and nodded.

"That addiction is ruining people here. The more a person uses, the more they need, and eventually it takes over entirely."

"Doesn't explain the blood," Hale snapped.

"Actually, it does," Tyrus said, his gaze down as though he were still working through the details. "The blood of demons—a lord or not—has healing properties. That is why we're stronger and heal better than damned or humans."

The merchant smiled, seemingly pleased to find someone smart enough to understand. "That's right. Now, I can't leave the Plains and demons can't get here normally, so it's been impossible to get samples. I've had a few angels willing to bring me demon blood, but it's costly and dangerous to trade with them, and they can only manage to get samples from the weakest of demons. That blood hasn't helped work out a solution, but perhaps yours will. I wouldn't suggest you taking Euphoria, but it's possible that your blood could help heal others."

"So all you want is some blood?" Tyrus asked.

"That's right. Just a vial apiece."

"Mine won't help," Yazmor said. "I'm not a demon. My blood isn't compatible with humanoid creatures like yourself. I mean, if you want some, I'll offer it up, but I'd suggest you only use it with people you really hate." Yazmor held his arm out, then sliced a sharpened nail down the inside of his forearm. Drops of blood escaped and landed in the soft dirt beneath us, and the merchant rushed for a vial, darting forward to catch it.

"If you're not a demon, what are you?"

Yazmor smiled, the one that had too many teeth, the one that unnerved anyone smart enough to see it for what it was. "A remnant."

Him saying that made my chest squeeze, a strange pleasure in it. Maybe it was because he'd hidden what he was for so long, so the idea of him coming right out and admitting it made me feel he'd moved forward, that he'd accepted himself at least a little.

"Then maybe your blood will help with something else."

"I'm bleeding for you—I think that earns us a real introduction, doesn't it?" Yazmor asked.

The merchant nodded, then gestured at the other vials. "Fill those up, please." When Hale, Tyrus and I followed Yazmor's lead and grabbed the vials, the merchant went on. "My name is Noah Bransky. You already know about everything else about me that matters—I'm a trader who brings goods from the city to the outer villages and outcasts."

"And why take that risk?" Tyrus asked.

"Because someone needed to. I did what most people do here at first. I waited and enjoyed the Plains for a long time. I indulged in everything I could, seeing this whole place as heaven, as my reward for a good life. I mean, sure, a few times I wondered if someone made a mistake, if they'd let me in by accident. I even had a few years there at the start when I kept looking over my shoulder wondering if someone would figure out I didn't belong, if they'd kick me out. Eventually I realized that the Plains isn't about who's good and who's bad, but more about who falls into line and who doesn't. I used to think they were the same things, but this place taught me differently."

"And now you're some sort of Robin Hood? Stealing from the rich to give to the poor?" I asked.

"Something like that." He held the vial carefully, catching Yazmor's blood before it slipped away, treating it as something precious. "I think I just can't imagine staying here any longer and doing nothing."

Tyrus and Hale sliced into their own arms as if it were nothing, but I hesitated. The idea of cutting myself seemed stupid as fuck, like something every part of my instinct said not to do. I distracted myself by speaking to Noah, my hand that wrapped around the knife trembling. "So it's just you against the world?"

"No. I have a family. Don't look at me like that's so hard to believe." Despite his words, he laughed as if my reaction amused him. "I think, if there is one great truth to the world, it's that people group up. Doesn't matter where they are or what's going on, they gravitate toward each other. Happens here just like anywhere else."

"Were they your family when you were alive?" Tyrus asked.

"No. They were born a long time after I had already died and come here. Still, when they did come here, when I met them, it felt like finding a part of myself I hadn't known was missing. Of course, it's just my wife and I, now, since kids move on."

I thought about Emma and Mae, about the family they'd made. Maybe Noah was telling the truth. Maybe he understood some underlying truth of the universe.

On Earth, people paired off. They created communities together. The same thing happened in the Chasm. Even with how violent and dangerous it was there, people found comfort in one another.

My gaze drifted to the men in the cave with me, as if that proved the point perfectly well.

A hand wrapped around my wrist, and I jerked in surprise until I realized it belonged to Tyrus. His vial sat on the table, a cork in the top to close it, full. He took the knife from me, then held my arm tightly so I couldn't move. "Just breathe," he whispered.

I stared into his familiar eyes, trying to let the darkness of them hold me, to keep me still. He ran the blade against my forearm, the action so quick that it took a long moment before the pain even hit me.

Looks like he's a man who can handle a knife.

He tossed the knife on the table, grabbed the empty vial and pressed it against my arm, the cut he'd left deep but small, so the blood flowed easily into the glass.

"Thanks," I said.

He nodded, the tightness remaining in his expression. "I do not appreciate harming you."

"So you're saying we'll leave knife play out of the bedroom?" I lifted one of my eyebrows, forcing a smile to try to relax him.

The laugh he let out didn't quite convince me, but I'd take what I could get.

The vial filled quickly, and before I knew it, we'd all done our duties and donated the blood he'd wanted.

"So, where the fuck is this amulet?" Hale asked.

"It's at my house. Come on—you've all helped me more than you know, so why don't you rest there? We can discuss your options for getting into the city, which

I'm guessing is where you're all headed?" He didn't seem to need us to tell him he was right, because he didn't wait to see how we'd respond. "The least I can do is put you up for a night. Besides, you can meet my family."

"You're going to trust us around your family?" Tyrus asked.

"Sure—why not?"

Hale gestured at himself. "We ain't exactly the 'bring home to your family' sort of people."

"Speak for yourself," Yazmor muttered. "People *love* me."

"You're thinking of hate, not love," I argued.

Yazmor's smile brightened more. "You're right, I am! That's right, people hate me." He paused, pressing his lips together. "Wait, so why are you inviting us? Aren't you worried about what we could do to your family?"

Noah laughed. "Don't underestimate my wife or daughter. If you wanted to hurt them, well, I've got nothing but pity for you."

And right then I knew I'd really like his family— they sounded like good people.

Chapter Five

The house where Noah lived seemed nice enough. It was cozy and warm, reminding me a bit of Yazmor's home in the Chasm.

It made me think that if I peeked in through the window, I'd see an adorable little family sitting down at the table to eat a dinner, which was a life I'd never understood or experienced for myself.

In fact, I expected that when we walked in Noah would say, *'honey, I'm home!'* and some sweet little wife would come rushing out in an apron to welcome him.

And there went my comfort. I would have much rather taken on an ambush and killers and thieves than this sort of happy family life.

Noah paused in front of the door before opening it, standing on the porch instead. He reached into his pocket and withdrew Mae's hair clip. He held it out to me. "You should take this."

"Why?" I didn't take it, unsure what he meant. "She only gave it to me to show to you. I don't know when or if I'll see her again — you should keep it. You can give it back to her next time."

"She gave it to you so you should keep it. You never know when it might come in handy. You see, it's a good luck charm. The person who gave it to Mae told her as much, and I have a feeling you need all the luck you can get. You hold on to it and when this is all done? Then you can give it back."

When he didn't seem willing to let me reject it anymore, I sighed and took the hair clip.

Except, before I could slide it into my pocket, a strong hand grabbed my wrist so hard that it hurt. Even when I tried to yank back, Tyrus didn't release, his gaze locked on my hand.

"Where did you get that?" His voice had taken on a strange edge, something both desperate and angry.

I didn't understand his question, but I found myself trying to answer anyway. "It's the hair clip Mae gave me. I told you that."

"You didn't show it to me, though." He turned his gaze to Noah, his fingers digging into my wrist so hard I feared he might break it. "Who gave this to Mae?"

Noah took a step backward, the first sign of fear I'd seen from him. It went a long way to show just how scary Tyrus looked right about now. "My wife gave it to her."

"And where did she get it from?"

"It was hers when she was alive. She had it replicated here."

"What's wrong?" I asked him, trying to ignore the pain in my wrist, his behavior so strange that I knew damn well that was the more important thing right now.

"I *know* this piece. I had this made as a gift when I was still alive."

A sinking feeling settled in my stomach, a feeling that usually came over me about a minute before things went to absolute shit around me. "A gift for who?"

"Tyrus?" The new voice came from the doorway, and I lifted my gaze to find a beautiful woman standing there. She wasn't dressed in the fifties housewife clothing I'd expected, instead wearing a pair of leggings and a long tank top that made her look like a modern mom on her way to yoga.

It wasn't her appearance that got me, though. Instead, it was the way she looked at Tyrus, the familiarity of her gaze, the way she spoke as if they'd known one another well.

I really hated the way she said his name.

Despite the fear inside me, I asked again, "Who was the gift for?"

Tyrus didn't look at me, his gaze locked on the woman, instead. "I had it made for me wife." He swallowed hard, then spoke softly. "It has been a long time, Emily."

Which meant this beautiful woman who stood before us, who spoke to Tyrus so gently, was Tyrus' wife.

Yep, I knew things were going to shit…

* * * *

Tyrus

Guilt gnawed at me as I recalled the marks on Loch's wrist. I hadn't even noticed that I'd gotten so rough with her, that I'd hurt her. My brain had stuttered to a

Jayce Carter

halt, my body acting without any true input from me. It was as if nothing existed except the sight of the woman who had died so long ago, who I had *watched* die at the hands of my youngest son, who had bled out before me just minutes before I'd taken my last breath as well.

And now here we were, facing each other again, in the living room of her home with another man.

Loch had excused herself, along with everyone else, leaving just Emily and me together in the quiet of the room that suddenly seemed far too small to hold all our history and all the questions we no doubt had for one another.

"It's been a long time," Emily said, her voice so familiar that I struggled to keep the past apart from the present.

"It has." I almost cursed at myself for the foolish, inane small talk. Didn't we have more important things to discuss than such trivial formalities?

Emily sighed and rubbed her palm against the top of her knee, the action taking me back to when she would do that before. Of course, back then she wouldn't have dared said a word. The world had been different, and women were mostly expected to remain quiet, to accept the opinions and desires of the men in their life above their own.

I had never mistreated her, but the entire dynamic was different than the world now. I was different than I had been then.

Judging from how she looks and what Noah said, she's different, too.

"You've been missing so long," she said, her voice hardly above a whisper. "I assumed you didn't make it to the Plains."

79

"I didn't," I admitted, unable to hold her gaze. Instead, I stared at the room, at the home she had made with another man. "I've been in the Chasm."

"I was afraid of that…"

"Well, if I wasn't here, that was the only other choice, right?" I paused, another thought occurring to me. "Unless you thought I had perhaps made it here but didn't want to find you?"

She shook her head quickly, an immediate rejection of the very idea. "No, of course not. I knew if you were here, you'd have found us. At first, I thought maybe you'd survived that night." Shadows rested in her eyes, as if that night still plagued her.

Then again, what she'd experienced would stick with anyone. I still remembered her shock when she'd looked at her own son, when the child who had grown inside her, the one she had fed from her own body, the one she had loved and raised had thrown that away in his desire for power. She'd died there along with her other child.

I'd had my share of nightmares from it, had remembered it when I hadn't wanted to, but that was different. I was hardened by that life already, whereas Emily had been protected from the truth as best I could.

"Did you eventually assume I must have died? When enough years had passed, you had to think I couldn't be alive anymore."

"I knew you died that night because Elliot told me."

My son's name, the one who had killed me, who had killed the rest of my family, made me sit up straighter and lift my lip in a silent snarl. He might have been my blood, but after what he'd done?

To say my feelings about him were complicated was putting it mildly.

"He's here?"

"Not *here*, no. In the Plains? I think so, assuming he's still alive. He came to see me, to apologize. He also wanted to tell me what had happened with you, that you hadn't survived the night. It was then I realized that you must have been in the Chasm. When did you sell your soul?" Her last question came out a whisper, a reminder of the woman who had never asked me anything when she was still alive.

She had followed my lead, had done as was expected of a woman in her position, had behaved admirably, by all accounts. The fact she asked me that now went to show how much had changed.

"I sold my soul before we married. I needed to have the power to protect you. I thought it a fair trade to give up my soul in exchange for the ability to protect what mattered most to me."

"Do you regret it?"

I considered that. Had I ever thought about it before? It was like asking if a person regretted gravity. It was simply a fact of life, and considering what it would be like without it didn't matter. It did not change a thing. I let out a soft sigh. "No, I don't. While I would have loved to have given you more, while I wish I had seen Elliot for what he was, my trade allowed us years of security."

The other part that I didn't say rested in my mind.

If I hadn't done that, if I hadn't given up my soul, I would have never ended up in the Chasm.

I wouldn't have met Loch.

Somehow, that seemed unacceptable and unthinkable.

Sure, life in the Chasm hadn't been perfect. A glance around this place gave a glimpse of what I might have had if I hadn't sold my soul, if I had come here with Emily.

Except, before that even fully formed in my head, my heart rejected it.

A life without Loch wouldn't have been worth it, no matter how cozy or comfortable it seemed.

"What about..." I couldn't bring myself to utter my other children's names, the guilt too thick, too choking.

Emily shook her head. "Our eldest did not adjust well here, and he passed on soon after we came here. Our daughter lives, though she prefers to remain in the outskirts, helping others."

"Is she happy?" I asked that one quietly, a part of me wondering if I even had the right to ask. My blindness with Elliot had led to her death. Even when alive, I couldn't say I had been the best father. Too often I had been blinded by work, by power, and did not spend the time with my wife or children I should have.

Emily smiled, the sight reminding me of so many years before. In fact, a part of me went back to when Emily and I were both young, when we were barely more than kids. We hadn't had any idea what the future would hold, had been content with one another, happy to face anything so long as we were together. "She is. In fact, I think she's happier than she ever was alive. She was always tough and smart — she has a lot of you in her — and that wasn't really allowed on Earth for girls at that time. Here, though? She's gotten to be herself."

I shuddered, surprised by how much that reassured me. Knowing that Emily had found happiness, that my daughter had, it lifted a weight from my shoulders that I had carried for so long, I failed to even notice it anymore. Even if our son had passed away, and Elliot lived even if he shouldn't have, just knowing that both Emily and my daughter had found a place for themselves reassured me.

"Good," I said softly. "I'm glad."

Emily smiled, the edges of it tense, a sure sign that despite our history, we had both changed. We lacked the comfort we had once shared with one another. "So you've been in the Chasm all this time? If you were anyone else, I'd say there's no way for someone from the Chasm to make it here, but you've always done things your own way and not given a damn about what was possible."

"Yes, I've spent this time there. I didn't know there was a way to the Plains, had never tried to get here before because I had assumed it impossible. Even if I hadn't, I wouldn't have come, to expose you to that danger."

Her gaze moved past me, toward the backyard where the others had gone. "But you came with her?"

Emily's voice held no jealousy, but whatever came out seemed like a close cousin.

And I had no reason to hide anything, not anymore. "Yes."

"Who is she?"

I struggled with how to answer that. Who was Loch? What was she to me? How could I explain what she meant to me to someone else? Did I even fully understand it?

I went with what I could, even if it fell far short of the full truth. "Loch is mine." I paused, then shook my head. "No, that isn't quite right. It is better to say that I am *hers*."

Emily just stared at me for a moment, and I wondered if I'd overstepped my bounds. Perhaps speaking about other romances in general was different than specifics, but I couldn't regret my words. They were true, and I refused to ignore or pretend Loch was less to me than she was.

Finally, Emily let out a laugh that was so unlike the woman I'd married, one more open and freer than she'd ever been in real life. "Well, I can see she's been good for you. When you talk about her, you smile in a way I've never seen before."

"Isn't such a conversation supposed to be awkward? Maybe I shouldn't say anything?"

Emily rose from the couch and went to a cabinet in the room. She opened it, then took out a glass bottle with a dark liquid in it and two glasses. "We're way too old to worry about things like that, don't you think? So let's have a drink to the past and to the future, then you can tell me what's happened since I last saw you and I will do the same."

She poured a glass, then handed it over to me, the scent of a fine brandy tickling my nose. This felt like a rare gift, like a chance to review the past, to put it to sleep finally, to move forward from it.

I had long ago known I didn't belong in heaven, that it had no place for me, so imagine my surprise to find my own salvation there.

Finally, I could bury my past and move forward with Loch knowing nothing held me back any longer.

* * * *

Loch

"You look fucking pathetic," Hale said just before he kicked the chair I sat in, shaking me awake from my musings.

I wanted to tell him he was wrong, but what was the point? I *was* pathetic. I couldn't help it as my mind swirled around the drain, focusing only on the fact that one of the men I loved was in there with his wife.

"Why couldn't she at least be ugly?" I leaned forward and set my elbows on the tops of my knees, then rested my face in my palms, knowing full well that I was pouting like a child. "At least if she was ugly, I'd feel better, but she's beautiful!"

"Want me to make her ugly?" Yazmor offered, his tone telling me he was serious. "I'll shave off her eyebrows and draw them on too high so she always looks surprised."

I smiled at Yazmor, knowing it didn't quite reach my eyes but not caring. "Thanks, but I don't think that'll make it any better. Still, how long are they going to be in there?"

"Want to spy?" Hale offered.

And fuck me but I was tempted. Still, the idea of getting caught spying on Tyrus and his...*wife* was far too embarrassing to risk. "No. I'll just sit here and see what happens."

"You're worrying for nothing," Yazmor assured me.

"You think?"

"Of course! How many people end up getting back together after being apart?"

"Um, that happens all the time..."

"It does?" He furrowed his eyebrows, then his eyes widened. "You don't get to talk to Gunnar anymore then!"

Hale smacked Yazmor in the arm, the sound loud enough to tell me he'd hit him hard. "You're not fucking helping, you idiot!"

I couldn't bring myself to hear anymore from either of them. If I sat here any longer, I was fucking sure I'd end up giving into their stupid plans and doing something I'd regret. I'd go in and haul Tyrus out, making a fool of myself and probably managing to strengthen Emily's case.

So instead, I got up and out of the chair.

"Where are you going?" Hale asked.

"A walk."

"You hate walking," he pointed out.

"Yeah, well, turns out I hate sitting out here waiting to see what happens even more."

"I'll come too, then," Yazmor said.

"No, you stay. I need to clear my head. I won't go far—I promise."

Neither Hale nor Yazmor appeared all that happy about the option, but Noah—who I had honestly forgotten was even there—spoke up. "It's fine. There's not much out here, so it's plenty safe. Besides, we should wait here for when Gorrin gets back."

If looks could cause harm, Noah would have a hole through his head from the glares of the other Demon Lords, but he didn't seem to notice at all. Instead, he focused on me. "Come back when it starts to get dark, okay?" He walked with me a few steps away, to where a gate in the back fence led to the forest beyond. When he opened the gate to let me out, I paused.

"I can see why Emily loves you. I wish I were as calm as you. How can you sit here while they're talking?" I asked.

Noah offered me a kind smile, and shockingly, I didn't sense the least bit of uneasiness in his gaze. He really wasn't worried at all, was he? "I trust Emily, and I trust what we've got. If she decided she wanted Tyrus, well, it'd break my heart, but you can't keep someone who doesn't want to be kept. She's got to make her choices and I have to make mine. All you can do is trust in what you've got."

I accepted his words even if they didn't quite make me feel better. Then again, he had a lot more years with Emily than I did with Tyrus.

Still, maybe after putting a little distance between the others and myself, I might feel better.

Probably not, but what the fuck else was I supposed to do?

* * * *

It was an hour later before I found a fallen log and plopped my tired ass onto it.

Are they still talking?

I had no idea, and I couldn't bring myself to return and check. It felt too dangerous, and I wanted to pretend nothing had changed at least a little longer.

A heaviness in my pocket drew my attention, and I pulled out the ring Gorrin had given me.

If we were revisiting the past, what better time than now was there to use this?

I ran my finger along the side just as Gorrin had explained, and the circle, which had been the size of a bracelet, grew to the size of a dinner plate. The inside shimmered and filled with blackness, reminding me of the well.

And what the fuck is wrong with me that I feel homesick suddenly?

"Loch?" The voice that floated through the black was distorted but still familiar. A moment later, Gunner's face appeared, relief spreading across his features when he spotted me. "Thank fuck! Where have you been?"

I smiled even if I didn't feel it. "Myers told you I'd be gone, didn't he?"

"Myers says shit all the time, but that's not the same as hearing it from you. How could you go off without even saying a fucking thing to me?"

He sounded like a jilted lover, and it made me even more ashamed of my jealousy over Tyrus and Emily. Was that what I sounded like?

No, I sound worse, I'm sure.

"Sorry," I lied. "It just happened fast. How is everything going?"

Gunnar sighed, and I could see nothing but his face. The ring didn't show me the rest of the room or anything beyond him, but I got the sense that he'd sat — probably on the edge of the well. "Myers is really fucking good at running shit. No one's even noticed you're gone."

"I knew I kept him around for a reason." I smiled at the thought of Myers keeping everything in order. Fuck, he was probably better at it than I would ever be. I'd bet the place was running smoother now than it ever did when I was in charge. "And you're okay?"

Gunnar didn't respond right away, as if weighing my words for meaning. "You don't ask about me usually."

"I guess I'm feeling nostalgic. If you keep being an ass, though, I'll make sure to never make that mistake again."

Gunnar laughed, the sound taking me back to so long ago, when I didn't know what an absolute fuckwit he really was. A part of me wished I could go back to then, to when things were simple, when they made sense.

Something about the past could be so enticing, and with Tyrus revisiting his own life, my mind wanted to do the same.

"It's quiet here without you," Gunnar said. "I thought that after you died, too. I had enough shit to think about on my own, distracted myself with work and women and booze, but fuck it—it was too quiet. Every once in a while, when it was dark, I'd sit there and I'd miss your laugh, your snarky little comments. Turns out silence doesn't suit me."

I dragged the toe of my shoe through the dirt to distract myself as I answered. "Yeah, well, I don't think either of us suits the other."

"I'm not so sure about that." Gunnar let out a soft sigh, as if we'd had this fight before and he didn't much like it. "I think you're just too hard on yourself—fuck, too hard on us. We've had a hard life, so it can't be that surprising that our relationship might be hard, huh?"

I thought about how things had been with Gunnar compared to later. With Gunnar, I'd been so sure we were soulmates. I'd thought we were meant to be, like modern-day Bonnie and Clyde, ride or die, idealistic bullshit. I'd accepted our fights and problems because I somehow thought it was all fate, all written in the stars.

Except, now with some distance, as I looked back, I wondered how I could have ever been so foolish. I'd mistaken obsession for love. I'd thought having someone—anyone—was more important than who they were or what exactly we had. I'd been so desperate to avoid being alone that I'd taken the first thing I could wrap my hands around, too afraid to let it go.

That comfort I'd found with Tyrus, the fun I had with Yazmor, the heat with Hale, the safety with Gorrin—those were things I hadn't had with Gunnar. Fuck, I wasn't sure we really had much of anything, but my stubborn ass had been unwilling to admit that.

Or maybe it was better to say I hadn't known any better. I hadn't ever seen or experienced a good relationship, so I had nothing to compare it to. It was like living off cereal as a kid, then trying eggs cooked in the microwave. It was gross to most people, but delicious to someone who had never had good eggs.

"It doesn't matter," I told him, trying to keep my voice gentle. Sure, a part of me hated Gunnar. That part always would, after all he'd put me through. Another part, though, it cared.

That was the part that had lived with Gunnar, the part that had shared so many years and memories with him. It was the part that remembered how his hair stuck up in the morning, and how grumpy he was before his coffee. It recalled the rainy nights when I'd snuggle up against his side and just listen to his breathing. I might know we weren't meant to be, that we didn't work well, but I still wanted him to find his own happiness.

"We aren't right for each other, and nothing is going to change that. We've got history, but that's it—history." I put my foot down, trying to offer him no room to think anything would happen.

It wouldn't. I wanted him to find some sort of happiness for himself, but it sure as fuck wouldn't be with me. I'd gotten to see what love looks like, how it felt, and I refused to settle for something subpar now.

Gunnar stared at me, even though we spoke through the ring and were far apart, I felt the uncomfortable weight of that gaze.

Then again, I got it. He'd died, had lost everything, and that was a hard change. It was a struggle to work out how to start over, how to move forward.

I'd gone through that when I'd died and gotten to the Chasm. I'd had to work through it myself, had to find my own place there—fuck I had to *make* my own place.

I couldn't do that for him, though. He had to do it for himself just as I had, or else we'd end up right where Gorrin and I had.

And I really didn't want to get stabbed for all my trouble.

"So you'll never forgive me, huh? One mistake and everything we had is just gone?"

"It's not about forgiving—it's about figuring out what future we want."

"And if the future I want has you in it? I'm just out of luck?"

So much for trying to go easy on him…

"Yeah, basically. I want to help you, Gunnar, to help you get your feet under you here, but I can tell you without any doubt that we are over with."

"What if things don't work out with the other Lords?"

"Even if that happened, it doesn't make you and I better. You're like a pair of shoes that don't fit anymore—even if my other shoes break, you'll just make my feet hurt worse." And there it was, the final bandage tearing off. If Gunnar bled from this, he'd have to build up a scab on his own.

He didn't sigh, and his expression didn't hold any real sadness to it. It was strange, because there was disappointment there, but it felt more like he was unhappy with the option given rather than that he was sad about *me*.

"I understand. So, when're you coming back?" His change in topic was clearly an attempt to hide, to move on, and I let him have at least that much. If anyone knew how necessary pretending was sometimes, I did.

"I don't know. Hopefully soon." Lying to him didn't chafe as much as I would have expected it to, but it wasn't like I trusted him enough to tell him what I was up to.

Even if he didn't screw me over, he might make a play I didn't agree with. Gunnar was way too manipulative to let my guard down.

He'd led to my death once — I didn't plan on letting him get a second try.

"Well, I'll keep things handled here," Gunnar said, his tone strained — not that I could blame him for that. Saving face always sucked. "Myers is on top of shit, so there's no problems yet. In fact, it's been strangely quiet in general. It's like the other Lords are all keeping things calm, too." Suspicion colored his words, but I refused to give him anything to go off on.

"Thanks. If you need anything, you can contact me through this. Just keep going for a little longer until I get back." I said my goodbyes, then ended the connection.

It left me exhausted, honestly. I rubbed my eyes, struggling to make sense of anything. Gunnar's feelings, Tyrus talking to his *wife*, all the bullshit that surrounded me.

Weren't people supposed to get breaks? Periods of time when shit got easier, when it wasn't such a big deal? When did I get that? When was my chance to just breathe, when I could catch my breath before the *next* disaster hit?

I glanced back toward the house, then down at the ring.

Before I knew what I was doing, I ran my finger along the side and reached out for Jay, hoping she'd answer, that I understood how to use this thing.

After a moment, Jay's face appeared in the center of the ring just as Gunnar's had, but my reaction was a lot fucking different. Whereas seeing Gunnar caused a general unease in me, Jay made me smile.

It feels like forever since I smiled.

And even longer since I got to see Jay. I hadn't realized she'd become such an important part of my life, but the relief at seeing her told me it was true.

"Loch!" Her bright smile said she felt the same. "Where have you been?"

"Just really fucking busy. So I take it Gorrin gave you this?"

Her lips thinned as she pressed them together, then nodded. "Yeah, he did."

Her tone made me narrow my eyes. "He didn't do anything, right?"

"Like try to buy my soul?" She laughed, the sound easing some of the tension. "No, nothing like that. I did throw something at him, but he's fine."

"What did you throw?"

"A large candle."

I snorted at the idea of Gorrin trying to ease a frightened teenager. He wasn't good at dealing with people in general, but teenaged girls were a whole different level of trouble. "He's tough. I'm sure he's fine."

"It was a lit candle…" Jay bit her bottom lip, and I lost my fight against breaking down into the sort of laughter that made my side hurt.

I couldn't stop thinking about how he must have reacted. Gorrin was a man who others feared, one used to having people fall into line, and he'd had to face off against a candle-wielding teenager who he couldn't hurt or intimidate.

I would have bought tickets to see such a thing.

Jay laughed after a moment as well, as though it had occurred to her for the first time just how funny the situation was.

"So, tell me everything that's happened," I said once I started to catch my breath again.

"Aren't you busy? You can't really want me to just ramble."

I thought about everything weighing on me, about everything I had to do, about how many people were relying on me, and it was almost crushing in scope. It had me nodded and moving so I sat in the dirt and rested my back against the log. "Oh, trust me, I do want you to ramble."

She beamed in return and nodded, then started to talk. I let myself get lost in her words, in the way her life was so easy, so normal.

It helped to remind me why I'd taken on so much, why it was worth it and why I couldn't fail, no matter how hard it got.

Chapter Six

I had no idea how much time had passed with me sitting outside, in the dark, by myself.

Talk about depressing.

I wanted to go back to Noah's, to check in with Tyrus, to stake a claim on him like some animal who wanted to leave bite marks on their mate as a warning to others.

Instead of giving into that childish desire, I kept my happy little ass right where it was. The last thing I needed was to make a fool of myself, to barge in there, open my mouth and say something I for sure should not.

And what if Tyrus ended up turning me down? Making a fool of myself was one thing, but what if I'd already lost?

And how could I have done anything but lose? I thought back to his wife, to how pretty she was, how sweet. They shared children and a past that I wasn't a part of, and it wasn't hard to see how good they looked together.

"My name is Emily and I'm just a perfect fucking little wife." I made sure to make my voice come out just as annoying as possible, even bobbing my head as if mocking someone who was essentially a stranger to me would somehow make this all better.

"And here I thought your name was Loch."

Busted.

I looked up to find Tyrus standing just in front of me, his arms crossed over his chest, his dark eyebrow lifted.

"Can we just pretend you didn't hear that?" I asked.

"Just this once." He sat on the log beside me, so close that his arm pressed against mine. After a long moment, he spoke softly. "She isn't perfect, you know?"

"I thought we were going to pretend."

"I am just talking about Emily here."

"Well, she sure as fuck seems perfect." *And you two look perfect together.*

My brain supplied a juxtaposition of her and me, beside Tyrus. She looked like the ideal housewife and me?

I looked like the delinquent cousin who gets shipped from family member to family member because no one wants to deal with me. I sure didn't fit by his side, and before I could think about it, I found myself touching my hair.

Tyrus caught my hand and held it tight, moving it away from the strands. "You worry too much."

"Pretty sure I worry the exact right amount." I took a deep breath, then forced myself to speak up, to say the things that swirled in my head. "So that's your wife, huh?"

"She *was* my wife."

I snorted. "We both know that 'till death do us part' isn't quite as final as people think."

"It was a very long time ago when we were together."

"Only because you were torn apart. Can you really say that if that hadn't happened, you wouldn't still be with her?"

He had the decency to not answer right away. Was he thinking about it? Considering what his future might have held if his son hadn't attacked him? The seconds ticked by, each one stretching out impossibly until I wasn't sure time moved at all.

"I don't know," he admitted, his tone soft. "I have changed in the years since I was married to her, as she has. It is impossible to say what would have happened if our lives took a different route."

"Convenient answer."

"Is it any different for you?" He turned to stare at me, an accusation in his dark eyes. "If you hadn't been killed, if you never sold your soul to Gorrin and came to the Chasm, would you not still be with Gunnar?"

I opened my mouth to tell him to kindly fuck off with that bullshit, but the words died in my throat. I wanted to say of course not, that I knew what a shitty person Gunnar was now, and I wouldn't have put up with that, but would I?

I understood those things only because I'd had the time and distance to see them. I'd suffered and grown and changed, and in doing that, I'd gotten a better understanding of both me and Gunnar.

But if that had never happened? If I'd never met the Lords, never gone to the Chasm, would things have been different? Would I have never grown past the naïve little girl I'd been?

My shoulders drooped and I let out a long sigh. "I guess I don't know either. So, what now?"

He furrowed his brows, as if my words made no sense. "What do you mean?"

"I don't like things that are uncertain. You didn't think you'd get a second chance, but that's different now, right? We have things we've got to do, but after that, you'll have options." I swallowed so hard that it hurt, but I plastered a smile I didn't feel as if it were armor to make it all a little less painful for us both. "So what now?"

Tyrus didn't respond at first, his expression not changing or shifting in the least.

I really am jealous of his poker face.

I could lie when needed, but the rest of the time? My face didn't have much of an inside voice, so whatever I thought often paraded right across my features.

Of course, I read Tyrus better now than I had when we'd first met. The tiny changes, the subtle notes, they gave me clues. The smallest of lines would appear in his cheek when he found something funny. He'd incline his head toward me, drawing a hair closer when he was nervous. A fire would dance in the depths of his brown eyes when he wanted me, when lust would overcome him even as he held himself back.

And right now? I spotted that fire.

"Are you telling me to pick her?" Usually when someone said something like that, I'd expect it to be in a pitiful tone, in something pathetic and sad. Tyrus must not have gotten that memo, because he asked it in a flat tone that screamed *danger*. His words looked more to me like a bear trap, drawing me in before it snapped shut around me.

I gulped hard. "I didn't say that. I just need to know where I stand."

"And if I said I wanted her? If I told you that I realized I was meant to be with her, that because we have a second chance, I want to take it, how would you respond?"

His words sliced through me as efficiently as my trusty bound dagger. Fuck, I was pretty sure his words did more damage than it ever could. Still, I owed him an answer. I'd brought up the topic, so no matter how much it hurt, I'd tell him the truth.

And I won't cry!

I almost laughed at that, because fuck knew I'd cry.

"I'd let you go. I want you to be happy, Tyrus. You deserve that. You know? It's been a crazy road to get here, right? I mean, so many things had to happen, things no one could have predicted. I had to get killed and draw you all to me, then I had to make the stupid choice of selling my soul. Gorrin had to push me too far and I had to try to kill him. Azael had to attack humans, and Kylie had to have taken that necklace from the Forgotten Caves. We had to decide to make a change, then survive the Path and figure out a way here. After all that, we still had to have met Emma, then get Mae to send us to Noah."

I shook my head as I thought about just how winding that road really had been, how many little offshoots we'd missed to keep on this path. "All of those things led us *here*, right? I don't know, I've never believed much in fate, but this has to mean something, doesn't it? Maybe I wasn't ever meant to have you—only to help you get where you should have been."

Something inside me broke as I said that, as I uttered the burning words inside me, the ones that threatened to sear away everything I had, to leave only pain and loneliness. I couldn't picture *not* having Tyrus, but I cared for him way too much to steal away happiness if he found it.

I'd seen Tyrus wield silence like a weapon so many times before, knew just how effective it was. He could force a person to admit anything, could let their minds run wild with fear while he just stared, letting them become their own worst enemy.

And fuck did I *hate* being on the wrong side of that particular skill.

Finally, he narrowed his eyes, the action making those flames I'd spotted roar brighter, taking over the darkness there. "Your foolishness knows no bounds, does it?"

I went to ask him what he meant, but I didn't get the chance. In fact, I couldn't even think about his words before he was on top of me, before the soft dirt beneath me pressed against my back, before his weight pushed me down after he knocked me backward, off the log.

A gasp escaped me, but he took my lips in an aggressive kiss that swallowed the sound before it could become free, as if he wouldn't allow anything of me to escape his clutches.

He spoke between the kisses, never drawing far away. "You would give me up so easily? Does this matter so little to you? Am I so disposable to you?" Anger filled his words at a level I had never heard from him before. He was often annoyed with me, but truly angry?

It felt like another side of him I got to see, but it was a side I regretted bringing out.

His eyes caught me as securely as his grip did, and I had equally small chances of escaping from either.

"I just—"

He silenced me with another kiss. It seemed he didn't really want to hear my excuses, and when he shifted one of his legs between mine, when he ground the top of his hard thigh against my cunt, I didn't think I wanted to make excuses.

Unless they wound him up like this even more…

"You are *mine*, Loch. How dare you try to walk away from this, from *me*."

"But Emily—"

"Is my past. *You* are my future. Have I been unclear about this in any way? Made you think for even a moment I would be willing to let you go?"

No, he hadn't. If anything, Tyrus had been surprisingly open about his feelings for me, about his commitment. Still, I couldn't seem to shake the image of Tyrus and Emily together, the tenderness and familiarity in their gazes as they'd looked at each other. It was easy to think he wanted me when I was his only option but now?

The little part of me used to getting passed over just couldn't accept it. I felt like that same little girl who had lived in the shadows of others, who had survived by avoiding anything dangerous, who had been written off by every person in my life.

No one had picked me over anyone else. Even Gunnar, who I had thought had loved me, had ended up just using me because I was convenient for him. It was how I'd felt in the Chasm, too. The Lords had wanted me, but they hadn't had a lot of other options, and I honestly thought that's why they'd ended up with me.

Now Tyrus had another option—a better one by all accounts.

Tyrus let out a sound of pure frustration before he slid his fingers into my hair and curled his hand into a fist. It forced my gaze to his, and he was only a breath away. "How can you truly not understand that? Even now, after all we have gone through, how can you not think I am serious about you? I always believed you were smart—foolish though you are—but then how can you be so clueless in this?" He leaned in and took my bottom lip between his teeth, leaving a sting in his wake before he tugged and released.

"I just want you happy," I said, my words breathless and embarrassing in how desperate they came out.

"Then you need to look no further than a mirror, because I have never felt happiness like I do when I am with you. I had no idea such contentment was even possible before I met you. Before you, I felt as if what I could give to people was all that mattered, but I never found peace, never found a person who made me feel at ease. Now, I don't want to hear another word out of your mouth unless it is to take back what you said, unless it is to tell me you will not ever let me go, that you will do whatever it takes to keep me."

"I'm never going to say that. What do you take me for? Some heroine in a teen manga?"

He smirked, the look downright sexy on his normally stoic face. "Well, that's fine with me. I'll enjoy you, and the more stubborn you wish to be, the longer I can indulge. I wonder who exactly can hold out longer."

And right then I knew that I'd already lost.

Tyrus

I shouldn't touch her when I'm this angry. The rational part of my brain — which had all but shut down at this point — screamed that I should back away. I should get off Loch and let her go, should take deep breaths outside until I could calm myself, until my actions were back under my control.

Except that rational part was far too weak now, especially when I wanted her this badly, when she'd pushed me this far.

Her words still rang in my ears like a cruel joke, the way she'd been willing to let me go so easily. The idea of allowing *anyone* else to have her drove me into a fury that promised a painful death for whoever would dare to touch what was most important to me in the entire world.

How then could she give in so easily? How could she walk away without a second thought and allow anyone else to have me?

Because she is a better person than you are.

That whispered in my ear, but even if it were true — and it was — it didn't change my anger. I did not care one bit for her relinquishing her claim on me so easily, and if she needed a reminder as to how much I cared for her, how much I wanted her, I had no problem reeducating her for as many hours and orgasms as it would take.

I moved my legs to outside of hers then rose so I could stare down at her. A streak of dirt rested on her cheek, and her hair was a mess between my gripping it and me pushing her down. Somehow seeing that eased me. Did I enjoy the idea that I had mussed her? That I had disheveled her? Perhaps it soothed the beast inside me by showing that I affected her in some way.

I grasped her shirt and pulled it up and over her head. She wore no bra — finding undergarments that fit out here was a challenge, after all — and it meant nothing obscured my view of her.

Her skin was pale, and even the scars at her stomach from the wounds that had killed her didn't detract from her beauty. Her breasts weren't large, but the rose-colored nipples that tipped them moved as she breathed, lures that drew me in. I set my hands on her ribcage, surprised as I always was by the difference in our bodies.

She was small in my hands, her body almost fragile. I moved up her narrow ribcage, her soft skin over her bones with very little muscle. It made her body giving and sweet as opposed to the hardness of mine.

I brushed my thumbs over the outer curves of her breasts, the touch surprisingly teasing given how ravenous I was.

"I'm sorry," she whined as she twisted beneath me. Except, she didn't move to get away, instead seeming to press herself against me more, to beg me with the action to keep going.

And that doused some of the anger inside me. In this way she was honest. Her body hid nothing from me. Our pasts, our fears, none of those things could exist when we were like this.

I cupped my hands on the outside of her breasts and pressed them together, then bent down to drag my tongue over one nipple then the other.

The moment I made contact, though, more of my control slipped from my grasp. She drove me mad, made it so I couldn't focus on teasing her, turning me into some base beast that wanted nothing more than to take my woman. I had prided myself for so long on my control, on my cool and calm nature, but Loch tore that away from me.

I shifted down, not caring that I was ruining my clothing, that I would have dirt caked to them and to me. I grasped the waist of her pants and tugged them down, taking her shoes and socks with them. It left her in only her panties, the plain white cotton making her appear almost innocent.

This green-haired vixen is as far from innocent as any person can get.

She gasped when I dragged a finger over the line of her panties, dipping beneath the elastic in a tease before snapping the waistband against her.

"You are mine," I said to her again, the words a mantra. They were perhaps the most honest ones I had ever uttered, the most basic truth I could guide the rest of my entire life by. "I will never let you go, Loch. You may run, someday — you may go as far or as fast as you wish — but I will never stop chasing you. I followed you to heaven. I submitted myself to a beast for you. Nothing will ever keep you from me." I leaned down and nipped the bottom curve of her breast, a red mark resting there as proof of my annoyance.

Before I was done tonight, she would be covered in such marks. She might feel she could walk away from this — from me — and make some clean break, but the love bites I left on her would say differently.

I shifted to leave another bite to her other breast, and Loch responded by carding her fingers through my hair, holding me tightly to her.

Greedy woman.

This was yet another reason I loved her, though. She knew what she wanted and didn't pretend to be chaste, to be embarrassed, to be some wallflower who didn't care for sex. No, Loch was the sort of woman who would dig her heels into my ass to force me deeper into her, to demand more from me.

And I would give her all she could take and then some.

I moved farther down her body, leaving hickies and bite marks over her ribs, her stomach, the points of her hip bones. Every inch of her body tempted me, made me hungry for more.

After removing her panties, I grasped her knees and spread her legs wide, not willing to let her hide anything from me. She squirmed, but I held tightly, refusing to give her an inch of space from me.

Even in the darkness, I could tell her pussy was drenched. I dragged my tongue along my bottom lip as though I could already taste her wetness and had already drowned myself between her thighs.

I kept my gaze locked on her cunt as I released one of her thighs so I could stroke my fingers up her slit. "You are more than I could have ever pictured having. You are my miracle, the goodness in my life I never expected to have, that I never could have earned, but that I will never let go."

She shivered, her eyes squeezed shut. I doubted she ever looked quite so lovely as she did at times like this, when overtaken by passion, when lost to her body and to her desires and to *me*.

I wrapped my hands around her hips, then pulled her up. I could have lain flat to gain access to what I wanted, but something about this pleased me more. I liked having her entirely under my control, liked forcing her to endure the pleasure. It made me feel like a beast eagerly devouring her.

And the first swipe of my tongue through her folds had me letting out a feral sound, the taste already hard-wired into my DNA so my body reacted.

She squirmed in my grasp, but I only held her tighter, plunging my tongue into her sweet pussy. I let my gaze roam up her body, over the dip of her stomach, the valley between her breasts, all the way to her flushed face.

She panted hard, her fingers digging into the dirt to find some way to anchor herself as the sensations washed over her, threatening to carry her away.

Not that I would let it. Nothing would ever take her from me.

I moved my tongue from the tightness of her pussy to her clit, to the swollen bundle of nerves tucked beneath its hood, waiting there to tempt me.

I swirled my tongue around it, licking without mercy, ignoring the way she struggled.

I knew Loch better than to think this would overcome her, though. No, not my woman. She was far tougher than that, and she could endure this.

She opened her eyes, and somehow locking gazes with her felt like she saw right down into my soul. Despite her being the naked one, her being entirely on display, I felt exposed. She was the only person who ever saw the real me, who I let close enough to know the parts of me I hid from everyone else.

And Loch had never once used it against me, had never made me regret that. Even now, even when she pissed me off by offering to let me go, she'd done it for my own good. She'd been willing to step away if it made me happy.

It humbled me as much as it drove me mad.

"I do not want Emily," I told her, even as a part of me screamed in my head that bringing up my ex right now was a poor idea. "You are my entire future—not her, not anyone else. Now let me prove it." I licked up her entire cunt, the action slow and deliberate, so she could see the filthy action clearly.

She swallowed, but if she planned to argue—and she sure argued a lot—she didn't get the chance. I snatched the words from her lips by focusing my touches on her clit. My hands were large enough that I used my thumb to pull the hood up, to give me direct access, to torment that sweet little bud with nothing in my way.

And like any good tactician, I never let an advantage go to waste. I latched my lips around the erect peak and sucked hard. She flailed, forcing me to grasp her tighter. With all the strength she had now, she could fight me like she hadn't before, but this was too important. I was a starving beast huddled over a meal, unwilling to let it go no matter what it took.

Loch shattered against my tongue so beautifully. She twisted and arched farther, the wanton cry from her lips making my cock ache with need. Her cunt pulsed, empty and needy and so damn wet. She panted hard as soon as her first orgasm faded away, when her muscles loosened, and the energy she'd shown before sapped away.

The marks I had left on her had darkened so she was a mess of tiny bruises like stars in a dark sky, each proof of my love, of my need. By the time I let her go, she'd wear even more, wouldn't have a single inch of her body untouched or unmarked by me.

But for now, I needed to sink into her tight cunt. I had to reach into the depths of her, to feel no space between us, to have her entirely. I lowered her hips to the dirt, then caught the nape of her neck and pulled her up and into my lap.

A quick reach between us undid my slacks, and a few shifts freed my hard cock, the tip already wet from precum.

I moved my hand from the back of her neck to her chin, the touch domineering and controlling and *me*. When she opened her eyes, when she looked at me, I offered her a rare smile. "Now show me, Loch, how much you need me. Ride me like a good girl, and I might just let you go after I fill you with my cum."

"Might?" she asked, her voice tired but showing signs of a second wind, as if my words dragged her back into the lust.

"That's right. If you don't do well enough, we will simply try again, over and over again, until I am sure you understand that you are mine forever. Should I tire you out? Well, your snug, warm body will please me just as much whether you are conscious or not." I bit down on her bottom lip, rewarded with a moan from Loch.

And just like that, I fell for her all over again.

Loch

As it turned out, despite all the shit I'd dealt with, all the terrible things I'd seen and experienced, there were still a few good things left in the world.

Puppies, caramel macchiatos and the sensation of Tyrus' cock sinking into me inch by inch. I dug my nails into his shoulders as I shifted down, as I took him deeper. He let me, not making me go faster, not forcing himself deeper. Instead, he moved his gaze over me as if the sight were just as good as the feelings.

And as always, I felt a tingle at the way he'd stripped me down but had remained dressed. Why was that so hot? I think I just enjoyed the differences between us, whatever they were. I got off on the power imbalance, especially because we were constantly switching who had the advantage.

Some of the time I shoved him down and took what I wanted, and other times he bent me over something and fucked me as if I were a plaything for him. Either way got me off, which left me to assume one thing—I just got off on him.

I let out a long, drawn-out moan when my body pressed against his, when I'd taken every inch of his thick cock. Already I teetered on the edge of another orgasm, my body still sensitive from the last. That was how it worked, though. That first orgasm was like priming an engine, and now I wanted to go all out.

The thought had me leaning in and taking his lips in an aggressive kiss, clinging to him as I rolled my hips. I didn't rise far, much preferring the feeling of him grinding deep into me, that full sensation that I couldn't seem to replicate with toys—no matter how much I liked to pretend otherwise.

He traced my bottom lip with his tongue, the touch leaving a streak of fire in its wake.

"I want no one but you," he swore, his words so honest that it seemed he'd opened himself to me fully, that he hid nothing from me. I couldn't even doubt him, no matter how much the jealousy inside me wanted to run free. "So never offer to walk away again—I will never allow that to happen."

His words should have been a threat, the sort of thing that teen dating articles would call a red flag, but fuck if red wasn't just my favorite color.

It'd be stupid to claim I didn't have just as many hang ups as him.

I grasped his face, my palm against his chin, my thumb on his jaw, and forced his dark eyes to mine. "Fine, then how about this? If anyone tries to take you — even Emily — I'll bury a dagger in their stomach."

He smiled, the expression far too sweet after what I'd just said. *We really are twisted, aren't we?*

Twisted or not, though, we worked well together. Fuck, maybe it was not despite but *because* of that shared twisted nature that we made sense.

"That's more like the woman I fell in love with," he whispered. "Now let me show you *exactly* how I feel about you."

And that sounded like a damn good idea to me.

Chapter Seven

Loch

Sitting across from Little Miss Perfect bothered me, but not nearly as much as it would have last night. Sure, she somehow managed to look like some fucking angel, despite the early hour, and I sure as fuck didn't look like that.

Then again, I hadn't gotten a lot of sleep last night, since Tyrus had kept me up until I couldn't stay awake. I had no idea when exactly I'd fallen asleep, but I'd woken in a bed in the house alone.

The alone part had started my day off poorly. It didn't really matter who I'd slept with, having them sneak out before morning always made me feel like some stupid booty call, and that moment of disappointment always made me cringe at my own weakness.

No doubt he'd done it for my comfort, had retreated to one of the two rooms that the men had slept in, so I didn't have to head out from a shared room, but I still didn't like it one bit.

I tried the food that Emily had made, the roasted vegetables and eggs filling the house with a heavenly scent.

And fuck her, they were good.

Why couldn't they have sucked?

"Do you not like them?" How was it that she could sound like a dog I'd kicked despite how put together she looked? That sort of honesty made my skin crawl.

She reminded me of Jay, and fuck, I didn't like that.

I sighed, then put another forkful of the delicious food into my mouth. "It's great."

"Why do you look upset, then?" Emily tilted her head as she sat across the table from me, her expression showing no understanding. Of course she wouldn't understand—she was far too good a person to get things like petty jealousy.

"I'd just been hoping your food would be terrible," I admitted.

"Why?"

"Because everything else about you is so perfect. I figured I'd be happy if something you did was horrible."

Her eyes widened slightly, the action shaming me as much as my words. It seemed she'd figured out what I meant.

It took Emily a long moment before she said anything else, and I tried to just focus on the food instead of her.

Yes, delicious food flavored with just the right amount of awkward and uncomfortable tension.

"Tyrus looks good," she said.

I lifted my gaze, struggling to follow her train of thought.

She offered me a sweet smile, a cup in her hands that she drank from while she hadn't served herself any of the food. "I remember when we were married. It was a long time, at least for a regular human life. He wasn't perfect, but he always made sure the kids and I were taken care of. We didn't see him as much as we would have liked, but he never let us down."

I swallowed hard, hating to hear about their perfect little family life. It was a life I could never have, one I couldn't offer to Tyrus.

No matter what I wanted, I couldn't give Tyrus kids, couldn't ever have a quiet little house with children and marriage and all that bullshit that people normally strove for.

Emily here had given him that, though.

That stung, the fact that I was helpless.

It didn't matter what I did, what I wanted, there were things that weren't possible for me.

It was the first time I'd really considered that, where I'd thought about what I could and couldn't do.

"Yeah," I said softly, hoping my voice didn't give away the aching inside me. I was pathetic enough without Little Miss Perfect seeing me like this. "I bet he was a good husband. No matter what happens, he always takes care of me."

Emily took a sip from her cup, then set it down, her gaze strangely focused. It reminded me of Tyrus in a way, how she remained silent while studying my reactions.

Then again, they *had* been married. Was it that surprising that she might have picked up a few things from him?

"Tyrus was always careful to fulfill what he saw as his role, his job as protector and provider for our family. I could never fault him for all he did, and right up until the last moment, he gave all he had for us." She paused, and it took all I had not to snap at her that I didn't need to hear about just how amazing their life had been. Except, when she spoke again, her words took me entirely by surprise. "Despite that all, I rarely if ever saw him truly smile. He did when our children were born, and on rare other occasions, but they were passing moments of happiness. I don't think I even realized it was missing before."

"He isn't much of a smiler," I admitted.

"Maybe he isn't, but I thought that was just his personality. I thought he just didn't show his happiness, or perhaps he just wasn't capable of it. He always did what he needed to, so I have no complaints about him as a husband, but he never seemed happy."

"Tyrus is hard to read. Fuck knows I have no idea what he's thinking most of the time."

Emily shook her head. "I just thought he wasn't capable of anything else, but I was wrong." She looked up at me again, meeting my gaze and locking in as if she wanted to ensure I didn't miss anything of what she had to say. "He smiles when he looks at you. It's subtle, but it's there. It's real. It's an expression I never saw from him, one I didn't think him capable of. *You* make him happy in a way I never did, in a way he never was before."

"I don't know about that," I muttered, unsure how else to respond.

"It's true. I get why you feel uncomfortable. I doubt either of you were expecting to run into me, right? Noah isn't much happier about this than you are, either. The truth is, though, that whatever Tyrus and I had is long over—and it wasn't really love anyway. It was duty and responsibility and mutual respect. I doubt either of us realized it wasn't love, not until we moved on and found real love. So, thank you."

I sat up straighter, unsure how to respond.

She smiled again, her expression softening. "I've worried about him for a long time and seeing him find someone who makes him happy eases me so much. Nothing I could say would really explain it to you, would make you understand just how much it means to me. Tyrus is a good man, no matter what he thinks, and he deserves someone by his side. I was never the right person for that because he always felt the need to protect me, to take care of me. He needed a partner, and I don't think I could have ever been that sort of person. *You* are, though, and seeing you together, it makes me feel like no matter how terrible things have been, the horrors I made it through, maybe it was all worth it. Maybe it all pushed us to right here, to where we belonged. Growth and change are hard and painful, but maybe it's worth it."

I snapped my mouth shut when I realized it hung open, when her words seemed to hollow out my brain and make it impossible to respond.

Thankfully, no response was needed, since a large yawn preceded a masculine voice. "Smells fucking delicious."

Hale plopped down into a seat beside me, the action breaking the moment and letting me breathe.

He cast me a questioning glance, which told me he'd probably noticed the atmosphere and had broken in to help me out. I smiled at him, a silent thanks.

Hale nodded, then served himself some food, signaling the end of Emily and my conversation.

At least, the end of it out loud. Her words still circled in my head, making me think about what she meant, about how sometimes the things we really wanted, the things we needed, weren't so obvious. We often didn't know what they were until we saw them.

I'd done that with Gunnar, hadn't I? I'd accepted things that weren't great because I didn't know any better, because I had no idea there was anything better or more out there for me.

So I ate my food in silence, our conversation repeating in my head, as the other men slowly made their way into the living room to eat as well.

Yep, one big happy, awkward family eating breakfast together in heaven.

Both life and the afterlife were really fucking weird.

* * * *

Hale

"We ready?" Loch came up, her damp hair suggesting she'd just gotten out of the shower. A breeze blew past her, carrying a citrus scent to my nose — must be her soap or shampoo.

"Just packing up," Noah said. "We'll pass through a few of the outer towns on the way to the main city."

"Why do we have to pass through anything? Isn't it faster to just go straight for the palace?" Gorrin asked, the amulet on his wrist and his lack of wings telling me that at least had worked.

Noah checked on the items in the back of the wagon, securing them with ropes, checking the knots. "You want everything to look normal, which means sticking with routine. I'm regular when it comes to my trading. If I show up when and where I'm supposed to, no one will think twice. If I change that, if I get into the city sooner than usual, if I miss my other stops, people will start asking why. It's best if we stick to what's normal."

"And you don't think anyone is going to wonder who your new buddies are?" Loch asked. "Because in case you haven't noticed, we don't exactly blend."

Noah nodded at the wagon as if to say, 'yep, it's all secure.' The action almost made me laugh, reminding me of the thing all men did when securing loads in the back of a truck. It seemed some things were so universal that nothing could change them—not even death. "The thing is, there *are* dangers to my work."

"At the cave, you said no one would dare steal from you," Tyrus pointed out.

"I didn't know anything about you at the time—I wasn't going to tell you anything important. The truth is that no one would steal the things in that cave, but I do have some rarer, more valuable items. I don't move them often, not unless I have a buyer already lined up."

"So you have one?" Loch asked.

"Sort of."

I furrowed my brows, hating when people talked in fucking circles. I tended to prefer things upfront and open, to know exactly where I stood with others. These games, just fucking around without any real information, it annoyed the hell out of me. In fact, it made me feel stupid, like I was just too dumb to keep up. "Get to the fucking point," I snapped.

Noah offered me a bored look that said he wasn't nearly as afraid of me as he should have been. "There's an angel in the palace who's wanted something. He paid me a finder's fee a long time ago to keep an eye out for it."

"So you're going to trick him and just pretend to have found it?"

"Oh, no, I found it a long time ago. I just don't like to deal with angels directly. I avoid them whenever I can."

"But you still took the finder's fee?" Tyrus asked. "That seems unwise."

"If I'd said no, I would have pissed him off. I don't like to be around angels, but getting on the bad side of one is far worse."

Tyrus ran his thumb along his jawline, his eyes narrowed. The bastard was a good strategist, and I had no doubt he was working this through from every angle. "Because the angel is from the palace, that will give you access to get us in. Additionally, because you will be transporting something so valuable, having security makes sense, thus few would think twice about you having others with you."

Noah snorted softly. "You all really are dangerous, aren't you? It didn't take long for you to work out exactly what my plan was. I guess I should be glad you're on my side, huh?"

His words struck me weird, causing a strange warmth in my chest at the idea of someone considering me an ally.

The other Lords and Loch, they were different. We had to spend time together for our goal, but Noah? He said that as if we were buddies, as if he trusted me.

And I had no fucking idea what to do with that. No one trusted me, least of all some spirit who was helping us for God only knew what reason.

"I packed lots of food." Emily came out, a large basket in her arms, the contents seeming heavy enough that she struggled.

Not for long, though. Noah was there a heartbeat later, taking the basket from her with a smile. "You should have told me, and I'd have carried it for you."

She brushed him off, a flush on her cheeks. "You have enough on your plate already. There's no reason for you to have to do my job, too."

I stared at the two of them for a moment, unsure how to handle them. I hadn't had a lot of relationships in my life — or my afterlife. Loch was about the extent of anything that lasted beyond a casual fling, and it wasn't like I could call what she and I had normal in any sense of the word.

It was passionate and violent and full of anger and questions. It made me wonder how it would feel to have something as easy as Noah and Emily had. How would I feel to have Loch rush toward me with a smile like that? Would it melt me the way it did when Noah looked at Emily?

Or maybe I was just lacking that gene, the one that made things like that possible.

"How long will you be gone?" Emily asked.

Noah placed the large basket in the back of the wagon and worked at securing it with rope. "I don't know. Normally, it'd take me a week there and a week back, but we're going to take some back routes to avoid the heavily patrolled roads. Then it depends on how long the city takes."

Emily nibbled at her bottom lip in a piss-poor attempt to hide her worry. "I want you to be careful," she whispered.

Noah cupped her cheeks. "I will be — don't worry. If anything happens, if you get word about anything going wrong or if I'm not back in two weeks, I want you to go to Mae and stay there, just to be safe."

Emily nodded, her eyes glistening with tears that she refused to shed. It meant she was tougher than she seemed at first glance. Then again, she'd been married to Tyrus, right? It took a tough bitch to survive being with him.

Noah leaned in and kissed her, the touch gentle despite the danger of the situation. It made me frown. In that position, I'd have kissed the ever-living-fuck out of Loch. I'd have been lucky to resist striping her down and having my way with her right there, in fact.

Noah, though, did none of that. Instead, he touched her gently, as though she were precious and fragile. Was that because he cared for her more than I did for Loch or less?

Or maybe just differently.

Emily pulled away, and after a quick goodbye to everyone else, took off back toward the house. She probably didn't want to have to watch Noah leave, to let him see her upset.

I gazed at Loch, the same questions plaguing me. I wanted to define and understand my feelings for her, my wants, but I never felt like I could get a grip on them. They seemed too big, too wild to figure out.

"Come on, get in," Noah said and patted the wagon. "I'll be up at the front with the oxen, but you all can sit back here."

Gorrin, Tyrus and Yazmor got in first, easily hopping into the back of the wagon. It creaked beneath their weight, but the two large oxen at the front shouldn't have a problem dragging all the merchandise and our asses. The three men shifted around until they found places to sit.

Loch grabbed the edge of the wagon and placed her foot on the wheel. She hefted herself up, but her foot slipped. She toppled backward, everything happening so quickly she didn't even get a yelp out.

Except, she didn't hit the ground. Instead, I moved fast enough to catch her, her small, soft body fitting into my arms so perfectly that the moment I touched her, I didn't want to let her go.

She had squeezed her eyes shut tight, as if she'd thought if she didn't see herself falling, it wouldn't hurt so much. She cracked one open, peeking out to see my face.

The smile she flashed me there made my heart stutter, time slowing from that look alone.

It took me back to when Noah had taken the basket from Emily, when he'd helped her carry it, when she'd smiled at him.

I hadn't thought that possible for me...but maybe I wasn't as far off as I thought. Sure, I wasn't Noah and Loch sure as fuck wasn't Emily, but we had our own softness between us. Even as fucked up as we were, as twisted, we somehow eased the darker parts of one another.

Unwilling to let her go, I held her against me with one arm and used my other to help me hop into the wagon. I plopped down near the back of the wagon, leaning against the closed gate, with Loch securely in my lap.

"I can sit on my own, you know?" she muttered in a sullen tone.

"You can't if I don't let you go." I whispered those words right into her ear, rewarded with a tempting shiver that ran through her. "And I don't ever plan to fucking let you go."

Chapter Eight

Loch

"My ass is entirely numb." I shifted, as if that would wake it up and stop the pins and needle sensation.

As it turned out, riding in the back of a wagon pulled down a rough dirt road was even worse than sitting on Gorrin's stupid throne.

And right now, *everything* was stupid. The throne. The wagon. The Plains. The Lords.

Well, maybe not them.

"Well, being numb there might just make things a bit easier on you," Gorrin said, a teasing note in his voice despite the fact his face showed none of it.

If he thought I'd blush, he'd be disappointed. Even if his words had shamed me, I wouldn't show it. I enjoyed defying expectations too much for that.

"You think I need to be numb? Don't you have a high opinion of yourself?" I let myself glance at his lap then quirked my eyebrow up in question.

Which was such a fucking lie I was lucky I didn't burst into flames right there on the spot. Implying that Gorrin's cock was undersized at all was a joke, but I couldn't stop myself from needling him. I enjoyed the back-and-forth too much.

He didn't rise to the occasion, only let out a soft breath of air that came out like a laugh.

Yazmor stood and pointed forward, reminding me of a child on a road trip who had just seen the amusement part we were headed for. "Look! Buildings!"

The wagon hit a small hole in the road, the action throwing Yazmor off balance. He toppled over the edge of the wagon, hitting the road hard.

No one even batted an eye since that was far from the first time the same exact thing had happened. In fact, I'd stopped counting when one hand wasn't enough to keep track anymore, especially because he just refused to learn.

His head appeared from the side of the wagon after he got back to his feet, Noah not even stopping the oxen anymore. Yazmor brushed himself off, staring forward as if he hadn't just fallen all the way off the wagon in front of everyone. "Are we stopping there?"

Noah shook his head, his expression holding a very special annoyance reserved for dealing with Yazmor. "Yeah, we are. It's the last stop before getting to the gates of the city."

And I really was looking forward to that. We'd done this damn trip for two days, stopping at multiple places, dealing with all sorts of people. Noah sure knew everyone, it seemed, and they all seemed fans of him.

He was well liked and respected from what I could tell, and he easily interacted with all sorts of people.

Some were nice, some reminded me of snakes, but they all welcomed Noah like family.

Still, we'd ridden through the night, making good time, and it was taking a toll on all of us. Noah had assured us that just before we reached the gates, we'd stop for a full night in one of the towns just outside the main city gates.

And I couldn't fucking wait. I wanted to stretch, to move around, to sit somewhere that didn't put my ass to sleep again.

I didn't really care where that place was.

The strangest thing about the Plains I'd noted was how much open space rested between the towns. In the Chasm, most souls had gathered together, existing in the one large city. They'd pressed in closer and closer until we almost lived on top of each other. That didn't seem true about the Plains.

Why?

I couldn't figure it out. Worse? The Plains had an underlying sense of dread, a tension running through everyone that was impossible to ignore. They were all on edge, all ready for something to go horribly wrong.

Yazmor walked the rest of the way — though for part of it, I swore he'd started to skip — and when we finally pulled into the small town, I could have dropped to the ground and kissed the dirt in thanks.

Except, after sitting for that long, I might have ended up unable to get back up, so I held the edge of the wagon for dear life instead.

"This place seems nice," I said to distract everyone from my current state.

Noah patted the oxen, then made his way back to where I was. "It's one of the quieter places outside the city. As we near the gates, the risks get larger in general.

You get people more desperate to get in there, more willing to do whatever it takes." He sighed, then looked me right in the eye. "We also have a much higher chance of running into an angel here, so guard your words and watch your step."

I nodded, unsure what else to say. Normally I'd have laughed and sworn up and down that I could handle anything that came my way. However, my brain went back to Azael, to how utterly outmatched I'd been there. It made me bring my fingers to that mark on my wrist, the shape of the dagger there a talisman that made me feel both safer and so much less safe.

Noah noted the action but said nothing about it—I liked a man who knew when to keep his mouth shut. "I'm going to go get our rooms set up for tonight. Meet me at the building there." Noah pointed at a large place down the road. "I won't be long, so order some food and wait for me there." With that, he took off in the opposite direction, toward what I could only guess was the inn.

Yazmor came over, a bounce to his step I understood. "So I hear we're going to go eat. I feel like there are probably fantastic places to eat here." He slid his arm through the crook of my elbow then tugged me forward, gaining us the glares of Hale, Gorrin and Tyrus who huffed but followed.

"I've never been here, you know," Yazmor said.

"Really? That surprises me. Since you can come here whenever you want, I figured you would have."

"I've been to the Plains before, but I usually stay farther away from the city."

"Why?" I peered in the direction of the city, close enough now to glimpse the top of a large tower—the palace from what I'd heard. "The city seems to be where everything interesting is."

"I don't care for following the rules, and that's the motto of the city. I prefer to stay away from there and enjoy the outer areas. The Chasm is home for me, though." He shifted his gaze toward me, a tension to his smile as if he was about to say something he wasn't sure he should. Still, in true Yazmor fashion, he went ahead and said it without thinking too deeply about any consequences. "*You* are home for me, now."

I tried to ignore the heat that sprang up on my cheeks, as though if I only didn't notice it, no one else would either. "That's not fair," I muttered.

"What isn't?"

"You're funny and chaotic and more than a little trouble. You're not supposed to be able to just whip out romantic lines like that. That's cheating."

Yazmor chuckled and leaned in, pressing a kiss to my check, the warmth of his lips teasing and soft. "As you often like to say, I'm a devil, Loch. We aren't known for fighting fair."

And just like that, my heart raced, and I had no idea how I was going to survive him, not when he could put me this far off balance.

* * * *

While surprising that Yazmor would be right about anything, he was totally right about the food in the Plains. It put what we had in the Chasm to shame. I'd thought before it had just been Mae and Emily's food, as if they were just wonderful cooks, but that didn't seem to hold true.

Maybe you're just so used to dust in all your food that now anything without hell-dirt seems gourmet.

That was fine. Low standards made life always feel so much more fun.

I sat at the table in the corner with the men, a large platter of food at the center of the table and smaller plates in front of each of us. They'd cooked what appeared to be a roast with vegetables, then brought the entire pan out to the table.

I would have normally laughed at how much food it was, but the men were already getting close to polishing it all off. In addition to that, a large pitcher of water sat beside the food, and it was so crystal clear that I could have cried out of joy.

Hale bumped his shoulder into mine. "You look happy."

"So?"

"So, when you're happy, you're usually planning something."

"Rude," I muttered. "Also, untrue."

Hale lifted his eyebrow to call me a fucking liar, and despite my attempt to be angry, a smile eventually spread across my features.

"Fine." I gave in. "I was thinking that this food makes this place really feel like heaven."

Hale let out a soft sigh, as if he didn't care for my words. "You're gonna be the death of me, I fucking swear," he said, his voice low and sullen.

I turned a confused look his way, but he'd dropped his gaze to the food in front of him as if he didn't want to continue the discussion any further.

Instead, Tyrus spoke up. "You have always been far too willing to believe that this place is good, that it is some ultimate goal."

"Just me?" I shot him a hard look. "Last I checked, we *all* suffer from our own issues about whether or not we're good people."

"I don't." Yazmor raised his hand. "I worried about whether my species was any good, but I don't worry about if I belong in the Plains or the Chasm."

Tyrus and I looked at Yazmor for only a split second before returning to our conversation as if he hadn't chimed in.

"I understand that," Tyrus said, "but you are more drawn to wanting to be seen as good than the rest of us. Even after all we've seen here, what you know about Hubis, a part of you still craves belonging here so badly. It's obvious when you talk about this place, as if it is the white pearly gates that you have always pictured. It makes me worried that you will value this place too much, that you will be unable to see the reality of it."

I blew out a breath, hating when they had a point. "I'll be careful, okay? I know nothing is perfect, that no place is ideal, but that doesn't change that this place *does* have some benefits. Whether it lives up to the hype or not, it was created as a reward to those seen as good, to give them a good afterlife. I saw Emma, heard Mae's story, I understand that it has its flaws."

Gorrin sighed and rubbed his temple with one finger. "This place has a much uglier side than you have even seen. Have you never wondered why I flourished in the Chasm so well? Because I learned cruelty *here*."

With that, the conversation dwindled, all of us just picking at the food because we had no idea how to get back the ease from before. Gorrin's words hung over the table, like dark clouds just waiting to open and drench us all.

"Got a place." Noah pulled up a chair and sat at the end of the table, then dropped a few keys on the table.

"At the inn?" I asked.

"No. They didn't have room. There isn't a lot of travel here, so most places only have one or two rooms available."

"So where are we staying?" Gorrin asked.

"We could camp out under the stars!" Yazmor said with a grin.

"There are no stars," I reminded him, then patted his shoulder when his smile fell.

Noah went on, already accustomed to Yazmor's little outbursts. "I was able to rent the entire barn where the wagon and the oxen are stabled. It has space on the second level to sleep, and since it isn't that cold today, it'll work. Besides, it'll keep you all together, under one roof, which is probably for the best."

"Are you expecting trouble?" Tyrus asked.

Noah shook his head, but the motion had a hesitation to it. "Not exactly. However, word of you all had already reached the owner of the barn when I was setting that up. You stick out, even when you don't cause any trouble. If everyone was in their own room, the odds of someone trying something would go up. With all of you together, though, only an idiot would attack."

I peered toward the window, where the light still shone. "So what do we do now?"

"Relax," Noah said. "I have some trading to do in town, and I won't return to the barn to sleep tonight. Seeing clients takes a while, and they usually want me to stay. We'll head to the city tomorrow morning, so take the rest of today and tonight to take it easy. You won't get the chance again, not after we reach the gates." Noah knocked his knuckles against the table then rose. After explaining where the barn was, he headed off, leaving us alone.

His words rang in my ears, the fact that we were so close to the end of this trip. It echoed in my head, a reality that I hadn't faced much. The end of this little trip had felt so far away for so long, but here we were, so close.

One way or another, this would all come to an end soon.

Chapter Nine

Gorrin

Loch smiling was something I didn't think I would ever get enough of. It felt strange, as it did each time, yet it loosened that constant tightness in my chest that I had lived with for so long.

She sat at the large firepit in the middle of the building that was a cross between a bar, a lodge and a restaurant. She could be surly and difficult, but she also managed to find friends wherever she went.

It was a talent I lacked.

As evidenced by the fact she had four people huddled around her while not a single person had chosen to speak to me.

Hale and Tyrus hadn't done much better. Yazmor, though, had somehow ended up waitressing, with an apron on and a tray balanced on his hand as he delivered drinks and food to tables.

What an odd bunch.

Laughter drew my attention back to Loch and her group, to the way she smirked at the woman across from her, cards in both their hands.

"She draws people to her wherever she goes," Tyrus said from beside me.

"She does. It is both her strength and her weakness, because she never sees people for who and what they really are. She fails to see the dangers they might pose to her."

"She sees it," Tyrus argued. At my look, he shrugged. "Loch knows that the people may harm her, that they might turn on her, but she accepts that risk. It is a foolish strength that she possesses, and it is often the core of her problems."

I nodded, unable to argue with him. I recalled when I'd spoken to her about Gunnar, how she'd been unwilling to listen to reason, how she wanted to help him.

I failed to understand why, when she gained nothing from it, but I had given up understanding every action she took. We were too different to hope for that.

Instead, I tried to accept the actions, to support her without understanding.

Obedience is needed, not understanding.

Hubis' words came back to me, the lessons he'd imparted on me over so many years. He had never cared what I thought, only that I did as I was told.

That had felt safe at first, but later had chafed. Would it feel the same with Loch?

No. Loch was different. She didn't demand obedience, had never attempted to force me to obey. She only stood her ground and did as she felt was right, and my response was always my own.

"We are nearing the end," I said.

"Yeah, I feel the same way. Maybe it is because we are nearing the gates, but it feels as if the rubber band we have pulled all this time will snap soon. No matter how it ends, this will all be over soon."

"Do you have any regrets?" My question surprised even me.

Tyrus took a long moment, as if he had to weigh his answer. Finally, he sighed and slumped forward. "More than I can count. I have done many things because I believed I had no choice, had walked down paths I loathed, done things after which I could not face a mirror the next day, all because I believed them to be necessary. I accepted the consequences because I was a man, because I would do what was needed. I did not think I would ever regret such things, but when I met her..."

Tyrus shifted his gaze to Loch, a softness around his eyes that I had never seen in the years before Loch had come to the Chasm. "I saw her stand up for what she believed no matter the risk, and it makes me wonder if my choices had been made from cowardice. She makes me regret many things in my life. You?"

I had asked him that question, yet having it turned around on me felt invasive. Why did it surprise me that he would ask me that back? Perhaps because I had so rarely had people in life one might call a friend that back-and-forth conversations were mostly unknown to me.

Still, I owed him an honest response. "I don't know. The things I've done, even those I am not proud of, led me here. Had I not lied to Loch, to you all, would things have gone differently? Perhaps, but perhaps that difference would not have led us *here*. If I had made other choices, perhaps I would have never been able to meet Loch, to have this time with her, to even bridge the gap between us. I struggle to regret the things I have done because they have brought me here, and no matter what here is like, it is better than the darkness from before."

The moment I finished speaking, I pressed my lips together, feeling far too exposed for my own comfort.

Tyrus didn't mock me, however. Instead, he let out a soft laugh and shook his head. "I wonder sometimes about the first time we met her. She was dying, nearly gone, and yet still filled with so much fire. Normally, a single human soul could not draw even one of us, let alone all of us, but she did. I think back to myself at that moment, and I wonder, did I know? Somewhere inside of me, did I know what she would become to this world, to us?"

"I did not. How could I? She was and is unprecedented. She is unpredictable and wild and stubborn. She is a fire no one sees coming, something painful and dangerous, yet after she passes? After she seems to tear so much apart, she makes way for something new and better."

I turned my gaze then to Loch, to her smile. She wasn't a light in the darkness because that was far too simple a thing. She was darkness as well, a mixture of good and bad, and perhaps a fire was the best description possible.

However, even if she was fire, I would never let go. I would let her burn me to ash to the very last moment.

* * * *

Loch

"You can't be serious," the woman, Maddy, said as she leaned in closer with a smile on her pink lips. Her eyes were wide, as if my story was hard to believe, but she enjoyed the ride just the same. We'd been talking for hours, and for the first time, the Plains had started to not feel quite so horrible.

"I'm totally serious," I swore. "I broke in and I stole the cow off the shop!"

"Why would you steal a fake cow? And *how* would you get it off the roof in the first place?"

I thought back to the story, to so many years ago when I'd been just a teenager causing trouble. So often my antics back then had been more about having to stay alive, having to outsmart people willing to kill me. Maybe that was why the cow story stuck with me so much, because it was one of the few things I did just for fun.

"The shopkeeper there was a dick. He'd always leer at the girls and had been known to have wandering hands. Still, it was one of the only little shops like that in the area, so it wasn't like we had a lot of other options. Because of that, we had to go there even though he was a complete asshat. He was so proud of that cow, and he'd always tell us girls when we bought something high in calories that if we kept eating that way, we could stand in for Betsy."

I remembered the bitter taste of those words, the way they'd stung even if I knew he was just a lecherous old man whose opinion shouldn't have mattered at all.

Now, those words wouldn't have meant shit to me. Some fuckwit thinking my ass was too big or my tits were too small wasn't an issue anymore. Back then, though? I'd still been impressionable, still wanted to fit in so badly that his words had stuck in my head.

"So," I went on, not wanting to get hung up on those unpleasant details, "I decided that I'd free Betsy. I showed up in the middle of the night, hooked up a pulley system, got a couple other girls to distract him, then lowered the cow into the back of a pickup truck."

The sparkle in Maddy's eyes pleased me, as if through it I could see her own backbone growing. It was like planting a seed of rebellion—and every woman needed that.

"Then what? What did you do with it?"

"Betsy hung out in a park a ways away from the store, the next town over. We poured some concrete to secure her in, and everyone just assumed someone else had planned for her. She's still there, and kids play on her, and I feel like it's a much better life for her. Plus, that asshole who made life hard for lots of kids finally got to give back."

Maddy blew out a sharp breath, as if she struggled to believe that such a story could be true. "How do you do that?"

"Do what? The pulley system? Before you get too impressed, there was a *lot* of trial and error before I got that right. I broke many things in the attempts."

She shook her head. "How do you just do what you want no matter the consequences? I mean, that man sounds like he would have done some nasty things to you if he'd found out."

"I just don't think much about it."

"How can you not think about it?" Maddy peered around the room, her lips tipped down. "I've seen a lot here, things that are terrible, and I *want* to do something, but it's like—I can't. My body freezes and I can't get it to move, to do anything." She let out a long sigh. "Maybe I'm just a coward."

I reached out and caught her hand, squeezing it once. "Don't be so hard on yourself. There are a lot of times in my life where I look back and regret what I did or didn't do. Life is scary, and not everyone has to be so up in your face. I mean… I dealt with a man who was abusing girls by stealing his fake cow. There are days where I think back and wonder why I didn't do more. Why didn't I try to turn him in? Why didn't I really stop him? Instead, I annoyed him, saw him ranting and raving for years after about his beloved missing cow, but I didn't really fix anything."

How often had I done something, but not anything that mattered? I picked the route that made me feel as if I helped but didn't do enough to actually change anything.

"I guess we all have regrets," Maddy said. "I just wish I was braver."

I released her hand and sat back, then took a drink of the crisp, cold water on the low table beside me. "Being brave isn't something you wish for. It's something that, when the moment is right, you just do. Eventually, you decide it's worth it to step up, that whatever is going on is so terrible, you can't stay still anymore. Bravery's just a matter of timing."

Maddy nodded, and the desire to warn her came over me. I wanted to make it clear that I was *not* exactly the best person to take advice from. I didn't have a great history of good decision making, so perhaps I should keep all my lofty ideals to myself.

The world did *not* need another Loch running, after all. Just the one was already threatening the very fabric of the universe. I didn't think it could bear the stress of two of us.

"How long are you going to be here?" Maddy asked.

"Just for the night. We're headed into the city tomorrow."

"The city?" the quiet way she said that screamed fear. "That isn't the sort of place you want to go."

"So I've heard, but I don't have much of a choice."

She shook her head. "You don't understand. The city is full of angels and those who follow the angels without question. No one else is allowed. It means you can't trust anyone there."

"I don't trust anyone anyways, so that's not a problem for me." I plastered a smile on my face to reassure her, but it didn't seem to help.

Her next words were whispered, as if she feared them spreading beyond the two of us. "You aren't just here to trade or protect Noah's goods."

"Why do you say that?"

"It's obvious. You and your friends don't belong here, you don't fit in. Just the way you walk, the way you speak, it all says that this place hasn't broken you. I don't know what exactly you're doing here, why you've come, but you won't find anything good in that city. The palace, the beings who live there, they only want to crush everything around them, to force them into the boxes they've created for them. You don't fit into a box, Loch, and if you go there, they'll destroy you."

I tried to smile, to reassure her. "You forget—I'm the girl who stole the cow. I'll be fine."

She sighed, the action telling me she didn't really agree. Still, it wasn't like I had another option.

So instead, I added something else, something truer. "I told you that bravery was just a matter of timing. What I'm doing, what I *need* to do, I can't back down from. It doesn't matter how dangerous it is, how little chance I have at succeeding, I have to try."

She nodded, but her expression still held hints of reluctance. Then again, it was easier to risk myself than it was to allow others to do the same, so I understood how she felt. Fuck, it made me respect her more, that she valued others that much.

I went to say something else, but the world stuttered to a stop around me. The door opened — not loudly, as if shoved with too much force, but that didn't stop it from somehow catching the attention of everyone inside.

And the reaction was for all sound to stop. No one moved — no one seemed to even breathe. I twisted around to find the cause of it.

There, at the door, entered a man dressed in a fine suit with a severe expression on his face. He exuded power, and the reason was obvious enough. The large, white wings that struggled to fit through the door explained not only the power I felt from him, but also the reaction of the other patrons.

And that went to show just how shitty my luck really was.

The last thing I'd wanted was to see an angel here.

Maddy shifted easily to the seat beside me, then set a hand on the back of my neck, forcing me to lean forward. It pulled my gaze from the angel and made me blend into the crowd.

Right, everyone had stopped moving so no one would draw the predator's attention. I allowed my gaze to move around, best I could, while I faced down at the glass of water in my hands.

"Just stay quiet," Maddy whispered.

"Who is that?"

"Orline," she said. "He is a lesser angel who patrols this area. He likes to come in here and ensure people are following the rules."

"Lovely—a Karen."

Line appeared in Maddy's forehead, suggesting she didn't get the joke. Then again, that was a newer joke, so it wasn't that shocking she might not get it.

Orline moved past us, then headed up to the bar. Yazmor was on the other side—was he bartending now? I squeezed my hand around the glass, hoping that for just this once Yazmor could just behave and keep his mouth shut.

Just pretend to be normal, please!

"A drink," Orline said, no pretense of manners as he said his order. The worst part was there wasn't even malice, as if Yazmor were nothing more than an automated drink machine that didn't deserve either manners or insults.

"What kind of drink?" Yazmor asked, his voice so careful that I struggled to believe it even came from him. I had no idea Yazmor *could* sound like that!

"Wine. Something from the top shelf. I don't care for the swill you serve to others."

Yazmor nodded, then caught a bottle of red wine from the top shelf. He took a wine glass from beneath the counter, then pulled the cork and poured the red liquid into the glass. He managed it so smoothly, I had to wonder if he'd done it before.

Orline took the glass and lifted it to his lips, sipping at it with an elegance I found more annoying than sexy. Sure, watching Hale drink whiskey or Tyrus drink fancy wine turned me on, but somehow Orline left me dryer than the Mojave desert.

"You all are quieter than usual," Orline said as he turned to look out at the entire room. Despite him moving his gaze from person to person, it almost felt as if he stared *right* at me. The gulp from Maddy said she felt that same thing.

Talk about an unnerving talent. This fucker would do great as a prison guard or a teacher.

No one answered, but his statement didn't welcome conversation.

Hale sat at a back corner of the room, a glass in his hand, his gaze hard but his body still. It meant he wasn't planning on attacking—at least not yet. Gorrin and Tyrus were only a table away from me, seated together, both avoiding looking at Orline.

And, thankfully, Orline's gaze seemed to move right over Gorrin, meaning his amulet worked to hide his angelic nature.

Orline took a few steps toward the center of the room, toward where I was by the fire pit. "Normally, you all at least try to pretend not to mind my visits. You put on a good face, acting as if you are not afraid or bothered by my presence. Today is different, though." He sat himself across from Maddy and me, but I didn't get the sense he was looking *at* us. It seemed more that he just wanted to be the biggest nuisance he could, which meant planting his ass at the center of the action.

"Aren't you going to say hello to me, Maddy?" Violence and threat dripped from his words, as if he'd soaked them in that malice before spitting them out.

"Hello," Maddy answered, her tone nothing like what I'd heard from her all evening. Normally, she was sweet, with a liveliness in her tone that made me want to smile. Now, though? She sounded dead, as if everything inside her had drained away. "Welcome back," she added on.

"How could I stay away? You all require my firm hand to ensure you remain on the proper path. I see you are wearing a skirt this time."

"You said the jeans were unbecoming," Maddy said.

And just like that, I wondered if I could stab him and get away with it. I could bury my dagger right between his ribs, and unlike with Gorrin, I really wanted *this* asshole to die.

A glance past him showed Tyrus shaking his head *no* in a single, rough jerk. *Right, that would just announce our presence.*

We needed to fly under the radar, and the way to do that was probably not by leaving angel bodies in our wake.

"Yes. The new styles on Earth are not fitting for the Plains, for the chosen who are fortunate enough to spend eternity here. A skirt is far more fitting for a female." His gaze moved to me, to the slacks I wore, and he made a soft *tsk* that screamed displeasure.

And what the fuck was wrong with me that I liked that? If he'd taken one look at me and been impressed, I was pretty sure I'd have felt slighted by that. Annoying him, though?

I had to fight a smile.

"And who is your friend? I do not believe I have seen her around before." He stared hard at me even though his words were clearly meant for Maddy.

"She's someone I met farther away from the city," Maddy said, her voice quivering but giving nothing away.

In fact, I was rather impressed by that. Maddy had seemed so fragile, I would have expected her to just crumble the moment anyone pressed. Instead, she held firm.

"So introduce us."

Maddy said nothing, so I spoke up for her. "I'm Loch."

"Loch? I certainly would have recalled if I had seen you previously." He caught my chin between his fingers, forcing my face up toward his. He tilted my face to see each side—no doubt to look at my tattoos. "These would stick out if you spent much time this close to the gates."

"That's why I don't come this close often," I said.

"Indeed. You are quite fortunate you ran into me and not anyone else. Others of my kind are less forgiving of people like you."

"People like me?" I winced as soon as the words escaped me, because I sure as hell shouldn't have opened my mouth and said something that came out like such a challenge. Still, it seemed my mouth moved a lot faster than my brain.

Orline smirked, as if amused by my statement. "Yes, *like you*. Those who buck against the order, who wish to stand out. What other reason would you have to wear your hair in such an unnatural color, to mark your face in such a way?" He dug his fingers into my face, but I refused to make a sound, to admit that it hurt.

I'd wear whatever marks he left, but fuck him if he thought I'd let him know he hurt me.

"I can't really change it anymore."

His smile widened. "No, you can't, can you? It is one of the things that people fail to recognize or accept, that the choices one makes on Earth follow them forever. You made poor choices there, and now you must live with the consequences. Of course, despite your looks, you have a draw I can't quite explain..." His words trailed off, as though he searched for a way to figure it out himself.

I pulled backward, and he released his grip to let me go. Soreness in my chin said he'd gripped me hard enough to bruise me, but I still ignored it. Instead, I lifted the water to my lips, going for casual and nonchalant.

Past him, I spotted Gorrin and Tyrus both all but on the edges of their seats, clearly wanting to jump in and intervene but holding themselves back.

The reality was that between the five of us, we could take the angel, but we didn't need this sort of heat. I met Gorrin's gaze, trying to beg him to behave himself.

And hopefully the same message was understood by the others as well.

In fact, I refused to even look toward Hale, because he was the *last* person we needed to draw attention to.

If I didn't look like I belonged, it was nothing compared to that walking train wreck of a person.

"So how long will you be here?" Orline asked, but his words felt more like a challenge than a conversation.

"Just the night."

"That is all? What a long trip just for a night."

"I was working for a merchant as security."

Orline lifted one of his dark eyebrows. "You must mean Noah. No other trader who works out this way would have enough goods to require security. You also appear *far* too little to be of much good. Security is a male's job, after all."

Security is a male's job. I repeated his words in my head using the most mocking tone I could possibly manage, just barely keeping myself from uttering it aloud.

Instead, I smiled far too wide, taking a page from Yazmor's playbook. "A lot of people have thought that. I welcome you to try and rob him and see. Fuck around and find out is my motto."

And just like that, Maddy's fear and Gorrin's absolute exasperation hit me all at once. Okay, so maybe it wasn't the smartest thing to say, but my leash on my mouth was only so long and this asshole had managed to snap it.

Instead of lashing out, he let out a soft chuckle, treating me like some bug who had done a neat trick. "I suspect this will not be the last time we interact. With a mouth like that, you clearly do not understand your place. It is a common issue with those who remain too far away from the city. I look forward to helping you find your place here." The perverted excitement of that statement chilled my blood.

I'd seen plenty of times just how much people who enjoyed such games could inflict pain, and I had no desire to experience it myself yet again.

"As much as I would like to do so now, I have, as they say, bigger fish to fry at the moment." He turned his gaze back to Maddy. "There are whispers about change."

"Change?"

"Yes. Such whispers reach even the city, the palace. There is a current on the winds, the scent of betrayal, of mutiny. I have smelled it wherever I go over the past few weeks, but it is getting stronger."

"I don't know what you mean," Maddy said. "But then, I don't have the powers you do."

Orline made a soft sound, as if he wasn't sure he believed her. He dismissed that so quickly, however, that I drew my free hand into a fist. He acted as if she were just a pet, something he was sure was so stupid and loyal that she would never betray him.

It took me back to how she'd asked me about how to be brave, and in that moment, I knew she had far more bravery in her than she realized.

"Whether or not you feel it doesn't change that it is there. Other angels have felt it as well. Something is coming, something that threatens the order we strive so hard to maintain here. However, it is far harder to know what is going on for us, since we try hard to not involve ourselves too much in the lives of spirits."

I fought the urge to roll my eyes at that.

Clearly, he didn't mean that shit in the least. From the fear on Maddy's face, from everything I'd seen, the angels had no issues involving themselves in everything they wanted to. What he meant was that he didn't want to have to know or give a damn about others.

It was like the cops in the worst areas of cities — they enforced rules, but none of the people who lived there would dare speak to them.

Which meant I suddenly understood why Orline had come, what his reasoning was. He was trying to gather information about whatever this change was.

And a laugh nearly spilled from me because *I* was the change he was looking for. Sitting here, right in front of him, was the reason for his unease, for his fear. Of course, he would never believe that. It was far easier for him to write me off as just some stupid woman with oddly colored hair.

"You are always speaking to those who come through," Orline pressed. "You make friends with every passer-by, involve yourself with every individual no matter how unwise it is. If anyone heard about plans, it would be you."

Maddy shook her head, her gaze down. "I haven't heard anything. I would tell you if I had."

"Neither have I."

"So how do you know there's anything going on then?"

Orline smiled, the expression sharp and unnerving. "Do you ever hunt?"

Maddy shook her head. "No. I do some gardening, but I don't hunt."

"When hunting dangerous beasts, there is a moment that you wait for. When you hear things, you can breathe easily. The moment things become silent, when everything stops making noise, that is when one must worry. See, predators go silent before they strike. Normally, my sources bring me plenty of information. They tell me all the rumors and gossip, most of it being entirely pointless. That has not occurred recently, though."

"Maybe there's nothing to know, then."

"No. The absence of information is like the absence of sound when hunting. There is something coming, and a lack of information says it nears. I can follow the path of quiet, from the outer edges of the Plains in, as though when whatever it is enters that space, no more rumors escape. It makes me wonder—is that an accident or are others protecting whatever it is?"

"Why would we protect anything?"

"Because spirits are foolish, and they never stay in their place long. They are always so eager to break free, to rise above their station, that they latch on to anything they think may help. They will see something that will spell their doom, and instead of resisting it, they see it only as a chance at change."

I swallowed hard, hating that he was far smarter than I would have preferred. Why couldn't he be an idiot? Why couldn't he just be some fool who couldn't see past his own nose?

Instead, I had some fucking detective over here, trying to work out our plan.

Though...his words also said that despite all the places we'd gone so far, all the people we'd seen, not even one had ratted us out. Even those who didn't know what we were doing or why, they hadn't spilled the beans, hadn't told the angels anything about us. In fact, Orline didn't even know how many of us there were or what we looked like.

He saw it only as some amorphous 'them' creature that he feared, even if he didn't want to admit it.

"I don't know what you want me to say," Maddy whispered.

Orline reached out, but instead of grabbing my chin as he had the last time, he caught Maddy by her hair and yanked her closer to him. He held her tightly, staring into her eyes. "Tell me the truth. You have always given in eventually, always told me what I wanted, given me what I desired. There is no reason for you to suffer first when we always end up at the same place."

His words turned my stomach, the lines I'd heard enough times from abusers. Fuck, they were the words I'd heard from Gorrin, back when he'd tried to force me to comply with him.

I pressed my fingers to the mark on my wrist, readying myself for pulling the dagger. I struggled to believe that Maddy wouldn't break, that she wouldn't give in and tell him about us. Why would she keep quiet when the risk to her was so great and she didn't know us at all?

If she said a word, I'd move fast. I'd slip the blade right into his chest, burying it to the hilt before he got the chance to even turn his head toward me let alone make a sound.

Sure, we didn't *need* a dead angel, but it was better than getting caught here.

Except, Maddy didn't do that. She kept his gaze, a tremble through her body that showed just how she feared him, but she still didn't give in. "I haven't heard anything—I swear."

Orline narrowed his eyes, the first real sign of anger from him. So, he wasn't nearly as dead to the world as he wanted to let on. Things still could get beneath that hard shell of his.

Like hopefully my dagger, even if it wasn't today.

"Is that your final answer? Think carefully, Maddy, because you know how I dislike having to reeducate people."

She gulped, the sound loud in the quiet of the room, then nodded. "That is my answer."

He snorted, then rose, not releasing her hair. He strolled toward the door, dragging Maddy along with him.

I got up, ready to leap at him, to stop him. In my head, I saw Jay, I saw myself, I saw so many times where someone was forced by those bigger and stronger.

I was *done* sitting back and doing nothing while others suffered. The entire reason I'd come here was to help others, to overthrow a bullshit system that I was tired of just watching destroy others.

A hand caught my arm, and I turned to find Gorrin with his fingers wrapped around me, holding me back. His sharp expression warned me not to do anything stupid.

Which, if I listened, would take away at least seventy-eight percent of my plans away.

I looked away from him, toward Maddy. She didn't struggle against Orline's grip, but she met my gaze and shook her head no with a single quick shake. I hadn't known her long, but that expression seemed to be universal one for 'don't get involved'.

"She remained silent. If you step in now, you will only make that sacrifice pointless," Gorrin whispered.

That last part stuck with me, made it so I stayed still and watched as Orline dragged Maddy from all of us, as he took her toward the unknown, and I had no idea if I'd ever see her again.

So much for being some sort of savior...

Chapter Ten

I tucked the communications ring back into my pocket after ending the connection with Gunnar. Things were going well in the Chasm from what he said, but he seemed far more interested in questioning me than giving me answers.

Then again, I'd learned a long damn time ago that Gunnar did as he pleased. He was like keeping an untrained and dangerous dog around — I had no idea when he might bite me.

"All done?" Hale sat beside me on the floor in the upper area of the barn.

The place had ended up nicer than I expected it to be. When Noah had mentioned a barn for us to sleep in, I'd thought I'd be picking hay out of my nether regions come morning. My head supplied the picture of a tall ladder that led up into a little hay loft, and sure, I had a few not so pure fantasies about Gorrin in a pair of overalls. Instead, it had turned out that the barn had stairs to the second level, and while it *was* open to the main floor where the oxen were, it had rooms and beds.

After spending time in the Path, anything with an actual bed impressed me.

I frowned as I stared at Hale.

"What?" he asked.

"You look different without your piercings."

Hale touched his face, where the lip ring would have been. "It feels fucking weird, like I ain't myself." He paused speaking for a moment, but he kept touching his lip. "Do you prefer me like this?"

I lifted one eyebrow, his question surprising me. Was he really that stupid? One good look said he wasn't kidding, that he really worried I might prefer this version of him. *What an idiot.*

A part of me wanted to tease him, like a small punishment for thinking me that shallow. However, his expression kept me from it. He just looked too damn anxious for me to get any enjoyment from pulling his pigtails. I reached up and slid my thumb across his bottom lip, pausing to tease over where the hole was. "I fell for *you*. Piercings, tattoos and leather are part of you, and I don't want you any other way."

Hale's expression softened, drawing me to lean in and brush my lips to his, to follow the same path I'd stroked with my thumb. When I pulled back, a red tint on his ears made me smile. Who would have thought that Hale would ever make such a face?

"So how's everything in the Chasm?" he rushed out, as if he needed to change the subject.

"Seems to be fine," I answered, trying to hide my smirk.

"So nothing on fire?"

"It's hell — there's lots of things on fire."

Hale snorted. "So you're telling me that there's just the right amount of fire."

"Exactly. It seems Myers and Gunnar are keeping my little corner in check."

Hale nodded, wincing a bit as he shifted on the hard floor. "Yazmor went back, and it seems everything is running smoothly. If anyone's noticed we're gone, they aren't talking about it.

"This is one of the only times when I'm glad I'm so unremarkable that no one notices me being gone." I let out a laugh, then leaned against Hale's side. "I remember a few years before I died, during one of the times where Gunnar and I were off again so I was living alone. I called Kylie up crying about how I was going to die alone, and my pet badger was going to eat my face because no one would notice and bury me."

Hale didn't respond right away, but when he did, it was with a laugh so loud that my cheeks heated. I didn't really like the idea that I'd amused him quite *that* much. Of course, the other part of me enjoyed hearing the sound.

We hadn't had a whole lot to laugh about recently, so even a glimpse of him seemingly uncaring, him having a good time, it reminded me of why I was doing this.

"It isn't *that* funny," I muttered.

"You really thought no one would notice if you were gone? *You?* Because as long as I've known you, you ain't never been the sort of person who doesn't make an impression."

"Yeah, well, that's *now*. Being important sort of goes along with the whole Demon Lord thing, doesn't it?"

"Not really," Hale said. "I haven't seen any other Demon Lords, since I was the newest before you, but fuck knows I've heard stories. There have been plenty who didn't rule long or didn't rule well. They weren't missed and unless they were bad enough to be a warning to others or a hilarious drinking story, they sure as fuck ain't remembered." He nudged me with his shoulder, the touch gentle and oddly sweet. "I don't think you've *ever* been the wallflower type who no one would miss."

I thought about it, the words nice but my brain not accepting them at all. "I think Gunnar was the only one who thought about me. I mean, I was friends with Kylie, with others, but we didn't keep in touch a lot. If I just stopped calling, I think only Gunnar would notice."

"Is that why you forgive him?"

I frowned, the question taking me off guard. It wasn't that it was unexpected as much as it was unexpected from *Hale*. He didn't normally involve himself with things like my other relationships. He might make some bitch-ass comments now and then, complaining or insulting someone, but he didn't usually just come out and ask me anything.

"I don't forgive him," I argued.

"If someone had done a fraction to me that he did to you, I'd have slit his fucking throat already."

"I'm not into throat slitting. I leave that to you."

"I'm serious here, Loch. I don't get it. I thought when he showed up and you didn't immediately toast him that you were just biding your time, that you'd off him within a few days. He's still alive though." Hale paused, then shook his head. "No, fuck that. He's not *just* still alive, he's *in* your life. He might be gathering some power, but he's just a damned. With his attitude, he'd be dead by someone else by now if you weren't protecting him, if you hadn't given him a place beneath you. So why? Why are you still helping him? Do you still love him or something?" His voice dropped lower at the last question, as though he really didn't like having to utter the words.

Or maybe it was better to say he didn't like what the answer might be.

I took a deep breath, then let it out slowly. Prolonging the conversation wouldn't make it any easier, but that felt like a future me problem. Eventually, breathing wouldn't delay the inevitable anymore, though, so I answered. "No, I don't love him. I don't think that I ever did."

"So why? You *know* he's a piece of shit, that he'd betray anyone to get what he wants, and that anyone includes you."

Those words should have hurt, but they didn't. Was that proof that I'd moved on? That I really had put to bed the old lingering feelings I'd had for him? Even during my years in the Chasm before becoming a Lord, as much as I'd hated Gunnar, a tiny part of my mind had thought maybe we'd end up together again. It had wondered if we had enough between us to survive even what he'd done.

I smiled softly at that lack of pain, because it meant I'd finally put that away, that I'd really moved on. Then again, how couldn't I have?

My gaze went around the open upper level, taking in where each of the men was. Hale beside me, Yazmor sitting on the bottom floor, one of the Oxen with its head in his lap, Gorrin and Tyrus sitting at a table across the way, deep in conversation.

These men had taught me what I really wanted, what I deserved, and Gunnar wasn't a part of that. In fact, he couldn't come close to living up to that anymore.

I forced myself to keep going, to explain it to Hale. "I need to save him."

A line appeared in Hale's forehead, and I could have *sworn* I saw him curing me in confusion without him having to say a word.

I could hear him in my head—*why the fuck do you need to do shit for him after all he did to you?*

"I know he isn't a good person, but you know what? Neither am I. Gunnar and I grew up so similar, got together when we were young. No one understands the real me like he does."

"Excuse the fuck outta me?" Hale snapped. "I'm pretty sure I know you a lot better than that fuckwit."

"Don't pout. I mean that he saw me at my worst, that he knows my past in a way no one else does. I know he'd screw over most people, but I don't feel like he would for *me*."

"And why do you think that? You're a smart girl, Loch, even if you make some stupid choices sometimes. You're way too smart to think he wouldn't turn on you if it suited him. In fact, I can see it in your eyes that you know the truth."

"Fine, I know he might betray me, but I have to believe he wouldn't."

"But why?" Hale's temper had slipped, and his anger almost had me smiling at the familiarity of it. How was it that him getting pissed made me feel all warm and fuzzy? "Why the fuck do you give him the chance to hurt you again? Why ignore what he really is? Why not just cut ties and let him fend for himself, even if I'd prefer to just snap his neck and be done with it—"

"Because that could have been me," I whispered, cutting him off. "I was just as bad a person. I've done some awful things, things that keep me up at night, but I'm still going, still kicking. The universe hasn't made me pay the price for all the shit I've done."

"Last I checked, you died, and all the shit that's happened since then? That seems like a big pound of flesh the universe has taken from you."

"It's not enough. I'm still here. I found you all. I haven't done enough to make up for any of the things I've done. When I look at Gunnar, I see my own sins, another flawed, broken person, and I want him to figure it out. I *need* for him to become better, to turn into a good person, because…" My words trailed off, dying in my throat when I struggled to voice the end of that statement.

Hale sighed, his gaze locked down on the main floor instead of on me. "You think that if you can redeem him, you've got a chance at it too, huh?"

When he put it into words like that, I felt both relieved and embarrassed. He'd managed to say exactly what I really wanted even when I'd been unable to explain it myself.

Still, I nodded. "I feel like if he can't be redeemed, if he really is just bad, then I am, too. If he can't become better, then I'm just fooling myself into thinking I can be anything more than what I've always been."

"But you ain't him, Loch. Just because he can't get his head out of his own ass, that doesn't have shit to do with you. You're setting up an impossible task here, thinking that the choices someone else makes somehow determined what sort of person *you* are. That's bullshit. We all make the choices we make, and we all do what we do, and we can't judge ourselves off someone else."

His words made sense — which was impressive for a man like Hale who wasn't known as a real introspective sort of person. Still, they didn't land as he wanted them to, no doubt. "You might be right," I admitted. "But it doesn't stop that I want to give him every chance. I want to prove that people can change, because without that, I don't think I can ever really believe that I can be more than what I've always been. You know? When I first got to the Chasm, I saw it all as a punishment."

"Well, you do call it hell."

"The thing is, the longer I spent in the Chasm, as I made a place for myself there, I haven't seen it the same way. Sure, I've suffered, but look at what I've gotten out of it. I'm stronger, more powerful, have people in my life who I can depend on. By all accounts, I'm doing so much better than I used to. Even with everything I've done, all the people I've hurt, I haven't *really* paid the price. It almost feels like all of this was a reward, but fuck knows I haven't done anything to deserve a reward. It's like…if I see Gunnar reform, then I think I have a chance, too."

He sighed again, then threw his arm around my shoulders, pulling me tighter against his side. "I can't say I really get it, but I've long since given up the idea of redemption. I don't believe in fairy tales like that anymore. However, I respect you enough to know I don't have to understand to support you. Course, if Gunnar fucks up, if he takes aim at you at all, there isn't anything in the Chasm or the Plains or anywhere between that'll keep me from skinning the fucker and gifting that to you."

"What am I supposed to do with a skin?" A smile tugged at the edges of my lips, despite the totally inappropriate conversation.

"I hear they make for good lampshades. Or what about a wallet?" He paused, then chuckled. "Let's use him like a bear skin rug and lay him out in your room — that way he can see me fuck you every night."

I lost the fight against the smile at that. It shouldn't have been nearly as funny as it was, given I was pretty sure he was serious, but I couldn't help it. The offer warmed me, a reminder that no matter how bad things got, how unsure I felt, I had people with me, those supporting me, those willing to skin my enemies and make rugs out of them for me.

"You ain't supposed to laugh when men offer things like that," Hale said, then nipped at my earlobe, the action blowing warm breath against me, making me shiver.

"Sorry. I guess I'm just not used to men offering me the skin of my enemies. It's sweet in a weird way, and it's something I'm pretty sure I'm not supposed to like."

"But you do, right? Look, any man can offer chocolates and flowers and bullshit like that. Those ain't my sort of thing. Instead, I'm the type who will swear that if anyone ever hurts you, I'll make sure they pay *dearly* for the mistake. I can't swear that no one will ever harm you, but I can fucking promise that they'll never get the chance to do it a second time."

"Well aren't you sweet in a terrifying and twisted way?"

He pulled me tighter against him. "Yeah, sweet, that's me. The skins of your enemies and orgasms — what more could a girl want?"

And sitting with him there, I had to agree. This sort of love might not have been expected, but it was a lot more than I ever thought I could have.

I'd do whatever it took to protect it.

Fuck knew I wasn't above delivering a few skins myself if anyone threatened the men I loved.

* * * *

The gates to the city stretched up so high that I craned my neck and squinted against the bright sky. I almost couldn't *see* the top.

Which seemed stupid since wings were all decoration rather than usable. It meant I had no idea *why* those walls needed to be that tall.

Still, I tugged at my cloak to ensure it covered my hair.

Getting past these gates would prove one of the biggest challenges, according to Noah. He could hide our presence outside of these walls, but there was no way for him to have us pose as guards once inside. The city was theoretically safe, so he'd have no need for security inside.

It meant getting past those gates was tricky, and while I knew what to do, it didn't stop my nerves from reminding me all the ways this could go wrong.

Noah played the part of distraction for us. It seemed he often had some items that even angels wanted, and he'd made sure to pack his wagon with such treasures.

If there was one big flaw the angels had, it was having *far* too much confidence in themselves and their superiority. Give them something to look at and they'd never imagine someone might use that to get past them. Nope, they were *far* too smart for something like that to work.

The main gates were open, but beside those main gates were several other smaller entrances into the city.

Some were used by angels or officials to bypass the long lines at the main gates, while others were used as underground entrances into the city.

If Noah could draw enough of the angels his way, the rest of us could slip through those other smaller gates. Our best shot was individually, since as a group, we drew far too much attention.

And yet again I realized how much I'd come to rely on the other Lords. On my own, I felt unsettled, my thoughts moving to each of them, wondering if they were okay.

Focus, Loch! If you don't get inside, how they are won't matter.

After scolding myself, I watched the angel at the gate Noah had told me to wait at. I mentally shoved at her, wanting her to go, to leave the gate unguarded for just a moment.

My chest burned as I held my breath, a nervous energy arcing through my body. I *hated* just waiting, but I had no other choice.

The angel turned her head and spoke to someone. She peered past the person, then took off in that direction.

Finally!

I walked forward, trying to move with a sense of purpose. People didn't tend to get involved with busy people, assuming they had business to deal with. If I just acted as if I knew what I was doing, others tended to believe it.

The gate was small—only enough room for a single person to pass at a time. Then again, that would make them easy to defend and secure.

I slipped through that space, the inside of the city coming into view.

And *fuck* was it pretty. I had a moment of awe as I took in my surroundings, the gorgeous cities that shone in the light as if they were made with tiny bits of crystals. It took my breath away, and for a split second, I forgot that the Plains was *far* from heaven.

The buildings were tall, and the walkways narrow but covered in cobblestone. It all had this strange combination of old and new, of traditional and modern, and at the center of it all?

The palace. Being here now, it was clear that no one would have missed out on it, would have not known what it was. The place stood apart from the rest, even the architecture different from the surrounding space. Where the other buildings sparkled, the palace seemed carved from pure marble, taller than even the walls of the city.

I should have been thinking about finding the meeting spot, but my attention remained locked on the palace, on my surroundings, on this place that I never thought I would get to see.

I was so focused on that, I didn't notice anything amiss around me. At least, not until a hand wrapped around my mouth, when someone yanked me against a large, strong body. From the corner of my eye, I spotted white feathers, and I almost relaxed. The sight of those wings reminded me of Gorrin.

"Aren't you a pretty one?" a lyrical masculine voice whispered into my ear, a voice that was for sure *not* Gorrin.

Which meant I had been caught by an angel, and I had a feeling anything he wanted with me was going to be something I was *not* into.

Just fucking wonderful.

Chapter Eleven

I looked down at myself and groaned at my attire. They'd taken my slacks, my nice shirt, everything I'd had on without a single word to explain why. Instead, the angel who had grabbed me had all but thrown me into a bath and left me to the care of spirits, none of whom had felt the need to explain or answer anything.

Still, I stared at a mirror on the wall, barely able to recognize myself. I wore a lace bustier, one that made even my subpar breasts look fucking amazing. I would have figured a pair of pants would have gone better with the rest, but instead, they'd given me a skirt that was *far* shorter than I would have liked. In fact, if I had to bend over, I was pretty sure everyone around would get a show, even with the black lace panties that I had on underneath.

Fishnet stockings finished up the look, along with a pair of heels tall enough to make me worry about the welfare of my ankles.

I looked like a biker's walking, talking wet dream. In fact, if I saw myself in a bar, I was fucking sure I'd try to pick myself up.

"I'm surprised you cleaned up so well." A woman walked into the room, her features lovely but her expression severe, as if she never smiled.

"What is this place?" I asked, for what had to be the hundredth time.

She let out a sigh that said I'd annoyed her, but could she really blame me? Who wouldn't want to know?

"You are at Willow's Flower. It is a prestigious establishment in the city, one of the more respected such places."

My steps slowed. "Yeah, '*such places*' and '*prestigious establishment*' don't make me all that comfortable."

"Comfort isn't something we worry about here, at least not when it comes to merchandise."

And just like that, my feet stopped. "Merchandise?"

Ollie stopped and crossed her arms, a displeased expression on her face when she turned back toward me. "Yes, merchandise. You are a product, like all of us. Come along. Your first lesson here is that tardiness and chaos are not allowed. Expect quick and severe correction if you do not follow the rules."

"Oh, but I'm not good at following rules."

"Learn." She turned and headed down the hallway again, forcing me to jog to keep up. As we'd gone through the large building, I'd spotted plenty of large and scary-looking men. I'd spent enough time in dangerous places to know hired muscle when I saw it. It meant that if I didn't follow, I had no doubt Ollie would call in help to deal with me.

And I didn't need that. I only needed to bide my time until an opportunity presented itself.

Ollie turned and headed up a staircase next. I hesitated for only a moment, the memory of those stairs at the base of the Path so similar that my brain juggled the two at first. When Ollie cleared her throat without turning, it got me back into gear, and I headed up the stairs, using my hands to try to keep the skirt in place.

If anyone was at the base of the stairs, though, they'd get treated to a show of my panties for sure.

"This is where you will sleep and spend your time when you are not scheduled for work." Ollie gestured as she gave me a quick tour, ignoring the other people around as if they didn't matter. "This is your room. You will have space there for clothing and any gifts you receive. When not working, we expect you to study and perfect your skills. There are more than enough books in the library to ensure you can entertain guests, along with space to practice other skills such as dancing or singing. There are baths at the far end—ensure you keep yourself clean at all times."

"What do you mean by *work*?" A sinking feeling in my stomach said I could guess. *Entertaining* had a very specific meaning in a place like this, where I was expected to bathe and dance or sing. It wasn't like I'd never sold myself before, but I'd expected that shit to be long behind me.

"Do not bathe or take off your makeup today, because you will have your first client in about an hour. At that time, someone will come up here to fetch you. Do not give them any problems, or I can assure you, your first day with us will be far less pleasant than it has to be." She left with the same haughty attitude she'd had before, as if my worries meant nothing to her.

It reminded me that angels weren't the only issue here—people were just as good at making a place hell as angels or demons.

"You're new?" a man asked, his voice cheerful.

I turned, expecting to find some lean, feminine-looking man. I mean, that was what I thought of when I considered male prostitutes.

Instead, I found a man who could have given Hale a run for his money when it came to looking dangerous.

He was over six feet tall with eyes so dark I couldn't tell where his pupil ended and his iris began. He had long black hair that hung loose around his shoulders, and he wore a simple pair of gray slacks and a long-sleeved button-up shirt. Even that clothing didn't come close to hiding his physique, though. He would have made me hella-nervous if I'd still been alive.

"Seems so," I answered.

His gaze raked over me, but it felt more like an appraisal than anything with lust. In fact, it reminded me *far* too much of how Ollie had stared at me, as though she'd been sizing me up, seeing how much I could fetch for them. Of course, this man didn't have quite the same edge. "I think you're going to end up being very popular."

"I thought the city was all about order. I mean, I wouldn't normally even be *allowed* in here."

"And that is exactly why they'll like you here. You are unique, something they normally don't get to touch, the forbidden. Anyone who spends all their time in the city is used to what we normally have, but you? You are different. You are something they won't be able to find elsewhere." He pressed his lips together and nodded. "Yeah, as long as you play your cards right, you'll have clients lining up and fighting over your time."

"Why would I want that?"

"Because job security here is a good thing. Play the part, be what they want and the clients here will make sure you have anything you want. Precious jewels? Fancy foods? Elegant clothing? Clients will give them all to you if you play them right."

Play sounded all sorts of bad. Also, I didn't *want* any of those things. Jewels? Fuck 'em, they were far too easy to steal or lose. I preferred low-key foods, the kinds of stuff purchased off questionable B-rated food trucks. And elegant clothing? No fucking thanks. I'd take jeans and a ratty shirt any day over this hooker outfit they'd put me in.

"Yeah, I don't think so."

The man caught my arm, pulling me to a stop. He leaned in closer, his voice dropping low, losing some of the cheer that it had before. "Don't be stupid."

"That's sort of my thing," I answered.

Still, he spoke quietly. Was he afraid of someone overhearing? "There is no way out of here, so you have two choices. You either play the game and stay on top as long as you can, or they force you to play *their* game."

"They can try."

He kept a hold of my arm—and I was sick of getting led around like this—and pulled me toward the back, where the baths were. I almost argued, telling him Ollie had warned me against messing up my outfit, but he pulled me into a side room that had no tub in it.

Instead, there were four people—two men and two women—on the floor. Three of them writhed together in what might have passed as an orgy, and the last man just rolled around on the floor while making a pained, broken whimper.

A frantic energy rested in the room, one that made my skin crawl. It felt unnatural, forced, like being the only sober person in the middle of a binge-drinking party.

The reason was so obvious, I didn't need the man to explain it. I'd seen this before, when we'd seen the man on Euphoria on the road outside of the city.

"They fought their place here. They didn't want to give in."

"So they were drugged?"

"Some were forced into taking it, others chose to do it to numb the memories and feelings. How it starts doesn't matter—it eventually turns them all into this. And since it takes more and more, since the addiction gets its claws into everyone, it will kill them at some point. This place only cares about getting their money out of them before the Euphoria destroys them entirely." He sighed, the first signs of true unhappiness from him.

It made me wonder if the rest was an act, just him playing the part he'd decided he had to. It made me hate him a little less.

"So you're telling me…"

"That if you don't fall into line, if you don't do what they want, they'll still get from you what they want. They'll give you Euphoria and you'll lose more than your pride—you'll lose your mind. This might not be the life you would have chosen, but you've lost that choice. Now all you can decide is if you're willing to give up your pride or your mind, because you can only keep one of them."

I licked my lips, my gaze locked on the people on the floor like some terrifying mirror into my future. I'd fought for so long to do as I wanted, to not allow anyone to control me, so the idea of losing myself like that was the scariest thing I'd had to face.

"New girl," called a voice that made me spin on my heels, assuming they meant me.

Down the hallway, a man I didn't recognize stood, his hulking presence telling me he was more of that muscle.

I knew I should go, but my feet remained rooted in place. Never had *it's time* come across as so ominous. The hope of the Lords showing up and saving the day dwindled away with each passing second.

Was I all on my own? Did I have to work through this myself?

I told myself I was a strong independent woman who didn't need any Lord to save me, but right now? I sure as fuck wanted them to.

"Go," the man who had given me the advice said, pressing his hand against my back to push me forward before he whispered into my ear, "Remember what I said."

As if I'd forget that. His urging got me moving, while his warnings swirled in my head, fear at what was coming, at whether or not I could stomach it, all twisted inside me until I feared I would shatter and break.

I didn't, though. I remained intact, even if for a moment, I wished I hadn't.

The guard escorted me down the stairs without saying anything to me. He must have figured he wasn't paid for making conversation. We took a different route than I had with Ollie, but the massive place had too many hallways, too many rooms for me to even hope to understand the layout. *So much for an escape.*

He stopped in front of a door, then gestured at it. "Go on in—your first client is waiting."

I took a deep breath, reminding myself to bide my time. I'd been through worse, survived worse. Anything that happened inside that room, I could deal with.

No matter what happened, I wouldn't let them see me sweat.

Chapter Twelve

Hale

Don't kill anyone.

I had to repeat that to myself as I stood there, my temper fraying more by the second as we waited in the small back room of the shop where we had planned to meet up.

"Where is she?" Tyrus asked.

We'd arrived at the meeting place as expected—all except for Loch. At first, I'd figured she had gotten herself lost. Fuck knew she was the type to get turned around and wander off, but after a few hours passed without her reaching us, I started to doubt it was so simple.

"Could she have gotten caught?" I asked.

Gorrin shook his head, his cloak hood off since he didn't have to hide his face from us. "I would have heard something when I stopped in at the Palace if they'd caught her — at least if they knew who or what she was. That sort of news would spread fast."

The door to the small private back room opened and Noah came in, his face pinched in lines that said he had some news he really didn't want to deliver.

I got to my feet, energy surging through me, helpless and useless but wanting to do something.

"You found her?" Gorrin asked.

Noah's complexion paled more, giving me the sense he really didn't want to have this conversation.

And didn't that tell me just how bad it was?

"Not exactly," he said.

"What the fuck does not exactly mean?" Maybe I could have softened my words, especially since Noah wasn't at fault for whatever was happening, but as it turned out, I really didn't fucking feel like it.

"I don't know exactly where she is, but I heard from someone that an angel found new merchandise to play with."

"Play?" Gorrin lifted one of his dark eyebrows as if to challenge Noah's choice of words.

"The angel was bragging about how much she was worth, saying she didn't look like she belonged here. She had green hair and tattoos on her face."

Fuck.

There weren't many girls in the Plains who'd fit that description.

And the use of *merchandise* told me what he didn't want to come right out and say.

"She'll be fine," Yazmor said with a wide grin on his face.

"The fuck?" I asked.

He shrugged. "Loch is plenty tough. Even if someone wanted to sell her against her will, she'd take

174

them apart. We'll figure out what place they took her and by the time we get there, she'll probably be walking out of the ashes! Really, I feel worse for whoever wants to try and force her."

His words made sense, at least somewhat. She was tough, so I doubted I had much to worry about.

Noah cleared his throat, the sound a nervous one that made me think he hadn't meant to say it.

It also said he had something to tell just what he really didn't want to say.

"What?" Gorrin asked, his tone harsh.

Noah let out a long sigh and slumped his shoulders. "Spirits who work at the brothels here don't do it by choice. The ones who won't play by the rules, who won't do as they're told, are made to obey."

Tyrus snorted. "Loch doesn't obey."

"They use Euphoria on any who don't fall into line."

My back went straight at his words, the memory of the spirit we'd seen before, all drugged out of their mind on Euphoria. The thought of Loch in the same condition made my stomach roll.

She was tough and smart and difficult as fuck—her being reduced to that had me slamming my fist down on the table, knocking the thing to the ground beneath the blow.

"How many brothels are there?" Tyrus asked, ignoring my outburst.

"More than I can count," Noah said. "Some are well known but beyond those, there are so many underground ones. There are even private collections. Normally, I'd guess that she'd be at one of the bigger ones, given how rare a find she'd be, but sometimes the more valuable an object, the more others keep it secret and to themselves. Going place by place could take weeks, assuming the places are honest about whether or not she's there."

"What will Euphoria do to her?" I asked. At Noah's questioning look, I went on. "We know what it does to spirits, but has it ever been fucking used on a demon?"

Gorrin let out a rare curse, the word sliding from his lips as if he hadn't thought of that yet. "Euphoria breaks down if it leaves the Plains, so I don't think it has ever been given to a demon."

Tyrus took a deep breath, then released it slowly. "Give me your best guess, based on what you know. How dangerous would it be to her?"

"Bad. Normally, Euphoria causes a spirit to become pliant and easy to deal with. It raises libido, lowers or eliminates inhibitions. It has never been administered to a demon, but it *has* been given to angels, back when it was first created. The results are far worse than in spirits, and if the angel doesn't work it out of their system, it can kill them."

"The fuck does 'work it out' mean?"

Gorrin swallowed hard. "The main purpose of Euphoria is as an aphrodisiac. A spirit will crave sex, but an angel will require it. Without, they can be seriously hurt or even die."

"So you're telling me that Loch might be given a drug that makes her fuck or die?" I asked, each word coming out darker than the last, more filled with anger.

"It is likely," Gorrin answered.

Yazmor had found Loch before, seemed to have some weird connection with her, right? Could he do it again? I turned toward him, ready to ask, but froze. "Where the fuck did Yazmor go?"

* * * *

176

Loch

Oh, look, I still fucking hate angels.

It only took one glance at the woman in the room to make it clear that Gorrin was a very big exception to my hatred.

Sure, when I'd first met Azael, when I'd first seen those wings and perfect features, I'd been smitten. Maybe it had just been some weird hold over from a lifetime of hearing how holy and wonderful angels were. Whatever the reason, I'd seen them as bigger than life, as more wonderful than I could possibly imagine.

They were something worth so much more than me, something I was desperate to touch.

That sense of wonder was long gone, now, and only revulsion struck me. The angel in the room leered the moment she turned her head toward me, her long blonde hair pulled back in a tight French braid, her eyes an impossibly bright blue that looked almost neon.

Every bit of her appeared beyond lovely, like a dream manifested.

"You *are* unique, aren't you?" she asked.

"So I've heard." I dragged my tongue along my bottom lip, my mouth dry and uncomfortable, my wrist itching as if to remind me that I still had the dagger there.

I had options, if I were brave enough to use them.

"Pour me wine." She turned her back on me as if she expected me to obey right away and she wasn't worried in the least about my response.

Then again, angels here were used to that, weren't they?

Well, sorry, I'm new.

I reached for the door handle, trying to be subtle, to make no noise. If I could just turn that, I could rush down the hallway. The guard had brought me here, but that didn't mean he'd be just outside, right? Why would he be if I were in here with an angel?

An angel could handle one little spirit, right?

Good fucking luck with that.

I turned the handle, but when I pulled, when the door opened the smallest of cracks, it slammed back into place.

I twisted back to find myself pinned between the angel and the now closed door, her hand above me, holding the door shut. Those blue eyes of hers peered down at me, hard and somehow still beautiful despite the malice in them.

How could someone still be that lovely even when I knew what they really were?

"They told me you hadn't been broken in yet. It was why they gave you to me. See, I prefer *breaking* spirits, for showing them their place in this world."

"Sounds like what someone who has no skills would say," I spat back.

She tilted her head, her bright red lips pulled into a smirk that screamed bad things were coming my way. "You are even more wild than what they usually have. I'm used to spirits who wait for their chance to run, who play the game, who cozy up to me and wait to stab me in the back. You are far more straightforward than that, which is rare. No wonder you're worth so much."

I refused to back down. She already knew I wasn't the type to do it, so it wasn't like it would help. "Let me make myself clear. I've sold my body in the past, and I won't do it again."

"No? Why not?"

"Because when I did it before, I didn't value it. I didn't value *me*. I did it because I thought I had to, and I hated every second of it. I've figured out since then that I'm worth so much more, so I'll never make that mistake again."

The words seemed to only please her more. She pressed in closer. "You think highly of yourself—much more highly than you deserve. Now, we can do this a few different ways, because we will do this. You can learn and obey, and this will be far more pleasant for you. Believe it or not, I do not find enjoyment from inflicting pain."

"Could have fooled me," I muttered.

She went on, as though she hadn't heard me at all. "I enjoy seeing spirits where they belong—beneath my thumb. How they get there, that matters less to me. If you choose to take your rightful place, if you fall into line, this will be an easy and even enjoyable time for you. However, if you want to fight, if you wish to somehow prove yourself, well, I am prepared for that as well."

"So you'll just beat me into submission? I'm guessing you don't get a lot of second dates?"

"Beating people into submission lacks creativity and skill. No—I am not into violence. Either you choose to submit, or I will make it so you are desperate to do so."

"And how exactly will you do that? Because your tits are good—no doubt about that—but even some perky C-cups aren't enough to make me forget about my pride."

"No, but this will." She lifted a vial, a shimmering liquid inside.

A crawling sensation in my stomach made me gulp, and a shaking started in my hands. I had a feeling I knew *exactly* what that was.

She smiled wider. "That's right. This is Euphoria. Just one dose is enough to make you beg me to take you, to turn you into the perfect little spirit so desperate to please. So, what is your choice?"

And I didn't have to think at all to know the answer to that.

I swung my head forward, her taller height meaning I nailed her in the nose. I would have preferred a crotch shot, but facing off against someone without junk there made that far less effective.

She loosened her grip, but when I tried to turn the handle again, to escape, she was back on me. She grasped my shoulder and yanked, sending me flying until I landed hard against the stone floor, the breath knocked from my lungs.

My other form shimmered inside me, clawing as if to get free.

Except, I was pretty sure that was the sort of thing I couldn't come back from, so I held it back, forcing my body to turn over, to move despite the way hitting the ground had shaken me.

The angel was on top of me a heartbeat later, so much faster and stronger than I wanted to admit. It again reminded me that angels could easily go toe-to-toe with me.

She grasped my chin, forcing my eyes to hers. The blue there danced brightly, like spotlights that spilled over me. She flicked the lid off the vial with her thumb, grasped my chin so tight I feared she might break my jaw, then tipped the shimmering liquid into my mouth.

Once it was all in, when I tried to spit it back out, she covered my mouth with one hand. Unable to help it, the Euphoria went down my throat, tingling as it did, and only once it was all gone did the angel sit up and release my face.

I stared up at her, the hatred inside me softening, drifting away, until I struggled to remember *why* I even disliked her.

The warmth of her body, her pretty eyes, they took over.

The edges of the world blurred until everything was okay, until I couldn't remember why I would ever feel unhappy.

Then a heat ignited in my lower stomach, a desire that burned and grew and seared me.

She ran a finger along my bottom lip as though I were a pet who had just pleased her. "Much better, isn't it? Finding your place in this world has benefits, and you will soon experience them all."

I couldn't even remember why that statement should terrify me.

Chapter Thirteen

Yazmor

Tyrus' words rang in my ears, Gorrin's warnings as well. The moment I'd recognized just how dangerous Euphoria could be for Loch, when it became clear that she might not have been able to fight that, my body had moved on its own.

I could find her always, but the need had never felt so sharp as right now. It drove me forward, my feet moving so fast I doubted the spirits or angels could have tracked my progress. They'd have sensed nothing but, at most, a rush of air as I passed.

But they didn't matter. The other Lords didn't even matter. The only thing my mind could hold or comprehend was finding Loch.

The draw took me to a large building near the center of the city, just across a large cobblestone road from the palace. The outside of the building was lovely, done in a similar style to everything else. It was spotless, as was everything else, but even the tile work that surrounded the windows and doors suggested this was a place for only the most important of clients.

And a desire to tear it to pieces struck me so strong that I had to take a calming breath to stop myself. I had to remind myself of everything at stake, that I could not fail it all just for my own anger.

Please do not let me be too later.

I inhaled, catching Loch's scent even amongst that of so many others. The breeze carried it, as if to reassure me that she still lived.

I closed my eyes, trying to feel for her, to sense where inside this maze of a building she was. It was too difficult to be sure, however, so instead, I moved around to the back of the building. I jumped easily to catch the ledge of a second-floor balcony, grateful again to not be human, to not be demon. It gave me advantages others lacked, ones others had no idea how to even counter.

I pulled myself onto the balcony, then slipped into the room.

Loch's scent. It hit me, pungent and drenched in anger.

Not in fear, no, not Loch. My lips twitched at how *her* that really was. I found her old clothes in a laundry hamper, telling me this must have been her room. It seemed they planned to keep her.

They should be prepared to be disappointed.

I moved from the room, following both the sense of where she was and her scent. Others moved around the space, but they only gave me the briefest of glances. Most had dead eyes, a sign that whatever this place had done to them had carved away a piece of them, something important, something they might never be able to get back.

A man got into my path, his eyes more cunning, more calculating. He missed that same piece, but it almost seemed as if he had grown scar tissue in its place, as if he'd adapted rather than giving in.

"You don't belong here," he said, his voice low.

I leaned in and breathed deeply. *Loch.* "Her scent hangs on you," I said, knowing my smile was too wide. Too many teeth, as Loch would have said.

He took a step backward. No doubt alarm bells rang in his head, that little piece of all living creatures that warns when danger approaches. "You mean the new girl?"

"If you harmed her," I said, feeling no need to continue that thought.

"Then what?" the fool asked.

"I have no idea. I'm not what you might call a planner. I prefer going with my gut, with the moment. If I find out you harmed her, I might tear you apart, bit by bit. I might flay you alive. I might just slit your throat like an animal because you deserve nothing else. Won't it be a fun surprise for us both to find out which it is?"

He wavered on his feet, and I feared for a moment I *might* have gone too far. I didn't care if he passed out, but unconscious people did not answer questions.

Thankfully, he seemed slightly stronger than that, because he gulped audibly, then leaned in so his voice didn't carry. "I didn't touch her. She was taken for her first client."

"And where was she taken?"

"I don't know for sure—they don't tell other merchandise things like that. However, because she's new, they probably put her in the large room on the bottom floor, in the corner."

I leaned in closer until I could taste his breath on my lips, until the sweet fear that escaped him rested on my tongue. "If I find out you're lying, I will return."

The sound of him breathing in deeply was a forgotten one when I turned my back and rushed down the stairs, following both his directions and my own senses, following the pull of her and her scent.

Bottom floor, corner room. Her scent escaped from under the door, telling me I'd found it.

The handle didn't turn, a lock stopping it, but I didn't break it. Without knowing what was on the other side of that door, I didn't want to risk her. What if by startling whoever was inside, they harmed her?

Instead, I waved my hand over the door, the soft click telling me it had unlatched.

I eased it open slowly, peering into the brightly lit room, my lungs frozen as I held my breath.

The sight inside had me going still.

Loch was on the ground, with an angel seated in a chair watching over her.

The *only* thing that saved the angel's life — at least for a moment — was that they were both still clothed, and I saw no clear injuries on Loch.

Perhaps I hadn't been too late. Maybe the angel hadn't given Loch any of the drug, or maybe Loch had even managed to hold her own long enough for me to arrive.

"I'm a *Demon Lord,*" Loch said, her voice slurred and arrogant. "At least, that's what they say. I don't feel all that Lordish, though. I wonder if that changes, if anyone feels like a Lord." She snorted as if to laugh, then looked at the angel. "*You* probably would. Angels are assholes, after all. Every last one of them!"

"You certainly have an active imagination," the angel said, a curl to her bright red lips that said she enjoyed watching this, as if Loch were nothing more than entertainment to her. "I don't think that any other spirit has been quite so amusing with their stories. Euphoria can produce illusions of grandeur in those who take it, and it seems you have some innate desire to be important, thus this fantasy that you are somehow a demon—no, more than that, a Demon *Lord.*"

I ground my molars at the tone the angel used, the way she dismissed Loch as unimportant.

Foolish, arrogant angel.

Loch was single-handedly the most important being in the universe at the moment, the hinge point that moved so many others around her. Even if this angel had not discovered this yet, the truth would be made clear soon.

Of course, the angel would not live to witness it.

Loch laughed, the sound almost soothing to me. Perhaps Euphoria would not affect her as badly as Gorrin had feared. She seemed drunk, at worst. "You have *no* idea. Then again, you remember what I said about angels, right?"

"That we are all assholes." The angel leaned forward, placing her chin on her palm, as though she found this all adorable. "Surely you have met at least one angel who you felt was not."

"Nope, not a one. I even love one of you! Doesn't change anything."

"You are telling me that this angel you love is an asshole as well?"

"A *huge* one, for sure!"

In any other situation, I would have laughed. Even drugged, even in this danger, Loch had a mouth that would never stop. Even if everything else about her changed, if I couldn't feel her, couldn't recognize her by sight or scent or voice, it would only take hearing her speak to recognize that iron will and loose tongue.

"And yet you claim to love him?"

"I do. *Soooo* much. I mean, I stabbed him once, but sometimes things like that happen in love. Gorrin's an asshole, but he's *my* asshole."

That seemed to get her attention, though, because the angel sat up straight in her seat. "Gorrin?"

"Yep. *That* Gorrin. I'm sure you know he's an asshole. Everyone who has ever met him knows it!"

"You are telling me that you know Gorrin? That you have some relationship with him?" She narrowed her eyes, as if putting together the pieces of the story that Loch had uttered.

Then again, Loch had given her enough tiny details for her to get it.

All angels knew where Gorrin had been before, that he'd taken over in the Chasm, that he had now returned. Even if they didn't know who the Demon Lords were—mostly because they didn't care—Loch had given enough bits of information to ring true.

The question was—was this angel smart enough to see the forest for the trees?

Uncertainty pinched her eyebrows, a line appearing in her forehead. She shook her head, as though to clear the thought away. "I wouldn't have thought you Gorrin's type, but perhaps he has enjoyed you in the past. People tend to let things slip when naked with another."

Was she assuring herself of the truth of her words, trying to convince herself that she was right, that the woman before her was crazy? That was a far safer guess.

She paused, though, her frown deepening. "How close are you with him? Would he care if another touched you?"

"Oh, he'll care. He's the least of your problems, though, because he doesn't like to kill other angels. Nope, nope. Tyrus would have you killed, quietly, so no one knew about it. Hale would do it himself and laugh the whole time."

"I see. And these men you imagine, they are the ones I should fear the most?"

Loch shook her head, crawling closer to the angel, then up and into her lap. The movements had a sensual edge to them that said the Euphoria had hit Loch, that it caused her mind to twist and distort reality.

The angel didn't react to Loch's closeness, but then again, why would she? She thought Loch was some drugged-up spirit, nothing but a toy to be used and discarded. If anything, Loch's actions seemed to ease the angel.

Perhaps she thought herself safe—she assumed Loch coming closer proved that the Euphoria worked on her.

She clearly has no idea who is in her lap. That angel shouldn't look as though she had a kitten in her lap, but rather like a tiger had just crawled onto her.

Loch set her hands on the angel's shoulders, staring down into her eyes with an intensity that made my skin crawl. Still, I waited. I gave Loch the chance to deal with it herself, to act.

I would step in the moment I needed to, but a part of me was reluctant to rescue her before she needed it. Loch wasn't the sort of woman to need nor welcome such interference.

"No. They'd kill you, of course, but the one you *really* want to watch out for is the one with the face of an innocent. He smiles with too many teeth, and he laughs when he shouldn't, and he is so much more than your little mind could even comprehend. You'd better hope I kill you first, because if Yazmor shows up? You'll *wish* I'd finished you off myself."

Her words rushed through me, my reaction surprising even me. I knew what I was, had mostly come to terms with it, but to hear her speak about me like that threw all my attempts at calm away.

She didn't talk about me as if I were something she put up with. She didn't pretend I was anything other than I was, either. She didn't lessen me, pretty me up, but rather accepted me for *exactly* the monster I was.

She accepted me as *her* monster.

And that was a position I would happily accept.

The angel moved, wrapping her fingers around Loch's throat and tossing her to the floor. "Bow," she spat.

Loch laughed, though the edges of pain bled into the sound. Her fingers curled against the stone floor, her knuckles turning white, the action seemingly out of her control. "I don't bow, and I sure as fuck don't bow to you."

The angel tucked her bare foot beneath Loch's chin, tipping her face up toward the angel's. "You feel it, don't you? The Euphoria swirling through your veins, stealing away your arrogance and your confusion and your fight. It replaces it all with lust, with a need for touch. I can see it in your eyes. You are nearly lost to that desire, nearly broken by it already. Just a little longer and you will be nothing more than the base animal you have always been, that all you humans are at your core."

Loch arched her back, a pained, broken sound leaving her lips. Still, she shifted her head. I nearly expected her to press a kiss to the angel's foot, but then Loch reminded me of who exactly she was.

She bit down on the side of the angel's foot, the sort of bite that was in no way playing, that intended to tear away a chunk of flesh.

The angel reacted by instinct alone, yanking backward, toppling to the floor when Loch wouldn't release her bite. The angle raised her foot to kick, which was the end of my waiting.

There was no way I would allow her to kick Loch, to injure her.

I would allow nothing in this entire universe to lay a finger on my woman.

Loch

Oh, she's going to kick me in the face. The thought didn't hit me so much as it floated by, just unimportant details.

It should have been important, all things considered. I didn't have the best teeth, but I'd really prefer the ones I had stayed in my mouth. Still, even as a part of my brain knew that, another part, the one currently in control, really didn't give a fuck about much of anything.

The blood in my mouth from biting the angel's foot, the racing of my heart, the lava that crawled through my veins, it played like background music to me.

However, her foot didn't make contact. I lifted my gaze to find a hand wrapped around her ankle, holding her still. I followed that hand to the arm, and to a familiar face.

A smile I couldn't help spread across my lips, and if I'd been in my right mind, I'd have slapped myself for something so obvious and embarrassing.

Still, never had the sight of Yazmor's face been so fucking pretty.

He smiled back, and it took me back to what I'd told the angel. He was far from good. He was as vicious as I'd said, as terrifying, and he was all mine. He offered me a smile that said exactly that.

The angel yanked, but Yazmor held her as if he couldn't feel her struggle. It again reminded me just how different he was from me, just how much stronger he really was.

Despite his looks, he was *far* from the young, innocent face he had.

"What do you think you are doing?" the angel asked, a haughtiness in her voice, but I sensed something beneath it. Fear? My brain was too addled to figure it out. Still, she went on. "Do you have any idea what you are doing right now? Who you dare to touch?"

Yazmor broke his gaze from mine, turning his face toward her. His smile never slipped. "Yes, I do. An insignificant bug, a useless creature who uses drugs to bend others to her will."

The angel opened her mouth, then closed it again as if she had never considered someone might speak to her like that.

Leave it to Yazmor to startle even an angel into silence.

Pain spread through me, fogging my mind, making it even more difficult to pay attention to anything around me. I could only think about that clawing, scratching need inside me.

I'd tried to ignore it after swallowing the liquid. I'd tried to put it out of my mind as need had grown, as desire had filled me.

Now, however, I couldn't pretend it wasn't there anymore. Maybe it was a sense of safety, of not being alone, or maybe it was just from seeing Yazmor.

The angel struggled against Yazmor's grasp once more, but when she made no progress, she panted hard. "What are you?"

Yazmor leaned in closer to her, his skin shimmering, a sign he struggled to keep his human form. "You heard everything about me from her — you should have listened."

"Yazmor?" she asked in a whisper.

Yazmor smiled even wider, so far that his cheeks had to hurt. "Yeah, that's me. And everything she said is true, but it isn't even all of it."

"I've heard that name before," she whispered, her gaze dropping. "I've heard all those names before." She lifted her gaze then, her eyes wide.

"That's right. Gorrin. Tyrus. Hale. Yazmor. You finally put it all together?"

"Who is she, then?"

"Loch. The demon who knocked Gorrin out of power, who took over his position, who clawed her way through the Path to get here, who helped to kill Azael. Those who stand in her way don't stand long."

"I'm sorry," she rushed out. "I didn't know."

"See, if you were just facing her, that might work. Her biggest weakness is forgiveness, after all, but I'm here now, and I do not forgive so easily."

"But—"

"Nothing. You use your power and target innocents beneath you. No, worse than that, you break people just because you enjoy it, and you are the sort who will never learn, who will never accept the truth that you are weak. You are not nearly so important as you think. The universe is so much larger and so much wilder and so much darker than you can comprehend, and you will never mean a thing in the waves of something so deep. Because you can't and won't understand that, you will always go back to this, will never stop. Even if I let you go now, you would lick your wounds for a day or two and after assuring yourself that this was just a fluke, you would target others again to soothe your own ego."

I might have said something, might have intervened, but the drugs in my system took away that option. Yazmor moved so fast that I couldn't track it, couldn't make sense of it. He grasped her chin in one of his hands and jerked, a deafening crack filling the room before her body collapsed as if it was nothing but a doll.

I should have thought about how terrifying it was that he could kill an angel so easily, but that never struck me. The Euphoria in my system took it all away, washed it clear because of the need inside me.

Yazmor grasped the angel's body and tossed it, it crumpling like a bag of trash out of sight.

My gaze followed him without me even meaning to, without me thinking anything that required more than two or three words strung together. He had dressed up more than usual, in slacks rather than ripped jeans and had traded his hoodie sweater in for a polo shirt. He wasn't built the way Hale or Gorrin were, his body smaller and leaner, but I saw beneath that all.

I saw his other form, his *real* one, and I wanted all of it. His twisted smile, his gentle fingers, his wicked tongue, this young, playful form and his real, monstrous one.

In fact, I didn't give a fuck what he looked like — I wanted him.

He turned back toward me but stopped, frozen in place. His eyes held a heat I'd glimpsed before, but was it his own? Did he want me or was he just caught up in how I felt?

Did I care?

I couldn't answer before the drug pulled me so far under that I gave up, I stopped trying to hold on to myself, onto my rational thought, onto anything.

With Yazmor here, I gave myself over to his safekeeping entirely.

I'd done that before, trusted others, and it hadn't worked out so well for me. I could only hope I'd survive it this time.

Yazmor

Keep a hold of yourself.

It was strange, as self-control wasn't something I had practiced much before, but right now?

It seemed Loch was my own personal weakness, the only thing I would truly hold myself back for.

And even the need to hold back surprised me. However, the look in her eyes drew out something I didn't know I even had.

I crouched before her, cupping her chin in my hand. The dichotomy of the action was far from lost on me, the difference between how I touched her and how I had grabbed for the same place to snap the neck of that angel.

Yet, if Loch saw that, she gave no sign. She relaxed into the touch, pressing against me as though to seek out more of my warmth.

It astounded me, humbled me as it always did.

"It hurts," she whispered.

"I tried to make it before she could give you the Euphoria, but it seems I ran a little late. I'm sorry."

She twisted to nuzzle her cheek against my palm, inching closer like a cat who wanted affection but refused to admit it. The action charmed me against my better judgment.

"She made me drink it all. It wasn't bad at first, but it's getting worse."

"What is? What hurts? What can I do?"

She shuddered, as if just the sound of my voice were too much for her. "You should go get the others."

"Why?"

"I need..." Her words trailed off, her gaze moving from me and to the floor. "You aren't interested, though, and I don't want to force you."

Her words touched me. Even now, even when wracked with pain, when out of her mind on a drug, she thought more about me than she did herself.

"We don't know what Euphoria can do to a demon. Clearly it affects you—Gorrin said it could be dangerous if you try to resist it, if you don't give in."

"So get them."

"You really think I'd leave you like this? That I wouldn't help you?"

She shook her head, tears escaping her bright eyes, wetting my palm. "I don't want you to do anything you don't want to do. I can't do that to you."

I pulled her closer, tugging softly until she moved into my lap. I used it to replace the way she had done with the angel, enjoying the way her weight pressed against me, the sturdiness of her body, the way it made her feel so much more real. "I thought we had this discussion. I'm not opposed if it is with you."

"I don't want you not opposed. I want you *wanting* me." Even as she said that, her lips seemed to have a mind of their own. The words escaped between the kisses she pressed to my throat, to the small V of skin from the open buttons of my polo shirt.

I slid my fingers into her hair, pulling her from me despite how she struggled against losing that touch, then forced her eyes to mine. I could almost lose myself in them, the blue deeper than eternity, as if I could slip into those depths and never have to surface again. I searched them for an answer.

Could I do this?

She was out of her mind, drugged and at the mercy of needs not her own. I could take care of her, but would it be right? She was in no place to make such choices.

But she told me before she wanted me, right? Did that make this okay? It was for her own good, to keep her safe. Without action on my part, she could be severely hurt, even die from it.

That answered it, did it not? Had I not decided that even if she hated me, I would never let her go? That I would never let her come to harm if I could help it?

I dragged my thumb over her bottom lip, the plump skin giving beneath my touch. It reminded me of how soft parts of her were. Despite her backbone, the iron core she had, her actual body was so giving that I feared I might break her.

"I wouldn't let you suffer, Loch, not if I can help it. So relax. Trust me. I will take good care of you."

"But—"

I pulled her in, silencing her with a kiss, repeating what she had done before. Something about her being so lost to need made this easier, removed any nerves I might have had. She moaned against my lips, opening for me, letting me have anything and everything I wanted.

And I wanted *everything*.

When I broke the kiss, I spoke again, taking the moment where her brain worked to keep up. "I want this. I have wanted this for a while. I want to feel you, Loch, to see every part of you, to see you in a way others don't, to have *this* between us. I may not have the same drive as others, but I swear, I will make you feel good. I will not hurt you." Saying that mattered.

Her believing me mattered even more.

And I knew the moment Loch stopped resisting—or rather, stopped whatever little resistance she could muster up—because she clung tighter to me, sliding one arm around the back of my neck as if afraid I'd escape her.

Touching her felt strange. A part of me feared hurting her, that I would be too rough, that I would use too much of my strength. That part of me warned me to go slowly, to use caution, but the thought escaped me when Loch yanked at her own clothes.

She moved as though not herself any longer, as if little more than desire and need made flesh. She pulled at the fabric that covered her, the overly sexy outfit showing off so much already.

I leaned back to watch, to savor each new inch of her skin she revealed. I'd seen her naked already, the first time back before it meant anything to me, when it was hardly a curiosity, but never had it excited me like this before.

The top came off easily after she unhooked fasteners at the front, exposing her breasts to the air and to my gaze. It was neither cold nor hot in the room, but her nipples still tightened into peaks, begging for my personal attention.

Her skirt was so short that it hardly hid anything, and the fishnets that covered her legs pressed into her flesh. There was time for that, though, so I focused first on what was exposed.

She needed touch, to give in to her desires, but I had no idea how far that needed to go. There was no reason to rush into anything.

I ran my hand up her bare sides, rewarded by goosebumps appearing in the wake of my touch. Her skin was soft and warm, and a gentle scent of citrus hung on her—the result of a bath? It didn't cover the scent I associated with her, though, the one I knew well.

I brushed my thumb against the heavy undercurve of her breast, surprised by the softness there, the way her skin gave.

Loch pulled her shoulders back and pressed more fully into my touch. I was so weak to her that I gave in easily to what we *both* wanted.

I shifted my hand to cup her breast fully, the weight of it surprising. She wasn't built like so many women in magazines or movies, the ones with perfect skin and huge breasts.

Yet, I found every part of her perfect. Her breast fit wonderfully into my hands, and when her nipple rubbed against my palm, she parted her lips and moaned.

I'd heard this before, the tempting sound that had escaped through the doors and walls when she had been with the other Lords. I'd listened, intrigued and curious but fearful.

Loch had chased that fear away.

Her nipple hardened beneath my touch, so when I pulled my hand back enough to trace the outer edge with my thumb, it stood erect.

A desire inside me that I couldn't even recognize had me leaning in and tracing with my tongue the same route my thumb had taken. I teased the tiny bumps that lined her areola, connecting them like stars, circling in bit by bit until she was panting and digging her nails into my skin.

Why was this so good? Why did I enjoy this so much?

Something about seeing her so undone pulled me in more than the physical sensations, more than anything else. It was headier than the strongest liquor, more beautiful than sights no other being would ever experience.

She shifted to get more, but I couldn't allow that. Instead, I caught her wrists together in a single hand of mine, her pupils spreading wider when she realized that she couldn't move.

I reached beneath her skirt, grasping the underwear she wore — or what little there was of them. They came down her legs easily, despite the way she squirmed to get more, to get closer. Her movements were uncoordinated, not using any of her Demon Lord powers, as if she'd forgotten she even had them.

I twisted the fabric of her panties around her wrists, careful not to make them too tight, then tied it to the leg of the chair beside us. She could have easily gotten out if she'd been in her right mind, but her frantic tugging did nothing.

"You need to behave yourself Loch," I whispered, surprising even myself with the roughness to my voice. I'd *never* sounded like that. It was deep and dark and masculine and full of so many desires I'd never felt before. Even if I didn't understand it, though, they all rushed out of my mouth.

Loch must have heard it as well because she reacted beautifully, going still and looking up at me like the best trapped prey.

I slid my fingers along her bare skin, teasing the points of her hip bones, her waist, her stomach. I moved along the old scars that sat there in her skin, the ones that showed how hard a life she lived, each one a reminder of how strong the woman beneath me was. They drew me in more, made me want to take her apart and watch her shatter, then gather the pieces together for her again.

"What do you need, Loch? Tell me and I will give you everything."

"*Touch me,*" she whined.

"I am." I used both hands, dragging each thumb against her nipples, rougher than before, testing her response.

Which seemed a useless task since she melted at each touch. Rough, soft, quick, slow, they all seemed to be what she wanted.

What a greedy woman. Why did I like it so much?

I straddled her, my knees pressing into the stone on either side of her hips and bent down. I took one of her nipples between my lips while I toyed with the other with my hand.

Loch arched up and off the floor, so I took the offer for what it was and sucked hard at the swollen bud.

Delicious.

It was everything I could have wanted and more. Her cries and panting breaths filled the room, along with her luscious scent. It was thick and hot, like fire that burned through the space.

She shifted her legs, rubbing her thighs together and lifting her hips. It let me know where she *really* wanted me to touch. She was too far gone to say much in words, but I understood her body just fine.

A noisy *pop* signaled that I'd released one nipple, then I worshiped her with a line of kisses, over the valley between her breasts, to her other nipple. *No reason to ignore this one.*

The chair shifted when she pulled her hands, her body writhing beneath me.

I released her other nipple and sat up, staring down at her, surprised by just how much I enjoyed this sight. I wanted it tattooed in my mind.

How often had I found *anything* I wanted to remember in my exceedingly long life? After surviving when so many others had perished in my world, I'd thought nothing else mattered. I'd thought nothing I experienced would mean a thing, would be worth carrying with me.

I'd discovered just how useless memories were, how fleeting. It had seemed that remembering things only caused pain, like moving a blade buried in the skin, where it only keeps cutting more.

Loch was the first thing worth savoring, worth holding with me, worth the pain of remembering forever.

"*Please*," she whispered, her eyes having lost any of the sharpness they usually held.

I scooted down her body, allowing myself to touch her as I wanted, enjoying the curves of her body, the warmth, even the roughness from scars and calluses. All of it was her and I adored every bit.

I traced the lines of her black fishnet stockings like they were a maze that I worked my way through them. They bit into her flesh, indenting the skin so I knew if I removed them, she'd wear red marks.

Strangely enough, though, I felt a reluctance against doing so, against taking them off and losing the pretty sight she made. "Between the panties that trap your wrists and these, you look as though you are all bound up, just for me. Maybe it makes me twisted, but I like that. I like you at my mercy, unable to run from me. Does that scare you?"

She blinked slowly, and for a moment, I wondered if my words could even filter through the drugs to reach her. Could she understand me at all? Just as I wrote that off, however, she shook her head.

A true smile touched my lips, but I'd bet it still had an edge, a threat to it. The threat wasn't to hurt her, but to do exactly as we both wanted.

I grasped her skirt and pulled it from her, leaving the heels on her feet. I'd never had much in the way of taste or preference when it came to what a woman

Jayce Carter

wore, but I adored Loch like this. The black of the panties was dark against her pale wrists, and a red flush colored her cheeks and her chest.

She didn't fight me when I took her knees in my hands and spread her thighs. The Euphoria had stripped away her modesty—assuming she had any at all—so she didn't try to hide anything from me.

I'd seen her naked, but never truly had the chance to look my fill, to study her.

Her body was so different from mine, and nowhere was it clearer than *here*. I stroked up her cunt with my knuckles, wetness remaining even when I pulled back.

Unable to resist, I brought that wetness to my lips and licked it off, the thick, heady taste calling to instincts I never knew I had. Even better, it increased her scent and made Loch lift her hips again in an impotent thrust.

My chuckle was dark, the sort of sound that would have frightened anyone else. Not Loch, though. She took her lip between her teeth and balled her hands into fists, appearing both broken and impossibly strong.

"You know me—I'm not the sort of man to stop after just a tiny taste of something I like. Be still, though. If you move, I stop."

A light in Loch's eyes made it clear she didn't mind the order, and it stroked the darkness deep inside me.

I shifted my body down to rest between her legs, coming face to face with the most private, vulnerable area of her.

Her scent filled my nostrils, and I let it wash over me. She was drugged by the Euphoria, but me?

I was no more sober because *she* drugged me. She brought me to my knees, and even more strange? I was happy there.

Maybe that was why ordering her around excited me as it did, because having her obey me played nicely with my darker side.

I teased gentle kisses to the insides of her thighs, first one then the other. I traced the top of her fishnets with my tongue, slipping it beneath the band that I then snapped with my teeth.

She gasped, and I didn't bother to fight my smirk at the almost yelp. "I plan to hear that sound many times. In fact, by the time I finally let you go, when I finish with you, you'll have no voice."

The sound that escaped her wasn't words—I doubted she could formulate speech anymore—but it still excited me. It was desire and lust and feeling.

I snapped her other fishnet, then peppered kisses into the crease of her leg, nearing what I knew she wanted, going slowly to torture us both. Even with how desperate she was, though, she stayed still.

Or she tried, at least. Her muscles twitched beneath her skin, a sure sign of the energy that rushed through her, that she fought against the needs to demand more.

So I rewarded her by swiping my tongue up her cunt, the thick taste so much better directly from the source. I explored her folds, dipping my tongue into each crevice, memorizing every bit of her body. Her pussy clenched like a trap trying to draw me in, and I'd happily be caught by it—by her.

Wetness covered my lips, and I drowned myself when I plunged my tongue into her, pressing it as deep as I could, wanting to take her, to own her. My nose ground against her hardened clit, not enough to get her off but enough to tempt her.

She squirmed, lifting her hips, straining for more, and I immediately backed off.

A growl of frustration left her, and I could almost see the release she'd been so close to simmering away.

I blew a stream of air across her drenched pussy. "I told you that if you moved, I'd stop, didn't I?"

If she could kill me with a look alone, I was pretty sure I'd be nothing but a pile of ash at that moment. That look made this *fun* though. It was a battle that I enjoyed, made this a game.

She settled again, her body tense but still. *Good enough.* I dove back in, not bothering to lessen myself, to go gently or slowly. Instead, I attacked her clit directly. It didn't take experience to tell what she liked, what she wanted and what she needed more of. I played her by seeing her reactions, by chasing each little catch of her breath, the barely there twists of her hips even as she struggled to not move.

And this time, when she neared that edge again, when every muscle in her body remained taut with need to obey my demand that she remain still, I gave her what she craved.

The sight of her burned into my memory as she came. I didn't stop teasing her clit while I stared up her body, each muscle of hers going hard and tense before snapping. She sucked in a deep breath then didn't seem to breathe again, as though even her chest had locked around her lungs.

A part of me wondered how that could be considered pleasant. It seemed far too overwhelming for someone to seek out, yet seeing it amazed me. It shattered apart her defenses, making everything fake fall away from her.

No more hiding, no more civility, no more past or future. The orgasm had broken through it all to reveal only the lovely, flawed incredible woman beneath it all, the one who had drawn me in a way nothing else in the universe ever had.

I pulled back enough to speak, but ensured my voice still blew air over her sensitive, twitching pussy. "I've seen worlds created and fall to darkness, but I've never seen anything as beautiful as that."

She probably would have blushed — or kicked me for the romantic words if she'd been in her right mind — but her skin was already flushed from her orgasm.

Romantic or not, though, I'd spoken true.

A darkness in her eyes, though, a question there sat so deep that I doubted she fully understood it. I did, though. "I enjoyed that," I swore to her. "Seeing you fall to pieces beneath me — *because of me* — was amazing. How about you show it to me one more time?"

I sank two of my fingers into her pussy, the tight clutching of her inner walls like a baptism. How had I thought I might not enjoy this? How had it never occurred to me to want this? To think about it?

I suddenly understood the drive that I had always lacked, the need for this. Maybe I didn't have the biological drive others did, but after experiencing what this felt like, the pleasure, the warmth of her pussy, the power as I drove her past thinking to only feeling, I knew this would not be the last time.

My fingers almost moved on their own, testing, seeking. Her hips rose, just tiny jerks as she struggled against moving, against losing the touch. When I curled the fingers inside her up to stroke against her there, she let out another moan, one loud and drawn out and entirely mindless.

"You're even more sensitive than before. I wonder how many times you can come, how many times you can shatter apart before it's too much? Before you're begging me to stop instead of continuing?" I knew my smile was far from innocent, the darkness inside me swirling and consuming both of us. "I wonder how many more I will force from you even after that?"

I didn't wait for a response, instead lowering my lips back to her clit, attacking without mercy.

Nothing in the world could pull me away.

* * * *

Loch

My mind cleared slowly. It was less like waking up and more like someone removing a bag from my head, my eyes adjusting to the light after darkness.

My body was sore and overworked, though at first I struggled to figure out why.

I gasped, my throat sore and my voice croaking as I came, the release so surprising that I struggled to make sense of it.

"That's right, love, I have you." Sweet words whispered into my ear, the voice dark and familiar.

Yazmor.

I recognized it immediately, and just after that, the shifting of something inside my tightening pussy brought so much back to me.

My vision cleared, slowly, and I found the familiar violet of his eyes in front of me. The rest of everything else came to me, bit by bit, like a dripping faucet. His bare pale skin, one of his hands clutching mine, his others on my thigh, his weight pressing me down, against a rug-covered floor.

A shifting of his hips then told me that last bit of information — that the thickness inside me was not his fingers.

"Yazmor," I whispered, my voice rough and broken from hours of crying out.

"Are you back with me now?" Worry colored his voice, as if he wasn't currently inside me, like we weren't apparently having sex.

Just how many times had I come? How many times had he gotten me off with these hands and his tongue?

More than I can remember...

Part of me wished I couldn't remember it all. The sounds of my moans, the way I'd dug my nails into his skin to pull him closer, the way I'd moaned and pleaded and growled out demands? I wanted to crawl into a hole and pretend I'd forgotten the whole damn thing.

He brushed his thumb against my cheek after letting go of my hip, staring into my eyes as if judging something. "Your pupils have shrunk and the purple is almost entirely gone. You seem to be coming out of it." He pulled his hand back, an odd uncertainty. "Do you regret it?"

"What?"

"Maybe now that the Euphoria is out of your system, you're sorry it was me? Maybe I should have gotten the others —"

I shook my head, clinging to him as if he might try to pull away right then. The thought of him moving even a breath away was unacceptable right now. However, when I did that, it caused him to shift forward, for his hard cock to stroke against me again. It made my pussy clench down around him, the action reminding me of how sensitive I was.

Yazmor groaned and dropped his face against my neck. His breath was rough and warm and uneven, telling me that he was far from unaffected.

Boy did that mess with me, making my heart speed.

"I didn't…" He paused, and him stumbling over the words had me glad he wasn't looking at me. "I held back, because I didn't want to, not when you were out of your mind."

Which meant Yazmor, who had never actually had sex, had managed to not come all because he worried I'd regret it? He'd done this all for me, but resisted so long all for me?

That melted away the worries that had plagued me, the part of me embarrassed by what we'd done, by the way I'd acted. His unexpected sweetness, the tremble of his arms as he still held back, it made it all the clearer just how much I loved him.

I turned my head, pressing a kiss to the side of his neck, moving until I could tease his ear. "It's okay," I whispered.

Yazmor pulled back to look me in the eyes, his eyebrows drawn together. "What?"

"You don't have to hold back anymore."

"But—"

"I'm okay, now. This isn't the Euphoria talking—it's me."

Yazmor swallowed hard, the action making his throat shift. Why the hell was *that* sexy? It reminded me of how he'd touched me earlier, when he'd been so confident, so take-charge. I guess that was an effect of me being out of my mind. "You're sure?"

"Why ask me that? You're the one without experience, not me."

He leaned in and rested his forehead against mine, the closeness making me close my eyes. "Because you matter to me. I never want you to look at me and regret anything, for you to fear me or hate me. I could tolerate anything but that."

I traced his bottom lip with my tongue, the action reminding me of all the ways he'd used these lips on me already. "I'll only hate you if you stop."

Yazmor released a long, drawn-out groan, one that screamed how close he was to that edge. Then again, I wasn't sure exactly how long we'd been at this, how long he'd resisted, but that was really fucking impressive. I wasn't sure anyone else could have managed that.

He grasped my hip again, holding me still before he took my lips in a deep, consuming kiss. That was my only notice before he shifted away, then plunged deep into me, hard. I tried to cry out, but no sound could escape, not with the way Yazmor kissed me.

He'd always been so careful with me, but that seemed like a different man from the one taking me now. He fucked me so roughly I would have slid against the floor if he didn't have a good hold of me. Still, each time his thick cock filled me, I only wanted more.

More of this passion, more of this man who wasn't like anyone or anything else in my life. I slid my arms around his shoulders, clinging to him, desperate for everything he'd give me.

"I didn't know," he said, his words strained and quiet, as if talking to himself. "I had no idea what I was missing. My world was covered in fire, and you? You feel like that same fire, like home. I want to burn with you."

I nodded as if he'd asked me a question, because that was exactly what I wanted, too. I pictured his world, the ash, the creature he was, and I held him tighter. Sometimes he felt too large, too wild for me to hold. He was far stronger than most people understood, ancient and powerful, and I needed that all.

He slid his fingers into my hair, cradling my head before he kissed me again, making me feel as ravenous for him as I had with the Euphoria, proof that he affected me just as much as that drug.

And I knew for sure that I'd never get enough of him.

Chapter Fourteen

Loch

The moment I entered the back room of the shop, I was reminded of just how over-protective the men in my life really were.

It was like in the movies when a college kid comes home for the holiday and gets swamped by parents and family. Hands touched me, pulling at my clothes, tilting my head this way and that, checking me for injuries.

It all happened so fast that overwhelming didn't come *close* to explaining it.

I swiped my hand, knocking them away and pulling backward.

It let me at least *see* them. Hale and Tyrus were before me, both wearing identical expressions — anger and annoyance.

Ah, that takes me back. I hadn't been gone for that long, yet it felt like seeing them after weeks apart.

Gorrin had gotten behind me, the sneaky bastard, and his fingers were still hooked into the collar of my shirt, pulling it down to peer at the marks Yazmor had left. Anger radiated off him, so strong I could feel it without turning to face him. "Who did this?"

I laughed, the sound almost hysterical. Somehow, it cracked me up that none of the three seemed to even consider that it could have been Yazmor to leave such marks.

Yazmor waved the others away, then pulled me past them and deeper into the large room. "You guys hover that much, and she'll run away. Give her room to breathe at least."

"What are you wearing?" Tyrus asked, a line between his eyebrows.

I couldn't have walked around looking like a stripper, so Yazmor had snatched an outfit from the upper quarters of the brothel. It wasn't fancy, just a long shirt that reached my mid-thighs, and a cloak with a hood to hide my hair.

"Look—the Plains doesn't have a lot of options, okay?"

"And what happened to your clothing from before?" A not-so-subtle threat ran through Gorrin's question.

"Apparently it wasn't brothel-chic."

And there goes their tempers again.

It charmed me a bit, the way they got so angry on my behalf. I was tempted to let it go on, but we'd never get anything done. Instead, I crossed my arms and faced off against the three worriers. "I'm fine. Yazmor got there before anything happened."

"So you weren't given Euphoria?" Gorrin asked.

"Oh, no, she was high as a kite." Yazmor plopped down onto a sofa in the large room. "Also, I think I like fishnet stockings. I wonder if they'd make my legs look good."

"They don't work as well with hair."

"I'm willing to wax!"

"So you were given Euphoria but you're okay?" Gorrin broke into the conversation, appearing fed up with Yazmor and my little sidetrack. "How are you okay? Did it not affect you?"

"I wouldn't say *that*."

"Then how are you all right? Who put those marks on you? Who got you through it?"

My gaze shifted to Yazmor, and he only smirked in response.

The room went silent, as though the three other men struggled to make sense of what the obvious answer was.

"Wait one fucking minute," Hale blurted out. "You're going to stand here and tell me that *Yazmor* fucked you?" He said the words as if he were suggesting a dog had done calculus instead of Yazmor and I having sex.

"That's right!" And damn did Yazmor manage to look *quite* proud of himself.

Tyrus frowned. "Really? But how…" Tyrus stared at Yazmor's crotch, then mine as if solving a complex puzzle.

"Well, you see, first I licked —"

I covered his mouth with both my hands, knowing full well that Yazmor had *no* sense of decency. Clearly, I'd need to sit down with him at some point and make a list of what was and was not okay to talk about. If I didn't, he'd end up giving a blow-by-blow description of what we did together in the Christmas cards each year. "It's private, right, Yazmor?"

He winked, the action unbelievably sexy when it reminded me of how his fingers had felt, how his gaze never missed a single reaction of mine, how focused he could be when he wanted to be.

It had me pulling away before getting caught back up in that, which surprised me as much as anything else.

Yazmor had never struck me as sexual, but now I couldn't seem to *not* see him that way. I couldn't ignore the memories of his touch, of how he'd driven me to that mindless place, how he'd stroked me and how I'd given into him completely. The fact he didn't have a drive for that only made me that much more impressed by just how good he was at it.

I turned my gaze to the others and boy did they look confused.

Not that I could blame them. If someone told me a month ago that I'd be standing here, wearing love bites from Yazmor—who looked *far* too proud of himself—I'd have called them a liar. Fuck, I'd probably have suggested they get some help because of all the unlikely things to happen, that had to rank near the top.

Yet here I was.

"Someone check in with the Chasm," Hale said.

I frowned, not even sure how to respond to that.

Hale continued, a smile spreading across his lips to tell me a moment before he spoke that he was for sure going to be an asshole. "Yazmor actually got some—hell must have frozen over."

"It's not hell," I muttered and crossed my arms. "And we're in the Plains, getting ready to attack God. You don't think we have anything more important to deal with right now? *Nothing* is more pressing than Yazmor's dick and what he does with it?"

"Well—" Yazmor started.

I jammed my finger toward him in warning, and while he stopped speaking, his smirk said he didn't much care if I scolded him.

Assholes, the lot of them!

Why did I put up with them? A dull ache in my body sent a rush of pleasure through me, as if my vagina itself was waving at me and reminding me of everything these men could do.

Right, that's why...

"You know," Tyrus said, stepping closer and running his fingers along my jawline in a touch so suggestive it should have been rated *R*. "You had us all rather worried. Maybe there's time to—"

I pulled away before he sucked me into his logic— and he sure as fuck could have done that—and spoke loudly to interrupt the thought before he could get it out entirely. "*Anyway!* We should get ready. I already saw Noah and said our goodbyes. He's out of the way so we don't have to worry about any splash back on him."

"I'm surprised he left," Gorrin said. "He seemed like the type to want to help more."

"He wasn't happy about leaving, but I told him we couldn't move freely if we were worried about him. So, are we ready?" I asked, steering us back on track. Normally Tyrus or Gorrin would have done that, but it seemed Yazmor's love life was interesting enough that even they'd rather focus on that.

"Yes," Gorrin answered, the first to recover. He really was the responsible one, wasn't he? "I have called a meeting with Hubis for tomorrow evening."

"And he just said yes?"

"I have rarely called meetings. Back at the start I was more involved, but over the years, prior to me leaving for the Chasm, they became less common."

"So you think he'll show up happily because he sees it as you falling back in line?" Hale checked.

Gorrin nodded once, quickly. "He has wished for me to become more involved, and he accepts this as my attempt to do so."

"What did you tell him it was about?" I asked.

"About my time in the Chasm. He doesn't like that I went there, but he will listen to what I learned, to anything that may prove useful. He will have his guard down, his ego eased by the fact I am doing as he wishes."

"And that'll be when we move?" Just saying that made it all real. Up until now, no matter how much I'd dealt with, facing Hubis had seemed so far away. It was like taking my first ice skating lesson while dreaming about the Olympics.

"Yes," Gorrin answered, a tension resting there between us all.

By the end of tomorrow, one way or another, this would all be over. We'd succeed or we'd fail, but the one thing for sure was that nothing would ever be the same again.

* * * *

I pointed my feet, stretching out in the massive bed.

And why the fuck was this bed so big? It had to be two king-sized-beds wide, and just trying to make a bed this large would probably constitute a cardio workout. Still, the ability to stretch out meant I could file this away in mysteries I didn't really give a fuck about.

I had a book of fairy tales in my lap, one I'd found on a shelf in the room. Anything was better than the worries that consumed me.

A knock on the door had me groaning and opening my eyes again. I called out for them to enter, and when I spotted Gorrin's face, I struggled to hold on to my annoyance anymore.

He was at least as stressed as I felt.

He closed the door behind him, but didn't move any farther into the room, didn't even meet my gaze. Instead, he stared at the floor as if the stone tiles were some puzzle he might figure out if only he looked long enough.

"I bet the floor here is the same as your room," I said, my voice feeling uncomfortably loud in the silent room.

The silence of the Plains freaked me out as much as anything else. The Chasm was always noisy, like this background hum that never quite went away. Earth was the same, where a person was never alone enough for complete silence.

The Path was similar to the Plains, but somehow, it was *worse* here. I knew there wasn't anything in the Path — well, other than Guardian — but here? Countless people and angels moved around, yet it was like the air itself muffled all the sound.

Gorrin's loud sigh drew a smile from me, surprising me again that even with what we faced, I could still feel joy, that I could still grin and be happy.

And fuck did Gorrin's annoyance make me happy.

I patted the bed next to me.

Finally, Gorrin left the doorway and crawled onto the bed beside me, turning to lean his back against the pillows. He wore a pair of sweats and a T-shirt, making him look dressed down. I was thankful for that, really, because I knew the next time I saw him, he'd be back in his uniform.

That made me sad, in a way, as if it would signal how far away he was. This Gorrin, the one who relaxed, who let his defenses down, was the one only I knew, the one reserved for me.

I leaned against his side, then rested my head on his shoulder.

"This feels weird." I kept my voice low, the action making the moment feel even more private.

"What does?"

"We're about to do something stupid."

"I would have assumed you'd be used to that."

I snickered softly at the jab. So long ago, when I'd first met him, I would have taken that to heart, would have felt hurt. However, the words now held affection, as though no matter how exasperated he might get with me, it couldn't change that he cared for me. "Yeah, but this is the last time, right?"

"You don't know that."

"You're telling me that you think we'll win?"

"I can't say whether or not we will win, but if I were hopeless, I wouldn't be here."

I elbowed him softly. "We both know that isn't true. You've followed me this far—I don't think you'd turn back no matter what."

He didn't react to the jab at first, then sighed. I expected him to tell me I was wrong, that my foolishness was my own, something like how we usually interacted. Instead, he shifted his arm so it went up and over my shoulders, pulling me against his side. "You are right, I think. Even if I knew this was hopeless,

I would still follow you, still remain by your side no matter what."

"Why?"

"I don't know."

I blew out a breath at the totally useless statement.

I snorted at how comfortable it was sitting beside Gorrin, never having expected to find myself here like this.

Another knock against the door had me letting out a sigh. Time alone was over in my life, wasn't it? I called for them to come in, but then Tyrus opened the door, he froze.

Hesitation played across his features, his desire to come in at odds with the fact Gorrin was already here.

I wanted to tell him to just come the hell in, but before I could, Gorrin spoke up. "Just come in."

The hesitation didn't last any longer than that statement before Tyrus closed the door and came over. He had also dressed down, wearing a pair of sweats and a long-sleeved cotton shirt, both black — *of course.*

He got into bed on the other side of me, pressing close until not an inch of space existed between our bodies. And damn me, because I leaned against him, enjoying the sensation.

I picked up the book from my lap, but before I made it even two full sentences, the door opened again — no knock this time.

Hale didn't hesitate as Tyrus had — no, not Hale. He didn't give a fuck who else would be there. He only cared about what he wanted.

And somehow, that reassured me. Hale, who was dangerous and scary and impulsive, but who also had cared for and tucked in Brendon so carefully, who carried so many scars from his horrific past.

He crawled into the bed, grabbed my legs, and put them over his lap. It trapped me between the three of them, but for some reason, a position that would have felt terrifying before felt safe.

When had that happened? When had these men stopped being — well, not dangerous, because I knew very well they were that — but comforting to me?

He gazed at the book, then gestured at it. "Go on."

"Go on?"

"You were reading, right? Heard your voice from out there."

I narrowed my eyes, not sure how to respond to that. The book was stupid, just a children's fairy tale collection, but here I had these three men all but enthralled.

It isn't about the story, is it?

The next time the door opened, I couldn't even feign surprise. Did these four have some sort of weird connection where they *knew* the perfect time to bother me? Or maybe they were just in it to bother one another, to ensure they proved themselves the biggest nuisance possible.

That I'd believe.

While the others had come in with some hesitation, or at least without a word, Yazmor always did things his own way. He barely spared a glance around before closing the door and jumping into the bed like an eight-year-old who'd had too much sugar. He shifted around, resting his head against my legs and Hale's lap, shifting into place like it was his right.

The action was *almost* adorable.

He peered up at me, his bright eyes peeking out from the bit of hair that had fallen over his forehead. It made him look young and sweet, that strange innocent side to him that always threw me.

He was ancient and powerful and almost disconnected from the world, but maybe that allowed him to keep that childlike side to him. The world didn't touch him as it did others.

"I like this story," he said.

"You don't even know what story I'm reading."

"Of course I do. It's the one with the penguin and the shark."

I pressed my lips together, annoyed when he'd guessed right. "Were you eavesdropping or something?"

"Of course not! If I were doing that, I would have just come in sooner. Who would stand outside a closed door instead of being in the bed?" He huffed a small sound, implying *I* was the strange one to suggest something so crazy.

"Then how did you know?'

"Because I know you. There are eight stories in that book. Four of them are about kids and not animals, and you wouldn't pick those. The other four are about all sorts of things, but *you* would have liked the penguin one best. The one about geese was about fitting in, and that isn't your thing. The frog story has a lesson about obeying your parents and *that* doesn't sound like you at all."

"What about the story about the ants?" I asked, annoyed that he knew me so well.

"That one tells people to prepare and think things through." He cocked up one of his eyebrows, a smirk on his lips as if to dare me to argue over that one.

And fuck him because I couldn't.

He chuckled, the sound soft. "The penguin one, though? It's about a cute little penguin that befriends a shark. All the other penguins tell it that the shark is dangerous, that it should avoid the shark, but the penguin makes friends anyways. Then, one day, a killer whale attacks the penguin, and they're almost caught. It's the shark that comes and saves the penguin. Don't you think that sounds like a story *you* might just like?"

Since I couldn't tell him he was wrong, I only tossed the book to the bed, beside Yazmor. "Well, now you've spoiled it anyways, so what's the point in reading it at all?"

Yazmor picked up the book and handed it back to me. "Because none of us are here to listen to a story about a penguin and a shark."

"Then why are you here?"

He peered up at me, a seriousness to his expression that threw me as it always did. "Because tomorrow, everything changes. Where else would we want to spend what might be our last night then here, listening to you. The words you say, the stories, none of that matters. I just want to listen to your voice for as long as I can."

I broke eye contact with him, glancing around to the others, half-expecting them to mock him, to point out he was a complete idiot most of the time, but that wasn't what I found.

Instead, Hale, Tyrus and Gorrin wore matching serious expressions. A moment of tense silence fell between us, as if for that one second, we all could admit that things didn't look good, that what we were facing was nearly impossible, and I suddenly understood.

If this was our last night, I couldn't think of anywhere else I'd want to spend it, either.

So I opened the book once more and started to read, thankful when the men didn't mention the tremble to my voice or the way I swallowed to try to calm my nerves.

And sitting between them like this, I could only be thankful that I'd chosen to fall for the sharks.

Chapter Fifteen

I pulled at the outfit I wore, frowning at the sheer stupidity of it.

"Stop fidgeting," Tyrus said before running his fingers through my hair to move it back into place after the many times I'd messed with it out of anxiety.

"Easy for you to say. You get to wear *that*." I scowled at his outfit, the need to rant and rave about sexism hitting me.

Tyrus wore the outfit befitting male servants in the Palace, which looked strangely like a butler outfit.

Me, on the other hand? I got my ass shoved into a dress with a long skirt and *ruffles*. Just thinking it almost made me gag. I looked like one of those old maids, the sort who would carry a candle and walk through the dark hallways of a haunted castle.

I'll take ghosts over this bullshit any day.

"Does your outfit really matter?" Tyrus moved his fingers over the laces at the back of my top, tightening the strings but not so much that I wouldn't be able to breathe. "If you wore anything that stood out, you'd draw attention to yourself."

"Yeah, because looking like an old-timey maid doesn't draw attention."

Tyrus tied the laces near my waist, the tightness of the garment almost reassuring. Or maybe my kinky ass just got ideas all on its own.

"Relax," he said, his voice soft. "You won't be alone."

"That's not the problem," I answered.

"Then what is?"

I didn't turn to face him, speaking being easier when I didn't have his dark eyes locked on me. "I've been alone a lot in my life. I can deal with alone. If I succeed or fail, I do it on my own. No one else must be involved."

Tyrus wrapped his arms around me, pulling me closer until I could feel his chest against my back, until his breath blew through my hair.

The touch got me to continue, to whisper the rest of what was in my head. "I got you all into this with me, and now I'm responsible for what happens to you all. I'm not worried about what happens to me—I'm terrified that something will happen to *you* and it'll be my fault. What's the point of this all if I succeed but I lose someone that matters to me?"

Tyrus tightened his arms around me, the touch reassuring. "You are talking about *us*, Loch. Do you really think something like this could take us down?" Even as he spoke with the surety he always used, I knew better.

It was easy to say that, but this wasn't a normal occurrence. We weren't ready to go up against something as mundane as an angel or Guardian or a

Karen. This was *God* we were getting ready to face against.

There were no for-sures here, no promises, nothing to prepare us for what we'd face.

Gorrin was already at the meeting place, waiting for Hubis. Hale and Yazmor were stationed in adjacent rooms — Hubis would recognize them the moment they got spotted. Tyrus would escort me once the others were seated and properly distracted. He would take place outside the door, as backup.

Which meant only Gorrin and I would be in the actual room.

My dagger would end Hubis, assuming I could get close enough. Gorrin had warned me not to draw it until the last moment, because Hubis would be able to feel the power when it manifested.

And why did *I* get to be the one who had to do the deed?

Because my dagger was the only thing certain to work the quickest, and the women's outfits included a hood, which would hide my identity best of all.

"Are you ready?" Tyrus asked.

No. That was an easy fucking answer, wasn't it? Of course I wasn't ready! Who was ever ready for something like this? There weren't self-help books that got people all hyped up for taking on God, were there?

If I survive this, I guess I know what I could do afterward.

Tyrus pressed a kiss to my shoulder through the fabric of my top. "You are thinking something foolish to distract yourself. I know that look. I suppose that means you are as ready as you will be."

I let out a long sigh, then finally turned to face him head-on. "If this doesn't go well—"

He leaned in and took my lips in a kiss that silenced both my speech and my brain. It was rough and possessive, pouring so many unsaid things into it that my heart sped and a part of me wondered if any of this was worth it.

I mean, I could just leave, right?

He broke the kiss, but stayed so close that his breath warmed my damp lips as he spoke. "We can't leave, Loch. For better or worse, we are in this now. I do not want to hear a goodbye from you, though."

I looked up and into his dark eyes, losing myself in them, in the feelings that ran so deep. When we'd first met, I'd thought he didn't feel anything, as though he were hollow and broken, as if old wounds had allowed everything warm inside him to leak out.

Over the years, though, I'd realized that wasn't true. Tyrus had as much depth as any person I'd ever met, he simply kept a tight hold on it.

So I nodded, accepting the truth he was trying to make me understand.

"I'm ready," I said.

He ran his thumb along my bottom lip, and even if he'd forbidden any goodbyes, that touch sure as fuck felt like one...

* * * *

Gorrin

My breath caught when Loch walked into the room. It was strange, because through my very long life, few times had I found people important enough for me to remember let alone get to know. How was it then that with Loch, even covered as she was, I recognized her.

I saw her in the way she walked, the slight sway to her hips, the set of her shoulders. I didn't need to see her face or her tattoos or her bright green hair to know exactly who it was.

However, now was not the time to let that get away from me, to allow myself to take notice of it.

Hubis sat across from me, his back to the door, his focus on me. "So you wish to resume duties here at the Palace?"

"Yes," I said, the lie heavy on my tongue but necessary. Even the thought of returning to Hubis' service, to do as he wished, made my stomach uneasy. The subtle rolling there, the general sickness, it said I could not go back to that life ever again.

However, it would set him at ease, which was exactly what we needed. This was too important to fail to play my part.

"You were so hesitant before," he said. "Why the sudden change of heart?"

"Even for us, we do not age, but we still learn. My time in the Chasm taught me much."

Hubis didn't remove his gaze from me. It was a common tactic he used, that intense stare that could unnerve even the most brave and foolhardy. "A drink."

For a moment, I thought he had asked me that, but a flick of his fingers said he'd meant it for Loch.

Right, she is in the outfit of a Palace servant. Of course he would expect her to wait on him.

Loch froze, her steps halting. However, she proved herself yet again when she moved toward the bottles set on a table to the side. Even the unexpected wouldn't get the best of Loch.

She poured one glass, then asked, her voice softer and sweeter than I had ever heard it. "And for you, sir?"

She means me? Her using that tone with me didn't sit right at all, made me feel like she saw me as others did, as my position rather than me as a person.

Still, if she could do her job, so could I. "No, thank you."

She nodded, the action showing from beneath the hood, then poured the drink from a large crystal bottle into a smaller glass. As she worked, Hubis continued to speak.

"Why now? What happened in the Chasm that taught you so much? When you left here, when you ventured out, you were so sure that you were right, and I was wrong. Even if you were too loyal to speak up, you think I—who made you—could not see what was in your heart? You thought you could change everything by yourself. Why has that changed?"

His words cut into me, the reminder of who I had been before, of how I'd wanted to do so much good. And what had it amounted to? Countless years in the Chasm and had I made it any better?

Not until Loch came and did what no one else could.

It solidified again just how much this mattered. It helped push me to continue.

"I left because I thought it was cruel to leave the Chasm alone," I admitted. "It felt like people could make one mistake and still find redemption, that they could still be better people."

"Do you still believe that?"

I opened my mouth to tell him, no, but the expected answer didn't come. Why? What was it about Hubis that made it more difficult to betray him? Maybe something inside me still wanted his respect because he has created me? *Pathetic.*

"I understand," he said, his voice lowering an octave. "You gave so much of yourself to that and what did it get you? Stabbed by one of the fallen you wished to save? I suppose that would prove to anyone that redemption wasn't a thing."

I nodded, his words ringing true. "I don't believe in redemption anymore," I admitted, the words honest.

I didn't believe in redemption, but not because I thought the people in the Chasm were lost causes. I didn't think they *needed* redemption. I didn't think people were good or bad in a way that required them to seek some form of salvation or change. Instead, everyone was a messy combination of good and bad.

Still, my words seemed to sooth Hubis, because he nodded and sat back, then held his hand out.

Loch gave him the glass, and he didn't even turn his head before taking a sip. He showed no signs of being aware of our plan or even on edge.

Perfect.

I didn't lift my eyes to Loch, couldn't risk tipping our hand too soon. Still, through my peripheral vision, I saw her shift. She set her hand over her wrist, and the wave of power as she took the dagger shifted through me like a soft wave, a warning that made the hair on the back of my neck stand up. I recalled that sensation a moment before she had plunged that dagger into me.

A tiny part of me didn't want this to do the same way, didn't want to see Hubis suffer as I had, but it was far too late to stop.

Loch moved fast, just as I'd told her to do, lifting the dagger to drive it down into him.

My breath caught in my throat as I watched it, as the horror of the moment washed over me. I *knew* Loch didn't want to do this, not in person. No matter what Hubis had done, she didn't revel in taking life, but she did it for so many others. She did it to help those she didn't even know.

The blade caught light from the candles in the room, and a hair from him, the blade stopped.

Loch's hand hung in the air, the blade clutched in her fist, with Hubis' hand wrapped tightly around her wrist.

"I am afraid that you came all this way for nothing," Hubis said, his voice still flat as if nothing had happened.

I rose, ready to sail forward, to help, to finish him off if that was what it took. However, before I could, he waved his other hand, a blast of power sending me backward. I crashed against the stone wall, and for a moment, I feared he'd push harder, that he'd crush me or send me through the wall.

It again reminded me that I was out of my league, that Hubis was not just a demon or an angel or even a remnant. Instead, he was the being who had shaped this world, who had given the universe form and function, and it seemed he knew exactly what we had been up to.

I was right that this would end one way or another, but it seemed we had no happy ending in our future.

Chapter Sixteen

Loch

My wrists ached, and even if I knew it was pointless, I still yanked at the binds.

Sure, my version of heaven would absolutely have some good old bondage, but I had a pretty good feeling that Hubis didn't intend to give me any orgasms along with the handcuffs.

"Where's Gorrin?" I asked, narrowing my eyes as I stared at Hubis.

He'd had other angels come in and take possession of Gorrin, slapping a pair of cuffs on him similar to my own. Once they'd gone on, my power had been all but gone.

Or it was better to say I could feel it, but I couldn't use it. Even my demon form had felt broken from me, like the pathways that let me access that were all cut.

Given how Gorrin had reacted when they'd gone on him, it seemed they did the same to him.

"He has been taken to the cells," Hubis explained as he poured more of his drink into his glass. "And because I detest false hope, let me tell you that alongside him in those cells are also Hale, Tyrus and Yazmor."

Those words crushed my hopes, turning them to dust inside me. I'd sat there, thinking that perhaps the others could have stepped in, could have provided backup, but now I found out that wasn't the case.

We really had failed.

Spectacularly.

Well, at least something I do is spectacular…

"You look sad." Hubis sat in front of me, our chairs so close that his knees brushed against mine.

This, in some ways, felt like the first real time we'd spoken. He'd talked to me before, in my head, as he'd inflicted his *lesson* on me, but I'd still been holding back then. I'd had plans I didn't want him to know about, had played my part, but what was the point in that anymore?

No matter how this went—and I was pretty sure I didn't get a say in that anymore—we were here, just the two of us, and there was no good reason not to say exactly what was on my mind.

It wasn't God and a Demon Lord. It wasn't someone from the Plains and someone from the Chasm. It was just two beings formed of the same universe.

"How did you manage this?" he asked.

"Manage what?" I shifted my hands, making the cuffs rattle. "It doesn't seem like I managed much."

"You did. Gorrin has had doubts for many years, but never would he have considered directly standing against me. He was always the most loyal of my angels, and yet for you, he was prepared to attack me directly.

He knew what that would do, what I was capable of, yet he moved without hesitation. Hale and Tyrus have never cared about anything but themselves, yet for you, they did the unthinkable. Even Yazmor, the troublesome remnant that I have tried to ignore, has never felt a need to participate in the world, yet for you, he does so? Why?"

I snorted softly at the absurdity of that statement. Sure, the Lords had followed me, but it wasn't about *me*.

"You find that question funny?" Hubis tilted his head.

"Yeah, I do. They do what they want."

"But you must agree that when what they want seems to revolve around you, it makes you a nexus. You befriended Kylie, drew her into a fight she had avoided for a very long time. You seem capable of changing people in a way you do not take full responsibility for."

"Kylie did what she wanted. I never asked her to do anything."

"You did not need to. That is the strangest thing about you. I can force others to comply, can use manipulation and strength to force my will, but you? You change what a person is without so much as a request."

I blew a strand of hair from my face since I couldn't use my hands to do so. "You really don't get it."

"So explain it. Because I am very old and have seen much, but you seem to have an understanding I lack. It is just us here, so please, explain."

"You can't force people to change. You can't force them to become something else."

"I have seen it happen. Kylie was not always what she is now. *We* were not always what we are now. She changed."

I shook my head. "No. I bet she didn't change at all, not really, not what matters. We are who we are — all of us. We make choices, we might choose to make different choices, but our core? That's not any different. It is what it is. She is the woman she has always been, and you are the asshole I bet you've always been."

He blinked slowly, the silence tense.

Then again, I'd bet not many people called God an asshole to his face.

After a moment, he shook his head. Had he expected me to apologize? Too fucking late for that. I was well past giving a damn about what he thought.

I had a feeling trying to kill him wasn't the sort of offense I could easily come back from.

"So you are telling me that Gorrin has always been this person? Despite having spent thousands of years with him by my side, with him following my will without question? That is the same man who was prepared to kill me just to save you?"

"Yeah, it's the same man. Gorrin is loyal to a fault, and that has never changed. The only thing different is *who* he is loyal to. At his core, he is the same man he has always been. Hale is the same nasty, short-tempered man. Tyrus is duplicitous and methodical, and Yazmor is a nutjob who is impossible to figure out. They're all the same."

"And you?"

"I'm the same idiot who sold my soul for a man. I'm *still* making the same mistakes I always have, because I am a hopeless optimist at my core." Just saying it let some of my energy rush from me. I'd come so far, done so much, but I was still the same woman I'd always been.

I had no idea if that made me feel better or worse.

"So if nothing changes, what is the point of any of this? You suffered so much and for what? To end up here, imprisoned, no closer to your goal than you had been? I feel as if my lesson did not take."

"Your lesson was just torture."

"It was not. It was perhaps harsh, but just like giving vaccinations to babies causes them pain, it is not torture as it is for their own good."

"And making me relive that was for what good? Because I don't know what the fucking point was." Just talking about it made that sickness roll around in my stomach. I swallowed to keep it down. While the memories had distanced some, while they didn't have the grip they had before, they still made me feel out of control.

"You truly did not understand, then. That was the tipping point. That was the event that ended my world."

"How could that have ended your world? It was fucking horrible, but it was *one* person."

"Then you do not know how the world works, how the universe works. Even one person can tip the scales, can change everything. That attack did so."

"How?"

He leaned back in his chair, and his expression took me by surprise. I'd expected him to look somewhere between smug and disinterested, but that wasn't what I saw.

Instead, it was as though he wasn't there with me at all, a sense of anxious nostalgia about him. "I believed as you did before. I thought that if I worked hard enough, the world could be better. I had those I wished to protect, and I thought I could do so if I only had enough power, if I were only strong enough. I believed in the basic good of most people, no matter how twisted our world became, no matter what horrors I witnessed. That changed that day."

"You knew the person who was attacked?"

He nodded, his eyebrows pinched. "I did. They were very important to me. I felt something was wrong, and when I went to them, I discovered them bloodied and broken and so fearful. They cringed away from me for the first time, and it was then I recognized that the filth in that world could not continue. Sometimes trying to save everyone only ensures obliteration. Sometimes cutting away the infection may hurt but will save the organism overall. When I looked into their eyes, when I saw that they had been broken, the rest of the world forfeited any rights to existence."

"So you took over and destroyed the entire world out of petty revenge?"

He shook his head. "No, not revenge. It wasn't out of anger, even. The world was flawed. No matter what I did to change things, to better them, it would be little more than a tiny piece of tape meant to hold back a cracked dam. The only true solution would be to wipe away what was and build something better. If there is a dilapidated home, shattered down to the foundation, trying to fix it is a useless task. Better to demolish it and start fresh. I could not save that person, but I could offer them a world where I would ensure it would never happen again."

I dropped my gaze, trying to make sense of his words. They were crazy, sure, but they were *honest*. Maybe the first honest things he'd said in so long. I couldn't agree, but I could understand it. I tried to put myself in his place, to think about how I would feel losing someone important to me, watching them hurt.

Could I destroy reality, destroy everything and everyone in it?

A pit in my stomach said I wasn't sure, and that was far more terrifying than realizing I could have done something so terrible.

"I don't know," I admitted. "But just because I don't know what I would do doesn't mean I think it's okay. And even if that *was* understandable, it doesn't excuse what you've done since. It doesn't change all the people who are hurt by you."

"People are hurt because existence breeds pain. No one can change that. This version of the world is better than the last, though."

"How is it better? Seems like it's just as bad. People suffer in life, and you make sure they suffer after they die, too."

Hubis waved his hand around as if to prove some point. "Suffer? I have created a paradise here."

"A paradise that those who aren't perfect are cast out of. Do you have *any* idea what the angels do to human souls here? How they mistreat them?"

A darkness entered Hubis' eyes. "I leave that to those I put in charge. I trust them to make the best choices. I cannot be expected to micromanage every little detail of existence."

"There are brothels in *this* city that trap human souls and allow angels to drug and abuse them. And don't you dare tell me I'm wrong about that—I was put into one. That is the heaven you made here while trying to condemn souls you felt weren't good enough to the Chasm."

"Those who sell their souls remove themselves from me, and thus are barred from paradise. That seems a logical result."

"But they aren't bad! You decide the only thing that matters about a person is whether they obey you. People's souls aren't that simple!"

Hubis tapped his finger on the top of his knee, the action surprisingly unnerving. "You are a fool who does not understand. You do not see the danger in chaos, have not yet lost enough to really see the value in keeping the things that matter to you safe. Perhaps eventually, when you see the Lords you so value fall, one-by-one, you will finally understand."

My mouth dried in an instant, all the saliva evaporating from the threat. "What are you going to do to them?" It took two tries to get the question out, only a scratchy noise coming at first.

"I will not allow chaos and disorder to continue. You have touched *everywhere* in this world—the Chasm, Earth, the Plains, even the Path. You have altered so many lives in your little mission, taught people that they can change things, that they can stand against me. That cannot be allowed to continue. It is only with your deaths that we can restore order, that we can dash that false hope you have infected others with. You will be publicly executed, the event broadcast to the Chasm as well. The Chasm will be run by a single demon of my choosing, one who has proven himself and his loyalty. He will be the one to end you all and ensure that this little rebellion dies with you."

"And who is this special little demon who thinks he can get the best of us?"

Hubis waved his hand, a shimmering portal appearing before us. A familiar face came into view, the portal like the communication ring I had used but larger, clearer. "I believe you are acquainted. At least you will see a familiar face when you die. That is more than most can hope for."

A smirk that I knew, one that had thrilled me before, now only crushed what was left of my pride, of my hope. "I told you I always come out on top," Gunnar said, his body twisted into a form I had never seen before, with large, leathery wings and pure black eyes, proof that Hubis had stepped in and elevated him from damned to demon.

Gunnar had been responsible for my first death—at least there was some cosmic balance in him being responsible for my second.

* * * *

Well, as far as cells go, this isn't so bad. No jail was ever like a hotel, but this place was a lot nicer than I would have expected, *especially* with someone as twisted as Hubis in charge.

"Loch?" Gorrin's voice had me setting my hand against the stone wall to the left of the door.

"I'm here!" I called back.

The stone muddled his voice, but I could still make it out when he responded in a tone full of relief. "Are you hurt at all?"

"No. He didn't hurt me."

I wasn't sure what he said after that, but I suspect it was something between a curse and a thank you—who he was saying them to, I didn't know. Finally, he spoke again. "We're all here, too. It seems like Hubis expected our attack because he was well prepared for it."

"Is anyone hurt?"

"A few bumps and bruises. No one was going to manage to take Yazmor or Hale without them...objecting." That last word held a surprising fondness, as if their stubborn streak pleased him. "Nothing serious, though. I do not understand how he could have guessed."

"Gunnar," I whispered, the pain as fresh as it had been when I'd seen him in the portal, when the reality had hit me.

Yet again, Gunnar had betrayed me. All the times that the others had told me to be careful, when they'd warned me about the dangers and I'd ignored them, that was all coming back to laugh at me, wasn't it?

When I'd seen him, I'd frozen. All the insults and threats I would have normally hurled had died on the spot, and I'd been unable to even speak. Why? Why was I still so shocked that he'd betray me, that he'd screw me over like he always did?

Because I wanted to believe he could be more, because that meant I could be more. It made me let out a hollow laugh, since I'd told Hubis that people didn't change. Why then did I expect Gunnar to?

"Gunnar?" The name was growled out, so low and angry that I swore I could almost *feel* it through the stone. My knees gave out, and I slumped to the hard ground, exhaustion tugging at me.

What was I supposed to do now? We were caught, and I saw no way this could possibly work out. No chance that this would get better, that we could come out on top. Instead, I saw only a future where I had to watch the deaths of the men I loved, my only solace that I would not live much longer.

I'd died once already—seemed about right to do it again.

"How did he even know?" Gorrin asked.

"He must have suspected it," I guessed. "He knew we were missing, so it wouldn't have been hard for him to tell Hubis. Hubis is planning on letting Gunnar kill each of us so all the Chasm ends up under his control."

"Why would he do that? It would make someone too powerful."

"He thinks he can control him. He probably can. Gunnar wants power, but he also knows a good thing when he sees it. If he can run all the Chasm as he pleases, why fight with Hubis?"

Another muttered sound floated through the wall, and I was pretty sure that time they were curses. Still, a smile didn't come. I couldn't bring myself to smile.

"We'll figure something out," Gorrin swore, but I knew better.

I heard it in his voice, too. He didn't believe it any more than I did. Sometimes it was time to just accept that we were beat, that we were fucked, that we had no more moves to make.

"I'm sorry," I whispered, letting myself collapse further so I lay against the cool stone. I closed my eyes, guilt tugging at me.

I saw what the world would have been without me. I'd been so damned egotistical to think that I'd changed things for the better, that I could be the thing that altered and fixed it all. Instead, I'd dragged countless others into peril.

Gorrin, Hale, Tyrus and Yazmor would die, because of me. If Hubis looked too deeply into our connections, all the people who helped us in the Plains might die, along with anyone loyal to us in the Chasm. I saw Myers and Koya and Jacob in my head. I saw Kylie and

Jay and Brendon. So many people whose lives were not made better because of me.

Gorrin called out to me, but I lacked the energy or strength to respond. If I opened my mouth again, I was afraid I'd shatter, that I'd sob and say so much more than would help any of us. So I ignored his calls and let the darkness of sleep take me.

I'd proven that I could only fuck things up worse — everyone would be better off if I just slept through it all.

Chapter Seventeen

Hale looks hot even like this.

The moment the thought came to me, I scolded myself for acting like a horny teenager at a time like this. Sure, Hale *did* look good, even with cuffs binding his wrists behind him, his chest bare to show off his tattoos, a pair of slacks hanging low on his hips, exposing his lean waist and his nipple rings. It also made me glad he hadn't removed *all* the piercings — just his facial ones. It took a special sort of person to look that good when all bound up and awaiting execution.

But now was hardly the time to focus on that. The men had been brought to the execution area first, and I was surprised just how the relief hit me upon seeing them. If I had to go, I was damn happy to see them one last time.

Maybe this life wasn't all that bad after all.

Yazmor gave me a smirk, then winked from his spot at the end of the line. As if that wasn't already totally inappropriate, he waved me forward as if he'd saved a spot for me at the movies. I went toward him, but the angels guarding me yanked me backward, their tight grips on my upper arms drawing a wince. "A little rough for my taste," I muttered.

"Silence," one snapped.

"Does that ever work? I mean, what are you going to do if I don't? Kill me? Because I think you don't have a lot of leverage anymore."

The angel who had spoken flushed, as if he'd never really thought about it before and didn't care for someone pointing it out. Instead of pushing anymore, though, he simply guided me to the end, beside Tyrus, and hooked my cuffs to a horizontal bar that ran along the length of the five of us and seemed sturdy enough to hold us—at least in our current underpowered forms.

"Are you all right?" Tyrus asked but didn't move his gaze from ahead, didn't turn to look at me.

It made me smile, the way that even now, even at the end, he could be so steadfast. "Yep. Just peachy."

He sighed softly, then lowered his voice. "I'm sorry."

"Pretty sure that's my line."

"No, it isn't. I wanted to protect you, but maybe I went too far, maybe I gave you too much room. I failed to keep you safe, and for that, I am sorry."

I heard the pain in his voice and had no doubt his mind had gone back to his family, to watching the die before him, to how he'd suffered through that failure. That probably made this hurt all the worse.

Before I had to say anything else, the crowd hushed, a heaviness filling the air to signal Hubis' arrival before he came into our view. When he did, I didn't bother to hide my own laugh.

The asshole had dressed for the occasion, hadn't he? He wore a uniform similar to what Gorrin had always worn, making me think they were some holdover from his world.

Sentimental asshole.

So why wasn't I more afraid? Maybe it was because fear came from the unknown. Fear was born in actions that created mystery, in the anxiety of what-ifs.

I didn't have any of those. I knew exactly what was happening, how this would go, and that made it a hell of a lot easier to accept.

It sucked, but when I had nowhere else to go, nothing else to do, I figured I might as well try to enjoy the ride.

And suddenly, Hubis didn't look so scary. He looked like a child playing with his toys, one who didn't know how to play nicely with others.

He walked up to stand before us and clasped his hands behind his back. It pressed his chest out, and for a moment, I could *almost* see who he might have been in the past. Before he'd given up, before he'd cracked and become twisted, I could nearly glimpse the strong, determined man beneath it all.

"You five stand accused of working against the order, of entering the Plains illegally, and of attempting to overthrow my order. Do any of you deny these claims?"

Yazmor lifted his hand, the chain hanging as if he'd broken it. "I didn't enter the Plains illegally since I'm allowed to be here."

"You entered through the Path," Hubis pointed out.

"So? If a place is *my* place, I can enter through the bathroom window. It's totally legal."

Hubis stared for a moment, then rubbed his temple and turned his gaze away from Yazmor. "Anyone else?"

Tyrus spoke up. "I am actually a fan of order, so I feel as if sowing chaos does not accurately describe my actions."

Hale twisted and brought his hands as far forward and to the side as the chain allowed, drew them into fists, then raised the middle finger on each hand. "I wasn't close enough to actually try and stab you, but I fucking wish I had been."

Gorrin stood tall, his pose mirroring Hubis, but fuck did Gorrin look so much better like that. "My only regret is that it took me this long to act."

My mouth hung open for a moment, the tense silence around us showing that *no one* expected them to speak up that way.

But why not? I knew these men, and even if they were going to their deaths, they weren't the type of people to go quietly, to be good little boys. They'd never been good before in their life — why would that change now?

In fact, it would have been far more shocking if they'd simply stood there and behaved themselves, if they'd just listened and not responded to this bullshit.

The silence around me, the way the crowd reacted, it finally got to me. Everyone was so fucking tense wondering how Hubis would react, but again, I remembered that he already planned to kill us. What the fuck was the point in paying his game?

Suddenly, it all seemed so funny. My laugh came out hard, like a sneeze, something I couldn't stop. The moment it started, it grew until I was almost gasping from it. The more I thought about it all, the funnier it got.

Especially as an angel worked once again to secure Yazmor's cuffs.

Hubis turned his eyes on me, fire dancing in the depths of them. "I suspect you fail to understand your situation."

"Oh, I understand it just fine." I bent forward slightly, my ribs hurting from the laughter. "You are a child—nothing more. This is just one big hissy fit from you."

Hubis stepped toward me, each time his foot striking the ground like a drum beat that signaled danger.

And I didn't fucking *care*.

When he stopped just before me, his gaze was hard and angry. He caught my chin and forced me upright to stare into his eyes. He whispered, his voice only carrying to me. "You are about to be extinguished—to move past this realm to the nothingness that follows. The only reason you could laugh at a time like this is because you think there is some way to avoid that, to get out of this alive. I assure you, there is not."

When I answered, I didn't bother to lower my voice, because I wasn't talking to *him*. Hubis wouldn't learn shit—he didn't want to. Instead, I wanted to talk to the crowd, to the angels and the spirits who watched, to those in the Chasm, to *everyone*.

"This world doesn't belong to Hubis," I said. "He might have formed it, but it isn't *his*. It belongs to you all, but you have to take it, to take responsibility for it, to risk everything for it. You can blindly follow the rules and order he puts in place, or you can decide you don't need someone to direct you anymore. He has power because we *allow* him to have that power."

Hubis narrowed his eyes and stepped backward, his nail scratching my chin as he pulled away. A trickle of warmth ran down my throat, and I had no doubt he'd intended to do it.

Talk about petty.

He lifted his hand to create an additional portal, one that appeared like the ones in the stone archway. It shimmered before a dark figure appeared as a shadow. Of course, I knew who it was even before they stepped through.

And when Gunnar did, when he showed up in his demon form, I didn't feel the same crushing pain I had before. It had only been a night, but it seemed I'd already come to terms with his betrayal.

Still, the gasps from the spirits said *they* hadn't expected to see a demon in the Plains.

"Do they still not realize who and what we are?"

Hubis held his hand up, silencing the onlookers. "I have made an exception to allow a demon into the Plains for this purpose. These five—Gorrin, Yazmor, Hale, Tyrus and Loch—are Demon Lords."

And there went the calm. Spirits backed farther away from the center. Funny, since they'd been all but crawling over one another, pressing tight to get the best view, but all of a sudden, they wanted to get away?

Cowards.

It also proved they didn't trust Hubis the way he wanted them to. If they'd believed in his ability to protect them, to care for them, they wouldn't worry. Or maybe it wasn't his ability that they doubted but his willingness.

Gunnar stared right at me, never breaking eye contact, a mocking half-smirk on his lips. What an arrogant fuckwit. The most disappointing thing of this all was the idea that he was going to get to kill me himself, that he'd take that power, and the fear of what he might do with that power.

Still, Hubis spoke louder, his thundering voice making the crowd quiet if not relax. "I have allowed this demon here since the power and souls that are bound to these five must be transferred somewhere. I have picked a person who can handle the job and ensure the Chasm runs as it should."

"You mean as *you* think it should," I yelled out.

Hubis tilted his head slightly. "My will is what created this world, what formed it, and thus my will is all that matters. What I say is right is right."

"Sorry, but that's not how things work. It doesn't matter how strong you are, how powerful—it doesn't make you right. You can force people beneath your boots all you want, but fear and obedience don't make you right. The absence of pushback doesn't mean you're right."

He narrowed his eyes and boy did I recognize the look when someone really wanted to hit me.

Not that it would stop me. I turned back toward the crowd. "You don't have to take his shit anymore. You don't have to live in fear. He has power because you let him have it. Stop being afraid—stop just giving in."

"And you think, what? That you will give some moving speech and they'll rise? They'll defend you and save you?"

I shook my head, my hair falling into my eyes for a moment. "No. Revolution doesn't start that fast. It takes time, takes people accepting they can change things. I don't think anyone will save me today — but words are a scary, dangerous thing. They worm their way into a person's head, simmering day after day, year after year, growing until they infect them, until they can't silence or ignore them anymore. It won't be today or tomorrow or maybe even within a hundred years, but one day, those words will come back, and they'll spur people to act."

"So if they won't save you, why do it?"

"I plant seeds even if I won't see the tree grow, because planting them, starting them, is worth it."

His expression told me what I already knew — he didn't understand. The idea of creating something for others, of leaving something behind that might not benefit me, it didn't make sense to him.

Even if he said he did this all, that he'd changed the world for someone else, it had been for him. It had been selfishness dressed up as if they were for someone else.

"That doesn't matter," Hubis said, his words sharp. I suspected he'd rather have refuted my statement, but he couldn't wrap his head around it well enough to do so. That made me smile and recognize I was a petty asshole as well. "None of you deny my claims, at least not in a way that would warrant a finding of innocence. For that reason, I deem you guilty of all crimes mentioned. The only sentence that can possibly be appropriate considering such heinous actions is death."

No murmuring, but that didn't shock me. It wasn't like people got dragged to the town center like this for a good tongue lashing.

I wish I'd had one more good tongue lashing before the end.

I giggled at my own thought, wondering if I'd lost my mind. Maybe this had become too much, had managed to snap my mind when I couldn't make sense of all the horrific things I'd suffered through and witnessed.

"Wait!" The voice made me freeze, and when someone broke through the crowd, I barely held back a curse. Mae stood there, her back straight, her eyes fierce. She had none of the fear I'd seen before from her, even surrounded here by angels.

Hubis frowned when he spotted her, as if he couldn't make sense of it. "You were told to never return to this city."

Mae didn't wilt under his look—though even I had to admit he lacked the anger I would have suspected. Then again, I recalled her past, that she'd been abused by an angel, and his mercy. *He probably sees her like the person whose memories he showed me.*

"I know, and if you want to kill me, you can. But these five came to the Plains, and they stayed with me."

"You admit to helping criminals? You understand that will incur a punishment of its own."

Mae nodded, not backing down in the least. "I know. The thing is, they were hungry and tired and clearly on the run. It would have been safer for them to kill me, to kill those under my protection, to take what they needed from us and move on. It would have been the wiser action. Instead, they took the bare minimum and did chores to help us before they left. They refused anything that might put us in trouble. You want to say they sow chaos, but they did more for us that day than anyone in this city has."

"Be that as it may—" Hubis started, but another person stepped out of the crowd before he could go on.

Noah. "I've sold goods in and outside of the city for a long time. Most of you know me, have worked with me, know I'm not the type to lie or rock the boat."

The most surprising thing wasn't his appearance, but the reaction he got. Where Mae had people backing away, looking at her with suspicion, Noah got no such negativity. Instead, it seemed clear how much others respected him.

"Be careful about what you say," Hubis warned, his tone like the rattling of a snake's tail.

Noah swallowed hard but continued. "These five had every chance to harm people here. They have been in the Plains for nearly two weeks, have been attacked in that time, harmed, but have yet to do that to others. Instead, they've offered help and have done what they can for those no one else gives a damn about."

"They're from the Chasm," another angel called out. "They're evil! There is no other discussion to have."

"If going to the Chasm makes a person evil, then maybe evil isn't what we think," Noah spat back. "Because I've seen people here in the Plains do some horrible things. So if those monsters are good because they're here but these people are evil just because they came from the Chasm, then the entire idea of good and evil is useless."

A soft whisper started, echoing through the crowd.

Another woman came through, stepping forward. Maddy, from the bar, who Orline had pulled away. She stood stall and spoke loudly. "This woman was willing to stand up for me. When an angel came asking about her, she was willing to risk herself to keep me safe." Seeing her made my knees sag, relief that she was okay after getting dragged away by that angel.

Hubis let out a low sound, one the crowd likely were too far away to hear. However, before he could speak up and get order again, a loud crackling filled the space.

Everyone turned just as multiple portals opened, ones that looked just like the one Gunnar had walked through.

Tyrus whispered to me, "Hubis had to take down the protection around the Plains to let Gunnar in. It seems others want to take advantage of it."

Before he finished his statement, several others stepped through those portals.

Koya, Meyers, Jacob, other damned that I recognized but couldn't even name. They came and lined before us, standing between us and Hubis.

"You *dare* enter the Plains?" Hubis spat, finally looking unsettled.

"You are the one who lowered the barrier that kept us out," Myers said, managing to not appear afraid at all, which was damned impressive. It reminded me that while Myers was an annoying bureaucrat, he was far from weak.

"The Chasm isn't what *he* wants to say it is," Koya argued, his voice loud and clear. "And the Lords aren't the monsters he wants to paint them as. They've run the Chasm for a long time, and no matter how hard it gets, how dangerous, how little they get in return, they have *bled* for us all!"

The whispers about Koya and Jacob's appearances were far from subtle, as if the crowd wanted them to hear it but were still too chicken shit to admit it themselves.

Jacob spoke up next, his voice less strong, which was shocking given how terrifying he appeared. "Loch helped me when she didn't need to. I was nothing to her, and she could have destroyed me. Instead, she helped me. She listened to me. She protected me, and she's done that for every person she's met. She isn't up here because she wanted power, but because she saw how many people were hurt by the system, by a God who's absent except when he's forcing others to his will. She's been willing to give up everything that matters to her for the benefit of others, even when the odds of success were almost nonexistent. So who will you back? Who are you going to support? The tyrant who declares himself king but turns his back on those beneath him or the person willing to risk everything she is and has for us?"

That seemed to sink into others, because all the murmuring had stopped. Even the angels peered around, uncertainty on their features. They weren't nearly so sure they had the upper hand anymore…

Hubis came forward, his gaze coming to rest on me.

Why was it that I was always blamed for everything? Somehow, it all ended up on my shoulders, as if *I'd* done this all myself?

Probably because I usually am at fault.

"This cannot happen," he spat at me. "You have caused ripples that will take hundreds of years to smooth over. You have created problems that I will have to remove. You stand here in defiance, but for what? I could wipe you all out with a wave of my hand, so this is all for nothing."

"My life doesn't matter in the scheme of things. Who am I? Just some green-haired asshole who doesn't listen and causes problems. I'm not arrogant enough to think I matter at all. If my life is what it takes to help others? Finally, I think that's a worthwhile trade."

"What about their lives?" Hubis didn't move, didn't break eye contact. "Not just the Lords, but all these other people. They've done more than enough for me to end them. I could pluck their lives away so easily, every last one of them, and end this here."

"You can't end things like that. Don't you get that yet? You only prove your tyranny more when you do that. You give everyone more reason to fight you." Even as I spoke, my gaze moved from his to look over his shoulder.

I saw the faces of all the people who had helped me, who stood here against *God* all for my sake. The real cost of it all hit me then, the heaviness almost enough to drive me to my knees.

It made me speak even softer, almost a whisper. "What if I trade my life for theirs?"

Hubis lifted one eyebrow. "Excuse me?"

"I'll accept my fate, and you can prove you are merciful by sparing their lives. You show everyone how powerful you are, you keep your precious order, and you don't make any more martyrs than you need."

"And you would sacrifice yourself like that?"

"In a heartbeat."

"What about your great revolution?"

"I spent a long time in those caves, seeing glimpses of old words. Want to know a secret? The universe will attend to itself. It doesn't need me around to keep it going. It's older than any of us and will outlast us all, so when it's time, you'll get what's coming to you. If my death saves this many, though? I'll take that."

"You'll apologize?"

"Not a fucking chance. But I won't fight Gunnar, I'll let him take my life and my power, and you'll get your spectacle."

Hubis pressed his lips together, his hesitation a sign he weighed the pros and cons of my offer. He must have come to the same conclusion I had — it was the best option available to him.

He nodded, then moved away. "Let it never be said I do not hear what people say. I will spare the lives of Hale, Tyrus, Yazmor and Gorrin."

Boy did he stumble over that last one. Clearly, Gorrin was the sticking point for him.

"They performed their duties for many years without fail. It was only when they were led astray by this newcomer that they faltered."

I should have stayed quiet, but it turned out the best I could manage was to mutter things under my breath.

It was always some woman blamed for everyone else's actions, wasn't it?

"I demand obedience, but I also understand that no one is perfect, that all fall short, and for that reason, I offer mercy when appropriate. Tyrus, Yazmor and Hale will return to the Chasm, where they are free to prove their loyalty to the order or suffer the consequences of disobedience. I do not offer second chances. Gorrin will have his angel nature stripped away and cast to the Chasm as punishment for his actions. Those who helped them, who spoke up today, will be forgiven their mistake since they were made in ignorance, because they had their minds clouded by the main disruption."

"What about Loch?" Jacob asked.

"Loch is the infection that caused this sickness to fester and grow. She must be cut out if the body is to survive and heal. Her life was forfeit the moment she decided to gather forces against me, against order and goodness. Gunnar will take her life, then take his place as Demon Lord."

"I thought I was supposed to rule over all the Chasm," Gunnar said, and I nearly laughed at his impudence.

Hubis was still just looking for a reason to dish out some more punishment, and Gunnar really needed to take a win when he could.

Hubis turned a dismissive look on Gunnar. "The situation changed. You are welcome to try to achieve full control of the Chasm yourself, and should the other Lords not fall into line, you will take over their positions at that time."

A twitch in Gunnar's jaw said he wasn't happy with that solution, but it seemed arguing with God was a step further then he wanted to go. It reminded me of his plan with Gorrin to take over the Kannor crime family, and how that had all fallen short. He kept coming up with bad fucking ideas, trusting people he thought he could use, and getting screwed because of it.

That soothed me more than a little. Sure, I was going to die, but Gunnar getting fucked over one more time because of his own stupidity made it easier to deal with.

Still, when Hubis didn't give in, when it was clear he wouldn't budge, Gunnar came toward me. The only negative? He was pissed, which meant he might not make this as quick as it would have otherwise been.

"Don't do this," Tyrus snapped, yanking at his binds. "You do not have to sacrifice yourself for us."

I turned a smile on him, one that amazingly didn't feel forced. "It's okay. This is my choice."

"This is fucking bullshit." The muscles of Hale's chest stood out as he struggled, but the chains wouldn't break. "What the fuck was the point of this if you just lay down and die? That isn't the girl I fucking love!"

"Does that mean you love someone else? What a time to tell me that…" I laughed at my own stupid joke.

"We can still figure something out," Gorrin added. "We've been through worse than this and we have always survived it *together*."

"I'd love to say that's true, but I'm pretty sure this is bottom of the barrel. Even the threat of tentacle sex was better than this. It's okay—I'm ready. If this is the price that has to be paid, I'll pay it."

"You can't," Yazmor whispered. His voice made me look down the line, to where he stood, having broken the chain again. Despite angels coming closer, none seemed to dare to touch him.

He stopped in front of me, peering into my eyes as if asking me something. He set a hand on my cheek, the violet one of the things I wanted to take with me to whatever was next. "You made me become part of this world. You drew me from my isolation, gave me something else, something more. You have to take responsibility for that. You can't just give up, now."

I leaned into his touch, savoring the warmth of his palm.

"I can't let everyone else suffer. If someone has to die, and it's got to be me, I'm okay with that."

"I'm not."

"Don't make this harder than it has to be," I pleaded. "Don't make me sad, not when I don't have much time."

Yazmor leaned in and brushed his lips against mine. "You drew me into this world, anchored me to it, finally gave me something after my very long life to care about. I have lived a long time just existing, not because I care about it, about anything. If you aren't here, that anchor is gone."

I turned my head and nipped his palm hard enough to leave a mark. "Don't you *dare* say something like that. If you do anything to yourself after I'm done, I'll kick your ass when you cross over to whatever is next."

He laughed softly, the sound hollow and full of pain. "Well, we wouldn't want that, would we? Fine. I will remain here until my time is up naturally. I'm old, as you like to point out, and I have existed this long. I can wait a little longer, knowing that whatever comes next, I *will* find you again."

Sorrow drenched his words, but the surprising part was the hope sprinkled on top. We had no idea what would come next, but he believed that whatever it was, we would be together again.

I would see them all again. It was only that belief that gave me the courage to stay standing.

"It's time," I whispered.

Yazmor blew out an unhappy breath, then turned his gaze on Gunnar. "She may allow this, but don't make the mistake of thinking *I* will forget it."

Gunnar's eyes widened, and a warmth filled me.

Good old Yazmor, threatening people with that chilling smile of his.

Still, he pulled away, moving a few steps back. The fact he could stand there and wait was beyond impressive. I doubted I could have done the same in his position.

Gunnar crossed the rest of the distance, a large fancy-looking knife in his hand. The blade was long and engraved, and while it wasn't as powerful as the weapon bound to me, I couldn't ignore the waves of power from it. At least that meant he'd probably get the job done quickly.

I didn't mind dying, but I wasn't a fan of unnecessary pain. This was one of the few times I hoped a man was really fucking quick.

"Funny, isn't it?" he asked. "This all started with us together. You remember the morning you died?"

I almost asked him how I could forget, but the truth was…I didn't remember much about it. Despite it being such a huge part of my life, despite how it had shaped so much of my future, it has stopped mattering years ago. I'd moved past it. "Yeah," I said, having no desire to fight with him. "I remember it."

"We were just two kids back then. I remember drinking coffee with you, having no fucking clue about everything that would happen, about how much of the world we didn't know shit about. What I did pushed you onto the path that made you a Demon Lord. It's kind of fitting that you're the catalyst to my becoming a Demon Lord."

I didn't bother to hide my chuckle at that. There was some truth to it, wasn't there? We had been entwined for so long, as if the universe forced us together time and time again.

Why? Probably so we could learn from each other, teach each other. Of course, looking back, I had to wonder if either of us had learned a damn thing. Maybe we were set so that the next time the world was made, we'd end up just fucking one another over again.

"You aren't going to beg for your life?" he asked.

"I'm not the type to beg, and I sure as fuck would never beg *you* for anything. If you want the power, get going and do it. It isn't like you'll hold the position for long. I give you a month, *tops*, before someone gets rid of you."

He narrowed his eyes, his anger tinged with affection, as if even he couldn't ignore our long past together. Still, I didn't doubt for a moment that he'd end up doing it, that he'd follow through, because Gunnar wanted power more than he cared for any other thing in the entire world—this one or any other.

He nodded once, then lifted the blade, setting it against the side of my neck, near my ear. It was surprisingly warm, despite how the steel should have been cold.

I met his gaze, refusing to look away, to hide from him or this moment. If everything I'd done had brought me here, I was fine with that. I'd accept it without hesitation, without regret.

Sure, I'd love more time with the Lords, to have seen what Jay grew into, to spend more time with those I cared about. Still, I couldn't bring myself to be sorry about it, because I'd done what was important, and I'd protected those I cared about.

Gunnar pressed the blade, but just as the tension pulled tight, as the sharp end threatened to slice into my skin, it was gone.

I blinked quickly, looking around to find a hand wrapped around Gunnar's wrist, pulling the knife away from me.

Standing just behind Gunnar was Kylie, her gaze strong, a reminder of all the times I'd seen her be one bad bitch.

And again I found myself jealous of the tough woman.

Chapter Eighteen

"What the fuck do you think you're doing?" Gunnar snapped, the tone he liked to take with women to put them in their place.

Silly boy. Kylie wasn't the sort of woman who could be put *anywhere* she didn't want to be, and certainly not by the likes of Gunnar.

He yanked his hand, but when he gained no ground, his eyes widened. It seemed Kylie wasn't quite as human as she appeared, given she could hold Gunnar despite his demon form. "What are you?"

"Kylie..." The name left Hubis' tongue like a prayer, one he almost feared to utter. It spoke volumes about their relationship, about what he felt for her.

Kylie turned her gaze to Hubis, and her expression didn't match his at all. Where his was longing and affection, hers held so much suspicion it hurt even me. Obviously, their relationship was far from good.

She slid her hand down from Gunnar's wrist to his hand, plucking the blade from his grasp and tossing it aside. It landed on the stone too far away for anyone of us to reach, and again went to show her strength. Gunnar wouldn't have easily or willingly given up his weapon.

He stumbled backward, putting space between them, but even the blind could spot the plans as his eyes darted around, as he searched for a way to get the upper hand.

Not that Kylie appeared to give a damn about him any longer. Instead, she turned her gaze to me and pressed her finger against the spot on my throat where Gunnar had nearly sliced me. She made a soft sound in her throat as if scolding me. "You are far too smart a woman to give yourself up for a man yet again. I thought you would have learned your lesson the last time."

"So I keep hearing," I replied.

Heavy steps against the ground signaled Hubis nearing us, but Kylie didn't seem to care. She reached behind me and grasped my wrists, then pulled hard, once, snapping the chain that held my cuffs to the bar. It didn't remove the bands that kept my powers trapped, but it let me move freely.

"You finally came," Hubis whispered in a voice I had never heard from him. Instead of the arrogance and certainty he usually exuded, his tone was all hesitation. It didn't even sound like the same man.

Kylie turned, keeping me behind her, pulling her shoulders back and meeting Hubis gaze head-on. "I thought that's what you really wanted."

"It is, but I never really thought I would get it. I thought you had forsaken me."

"Yet you never failed to check up on me, to send your lackeys into my life."

"I was looking out for you. You may not want me, you may hate me, but that does not change that I will protect you forever."

"That's always been your problem," Kylie snapped back. "You've never *listened* to me! You never bother to stop and listen to me."

"You were afraid of me. When I tried to see you—"

"I was terrified of everything. Of the world, of myself, of the future. Instead of giving me time to work through it, instead of being there for me, you destroyed my entire world!"

Her words struck me with the weight of a sucker punch. Everything slid into place, all the bits I'd had but hadn't known what to do with.

The memory I'd lived through, the one Hubis had shown me, hadn't been some random person he'd known. It had been Kylie's pain, her trauma, and I'd experienced it along with her.

Hubis had destroyed the previous world because Kylie had gotten hurt, because his anger and fear had run so deep that he'd re-formed *everything* to make a place for her he thought was safe.

"You don't understand," he said. "I pray you never understand the pain of seeing the one you love so hurt, seeing them in pain, and wanting nothing more than to find a way to keep them safe, to ensure they never suffer that again. Of course I did what I had to."

Kylie shook her head, and I got the sense this was a fight they'd had before.

Or, maybe it wasn't that they'd had the discussion together so much as they'd fought this out in their heads so many times, frustration eating away as they were so sure the other person wouldn't understand.

Kylie peered around, then pressed her lips together. Had she just realized she wasn't alone? That a conversation *this* personal was occurring in the middle of a group of onlookers?

A line appeared between Hubis' eyebrows before he waved his hand, the ground disappearing beneath my feet. It felt as though I tumbled into the darkness, nothing having form or shape around me, until I struck something hard.

"I really hate getting thrown around," I muttered as I flattened my hands against the ground beneath me and pushed up, squinting at the bright light that assaulted my eyes.

I found myself on a stone floor, with a huge, open window on one side. Was this a bedroom? It had a seating area with a sofa and chairs along with a large bed against the far wall.

"I thought you would feel more comfortable without an audience."

I spun around at Hubis' words, frowning because he hadn't ever seemed to give a fuck about what I wanted or how I felt. Except, when I turned, it all made more sense.

His gaze wasn't on me, but on Kylie.

I lifted my hand like a kid in class. "And why am I here?"

"Because I also thought she would feel more comfortable not being alone with me. I would spend no more time in your presence than I must, but I am willing to tolerate even you for her benefit."

"Harsh but fair." I rubbed at my wrists, surprised to find the cuffs gone.

Right, he probably figured I didn't need them anymore since he's watching me personally.

"I missed you," Hubis said, coming no closer as if he knew Kylie wouldn't welcome it.

"You've always known where I was. You've followed me no matter where I went, no matter how I tried to hide from you. Don't act like I've ever been away from you."

Hubis didn't argue that point. I was so used to the way he ignored all points contrary to what he said, the way he trampled all over the opinions of every other person. Maybe that was why my mouth hung open when he collapsed into a chair across the room and leaned forward, hanging his head.

Then again, I recalled how Gorrin would hear me when he listened to no one else, the way Hale was sweet with me when he showed no one else that side. As difficult as it was to think of Hubis as a person who might love someone, the idea was less far-fetched than it had seemed at first.

"I wanted to make sure you had what you needed, that you were safe. It was why I gave you that dagger, why I ensured you had help should you require it."

I brushed my fingers against my wrist, the very dagger they talked about there. So that was how it was created, as a gift to Kylie, a weapon capable of killing anything.

Including Hubis himself.

"I never asked you to do any of that."

"You never ask me for *anything*. That is the problem. I had to do what I could, what I thought might help, because you refused to speak to me."

A rushing of power filled the room, and I cursed softly as I suspected another one of those plunging falls that I loved so much. Thankfully, whatever these two beings had done was different this time. The room remained, but what seemed like a hologram between us played, like a movie in real time.

It was still strange to try to compare the Hubis and Kylie I knew, the way they appeared, with their real forms. Worse, just seeing those blue creatures threatened to shut my throat down, to take me back to the fear and pain I'd experienced from Kylie's memory.

Pull it together, Loch!

I took a deep breath and swallowed down the bile that crept up my throat.

Before me was the image of a large bed and the damaged, broken body of what had to be Kylie. I'd experienced what she had, but I hadn't seen the aftermath, hadn't seen it from the outside. It seemed so much worse looking at her, wondering how she could have survived it at all.

Through the doorway, in the memory, another walked in. While I wouldn't have recognized him, it had to have been Hubis. Something about a power there that I could feel even through the memory told me that much.

Kylie appeared unconscious, with another beside her, checking wounds.

"How is she?" Hubis asked.

"Resting. She is lucky to be alive. I don't think they intended to kill her, but the injuries were so bad…" The healer shook their head. "It is a miracle she dragged herself back to the dome. Did they catch those responsible?"

"Yes." A darkness in Hubis' voice sent a shiver through me. I knew violence well enough to know what he didn't need to say.

They hadn't just been caught, but he had *personally* dealt with them.

"When will she wake?"

The healer rubbed their hand over Kylie's forehead, the touch gentle. "I don't know. All we can do is wait. However…"

"What?"

"Even when she wakes, you need to prepare yourself. She may not be the same as you remember. People who suffer like this, who go through something like this, it changes them. It causes wounds that even I can't heal."

Hubis looked down, his hands drawn into fists, and a part of me wanted to move forward. I wanted to set my hand on his shoulder, to offer some sort of reassurance.

I knew that loss was horrible, but nothing was worse than helplessness, than watching those we love suffer and knowing we can do nothing to fix it.

This wasn't Hubis, though. It was a memory, a snapshot in time that was long gone.

"You were there?" the real Kylie asked. "I don't remember much after it happened, just that I woke up alone."

"After tracking down those who harmed you, I did not leave your side, not until you woke."

"You weren't there when I woke up," Kylie pressed.

"Yes, I was—the first time you awoke. You looked at me and you screamed. I had been holding your hand as you slept, and when you woke, you pulled away, frantic, crying."

"I don't remember that," Kylie whispered. "I was just confused, still not all together yet. You can't blame me for that."

"I do not blame you, not for any of it." He let out a long sigh, then rubbed his hands over his face. "I did not even consider gathering the power needed to change the world at first. Even after your attack, after punishing those who had dared to touch you, I had planned only to remain by your side, to do whatever it took to help you recover. When you screamed, when I saw your fear, everything changed. When I looked around, I realized that the entire world was impossibly flawed, that what happened would happen again, that without *true* power, I could do nothing to help you. Our world hurt you, broke what we had, and without that, all I had left was a drive to protect you."

Kylie walked closer to Hubis, the first time she had made any move toward him. "You're trying to tell me that you destroyed our *entire* world, that you obliterated everything we knew, everyone we loved, all because you thought that someone had gotten between us?"

"I did it because I thought I could give you a good world, that I thought if I implemented my order, you could live safely and happily. It was my penance for not keeping you safe. You were worth more than the entire world to me."

Kylie crossed the rest of the distance between them and grasped his chin, forcing his gaze up to hers. "You're an idiot. You could have had a future with me. We could have been together and lived happily, but instead, you took everything from me and left me all alone."

His hand twitched, as if he wanted to touch her back but held himself back. No doubt he feared if he moved, she'd disappear like a mirage. "You were never alone. I was *always* here, waiting."

She shook her head. "I was so terribly alone. You only cared about the world, about your precious order.

I had to recover by myself, start over again and again. Do you know how many times I went to the Forgotten Caves? Just to catch a glimpse of our world? I caused the problem with possessions because I took from the Forgotten Caves a necklace, one with a blue crystal."

He furrowed his brow. "You mean the one I gave you?"

"That one was gone, but I wanted to hold it again, to feel like I wasn't completely alone in the world. You always said I was too sentimental."

"Then so am I." He shifted slightly, brushing against her fingers still on his chin, as if he craved touch with all he was. It was weird to see him like a kitten seeking affection. "I built this entire Palace around the crystal. It was stolen," he said. "I care little about many things. I thought it some form of punishment that one of the few I did care for would be stolen."

I frowned as I thought about that. A blue crystal…
Gorrin…

I stood, then gestured at the door. If this was Hubis' room, then Gorrin had said he had his on the same floor, right? "Gorrin's room is next door, right?"

Hubis nodded, but a sharpness in his gaze stopped me before I could move. "Do not even consider running away."

"Don't worry. I never run—I hate cardio. I'll be right back."

I left the room, then went into the next door. Just stepping into it told me I'd gotten the right place. Each piece of décor was all Gorrin. Simple, organized, everything in its place.
Really fucking boring.

Good old reliable Gorrin. I went to the safe he had mentioned, the one behind a painting. It didn't have a lock on it, using camouflage rather than codes. Inside was a crystal hung on a lovely silver chain, one that looked exactly like the one I'd returned to the Forgotten Caves.

Or, rather, it was like the reality that the other one had tried to replicate but fallen short of. With it in hand, I rushed back to the room.

I found Kylie and Hubis in the same exact position, as if neither had dared even breathe without their witness.

I held the necklace out to Hubis, and he took it, a tremble in his hand. He stared at it, longing in his features. "If you were anyone else, I would ask how you could have had this, how you possibly could have gotten it, but you have done enough impossible things by this point that I know better than to ask."

"Good idea, especially since I rarely know what I'm doing well enough to explain it."

"You kept it?" Kylie asked.

"I always hoped that after you left this, when you ran from me, you would come back. I placed it at the top of the Palace, like a beacon to guide you back." He lifted the necklace and blew over it, the action causing sparkles to come alive and dance inside of it, as if woken by his breath. "But I wonder if too much has happened to ever get that back."

She moved her hands to cup both his cheeks, touching him with a gentleness that showed her feelings were far from gone. They might be complicated, but they hadn't disappeared. "I can't be here, in the world you created. I miss what we lost, who we were. There's too much pain between us, too many years."

"So after everything, I still cannot have the one thing I truly want?"

"Not *here*," Kylie pressed. "You have followed me for so long, always my shadow, always there. What if you follow me one more time?"

"*Anywhere*," Hubis assured her without even a moment of hesitation. Except, her meaning seemed to dawn on him as he sat there, when concern pinched his features. "You don't know what exists there. Even I don't know what comes after."

Kylie nodded. "I know—but we've broken us too much to fix here."

"Aren't you afraid?"

"Not anymore. I'm tired, Hubis. Tired of running, or being alone, of holding onto what hurts just because letting go is scary. If you are with me, I can face whatever comes next."

"But this world—"

"Can attend to itself as it always has. Many worlds came before this one, many will come after. Our time has long passed, and I'm ready to let go." She shifted her hands from his cheeks and held one out to him. "I'm ready to let go of everything except your hand."

He blew out a long breath, then took her hand in his, the answer clear. Then again, seeing him like this, I suspected the answer had always been clear. No matter how twisted he was, how wrong he was, he cared for nothing more than Kylie.

Hubis rose, then they both turned toward me.

"Does this mean I'm not dying?" I asked hopefully.

Kylie laughed softly, though the sound struck me as bittersweet. The reality hit me—I wouldn't hear that laugh much longer. None of us knew what came after this world, but we knew that once crossed, no one came back from it. Whether that meant reincarnation or another realm — it was anyone's guess.

But it meant I'd lose her.

"So it seems," Hubis muttered. "As much as I would love to remove you — I find you a troublesome influence who causes nothing but problems."

"Not the first time I've heard that," I agreed.

He narrowed his eyes, and I could almost hear him telling me that I should just shut up when I'm ahead. Instead of saying that, he spoke as though I'd said nothing. "However, this change, it is due to you. You shake the status quo — whether for good or evil is yet to be seen."

"That's the nicest thing you've ever said to me. It might be the nicest thing anyone has said about me."

He shook his head as though my quips had started to reach the far end of his patience. I tried to remind myself that until he *actually* left, he could still smite me if he wanted to. Pressing my luck was probably stupid.

Kylie released Hubis hand and threw her arms around me. She hugged me so tightly I could hardly breathe. "Thank you, Loch, for everything. I'll miss you."

I hugged her back, words sticking in my throat. I hated goodbyes — there really weren't any good words for something like this. As if she understood it, she pulled away and smiled. It was strange how she could face something so scary without the least bit of hesitation.

Maybe that was what happened when a person lived that long, when they were truly done. She peered over her shoulder at Hubis. "You'll follow?"

"*Always,*" he repeated as he had before. "I will be right behind you."

Kylie nodded, took a deep breath, closed her eyes, then exhaled slowly. As she did so, her form shimmered. It shifted between the human one I recognized and the blue creature she really was, growing dimmer and dimmer. I had to fight myself from reaching out, from grabbing her and trying to hold on to her.

I had to let her go, let her make her own path. No matter how much it hurt me, I couldn't force her to stay. Between one blink and the next, her form disappeared entirely, fading to nothing until not even the sense of her power lingered.

"How…" I whispered.

"Remnants remain because we cling to life. The moment one releases that hold, they move on to whatever is next." His gaze remained locked on where she had been, as if he could still her even though she was gone.

"Not to be rude," I said, "but you're going, too, right?"

He snorted then looked at me again. "You press your luck. Still, I leave you with a gift, a curse and a hope for the future."

"Can I decline them all?"

Hubis reached out so fast that despite me yanking backward, he grasped me by my throat easily. "I have discovered that people never truly understand what they are capable of until in the situation. We do things we never expected, never planned on, never thought ourselves capable of. I hope that even if I cannot return to this world, I will be able to watch, because you will learn this very painful lesson. People take power, and they keep it, and they use it. So my gift is your life, my hope is that power destroys you as it does all those who wield it."

"And your curse?"

He smiled for a moment, the expression chilling, a reminder that while he might love Kylie, while it seemed he would leave, there was no doubt he was twisted, that he held a darkness inside of him that ran deep. He didn't answer me, however, before a pain filled me so strong that it felt as if every cell in my body were splitting apart and remaking themselves.

Darkness took me, pulling me under so quickly and fully that it was as if my entire body had shut down in a split second.

I didn't dream, didn't think, as if floating in a sea of nothingness. Only Hubis' confusing words echoed in my head, as if he'd recorded them and played them on repeat.

* * * *

"Loch?" That voice… It called to me, drew me to it, made me swim through that darkness to reach it.

Warmth brushed my forehead, causing me to open my eyes, finding myself on a bed.

Not just any bed, but my bed… I was in the Chasm, in my own room there. And with me?

Tyrus sat on the bed beside me, his hand on my forehead. Yazmor sat in a chair, his feet up on the desk, a book open in his lap. Gorrin paced the floor, and Hale stretched out on the couch, his eyes closed and head back.

"What happened?" As soon as I croaked out those words, my throat dry, I recalled the pain that had overtaken me, and the moments just before I'd lost consciousness, where Hubis had faded away just like Kylie had.

When I spoke, it was like the Lords had waited for just that moment. I hadn't finished the second word before they were all on me, leaning on the bed, pressing close and checking me for injuries. They looked into my eyes, grasped my chin and tilted my head, seemingly searching for *something*.

"How did I get here?" I asked after swallowing to try to wet my dry throat.

"You transported yourself here," Gorrin said, his tone quiet and careful. "You also transported the four of us here and removed our binds, but you were unconscious."

"How did I do that?" Even with the barrier down around the Plains, demons couldn't transport there.

Unless…

I hope it destroys you.

Hubis' gift. I held my hand out and stared at it, the truth revealing it to me in the way I felt, my connection to things I couldn't even understand yet, as if I felt things deeper, knew more than I should, could touch things so far away from me.

God was gone, and his power had to go somewhere.

"That is what I feared," Gorrin whispered.

"The fuck do you mean?" Hale asked. "You didn't say shit."

"I felt it, but I didn't want to say anything until she woke, until I was sure."

"Say what?" Tyrus asked.

Yazmor didn't ask, but the way he stared at me said he didn't need to. He already knew, just like Gorrin. Yet neither spoke up.

"What the fuck is it?" Hale snapped.

"Hubis is gone," I said. "He moved on to whatever's next."

"So his power...?" Tyrus asked, trailing off as if he'd worked that out as well.

I swallowed hard and nodded. "Yeah. Looks like I'm God, now..."

Talk about jobs I'm not qualified for...

Chapter Nineteen

As it turned out, explaining how and why God died and left me in charge was a more complicated conversation than one would expect. Even still, the Lords remained silent as I went through the events.

It seemed that when Hubis had transported the three of us, he'd closed off the entire floor of the Palace, keeping everyone out of it until that barrier fell — about the time he gave me all his power.

"How do you feel?" Tyrus asked.

"Okay, I think." At his raised eyebrow, I shrugged. "I don't know what being God is supposed to feel like. I can tell you it fucking hurt to start with, but that's gone away."

Gorrin stared at me, having said nothing at all since I started my story. I opened my mouth to ask him why, then shut it.

Asking a question I didn't know the answer to would open me up to potential heartbreak. What if he said that this changed things between us? What if he decided that I was too different now, that he no longer wanted me? All those things swirled through me, the worries consuming me until an odd sound came from outside my room.

Hale went to the wall that rested on the outer edge of the building and pushed the shutter open. "Um, Loch? It's raining."

Rain? It didn't rain in the Chasm.

Yazmor started to laugh, the sound stopping my spiraling thoughts. He wiped a thumb under his eyes to clear away the tears from laughing so hard, and at my glare, he answered. "I'd say you'll be God when hell freezes over — well, with the rain, you're halfway there!"

His randomness in the face of such change walked the line between annoying and amusing, as was usual with him. It tipped toward amusing, probably because I needed a good laugh.

Yazmor leaned in and pressed his lips to my cheek, the touch surprisingly sweet and chaste. "You look better when you smile," he whispered, then pulled away as if he hadn't tried that lovey-dovey bullshit in front of everything.

Another detail hit me. "Did Koya, Myers and Jacob make it back safely?"

Tyrus answered. "Yes. They are all back in the Chasm, and Gorrin ensured that angels he knows and trusts are watching things in the Plains for now."

"I guess I'll have to be nice to Myers now, huh? I mean, he went to heaven and stuck up for me. Mae, also, and Noah. Maybe we'll throw a big party to say thank you all at once."

"Kill God then have a party?" Hale smirked at me, leaning his back against the stone wall beside the window. "That's pretty metal."

I nearly made a joke about Hubis looking the part to play the music, but the words stuck in my throat. I wasn't sorry he was gone, but it again reminded me of just how much things had changed.

A knock on the door had Tyrus sighing. "Hubis' absence has created several issues. I have left what I can to Koya and Myers, but word has spread about what happened. I didn't want to leave you, though..." His words trailed off, the fear in them telling me just how worried he was.

And how much he'd grown. In the past, he would have ignored what happened with others in exchange for what he felt he needed to do. Instead, he had pushed off those problems just to stay with me until I woke.

It made me smile, and I didn't give a fuck if it was a goofy one. "I'm okay now. You can go." I tacked on afterward, in a small voice, "And thanks. For staying with me and for taking care of so much."

He pressed a kiss to my cheek, the other one from where Yazmor had, and it made it so both sides of my face tingled. "All right. I will come back as soon as I can. Try to rest—we have no idea what taking all that power into you might do, or what sort of toll it could take on you."

"You're such a worrier."

"Of course I am. Look at who I am stuck with." Tyrus gestured around the entire room, making it clear he didn't *just* mean me.

It let me believe that I wasn't even the worst offender, but who the fuck was I kidding? No doubt I'd have given him *way* more gray hairs than the others — if his hair grayed.

That made me press my lips together, wondering how Tyrus would look as a silver fox. Hale couldn't pull it off, Yazmor neither, but Tyrus? Some silver at his temples would make him look even more regal, like some bad ass who had been around the block a few times.

"I know that look," Hale said with a suggestive leer.

My cheeks heated. "Don't tease God. It isn't nice and probably isn't smart."

"When is anything I do smart?"

"Fair enough." My fingers went to my neck, to the place Gunnar had pressed the blade. No mark rested there, since he hadn't broken skin, but it almost felt like some phantom of that moment had stained me. It also made me realize the one last hanging detail. "What happened to Gunnar?"

It was hard to believe after his actions that anyone would let him walk away.

Tension filled the room, and it was Yazmor who answered. "He got away. As soon as he saw things going bad, while we were dealing with trying to find you, he went back through the portal. Once in the Chasm, he could transport to Earth. Don't worry, though, he won't get far. We'll track him down."

I shook my head. "No need. Once things settle down, I'll summon him."

"You'll just fucking let him do what he wants until then? After the shit he pulled?" Hale muttered something ugly under his breath, and a few *fucks* and *shits* were all I caught. "You're still too fucking soft on him."

"I'm not soft on him. Trust me, I'm past trying to save his stupid ass. He's just at the bottom of the list of things that need to get done right now. We have to deal with the angels in the Plains who are out of control. We have to take care of the outcasts in the Plains, rework the broken parts of the system, get control of the damned here in the Chasm, find a way to bring the two groups together..."

My voice trailed off, not because I was done but because there was so much more to deal with than that and I wasn't even sure where to start. I shook my head, frustrated that even when I was God, I still didn't have all the answers I wanted. "He's small time at this point."

Yazmor nodded, though an edge there said he might not agree. Then again, if Gunnar had targeted them, I doubted I'd be so quick to ignore him. "Well, I've got a few things to deal with. I need to see if the crocodiles ate anyone while I was gone." Yazmor waved as he walked out.

Hale pushed himself off the wall. "Guess that means I better go deal with shit, too. Been away for weeks now, and unlike the rest of you, I don't have some little lacky to take care of all my tasks for me." He came over, but unlike the others, he didn't just leave a kiss on my cheek. Nope, not Hale. He tipped my face up and gave me the sort of kiss I was thankful I was sitting down for. He claimed my mouth, pressing his tongue past my lips as if making up for lost time.

Then again, with that kiss he also made it perfectly clear how worried he'd been, how glad he was that I was okay. He closed his teeth on my bottom lip and tugged softly before pulling back. A confident smile on his lips said he knew exactly how it had affected me.

"Couldn't risk someone else getting your first kiss as a God, right?" The arrogant bastard didn't wait around for me to catch my breath or gather my thoughts. Instead, he sauntered out — an honest-to-me saunter.

Which left Gorrin and me alone, and again reminded me that he'd yet to say anything to me since realizing what had happened.

The silence threatened to crush me. How could unsaid words be so heavy?

I'd never dealt with quiet well, so I opened my mouth and let whatever bullshit sat inside there out. "Do you hate me now?"

His eyes widened. "What? Why would you think that?"

"Well, you won't talk to me. I thought maybe you saw me differently, that things changed now. Hubis *created* you, so maybe this feels like some weird pseudo-incest thing? Like some weird who's your daddy thing where I took the position of your dad? I mean, I'm up for weird games if you want, but maybe it's too far for you?"

I should shut up. I knew it, and really the second the words 'who's your daddy' left my mouth should have triggered some automatic shut down so I couldn't dig myself any deeper into this pit. Still, I'd never managed to stop talking, especially when I felt unnerved.

Gorrin came over, even as more nonsense spilled from me, and pressed his finger against my lips to silence me.

Just the sensation of him touching me helped calm my racing heart.

"I don't hate you," he assured me, and I detected no lies in his voice. "I'm not angry with you, and I do not view you as some father figure now. I can assure you, the things I want from you are *not* things appropriate with that sort of relationship."

"So why aren't you talking to me?" I spoke even though he hadn't moved his finger away.

He pulled away but took a seat on the bed beside me. He let out a long sigh, then spoke softly. "I am not sure if I ever truly thought we would succeed, because it never occurred to me what would happen afterward. I never thought about where his power would go, or who would end up in that position. Now that it is you..." He went quiet for a moment, the question dragging on. "I am unsure how I still fit into your life."

The made me jerk my gaze to him. "The fuck?" That was certainly the last thing I'd thought I'd hear from him.

"You now will control so much. You will be responsible for so much. The others, they are still Demon Lords. You may be above them now, but they make sense. Me? I am not a Demon Lord. I have no place here. I fear that you will wonder what I add to your life."

I couldn't see my face, but I suspected if Yazmor was still here, he'd have laughed at me. I could feel the pinching from my eyebrows pulling toward each other as I tried to work out just how someone as smart as Gorrin had come to such a stupid conclusion. Finally, when it became clear he wasn't going to figure it out on his own, I spoke up. "You're an idiot." *Not the best start, Loch!* "You have a place here. You will *always* have a place here."

"But I am not a Lord."

"You have a place with *me*. In case you've forgotten, I wasn't even with you until after you weren't a Lord. I never cared about that at all. I want you in my life, and nothing about this changes how I feel."

"You say that now. What if that changes? What if you see me as deadweight later?"

My gaze moved down his body. "Not to be crude, but I've fucked you a few times. You haven't been deadweight there."

"So you are telling me that so long as I can give you orgasms, you do not care if I've got power elsewhere?" Some of that mood had shifted, and a smile pulled at the corner of his mouth, that subtle almost-grin that only I knew.

"Hey, now, don't underestimate the value of good orgasms!"

Gorrin laughed as if he couldn't get over how strange I really was. That was fine by me, if it kept it around just so he could try to figure me out.

"Besides," I added on, "you are plenty helpful. I didn't even run the Chasm that well on my own, and fuck knows I can't get along with Myers. Hell, maybe it's best for you to either take over my portion of the Chasm again or to keep an eye on the Plains. This job is way too big for one person. Don't think for a moment that I don't need you."

His expression softened. Then again, I knew well how much feeling useless sucked. I hadn't lied, though.

"You know," he said as he rose, "there is something you haven't talked about."

"Well, we already talked about pseudo-incest, so I feel like we don't need any more novel conversation topics."

Gorrin shook his head. "I've taken time to talk to Yazmor, to learn as much as I could about the previous worlds. The reality is that so far, every person to take your position has remade the world. They have reshaped it as they pleased, to better it, believing they can create something perfect that others have failed to do." He didn't ask me if I planned to do that, but the question rested there in the space between us.

He didn't need to ask, though. I answered him. "I wouldn't do that. I saw Kylie hurt from losing everything. Doing that is selfish." Hubis' words came back to me, that mocking tone as if he'd known what would happen. "Hubis said that the power was a curse, that he hoped he could see me struggle and get torn apart by it. He said I wouldn't ever understand him or what he did until I was in that position, but I still don't get it. I can just fix things—I don't have to destroy it all, first."

Gorrin nodded, but his expression didn't scream confidence. He pressed a kiss to my forehead, the touch gentle. "I will go check with Myers and ensure things are running smoothly. You should sleep a while longer."

Once alone, I stared at the window, at the rain that fell outside of it, breathing in the strange scent of water and ash and dust.

Usually, my position in life had been at the bottom. I'd had to struggle constantly to get what I wanted, to settle for what I could get, to accept things I couldn't change. Now, however?

I had all the power in the world, but not enough answers. I didn't know what the right choices were, what I wanted, let alone *how* to get it. Instead of struggling against the man, I *was* the man.

I lay back in my bed, snuggling under the covers and closing my eyes. The sound of the rain falling outside lulled me back to relax, and for just a little while, I let the peaceful darkness of sleep take me.

Even God deserved a break, right?

* * * *

I yawned, covering it with the back of my hand as I sat in the throne room in the Chasm.

This sucks.

I hadn't gotten a moment of peace after waking up. Word of my ascension had spread far and wide, and if I'd thought becoming a Demon Lord had been exhausting, it was nothing compared to this bullshit. Because we had left the barrier down between the Plains and the Chasm, the residents of both had started to mingle.

Fights had happened, and mostly those in the Plains had complained, but the Lords had worked hard to keep the violence to a minimum.

However, it meant I had not only damned but spirits and angels now lining up to see me.

I'd *tried* to put Whalebert in charge again, but it seemed spirits and angels were less likely to accept a stuffed animal. Myers had tracked me down after an hour of that and made me come to the throne room myself.

And six hours later, I still couldn't see the end of the line of people wanting to talk to me.

Everyone wanted something. Some just wanted to meet me, as if they'd get some special points for that. They gave me empty platitudes — the same people who had counted me out before I'd gotten any power. They now pretended I was different, like I was special, like they'd always known it.

I rubbed hard at my eyes as yet another angel dropped to their knees in front of me, prostrating themselves until their forehead pressed against the stone floor.

"That's enough for right now." Gorrin's voice echoed through the room. "We will break for two hours, then resume."

I hadn't even realized he'd shown up, but I was really fucking glad he had. I'd take whatever break I could get.

Who knew running the universe could be *this* exhausting? It wasn't even from using my powers! Except for a few small things—such as stopping the rain, fixing Mae and Emma's house, and summoning myself one of those tasty white chocolate mochas—I hadn't used my powers much.

Instead, it was all this administrative shit. It was the well-wishers and the petitioners and those who just wanted to gawk at the green-haired wonder that made me want to hide under a blanket.

Those in the room grumbled, but all kept their voices down because they didn't want to be the ones to catch my attention. Still, they left the room, though the line outside didn't shorten. Seemed like no matter how long it took, they planned to wait.

Gorrin brought a glass of water to me, and it wasn't until I took the first sip that I realized how thirsty I was. "Why didn't I notice I needed water?" I asked, then frowned. "I'm also not hungry even though I haven't eaten in…I don't know how long. I'd ask if I'm still alive, but I'm pretty sure that's a dumb question since I remember dying."

"Hubis never needed to eat or drink. Or it may be more accurate to say he didn't have to do so. He could draw off the power he held to keep himself healthy and energized, but eating and drinking meant he didn't have to use power for that. Since your body will use the power, you won't feel those hunger or thirst pangs."

"Well, isn't that useful?" After that, I gulped down the rest of the water in the glass.

Gorrin went to take the glass back, but I kept it and stood. "I could use stretching my legs some." I took the glass to the small table at the side of the room, then hooked my fingers together and stretched my arms above my head.

The tightness in my muscles eased as I moved, bending to the left first, then the right. Along with it, I exhaled slowly, trying to push out all the stress that had accumulated inside me.

Administrative stuff was *never* my strength. I had another moment of wondering just how I'd ended up in this position. I wasn't cut out for being 'in charge.' I'd always gotten along, done what needed to get done, but never had I really wanted to lead anyone. I didn't like being responsible for others, yet here I was, steering the whole damn thing.

Before Gorrin saw my worries—and he would, because he was one observant bastard—I tried to clear it from my mind. This was the first week—it'd take time to work it all out, to settle in. I just had to keep moving, one step at a time, and trust I could figure it out as I went.

The door to the throne room slammed open, forcing me to turn toward it along with Gorrin. For the most part, people had been exceedingly careful around me, as if I might smite them for a single step out of line. There were only a few who would dare to enter a room

I was in like that, and those were mostly the men I was sleeping with.

I froze when I spotted who it was.

I guess a man I used to sleep with would dare, too. Gunnar walked into the room, and the sight of him brought back that phantom pain on my neck. It took me back to everything he'd done—not just the most recent shit, either. Yazmor had filled me in on how Gunnar had even orchestrated my attack by the Sand Snakes, when they'd tortured me. He'd set me up then, had worked against me the entire time, had only gotten closer so he could drive the blade in deeper.

If I'd had a speck of feeling for him, it had disappeared with the truth.

I nearly slaughtered him on the spot, except when he continued into the room, he hauled someone with him.

Not a damned, but a spirit. The sight of them shocked me so much that it took longer than it should have to fully recognize them, to accept the truth before me.

Gunnar strode up the center of the throne room, hauling the stumbling girl with him. The blonde hair, the blue eyes, the familiar face, the scar along her throat that showed how she had died.

It all came together to mean only one thing.

Gunnar stopped just in front of the throne and pressed the same dagger he'd tried to use on me against the girl's throat. "If anyone makes a single move, I'll slit her throat again, and since this'll be her second death? Well, you'll have to say goodbye to your precious Jay."

Chapter Twenty

I wished what I saw was the result of some bad acid trip. Maybe it was all like the time I took *way* too many of those special cookies and ended up certain that the horse next door was planning to break in and steal the carrots out of my fridge.

I closed my eyes tight then opened them again, praying that I'd find everything different.

Nope. Still the same.

"Loch," Jay whispered, her voice cracking.

Dying shook up even the bravest of people.

"It'll be okay," I assured her.

"That's really up to you," Gunnar said, pressing the blade tighter against Jay's throat. "This is the dagger Hubis gave me. It isn't as good as the one you have, but it'll do the job. If it breaks the skin, it'll kill whatever they are. If it can take out a Demon Lord, I've got no doubts that it can handle one little spirit."

I met Gunnar's gaze, finding his eyes full of so much more madness than I'd ever seen before. It was like he'd finally broken, that he'd failed too many times to hold on to his sanity. I knew what he'd done before, yet somehow, him harming Jay still managed to surprise me. "You're making a very bad choice right now."

"*You* left me without options. This is all your fault. If you'd just died like you were supposed to, everything would have gone right. You keep screwing up my plans! You got in the way when I was supposed to take over the Kannor line and got me killed. You refused to give me anything but crumbs here. Even when I tried to work with Azael, when I made sure you'd be the one to face him, you survived that. Then I thought I'd *finally* gotten my break, when Hubis agreed to my terms and told me I could kill you, but no. You somehow twisted that to your advantage."

"That has nothing to do with Jay."

"Of course it does. This all started because you thought she was special, because you wanted to save her. Now that I'm on the chopping block—and don't even try to lie and pretend like you or your fuck buddies weren't going to come after me—I figure she's about the only bargaining chip I have left."

Through the door, Hale, Tyrus and Yazmor rushed in, their serious expressions screaming that they knew something was wrong.

Myers must have seen Gunnar and contacted them.

The backup made me feel slightly less frantic. It did the opposite for Gunnar, who twisted and backed away, so only the wall was behind him, and no one could flank him. He shifted the blade to draw attention to it. "Come any closer and she's gone."

Everyone froze, and I gestured for them to back away. I could kill Gunnar where he stood with ease, but with that blade pressed so tightly against Jay's throat, I couldn't guarantee that he couldn't nick her, first, and if that was all it took to kill her?

Unacceptable.

"You've got my attention. What do you want?"

He peered around, his eyes wild and dangerous. "I want what I've *always* wanted. I want to rule. I've earned it—I deserve it. That power you have? You shouldn't have it at all! You aren't strong enough to be in charge, to make those choices. You have to give it to me."

I could feel the desire from the others to banter back, probably to tell him to go fuck himself or to threaten him with some creative and violent retribution. However, they remained silent, thankfully.

We didn't need to push him any further. Who knew what he'd do...

So instead, I softened my voice. Being calm and reassuring wasn't exactly in my bag of tricks, but for Jay's sake, I could give it a try. "Okay, let's discuss this. What do you think is going to happen here?"

"You give me the power you have, I let Jay here go to the Plains and everyone is happy."

"That isn't possible," Gorrin interrupted. "The power Loch has cannot just be given away. Hubis could only because he was already planning to pass on. The damage that would occur from that is too great—she would never survive it."

"So?" Gunnar's response came out in a growl, the malice inside of it shocking. Sure, I'd accepted that he didn't give a fuck about me, but I hadn't ever thought he'd hate me like this. "She was ready to give up her life for you all—I'm pretty sure she'll be happy to do it now for Jay."

"And how do I know you won't just hurt her afterward?" I asked. "If you get all this power, you could do whatever you want. It wouldn't *just* be Jay in danger then—it'd be everyone and everything."

Gunnar pressed his lips together into a thin line. Had he not thought about that at all? Even for Gunnar, that was short-sighted. Except, he shook his head like he was clearing away the unwelcome thought. "It doesn't matter. You'll have to trust me because you don't have another choice. I know you, Loch. I've known you for a long time. You might fool these other idiots into thinking you're some tough bitch, that you've got a handle on shit, but I know the real you. You are terrified of being in charge, so you'll happily hand that over to save Jay."

I hated how right he was. I hated that he knew me, that he saw through all the masks I wore and knew how afraid I was of my new power and responsibility.

"Don't do it," Jay said. "Not for me. If he gets that power, he'll go after my dad and my brother. He'll hurt so many other people. My life isn't worth that."

"I'm not going to let anything happen to you." I had no idea how I was going to do that, but it didn't matter. I couldn't accept the idea of losing her.

Jay was like my moral compass, which had been cracked and broken for a long fucking time. Seeing her and protecting her was like caring for a part of me that had withered and atrophied for so long. Watching her live the life I couldn't mattered to me.

Gunnar swung his gaze around, a tremble to his hand as if he had just realized what a last stand this really was. Either he succeeded and I gave him what he wanted, or he wasn't walking out of this room. It made him even more dangerous than usual—he had nothing to lose.

"Is this really who you want to be?" I asked Gunnar. "A man who murdered an innocent girl? Who kidnaps a child? Who sets up the torture and murders a woman he once loved? Is *that* who you are?"

"Don't you talk to me like that," Gunnar snapped back. "Don't act like you're better than me! I've seen you steal, Loch. I've seen you hurt others, and I've seen you sell your ass to others for whatever you wanted or needed. I've seen you do so many terrible things. You and me? We're the same—I'm just better at it than you are. I'm just willing to do whatever it takes to get to the finish line first. I'm done playing games. Last chance. You either give me your power or you say your goodbyes to Jay."

I drew my hands into fists, backed into a corner. All this fucking power and I could do *nothing* about this? Even if I gave him an order, he could cut her before it took effect. I couldn't just hand that sort of power to him, couldn't risk the men I loved or the world I'd worked so hard to save, all for Jay.

Especially because she might not be safe at all.

"I can't do that," I whispered. "But I'll grant you your life. I *can* do that. Let her go and you walk away. You're already a demon, so you can go between Earth, the Plains and the Chasm. You can do whatever you want, and I will promise that none of us will come after you or touch you." My offer came out in a desperate rush.

It was, by all accounts, a good fucking deal for him. He'd done more than enough to deserve death—a horrible one if Hale, Tyrus, Yazmor or Gorrin got ahold of him first—so offering him the chance to live was something he should thank his lucky stars for.

His expression said he didn't agree. "That's just table scraps. I've lived my life in the shadows of others, climbing the world through sheer hard work and blood and sweat. You think I could be happy to live like some useless, forgotten thing? Fuck you, Loch. Fuck you and your bullshit offer and everything else. I might die here, but you know what makes me laugh? You'll have to keep living for fucking *ever* and you'll have to remember all that time that her death is on *your* head."

I rushed forward, my body moving so fast that I doubted anyone could see me. Maybe it was fast enough? Maybe I could knock him away from her?

I swiped my arm, striking him hard in the chest, flinging him away so he struck the far wall. If we were anywhere else, I would have been shocked by my own strength, by the reminder of how powerful I was, but I had bigger things to worry about.

Gunnar hit the floor, and his crushed, twisted body told me he wouldn't survive. Even if I thought he might, Yazmor grasped his chin and yanked, separating Gunnar's head from the rest of his body with a far-too-satisfying crack.

Jay collapsed, her knees giving out, and I cradled her body to soften the fall. I peered at her face, hoping it was just shock, that this was nothing more than surprise that had gotten her.

A tiny trail of blood that streamed from a scratch on her throat proved that wrong.

"Jay…" I whispered, staring at her, feeling that old helplessness as her face grew pale.

I watched her life slipping away, her eyes dimming, her body going lax.

Wetness tracked down my cheeks. I'd worked so hard, given up so much, all spurred by this girl. All because I'd wanted to protect her, to give her a future, and at the end, when it seemed like I'd gotten all I wanted, I lost her.

"How can I save her?" I asked, unwilling to turn my face away, to pull my gaze from her for even a moment.

"You can't…" Yazmor said, crouching beside me with Gunnar's dagger in hand. "There is no power that can fix a wound from this."

"Gorrin survived a dagger like this."

"Because you hadn't wanted to kill him, and he was both a Demon Lord and an angel. Gunnar wanted to kill Jay, and she's only a human spirit."

"No, I don't accept that." I shook my head. "I'm *God*. I'm supposed to have unlimited power, the ability to do anything." I focused and poured power into Jay, to heal the wound, to stop the bleeding and the way she seemed nearly out of reach.

A hand rested on my shoulder, and Gorrin's voice came out soft. "It isn't working. There are things even God can't do. This world has rules, and you must abide by them. It doesn't matter how much power you push into her, you cannot heal that wound." His words were harsh truths that I didn't want to hear, and him using his gentle voice didn't truly soften the blow at all.

I shrugged, knocking his hand away. "No. I don't accept that. What is the point in doing any of this if I can't even protect the things that matter to me? What is the purpose of this fucking world if the good things in it can be so easily snatched away? I haven't given in to anything else in my whole fucking life, and I sure as hell won't start here."

I took a breath so deep, my lungs ached, before closing my eyes and throwing myself into my powers—all of them. The ones I'd gotten from Gorrin as a Demon Lord, the ones I'd gotten from Hubis. Whereas I'd hidden from them before, too afraid to truly do anything, I couldn't do that anymore.

I reached out, through the energies that swirled around us, that formed the world to its very core. *There.* Almost too far away, I felt Jay's essence.

It had grown so distant, going somewhere I knew I couldn't follow, but fuck it. Following rules was for suckers. I grasped her soul, the part of her that existed outside of the world, and I held it tight.

It pulled, like something on the other side yanked her, but I didn't give up.

The room shook around us so violently the Lords only just barely remained on their feet.

It didn't matter, though. I held Jay, my hand around her wrist, clutching her. She looked at me, us somehow both there in the room but also somewhere else, as if we existed in both places at once.

"What are you doing?" she asked.

"I'm not going to let you go," I swore to her. "I told you I'd protect you and I'm damn well going to."

"You are tearing apart this world," Tyrus shouted, his voice barely audible over a thundering crack as the world shook.

I don't care! I couldn't seem to answer back, all my focus on this moment, on holding on to Jay despite the way some force drew her to somewhere I couldn't follow.

I'd promised her that I'd protect her. I hadn't made many promises in my life, and certainly none that I'd cared about keeping—none but this one.

I could almost hear Hubis laughing at me, the sound feeling so real I wondered if it really was him from the other side.

"You are going to pull reality apart," Yazmor said, his voice somehow quieter and closer than Tyrus, as if he could speak to me directly despite the noise surrounding us.

"Souls move on after their second death, going to whatever is next," Gorrin pressed. "You cannot change that basic fact of this world."

"Then I'll change the whole world," I responded, gripping Jay tighter, refusing to let go, to give an inch. "If *this* version requires things like this, if this version means someone innocent like Jay dies and disappears, is it even worth saving? Why not start over?"

That laughter echoed louder, and Hubis' words came back to me.

Everything quieted for a moment, as if time had stopped between the ticking of the seconds.

"You can't do this." Jay stood before me, my fingers wrapped around her wrist, but she didn't look frightened as she had before.

"I'm not going to lose you," I argued, squeezing hard. "I don't care what else happens, I'm not going to let this fucking world win this one. I can't."

Jay shook her head, laughing softly. "You have to let me go. This isn't you. You know better than to risk everything for just one person."

"You're not just one person," I admitted. "If I can't even save you, why did I do any of this? What's the point of being God if I can't protect even one person? Don't ask me to let go."

Jay set her hand on top of mine and squeezed gently. "You didn't fail. You gave me more time with those I care about, helped me see my own worth. I can't stand the idea of you breaking your own rules, of you making others suffer just for me. I don't want that. I'm not afraid."

I swallowed hard, then whispered back to her, "But I am. I'm afraid that without you in the world, I can't even think I can do this. If I lose you, it's proof that I'm damned right from the start."

Jay sighed softly, though it held fondness. "There is an *entire* world out there you're responsible for now. A world you need to watch over and take care of."

"But this world is broken."

"The universe is always broken. People are broken. Nothing and no one is perfect. I can glimpse beyond the veil, to whatever is next. It's calling to me, helping me to understand. It's the universe, Loch, what made all of this. Do you know why the world gets remade? Because each person thinks they can do it better, that they can perfect it, but you can't do that when you start with something flawed. You can't shape something imperfect into something perfect."

Again, Hubis came back to me, his words, his mistakes, his arrogance. I thought about him sitting there with Kylie, how she'd lost so much even if he'd done it all for her.

Hale. Tyrus. Yazmor. Gorrin. Their faces flashed through my mind. Somewhere else, back where my body was, I *felt* their hands on me, as if they tried to hold me together as well. Even now, they didn't abandon me, following me even if I wanted to destroy everything.

They could have killed me, could have stopped me, but they didn't. They were the same steady presence they'd been in my life since I'd met them, willing to trust me.

Hubis said that if I ever understood, I'd become just like him. Gunnar had said the same. I'd fought so hard because I'd believed people weren't good or bad, that we were nothing but a selection of choices, and here mine was before me.

Destroy everything out of ego and fear and selfishness, or risk the unknown and trust that I could survive whatever this fucked-up world threw at me.

"You'll be fine," Jay said, her expression appearing so much wiser than it had before. Then again, she'd said she already felt connected to whatever was next. She looked away, peering over her shoulder as if she saw where she was going. "And you know what? I will too."

I nodded, words clogging my throat, making it impossible to speak. I forced, "I'm sorry," out as I released her wrist. The moment I did, she was pulled away, farther and farther until I lost sight of her.

Just as quickly, I found myself back in that room, her cold, unmoving body still in my arms. I could sense nothing from her, no sign of her spirit at all. I didn't allow this sight, though, the one of her lax face, her lifeless form, to stay with me. Instead, I tattooed that smile she'd given me when she'd said she'd be okay instead, to trust the unknown, to trust us *both* to come out the other side okay.

"Well fuck..." Hale muttered on an exhalation, as though he'd been keeping it in that whole time.

And I couldn't say I disagreed...

* * * *

I was *not* going to cry.

Sure, I'd put on my best waterproof mascara, the shit a girl wore like armor when she expected her boyfriend to break up with her, but that didn't mean I'd just give in.

I'd cried *more* than enough tears.

That was the plan, at least, until I took one look at the black marble on the ground, the name sticking out as though lit up. *Jaymie Kannor.*

I hadn't come for the service — that wasn't my place. I couldn't face her father, her brother, all those grieving family members who had no idea what had happened or why. Her service was for those who loved her, and I knew I didn't deserve to be there.

I hadn't told the Lords where I was headed — they would have insisted on tagging along. Funny that even as God, I still couldn't manage to get my way. The thought of doing this, of closing this door officially with an audience had seemed far too painful.

"There you are." The voice made me jump, and when I turned to find Charles Kannor, Jay's father, I dropped my gaze immediately.

"I can go," I offered quickly, already taking a step backward. "I don't want to interrupt."

Charles didn't bother to stop me, to grab me, but then again, I had no idea what exactly he knew. He was headed to the Chasm when he died, had sold his soul long before I'd ever known about this world, so maybe his connections had told him everything that had happened. Instead, he stopped me with his voice. "You should have come to the service."

"That was for family."

Charles offered me a strained smile, the sort of look when a person hurt but was trying to put on a brave face. "We wouldn't have a family without you. I know a lot went on that I don't know all the details about, that I will never really understand, but I also know that Jay cared about you. She looked up to you a lot. My daughter never understood how she fit into the world, but after she met you, she changed a lot. She grew up, started to trust herself. No parent should lose a child, but I can say that I'm glad you were a part of her life, no matter how short it was."

I swallowed hard, not sure how to respond to that, what to say back. 'Thank you' didn't seem nearly enough, and 'I'm sorry' was hollow.

Charles came forward and set his hand on my shoulder, squeezing in a way that felt so damned fatherly I nearly broke down. "I'd really like if you stopped by sometime. Brendon has been asking about you and Hale, and I think it would do us all some good to get together. Maybe dinner?"

I nodded, blinking away the tears that had gathered in the corners of my eyes. "Yeah, I will."

He squeezed once more, then walked away, headed toward a large town car parked a way down the road. Had he been waiting here for me?

It was a strange feeling that simmered inside me, something warm and foreign for me. Was this what a family felt like?

I pushed it away and turned back toward the gravestone, flowers clutched in my hands. I had no idea what to say. Even after the week since she'd been gone, since I'd let go of her, when I hadn't known what to say, I hadn't come up with anything.

Nothing I could say felt like enough.

I couldn't bring myself to set down the flowers, either. That seemed like the end, like something final, so instead my knuckles ached as I held the stems of the flowers.

Someone stepped past me, and nothing but a black suit caught my attention at first.

Tyrus. He crouched down and set a flower on the gravestone, then ran his fingers across the tombstone. He said nothing but rose and stood beside me.

Another black outfit, another person, this one Gorrin. He repeated Tyrus' action, then took a spot on my other side. I'd never seen him dressed like this, but it suited him.

It no longer surprised me when a flash of violet hair passed me, though the fitted black suit still managed to. Yazmor didn't carry a rose as the others did, instead setting a black and red flower I'd never seen before. It was lovely in an ethereal way, like something magical that didn't fit here. It reminded me of him, making me suspect it was a replica of something from his world. After placing it with the others, he turned and gave me a sweet smile and stood along with the rest of us.

I tried to steel myself, but nothing I could do would make the sight of Hale in a suit any less jarring. The fact he'd worn an actual collared shirt under the jacket was even more shocking. Still, no matter if I never planned to admit it, he looked good in a suit. His tattoos peeked out at his throat, his knuckles, but he'd put himself together so well that only the wild glint in his eyes was the same as before.

He placed a pink rose on the grave, remaining crouched longer than the others had.

Where the others had taken only a few moments, Hale remained there, his fingers on the black marble.

Then again, Hale had known Jay better. He'd come with me to visit her and her brother, had interacted with them. According to Charles, he'd even visited with Brendon since... My mind struggled to even admit Jay was gone.

Hale remained still for what felt like forever before rising and taking his place with the rest of us. We stood there, silent, each seemingly in their own world.

"I miss her," I whispered. "She was braver than most, and she never really saw that in herself. She was willing to sell her soul for her brother, she never ran from any of us, never feared us, and in the end, she was willing to sacrifice herself for everyone else. She didn't even hesitate. Fuck, she was more worried about me not feeling bad about it than about herself."

I went forward and dropped to my knees, a position I often said I'd never take. I'd often sworn to those who tried to put me here that I'd fight it, that I'd never willingly do it, yet here I was.

I set my flowers down with the others. "I'm sorry that your life was cut so short. You deserved so much more than this. But thank you. You changed a lot for me, taught me about myself, about what mattered. Before you, I let life just pass me by. I tried to stay out of things, to not interfere, to not rock the boat too much. *You* taught me that there are things worth standing up for, that the world was worth changing and fighting for. I couldn't ever really explain how much that meant to me, but I can only hope you know that, wherever you are."

A calming warmth filled me, something strange and familiar. It was impossible as far as I knew, but it *felt* like she was there, so similar to when I'd let her go, when she told me that we would both be okay. Was this her? Maybe, wherever she was, she wasn't totally gone? I recalled that laughter from Hubis I'd felt, so maybe people who moved on weren't as gone as we'd always assumed.

I took that warmth as a sign, like she was telling me it was okay to let go. A single wet spot appeared on her tombstone, and for a moment I thought it had started to rain. When a second joined the first, I realized that they were my tears.

I took a deep breath, then said what I'd fought myself from saying, the one phrase I really didn't want to utter. "Goodbye."

My legs wobbled when I stood, and for a moment I feared I'd fall. However, before it happened, an arm wrapped around my waist and pulled me against a large, warm side. *Gorrin.* Hale took my other hand in his, squeezing tight, while Yazmor set his hand on my shoulder and Tyrus rubbed his hand against my back. We were all pressed so close together, but for the first time in the last week—no, longer than that—I felt safe. I felt like the ground beneath me wouldn't crack and swallow me whole if I took a single step.

Why?

Because you finally know you aren't alone.

I wasn't facing the future on my own. I knew, without a shred of doubt, that I had others with me. No person was perfect, no one could do everything themselves. Trying to do so would destroy and twist a person.

It was our connections to others that gave us true strength, that kept us from falling to our worst natures.

Which was the same thought that had swirled around in my head after I'd gotten Hubis' power. So many times before people had tried to rule on their own, to run everything their way, and they'd all failed.

I had nearly fallen to that same trap, saved only because of Jay's strength.

I can't risk that again.

I pulled away from the men so I could turn and face them all. "I need you."

Yazmor lifted his eyebrow, then shrugged. "This isn't the normal place for that, but I'm game."

I hit his arm softly—I'd learned my strength was far greater than it used to be after accidentally knocking Myers against a wall when I'd hit him with a door as I'd rushed into a room. "I don't mean it like *that*. I want to break the system."

"Didn't we just go through that?" Gorrin asked. "You nearly destroyed and remade the world, and I thought you realized you didn't want that."

"I don't want to destroy anything. I want to fix the real problem, what has *always* been the real problem. No one person is meant to rule. The world is just another form of the universe, and no matter how many times we remake it, it's still made of the same. It doesn't need one person trying to steer it."

"I've never been the smartest," Hale said, "but that makes no fucking sense to me."

I laughed at Hale's willingness to admit when he had no fucking idea what I was talking about. Even with where we were, with the tense conversation, his ease helped solidify my choice.

"No one person should sit at the top of this sort of power. No one should have this much power all to themselves. It's too easy to slip, to start thinking your way is best. I nearly fell into that very trap, and I don't trust that I won't in the future. This whole world—all the worlds before—relied on this idea of a hierarchy, of people selling their souls to others and that's been the big problem. I want to stop that."

"How do you expect to do that?" Gorrin asked.

"I want to sell my soul to you." I pointed my finger at Gorrin. "And in exchange, I want you to sell yours to Hale, and him to sell his to Tyrus, and back and forth until we have no top."

Tyrus frowned, that look in his eyes I knew so well, the one that meant he was working through a complex problem. "So you want to create a loop? To cut the top off the power structure by ensuring there isn't one."

"That's right. By doing this, we remove any of our abilities to hold all the power ourselves, to be tempted to abuse that power in the future. We give that power back to the people and break this whole system. We've already connected the Plains and the Chasm, already removed any difference between those who sold their souls and those who didn't. By doing this, we break the rest of that system. Without a real head, no one will hold that power."

"Will that work?" Gorrin peered to the side, at Yazmor.

Yazmor shrugged as if we were talking about something as simple as tying down furniture in the back of a truck instead of changing the very fabric of our world. "I don't know. As far as I'm aware, no one's ever tried. Power isn't the sort of thing people usually give up, so I doubt it's ever happened before. Theoretically? By doing this, we will have *all* the power from souls split between us, and because it breaks the chain of command, selling one's soul won't matter anymore. It won't affect anything."

Which was exactly what I'd thought as well. "So, what do you say? I can't force you to do this, won't push you into it, but it's what I want."

The four men peered around at one another, because it was a risk. They were removing their own positions, changing their entire lives. They'd gain power, since I had more than any of them, but they would lose their ability to control those under them, would alter the entire way they interacted with the world.

"Fuck it, I'm in," Hale said first.

Gorrin let out a long sigh, the sort he used to do when I annoyed him. "Leave it to you to break everything I understood. Of course, you have been doing that since the day I met you, so I suppose I am used to it. I agree."

"You know me," Yazmor said with a smirk. "This is new, and at my age, new is rare. I wouldn't miss it for anything."

Tyrus ran his fingers through his hair, more uncertainty on his face than the others. Then again, he was the one most accustomed to the order of things, the one who most enjoyed his position of power. He peered at me, then offered me that rare half-smile I so cherished. "I have followed you through so much already. I won't leave you now. Let's do this."

My breath rushed out from my lungs, relief swamping me. I really hadn't been sure they'd agree so readily.

"Should we go elsewhere?" Tyrus asked, his gaze shifting over to the tombstone.

"No. Jay would have supported this. We should do it here." In fact, it almost felt like the best gift I could leave for her, better than the flowers or my inadequate words.

The process of selling one's soul was, at its core, easy. It was all about intention, about trade. I put my hand in, like some weird cheer. Hale set his on top, with Gorrin next, then Yazmor, then Tyrus.

I closed my eyes, forced to trust them. We were *all* forced to trust one another. If any of us wanted to fuck over the others, we could, since if even one didn't go all in, didn't offer their own soul up, it wouldn't work, and they'd get the benefit of the power from the others without giving anything back.

But I didn't hesitate in the least. We'd all proven that we were all in time and time again, after all we had been through.

"Now," I whispered as I did what I'd promised. The action felt rushed and crowded, and the push and pull of power nearly made me fall away, knocked down by the unprecedented action.

I twisted my arm to wrap my fingers around Hale's wrist, and the others did the same, clutching each other so the power didn't knock any of us away until it was done. Each new link settled, the power shifting from person to person, the pain bad enough a split second of my brain thought this was a bad idea.

Maybe we'd end up just frying our brains? Maybe this couldn't be done.

Anything this important is worth that risk.

While it felt like forever, it must have only lasted a few seconds before that power settled, before it stopped rebelling and fighting.

Before, the power had felt like a stagnant pond inside me, something deep and dark and full of things I couldn't see. Now? It seemed to have cleared, moving like a stream between us, from one to another, calm and gentle and peaceful.

Is this the way it was always meant to be? Maybe so long ago, people had perverted the rightful order of things, had hoarded power for themselves and poisoned it all in the process.

I blinked slowly as I looked at the other four, each with a similar surprised expression. They must have felt the change as well.

"So what now?" Gorrin asked, no one pulling away, our hands still linked.

"Chicken wings!" Yazmor answered.

"You are still so fucking weird," Hale muttered.

"Nothing will ever change that," Tyrus said. "But he isn't wrong. Chicken wings actually sound good."

"Mr. Fancy Pants is going to eat chicken wings? Talk about a fucking miracle," Hale added on.

"You are all like children," Gorrin scolded. "We change the very fabric of how our world works and you are thinking about food?" Just as he finished his statement, a loud rumble came from his stomach as if it wanted to chime in as well.

I let myself laugh, feeling as if it had been *far* too long since I had.

"All right, all right. We saved the world, we all became gods, we've earned chicken wings!"

Epilogue

Tyrus

I stretched my back as I looked over my bar, the familiarity of it reassuring. Koya stood behind the bar, serving drinks to the regulars. He created a sense of continuity for this place.

However, there wasn't as much for me to do as before. Since changing so much, the Chasm had lost some of the darkness, the danger. It was as if when those here had learned that they could get to the Plains, that they were neither damned, forgotten nor forsaken, some of the violence in them had dissipated.

We still had fights, of course, but the desire to collect souls, to climb the ladder and step upon others for strength had gone away.

It had left a sort of peace at my bar, and now even angels and spirits came in.

As proven by the white-winged woman at the bar who spoke to Koya. The woman leaned in, a smile on her lips, one that Koya returned.

Interesting.

Koya certainly deserved happiness in his life. He had devoted so many years to me, had supported me without question or failure, risking his own life more times than I could count while never stepping over a line or harming others.

The thought of potentially losing him, of him leaving the Chasm with some angel made me rub at the center of my chest, but I pushed that away. I wanted him happy, and if he found it in the Plains, I would simply plan to visit him there. It wasn't as though I didn't go often.

My job of overseeing things in the Chasm often led to me returning there, meeting with Gorrin and others to facilitate better living conditions everywhere.

Figuring out what we all should do hadn't been as difficult as I would have at first assumed.

Gorrin had been the obvious choice for taking over the Plains. He understood there better than anyone else, and given he was dealing with mostly angels and spirits, it made sense for him. They still doubted and feared most of those who came from the Chasm.

I had the best grasp of the running of the Chasm and the most connections here, which meant that job landed in my lap. It was strange to see the Chasm as a single organism now, instead of the fractured war zone it had been before. The days of struggling against the other Lords for power and position had been replaced by a sense of solidarity.

Hale had taken over Earth, ensuring no one created problems there. It suited him, as the youngest, and he seemed happy there.

Well, as happy as Hale ever seemed, at least.

As for Yazmor, he had chosen to take a backseat in terms of leadership, instead focusing on recording events and history, of gathering and keeping knowledge to ensure we never slid back to the darkness from before.

A silence in the bar, a tense moment of change made my gaze shift in that direction.

There was only one being who drew this reaction from so many.

Loch.

She had dressed up, wearing a black floor-length skirt that shimmered when the lights hit it and a long-sleeved black shirt, snug enough to show off her lovely form. Her hair, a shade of green I never thought I would like, but one I missed when I went days without seeing her, seemed even brighter when paired with the all-black outfit.

She didn't look my way, instead meeting gazes with Koya and walking to the bar.

And *just* like that, I considered removing Koya's head. The desire hit me so fast that it shamed me. I trusted Koya, knew nothing was between him and Loch beyond friendship. In fact, I appreciated their relationship, their sibling-like closeness, because she could use all the friends she could get.

However, that didn't change the spark of jealousy when she didn't even *notice* me, and instead went to speak to another man.

"Don't you look pissed?" Hale's voice from beside me made me narrow my eyes into a glare. Behaving so shamefully was bad enough on its own, but the fact that Hale witnessed it made it worse.

"I don't recall asking for your opinion."

"I don't fucking recall asking to give it to you, either." He stole the glass from my hand and downed the whiskey that filled it in a single noisy gulp. He was one of the few who would dare to treat me so casually.

And no matter how much I did not want to admit it, I had come to appreciate that ease between us.

"She makes friends so easily," he muttered.

"It is one of her benefits. Others are drawn to her because she has a good heart."

It was what had drawn me, no doubt. Loch, even if she did not see it herself, was fundamentally good, unlike me.

"How long's it been since you saw her?"

"Three days." Even I couldn't smooth my voice over that, the annoyance at her absence like a bruise that ached each time it was touched, impossible to ignore.

Hale whispered lowly, "That fucking sucks. Girl's busy, though. Splitting her time ain't exactly easy, and she's getting pulled in every direction. Everyone seems to want something from her."

"She takes on too many responsibilities, tries to shoulder too much all by herself. It runs her ragged."

"I've said the same but our girl ain't the type to listen." Hale took the glass that a waitress dropped off for me—she had noticed my empty glass, no doubt. He drank that one with the same method he'd use the first, which was a travesty given just how good a whiskey it was. It should have been savored slowly, enjoyed, but Hale wasn't the sort of man to understand that. "Been four days since I caught a glimpse of her," he admitted, a pout in his voice.

"She clearly came to speak with Koya. When their discussion is over, we could tempt her to join us upstairs," I offered.

"Tempt?" Hale snorted softly. "I'm more of a 'throw her over my shoulder then fuck her silly until I ain't so annoyed about missing her anymore' type of person."

"You have still failed to learn any patience? What a sad state you are in." I caught his chin, rewarded when his breath stilled and his pupils grew. It reminded me that while I missed Loch, she was not all I missed.

We had all gone to deal with our own issues, to form some sense of cohesion and calm after such a large change, but a part of me feared we had lost something in the process. I had not seen Gorrin in well over a week, and I had no idea where Yazmor was. What had been a tight group had now spread out, and the space between each of us stretched out cold and deep.

"I might not have patience, but I don't recall hearing anyone complain when I'm done," Hale whispered back before he dragged his tongue along his bottom lip, the action shifting the ring there.

"So shall we capture our little demon?"

Hale's blue eyes shifted to the side, to Loch, before a line appeared between his eyebrows. He shook his head and pulled back from my touch, then took one last drink to drain the rest of the whiskey in the glass. "Nah. You ain't seen her in days. You should get some time alone."

"I don't mind," I pressed.

"It's fine." Hale rose from the table, then offered me a smirk. "And what can I say? I don't mind the idea of fucking her when she's still got your cum in her one bit."

"Pervert."

"You know it." He offered one mocking salute before disappearing, our new shared power making transporting from one place to another so much easier since we didn't require soil anymore.

Loch still leaned over the bar, having taken a seat on one of the stools, as she spoke with Koya. I had been content to wait until she noticed me, but something about my exchange with Hale made me dissatisfied with that anymore.

Instead, I abandoned my drink and my place in the corner, stalking Loch like prey. Despite her power, despite how she could easily stand against me, times like this I never failed to feel like a predator.

She didn't notice me until I grasped her shoulder, turned her in a quick jerk, and took her lips in a kiss meant to silence any objections she might have.

She kissed me back, though I got the sense it was instinct rather than thought. I was surer when, a moment later, she pressed her hands against my chest and shoved me backward.

Her glare made me want to smile, reminding me I had not grown much from a young man who liked to tease the girl he liked. "Really?"

"You came into *my* bar and yet failed to even notice me. You instead spoke to another man. I believe my reaction was rather restrained."

She let out a long sigh. "You're kidding me, right? Last I heard, you were supposed to be meeting with community leaders today."

"It was moved to tomorrow."

"Well, how was I supposed to know that?"

"You should have felt me here. I always know when you are around. The moment you enter a room, it is like an electrical shock runs through me and I can't even take my eyes off you."

"That's because you are obsessive."

I turned my gaze to Koya. "Are you finished with your discussion?"

Koya snorted softly, a smirk telling me the exchange amused him. "Only an idiot would say no. Anything else we need to talk about can wait, boss."

"Good answer."

"Wait—" Loch only got that out before I cupped her cheek and pulled her in for another kiss, taking the chance to transport us up to my room.

Loch broke the kiss and turned her head, peering around to realize what I had done. "Seriously? I was having a conversation!"

"You have been gone too long, and after what just happened, it seems to me you have forgotten about me."

Her gaze softened. "I would never."

I ignored her objection. "I believe I need to remind you who you belong to, to ensure you are just as *obsessed* with me as I am with you. My need for you is like a madness, something deep and consuming, and I plan to infect you with it as well, to drag you into it with me." I slid my fingers into her hair, gripping it tightly to keep her still before I kissed her again, pressing deeper, trying to ensure no space existed between us.

And, if Loch had ever planned to resist, she stopped there. She clung to me, pulling at my suit jacket, uncaring if she tore seams or snapped buttons so long as she got to feel my skin.

It reminded me of my fortune. After a life I was far from proud of, an existence where the accumulation of power was all I had cared about, I finally had something more. Loch was the one bright point for me, the only good thing I'd ever had.

It explained why I was so ravenous for her, why I needed her as I did. Without her, I felt that crushing loneliness I had lived with so long, that I hadn't ever even recognized before her.

"I need you," I whispered to her between the kisses, the truth I would never dare speak aloud at any other time.

Loch pulled back far enough to stare up and into my eyes, to give me that smile I so cherished. "Lucky for you, then, I need you too, and I have no plans to let you go."

"That is a deal I am more than happy to accept," I answered before lifting her against me holding, tight to her and walking the few steps to the bed.

It didn't matter if we had broken the system, if people could no longer sell their souls, because I knew without doubt that at the end of the day, I had willingly given what little of a soul I had left to Loch.

* * * *

Gorrin

I breathed the crisp air of the Plains deep into my lungs and closed my eyes.

"You look happy."

I didn't bother to even turn toward Loch when she spoke, because she had a knack for finding me no matter where I went. Of course, I hadn't gone far—only to an open space outside of the main city in the Plains. "I missed the air here," I admitted, then paused. "No, that is not quite right. The air feels different now. It was choking before, so while it was familiar, while it was home, it never felt free. Now, however, when I come here, it feels as if I have finally come home again."

Warmth pressed against my side as Loch slid her hand around my arm, leaning against me. This was one of the things I needed, one that pleased me beyond measure or explanation. She never hesitated around me, never treated me as though I were different or broken.

Instead, she treated me like a man, no different than any other. When she shivered, I spread my wing wider, shielding her from the breeze.

Loch snorted softly and cuddled in closer to me. "Isn't that useful? Well, I mean, I've found a lot of *other* uses for them, too."

I couldn't help it when my cheeks warmed at her comment, when it brought back so many precious memories, all detailed because each time I touched Loch, I tried my hardest to memorize every last part of it no matter how small or trivial. I thought about how I had dragged the white feathers over her bare skin, how I had teased her pebbled nipples until she'd cried out.

I wasn't an overly shy man, but something about Loch's aggressive side, her greedy side, made it impossible to remain calm when she brought up such things, especially with that hunger in her eyes.

Even as I reached for her, she tipped her head up, offering me her lips without reservation. I had never needed to prompt her, to force her, to even convince her. No, not Loch. She was always just as eager as I was.

So when our lips touched, when I leaned down to cross the distance between us, I held nothing back.

Neither did she.

I slid my hand to the back of her neck, pulling her against me, savoring the way her soft body molded against me. The differences between our bodies excited me, the way she was so different from me. I would have never fallen for someone like me. I was reserved, focused on goals to the exclusion of the feelings or needs of those around me.

Someone like me would have bored me, at best. I could suck the fun out of life, which was one reason Loch mattered so much to me. She was fun, and I had experienced little of that in my long life. I had never truly just sat and felt content, felt joy at my life or excitement at the future.

Loch had changed that.

She pulled her lips from mine, her eyebrows drawn toward one another in confusion. "Are you really bored already?" she asked, taking her full bottom lip between her teeth. Even with her playful tone, her true anxiety beneath shone through.

I stroked her cheek with gentle strokes, hoping to somehow explain just how much she meant to me. I wasn't the sort to know what to say, to have fancy words, to expose the parts of myself I normally hid, but for Loch, I would try. "I was just thinking of how fortunate I truly am to have you."

Her cheeks turned red, and the action made me chuckle softly. She could do the filthiest things, speak words that would shock most people, yet such an innocent statement embarrassed her?

Yet another thing I love about her.

And since she remained quiet—for once—I used that to my advantage and went on, needing to say the things I had locked away, the truth of what she meant to me. "I learned through this all how fragile life truly is, and how quickly it can be taken away. It forced me to recognize what matters to me, to take stock of what in my life I value, of what makes it worth living. For me? That is you."

"You know, this isn't the Chasm," she whispered. "You aren't supposed to torture people here."

I leaned down and placed my forehead against hers, the closeness allowing her to close her eyes. Perhaps that privacy would ease her, would let my words sink into her. "You are mine, Loch. You are the only thing that I cannot lose, that makes all the painful things in life worth suffering through. You gave me purpose when I had none, taught me that I could have a place where I connected with others, created a home for me where I could belong, where I could be accepted."

"You're being embarrassingly romantic," Loch whispered. "You're lucky no one else is here or you'd never live this down."

"I would never behave this way around others. You are the only one who has the privilege of seeing me like this, the only one I would let my guard down so fully around. Tell me you accept me — even this pathetic part of me."

She exhaled slowly, then pulled back. The loss of her warmth made my heart speed, made me worry she might reject me. No matter how long we had been together, no matter how deep I knew our connection, a part of me feared she would eventually grow tired. I could not imagine spending eternity with someone like me, so the thought of her doing so was difficult to fathom.

Except, when she lifted her lovely blue eyes to me, no speck of hesitation sat there. "I accept you. I know every part of you. I know how you throw yourself into work to the point of exhaustion, and I know you're paranoid and controlling, and I know your humor is so dry it could make jerky, and I know you're secretly amused by things I do even if you like to roll your eyes." She set her hand flat on my chest for balance and went up to her tiptoes, brushing her lips against mine in a touch so light, it wasn't truly a kiss. "I've seen you grumpy when you're hurt, and I've seen the disaster you call cooking. I know every bad habit you have, and I'm still here. I still love you. If you haven't scared me off so far, there's really nothing you could do to get rid of me, so stop worrying so much."

Her words soaked into me like a salve on the deep wounds I held, the ones that still reared their heads when I struggled to understand how I could have been this fortunate, to have found this level of happiness in my life.

"Then again," she said, a familiar, mischievous smile appearing on her lips, "I *did* stab you. So I mean, if I ever get really tired of your bull, I have options."

I snorted out a soft laugh before moving quickly enough to startle her. I pounced on her, wrapping one arm around her waist to pull her against me, my other hand going to the back of her head to ensure she did strike it on the ground. My wings slowed us so instead of slamming into the ground, we landed softly in the grass, her body beneath mine.

She slapped my arm, a glare having replaced that smirk. "You aren't supposed to manhandle God like that!"

"Aren't we all God now?"

She let out a sigh, and for a moment, I felt a thrilling reversal of roles. Normally, she was always the one causing trouble, the one pushing my buttons and making me feel as if I were playing catch up.

However, with her pinned beneath me, that exasperation on her face, I finally understood why she enjoyed being a problem so much.

"Fine, we're all God, but that doesn't mean you should manhandle me!"

I shifted, my lips drawn to the angel wing on her cheek before moving down to her throat. When I spoke, goosebumps appeared on her pale skin from my warm breath. "No? But I wish to worship you, my goddess." Her pulse raced beneath my tongue as I licked across her neck. "I plan to show you the utmost respect, the depths of my reverence for you."

"Fuck," she whispered when I latched my lips over her skin and sucked softly, increasing the pressure until I was sure to leave a mark. They didn't last long, not with the power she had, but that simply meant I had the chance to place them more often.

"I never realized you could be *this* difficult," she said, the last word drifting into a moan when I moved my fingers up her side, teasing the curve of her breast through her shirt but avoided where I knew she really wanted me to touch.

"Perhaps I learned from you," I said. "What better way to prove my devotion to a goddess than to emulate her behavior?"

She arched up against me, but even still, I didn't give her what she craved. I danced my fingertips closer and closer to her nipple, but skirted away before contact each time, rewarded with the lovely sounds of wanton frustration that fell from her. I moved my lips down her throat, then took the neckline of her shirt between my teeth. I tugged teasingly at it, then left another mark just below.

Tiny bits of pain sparked in my back, which told me she'd dug her nails into me. No matter how I joked about my worship, the exchange pleased me. While I would forever worship her, spend my eternity paying homage to her, the fact she gave back excited me. She left her own marks on me just as I had on her, and that helped prove that as much as I was hers, she was mine.

She was perhaps the first and only thing that had been mine, the only thing I would never let go.

"Stop toying with me," she snapped. "I'm not the sort of girl you should piss off."

"Having been stabbed by you before, I know that better than most."

Her smile fell at that, at the reminder, at that painful point in our past that would never fully go away. "I'm sorry for that," she whispered. "I wish I could take it back."

"I don't." I grasped her chin and forced her gaze to mine, refusing to let her get away, to avoid me for the briefest of moments. "That was the catalyst that brought us here. I would allow you to stab me a hundred more times if it meant I got this, that I could have you."

She blew out a breath as though I spoke in riddles like Yazmor. "Yeah, well, then how about I promise I won't ever stab you again?"

I shook my head and traced her bottom lip with my thumb. "No. Promise me you will never leave me. Stab me if you must—I would accept that over and over again with a smile so long as you never leave me. If I anger you, if I hurt you, if I do not live up to what you need, I will hand you a blade myself—just give me the chance to make it up to you afterward."

She blinked slowly, silent for a long minute as if those words had taken her by surprise. A smile tugged at one side of her mouth before she offered me a rare, shy smile, one that said my words had reached her. "You know, normal people don't have stabbing in their romantic declarations of love."

"But we are not normal. We did not start normal, and we will not end normal. I can think of no more apt way to express my feelings."

"I can think of one way." Loch lifted one of her eyebrows, that troublesome look reminding me that no one could tame her—not even me.

"What is it? I will do anything."

"Well..." Her voice trailed off for a moment as she moved one hand down my chest, over my stomach, in the narrow space between our bodies. She cupped my groin through my slacks, her small hand feeling impossibly good against my hard cock. "You said I could stab you, but I don't think I'd mind it at all if we reverse that."

It took longer than it should have for me to get her point, and my reaction bounced between embarrassment, disbelief at the clumsy come-on, and lust because I wanted to do *exactly* that.

Loch was so many things, and most I would have never thought I'd wanted. If I'd created my perfect mate, she would have made it nowhere on that list.

And I would have been wrong.

"Very well," I whispered before claiming her lips in a deep, passionate kiss. "Let me show you just how I worship my goddess."

This troublesome problem-maker of a woman was everything I needed, and I would never let her go.

* * * *

Hale

I felt her before I saw her, but it was always that way with Loch. When she got closer, my body turned restless, like a predator who sensed prey around and wanted to chase.

However, like a good boy, I kept my happy ass exactly where it was rather than chasing her down.

See, Tyrus, I've learned some patience.

It didn't take long before Loch walked into the large backyard, and I had to admit, the girl looked good on Earth.

Actually, she looked good everywhere, who the fuck was I kidding?

Still, seeing the actual sun shining down on her, brightening that green hair of hers, it fit. In the Chasm she looked like some dark goddess, and she seemed downright angelic in the Plains, but here? Here fit her best.

She smiled brightly when her gaze landed on me, and *fuck*, that got me. Was there anyone else in the whole damn universe who lit up like that when they saw me? I was used to fighting so hard for everything I had, and people hated me for it. They put me down, they feared me because of how I looked and how I spoke and how I had a tendency for stabbing people.

Not Loch, though. She brightened when she saw me, as if she liked me. I didn't think I'd ever get used to that.

Even if it felt strange, though, it warmed me.

Loch walked toward me, and it reminded me of just how long it'd been since I'd seen her. I'd spotted her for a moment the day before, in Tyrus' bar, but it hadn't been near enough. I hadn't gotten to touch her, to hear her, to really savor her the way I'd wanted to.

The laughter of children around said I wouldn't get to quite *enjoy* her as I wanted now, either.

Before Loch reached me, a kid ran toward her with the sort of short-sighted excitement reserved for children and drunks. If Loch were human still, the excited six-year-old would have taken her down. In fact, I nearly was off the bench and over to her in a heartbeat to intervene.

However, Loch taught me again that she didn't need to be saved when she twisted, crouched just enough to catch the kid and lifted the girl into her arms with a spin.

"Loch!" the little girl, Hazel, said with a wide smile, her front tooth missing. "You said you'd come back sooner but it's been *forever*."

"Sorry." Loch crossed the small distance to where I was, Hazel on her hip. It was rather funny, because Hazel was a big kid and Loch was a small woman, but if Loch struggled at all, she didn't show any signs. "It's been really busy."

"Are you staying for dinner?"

Loch moved her gaze to me, her eyebrow lifting. "I don't know. Am I invited?"

I smiled, having missed her snark and our banter. "I don't know. Can you make the garlic bread?"

"Ohhh, hard bargain."

"I'll help you with it!" Hazel offered, eyes bright. "I know how to make it, and I'm really good at it."

I stood, then took Hazel from Loch. "You are a little troublemaker, ain't you? Go on, the others are getting pissed that you abandoned their game." I set the girl down and ruffled her strawberry blonde hair once, then pushed at her back to get her going.

Loch watched the girl go, a strange longing in her eyes. "If anyone had told me when I first met you that you'd end up running an orphanage, I'd have said they were on crack."

"Yeah, well, to be fair I probably *was* on crack back then." I sat again and patted the spot beside me. "And besides, I'm not running it. There are people who do that—I just make sure the bills are paid and stop in sometimes."

She smirked as she took a seat beside me, "Really? Because I'm pretty sure you're sleeping here almost every night."

"No reason to have a different place. Just have to deal with the bullshit of upkeep myself."

Her snort called me a liar, but we both dropped it. The truth was that I liked to stay here, to see kids running around these halls again, to know that there was a place for these kids to keep them safe.

Especially because I'd fucking *ensure* they were safe. I hadn't had someone looking out for me at that age, had been left to try to protect others when I was just a kid myself, but now?

These kids were the safest on the whole face of the Earth.

"So, you staying for dinner?" I asked.

"How can I say no now? Hazel has a mean glare when she gets mad. Pretty sure she learned it from you."

"We practice that in the evenings. Six p.m. is pick-pocketing and seven is mean-mugging."

"So you've got all the important life skills covered, huh?" She leaned against my arm, the action so gentle it made me suspect she hadn't even thought about it.

Maybe she really had missed me as much as I'd missed her? It was strange to think, since she was so busy, since she split her time between so many places and people.

"Of course I missed you, too." Her whisper was quiet, and at my startled look, she smiled. "You're easier to read than you used to be. I'm sorry I haven't been able to come visit more. I'm so tired, and stretched so thin, but I still miss you."

"Even though you've got others?" I knew my words came out sullen and childish, but I couldn't help it.

She took my hand in hers and squeezed tightly. "Yeah. *You* are Hale, and no matter what time I spend with anyone else, they aren't you. So of course I miss you when we're apart. I'm hoping everything settles down soon, that we can spend more time together, but it feels like each time I think that'll happen, it doesn't."

She let out a sigh and leaned her head against my shoulder.

All the annoyance I'd felt dissipated in the face of her exhaustion. She had a *lot* on her plate and kicking her when she was down was just fucking mean. I might have been watching over all of Earth, but that girl had to coordinate *everything*.

"Why don't you stay for dinner, then, and take an evening off?"

She nodded, letting out a long breath as if relaxing into the quiet.

* * * *

"I feel like a fucking prison warden sometimes," I muttered after finally getting the last of the kids to bed.

Bedtime didn't normally take this long, but with Loch there, everything had been harder. Every kid wanted a tuck-in from her, wanted a story and extra water and the second we thought we had 'em all down, one would pop back up like a meerkat and get them all riled.

"And I thought herding damned was rough." Loch collapsed on the bed in my room, appearing just as winded as I felt.

"Being a Demon Lord is the only real training for a job working with kids." I sat on the edge of the bed, then twisted to look at her.

She was lovely. It hit me sometimes, as if I'd forgotten and it surprised me again just how beautiful she was.

In the past, I'd always seen women as tits or ass or anything in between those two points. Women weren't lovely — they were hot. Loch was the first I'd ever really seen differently, the first who had made my breath catch, who I saw as a person I couldn't live without.

Guess that's what love does, huh? It was like I saw her strength, saw something deeper than just her body, and it all drew me in.

I twisted to lean over her, caging in with her by putting my hand on the mattress on the other side of her.

Loch had a beast above her, trapping her, but she didn't show a fucking sign of fear. If anything, a heat burned in her eyes as if this excited her.

Then again, Loch hadn't ever needed me to gentle myself or pretend I was anything other than I was.

"I missed you," I told her. "I don't like going this long without seeing you, without touching you."

She bit her bottom lip, the action making me want to taste that spot. "I know—I missed you, too. I'll do better, I promise."

I shook my head and leaned in, brushing my lips to hers. "I ain't attacking you, not saying you're doing shit wrong. There's only so much we can do. I'll try harder, too, make sure I make it to the Chasm or wherever the fuck you are. You're more than worth the effort."

She slipped her hands up to the nape of my neck, using the leverage to pull me down toward her, to kiss me back. She didn't need to tell me anything because the kiss said it all. It screamed that she suffered as much as I did, that while so much of our lives was going well, we were making the changes that needed to be made, the personal piece of that puzzle wasn't quite straight.

I didn't know how to fix it, but I knew we would. After all we'd gone through, all we'd sacrificed for one another, we could fucking figure this out, too.

However, that was for the future. That was just part of the path we'd have to walk as we worked out the details of our relationship. I sure as fuck wouldn't waste a second of the time we *did* get together worrying about it, though.

Her gaze darted past me and toward the door, a hesitation on her cute face.

I left kisses along her jawline, amused by her reaction. "Don't worry—I locked the door and the room's soundproofed. You can be as loud as you want, and no one will bother us."

She nodded, the hesitation drifting away as she tugged at the waist of my shirt. I sat up long enough to pull the shirt off, willing to give her whatever she wanted.

She sat up—Loch hadn't ever been some passive lover, after all—and brushed her thumb over my nipple, teasing the ring there. I sucked in a breath at the sensation, at the pleasure that simmered through me.

She smirked—a sure sign she'd noticed my reaction—then she leaned in and took the ring between her teeth, tugging gently. The wet heat of her mouth, of her breath as she exhaled, all caused my nipple to tighten, to arch forward.

Before Loch, I'd always assumed I oversaw everything. I'd been fucked over too many times, hurt because others had been stronger and all too willing to use that strength against me. I still wore the scars on my back, the proof of what I'd suffered and survived, and it had taught me to bite first, to keep others from ever getting close enough to hurt me.

Until Loch.

She'd slipped beneath those fears, those defenses, and she gave me the only place in my entire life where I could just let go. I could put down that fear, drop those walls, and just be myself with her.

I groaned, the sound embarrassingly loud, when she shifted to my other nipple, her fingers moving to the one she'd abandoned, toying with the ring, tugging at it to keep me on edge. My cock ached, full and heavy and desperate.

Loch moved, slinging her leg over my lap and pushing me down so my back hit the soft mattress. She was so much smaller and lighter than I was, but she managed to move me without worry, to restrain me with her presence alone. She'd always done that, never afraid to push at me, to pull, to somehow manage to be in charge, even back when I was stronger.

"I will do better," she whispered just before she took my lips in a deep kiss, her hands pressed flat against my chest, her thumbs still teasing my nipples. She spoke in the brief moments where her lips left mine. "I'll come here more, make sure we have more time together."

I caught the nape of her neck, using my thumb to tip her face up, to make her look into my eyes. "I love you, Loch, more than any other fucking thing. I want you all the time, but you know what? I'll take whatever time you've got, and I'll be fucking thankful for it, because you're that important to me, because even a tiny fraction of you is more than I thought I could ever have, than I could ever deserve."

Her gaze softened, the sweetness there drawing me in more than anything else could have. She slid her tongue along my lip ring, shifting it as she ground her hips against me, the action rubbed her cunt against my hard cock even through our clothes.

This was the woman I loved, and no matter what challenges we might face, no matter how hard shit might get, I knew without a doubt she was worth any amount of trouble.

I was *never* letting her get away.

＊ ＊ ＊ ＊

Yazmor

I set out the coffee, shifting it on the small table out back until it was perfect. The whipped cream on top had a drizzle of white chocolate with dark chocolate shavings.

I didn't normally worry about things like this, but this was the first time Loch would be coming to my place in a very long time. I wanted everything to be perfect, to draw out one of those precious smiles of hers, to bask in that sense of home she brought everywhere with her.

She hadn't *told* me she was coming, of course, but that sense I had of her, the one that reached through every realm to let me find her, said she was nearing me.

Besides, it had been too long since I'd seen her. She'd been busy, drawn from place to place, pulled in a million directions by a million different problems, so focused on taking care of everyone else that she had barely had a moment's peace.

It meant that I wanted to give her that. Even if it wasn't for long, I wanted to offer her somewhere to take a breath and just be.

The hinges of my back door creaked, signaling her arrival. Even if I didn't work as a Demon Lord anymore, people knew better than to walk into my place at all, let alone unannounced. It meant it had to be her, even if I hadn't sensed her.

I pulled out the chair at the place I'd set up for her and offered her a smile, one that I hoped drew her in. She often told me I smiled too wide, that it appeared I had too many teeth, but I couldn't change that about myself.

Thankfully, she smiled back, which showed she'd accepted that strange part of me. To be fair, however, she'd accepted all parts of me, even those I struggled to accept.

"Déjà vu," she muttered as she picked up her cup.

"Is it?" I peered around. "I don't think you've ever seen my backyard."

"Because that's where you keep the crocodile?"

"No. They'd like you, I bet. You just haven't been by enough for me to show you."

She sighed, and it showed the cracks in her façade, the fact she tried to put on a brave face despite her obvious exhaustion. "The coffee's what gives me déjà vu. How many times have we had coffee together?"

"Over the years? Four hundred and three times, if you count anytime either of us drank coffee around one another. If you mean when we get together and both have coffee, three hundred and twenty-six." I paused, then added, "three hundred and twenty-seven after today."

"How do you remember that?"

"I remember everything important. My time with you's important, so I refused to forget a moment of it." I set my elbow on the table and rested my chin in it, staring across at her. "You don't look very good."

"That's not nice to say to girls."

I leaned across the table and ran my pointer finger over her cheek, just below her eye. "You have dark circles here. Your smile isn't as wide. If you *could* lose weight, I bet you would have."

She swatted my hand away and glared, even that expression somehow adorable. "I've just been tired.

Sorry I'm not keeping up enough on my beauty regimen for you."

I sat back, frowning as I stared at her for a moment. How was it that for as smart as she could be, she failed to understand something so simple? "You are always beautiful to me," I said, not adding any joke to my voice, nothing to allow her to misunderstand my statement.

"Not fair," she muttered. At my raised eyebrow, she explained. "You're hard enough to deal with without using corny lines like that. You're supposed to be odd and random — *not* romantic."

I laughed at her pout as I picked up my own coffee and sipped it, studying her, noting the changes. We'd all worked hard in the weeks since Hubis had left, since we'd reworked the fabric of our universe. That would take its toll on anyone.

And where I never cared before, while the strain on others would have felt like none of my concern, I did care this time. Loch was exhausted, Tyrus isolated, Hale overwhelmed and Gorrin adrift. Each time I saw any of them, they seemed further from that happy place we had found before Gunnar had thrown a chicken into the workings.

A black ball of fur jumped into Loch's lap, causing her to nearly spill her drink. She frowned down at the cat. "Is this..."

"Her name is Iris."

Loch scratched the cat behind its ear as she stared down at it, shifting as if trying to figure it out. "Did you steal her from that pharmacist?"

"I wouldn't say *steal*."

"You took her?"

"Yes."

"And she wasn't yours?"

"That is correct."

"But that isn't stealing?"

I lifted my hand and shifted it side-to-side in a *kind-of-sort-of* gesture. "It's a gray area since she wanted to come with me. Besides, he had physical therapy to deal with after something happened to his leg, and after what I saw on that screen, I don't know if that was the right home for Iris. So now she lives here."

"And the crocodiles don't eat her?"

"Of course they don't! They know friend from foe. Crocodiles are very smart creatures." I shifted to catch Loch's gaze. "And you avoided the conversation about you being exhausted."

"I avoided it because I don't know what you want me to say about it. Yes, I'm tired. I could use a week at a naked beach, just resting in the sun, but that isn't going to happen, so I'm dealing with it." She let out a long sigh as she petted Iris, and I got the sense that just stroking the cat's fur helped her to keep talking when she otherwise wouldn't have. "No, it's not just that. We worked *so* hard to save everything, and that was supposed to make it all better, right? It was supposed to fix everything."

"You know better than most people that isn't how it works. Life isn't ever perfect, no matter how much it feels like we've earned it."

"I'm not looking for perfect—just better. I keep thinking things will calm down, but they don't. I'm starting to think they won't ever. So we did all this, grew so much, came so far, and for what? So I can be just as lonely as I was before? So we all go to bed alone at night? It's not just me, either. I see it wearing on everyone. But even if I know *what's* wrong, I don't know how to fix it. We're all needed in different places—we can't just abandon that all and playhouse.

So what am I supposed to do? How am I supposed to fix this? Or am I supposed to just accept this is what life is supposed to be now?"

My heart ached at the hopelessness in Loch's voice. Even if I'd just said that life wasn't fair, that we had to accept that we didn't always get what we wanted, that suddenly felt inadequate.

She *deserved* happiness.

Don't we all?

I wasn't sure what to do, not yet, but if anyone could think outside of the box and fix this, it was me. I'd lived long enough, seen so much, so I could find a solution to this, one that would put a smile on Loch's face.

"You're up to something." Loch narrowed her eyes, suspicion all over her pretty features.

"Who, me?" I set my hand on my chest, and widened my eyes, trying to appear both surprised and offended by such an allegation. "I would *never* be up to anything. Now, you're done with your coffee, right?"

She pressed her lips together, showing no signs of letting me off the hook just yet.

I rose and held a hand out to her, bowing slightly. "Come on."

"Where?" Even as she asked, she gave me her hand, the trust something worth savoring.

"I haven't shown you all my house. You've seen the backyard now, the living room, the kitchen."

"The basement?"

"I could show you, but there aren't any crocodiles there. Mostly, though, I think I'd like to show you my bedroom."

She lifted her eyebrow. "Your bedroom?"

"Of course!"

"You have a bedroom? Like, with a bed?"

"Where else do you think I sleep?"

"I don't know. Maybe upside down like a bat?"

I pulled her against my side, wrapping my arm around her, laughing softly. While I'd laughed many times in my life, taking most things as a joke, I wasn't sure if I'd ever really enjoyed my time as I did with Loch. It was like she'd added depth to my humor, so my laughter wasn't so hollow, so empty. She made life fun and exciting and interesting, which I never thought I'd experience again.

"To be honest, I bought a bed when we got back from the Plains."

"Oh yeah?"

I leaned in and pressed a kiss to the side of her throat, enjoying the way her scent tantalized me. It reminded me of the sounds she made when I touched her, the way she gave herself fully over to me. I still didn't have the same drive others did, but that didn't change at all how much I valued those times with her, how much I enjoyed the vulnerable way she reacted, the honesty in every touch, every kiss, every caress. "I never had a need for one before, but I picked one you would like. In fact, I picked a black bedding set that will look amazing against your skin. The sheets are silk, and I've been *waiting* to see you in them."

Her cheeks flushed, the reaction beyond adorable. Even still, I waited at the doorway, wanting her to make the choice, to accept me, to *want* me. It was the thing that she gave me, at the end of the day, the priceless gift that I could never repay.

Loch turned toward me and pressed her lips to mine, taking the initiative, before curling her fingers into the fabric of my shirt. Without breaking the kiss, she stepped backward, pulling me with her into the room.

And just like that, she brought me to my knees again. She made a home for me, a place in the world for me, and it was by her side. No matter what happened, no matter what tried to tear us apart, I wouldn't allow *anything* to touch what we had.

I had lived a long time, accumulated untold power, and I would use that all to spend every day I had protecting the woman I loved.

* * * *

Loch

Talk about dragging ass.

I yawned, which seemed really fucking unfair. I was one of the rulers of the whole damn world — why was I so tired?

The reason was obvious enough from the never-ending pile of documents on my table. I'd started with a desk, but when the files became too much, I'd had Jacob drag in a table large enough to seat twenty. Each time I thought I'd made a dent in them, it never lasted.

Not that I minded it all that much. The work wasn't that bad, it was just that I felt like I lacked any real balance of work and life. I was back at Gorrin's old place in the Chasm, using that as my home and office. The bed felt lonely all by myself, though, so I usually just worked until I ended up falling asleep right here.

And the aching in my neck said I'd done the same damn thing again. I rubbed at the knots with an aggressiveness usually reserved for door-to-door missionaries who always showed up when I was masturbating.

"There you are!" Yazmor came into my office, a skip in his step that told me he'd done something that made him proud.

Anything that made Yazmor proud should make everyone else *very* nervous.

Still, even with that grin, even knowing I probably had one hell of a headache coming my way soon, I couldn't stop the rush at seeing him. It had been... I sighed when I couldn't even remember how many days it had been since I'd seen him.

Guilt gnawed at me.

Yazmor caught my chin and pressed a sweet kiss to my forehead. "Stop frowning. Come on."

"You always want to just take me places, you know that?"

"And you always have fun."

I sighed when I couldn't argue that point. He did make life more fun, and I hadn't had nearly enough of that lately. "I have work."

"You want to know the ultimate truth of the universe? You'll *always* have work. Even if you spend every second working, you'll find more to do, so it'll keep. *Trust me,* this will be worth it."

It was clear that he wouldn't give up, and I'd learned that giving into him usually made whatever nonsense he had in his head less painful for us all. Nothing in front of me was all that time sensitive, so I could take a little time away.

Yazmor pulled out my chair as I stood, the action old-world and strange from a guy who looked like a college student still living off Mommy and Daddy. He moved behind me and set a hand over my eyes.

"What are you doing?"

"It's a surprise! You can't see until it's time."

A smile tugged at my lips despite my best efforts to resist. Even if I knew how absurd Yazmor was, I couldn't help but get into the fun of it all. He was like a kid, seeing things with a magic that only the young and innocent usually had.

So I gave in. Even if the worries of what I needed to do, the stresses of the last few weeks all hadn't gone away, Yazmor's contagious excitement distracted me.

"Good girl," he whispered, his breath teasing my ear and heating me up. It reminded me of the last time we'd been together, when he'd shown me his black silk sheets.

His laughter was soft, but he said nothing. Still, that chuckle said he'd guessed exactly what I'd been thinking about.

When strange sounds filled the room, I furrowed my eyebrows. *What is that?* If I weren't with Yazmor, I might have worried, but the reality was that if it wasn't something he could handle, it probably wasn't something I could.

The sounds were like sparking electricity, and waves of power stroked against me, especially since after getting Hubis' power, I was far more sensitive to when others used powers. Yazmor's always felt strange, a holdover from an old world, but it comforted me, too.

When the noise stopped, he pressed me forward, guiding me without removing his hand. Even then, I trusted him not to run me into anything, to steer me safely.

Stepping through any sort of portal created a vacuum sensation inside me, a split second where it felt like I was nowhere then in two places at once. That hit me, telling me we'd stepped through a portal rather than transporting.

Odd.

There weren't many places a person would go that required portals, especially for us. Others used the main ones between the Chasm and the Plains, but we never did.

So where the fuck are we going?

"Just wait," Yazmor said, his tone playful.

I hoped he could feel me roll my eyes, even with my lids closed and his hand there. When I inhaled deeply, fresh, clean air filled my lungs. It felt like we were outside, but the world around us was eerily silent.

"Ready?" he asked, bobbing up and down behind me as if bouncing his weight from foot to foot. After I nodded, he pulled his hand away with a flourish.

And before me was...

I wasn't sure. It took a long moment for me to make sense of any of it. It was a large home, one made of adobe with sharp, modern lines and huge windows. Desert stretched out around the house, the sky a lovely mix of pinks and purples that sat against the browns of the sand and the mountains in the distance. No sun hung above us, making me pause. "Where am I?"

"Home."

I turned to face Yazmor. "Excuse me?"

Yazmor tucked his hands into the large pocket of his hoodie sweater. "You've been exhausted, right? You've been sleeping at your desk if not at one of our places, and you're running yourself into the ground trying to figure out how to balance it all. You needed a home."

"Where are we?"

"A tiny pocket. Think of it like the Path, an offshoot, a section of space that sits between Earth, the Chasm and the Plains."

"Why make this here?"

Yazmor took my hand and pulled me toward the house, then turned us around when we reached the porch. From this distance, I spotted five shimmering spaces, each with a stone arch surrounding it. We must have walked through one of them. "Those connect to the places that each of us live. Tyrus' penthouse, Gorrin's room in the Plains, your office, my house, and Hale's room in the group home."

I frowned, struggling to catch up. "Why..."

Yazmor's smile widened farther, the way it always did, but he looked so damn proud of himself. "This way we can all get together at night. We have to be apart for work, to do the things we need to do, but when we're apart too much we are...*lessened*."

I stared at him, unsure how to respond. "You did this for me?"

"Not only you. I did it for us all," Yazmor admitted, for once looking shy. "This distance hasn't been good for any of us. We all work so hard, but apart, we can't rest or recover. Finding time to meet up is hard, especially between five people. You gave me a home, Loch—you *all* did. I wanted to give you one back."

He spoke with such earnest words that I couldn't stop myself from throwing my arms around him and kissing him. It was probably too much, too fast, but I couldn't help it. The thought of him doing this for me—for us all—meant the world to me.

"You see—being in our own realm has benefits. You can't fuck on the porch if you're living in a city." Hale's words made me break the kiss, embarrassment hitting me at getting caught.

"If you hadn't said anything, we could have watched for longer," Tyrus complained as he walked out from the house along with Hale, his comment paired with that half-smirk he liked to give.

"You all are perverts," Gorrin muttered, moving past the other two to step onto the large porch with us.

"*We're* perverts?" Hale asked. "Last I checked, you were the one who likes to put it in her—"

I put my hand over Hale's mouth because *no one* needed to hear the end of that statement. A playful light in his blue eyes said he'd done it on purpose and enjoyed watching me react.

Bastard.

I let him go when I was pretty sure he wouldn't continue with the line of thought. That, of course, left me there with the four of them and more uncertainty than I would have expected.

Did they want this? It felt oddly official. *Sure,* we had a lot of history between us, and we were bound in a way that couldn't be broken anymore, but this shit felt domestic and new and scary.

Would they say no? Was this just Yazmor coming up with random shit all his own?

"She sure worries, doesn't she?" Hale said, crossing his arms.

"It's like the spectrum of emotions, one right after another," Gorrin added.

"How long do you think she will continue until she works through it all?" Tyrus asked.

Yazmor snickered softly but didn't pile on.

"Wait, are you saying you do want to live here?" I tried to keep a hold on my own hope—I knew exactly how dangerous a thing that was.

Gorrin shook his head and grasped my wrist, pulling me closer. "The chance to sleep in a bed with you every night is something I would not give up—not for anything. Yazmor often does unwise things, but this time? He got things exactly right." He cupped my chin and tipped my head up, then took a kiss that said just how much he'd missed me, how difficult the time apart had been.

When I pulled back, my breathing uneven and quick, I turned toward Hale. He was a man who liked his freedom most of all. Surely, *he* wouldn't be okay with living with the others like this.

Except, he shook his head at me, as though I'd gotten it all wrong. "You know the weirdest shit? I miss you, yeah, but I fucking miss the noise. I miss Yazmor's stupid fucking jokes, and Gorrin grumbling about cleaning and I even fucking miss Tyrus stealing shit because he wants to make sure he can stab me if he needs to."

"I thought you didn't like to be around others."

"I don't, but you all? You ain't *others*, and my life doesn't feel right anymore if it doesn't have you all in it—even these fuckers." He lifted his eyebrow, the action causing the ring there to catch the light from the sky. The look was a question, an offer, and I knew the answer. I went to him, but instead of a kiss, instead of going to my tip toes and pulling him down, I pressed my lips to the side of his neck and bit down.

I didn't do it hard enough to break the skin, but I sure as hell left a mark. When I released him, I soothed the spot with a stroke of my tongue, then pulled back. The sight of that mark filled my chest with warmth, and when I lifted my gaze to his, fire danced in his bright blue eyes. Hale didn't move, but a promise blazed there. "You are in *so* much trouble, Loch," he said in a voice so low it rumbled out like a growl. "Hope you don't expect to get any sleep, because the second I get you inside, I'm gonna show you *exactly* how much we're gonna enjoy living together again."

I gulped, suddenly unsure if I might have pushed things a little too far.

Talk about writing a check my ass can't cash.

A hand on my arm pulled me from Hale, which was probably good because otherwise, I doubted I could have broken the standoff myself. Instead, I found a hand on my chin and dark eyes staring at me.

Tyrus brushed his finger along my bottom lip, the touch melting any resolve I might have had. Suddenly, sex on the porch sounded like a great idea to me. "I had a family a long time ago, but I never truly cherished it. I never understood how important they were, not until I lost them. I will never make that mistake again, and whether it is the family I had expected, this *is* my family now."

He came closer, so close that his breath spilled on my lips, but he didn't kiss me. Instead, he spoke, his words soft. "So living here, having you all in my day-to-day life, this is what I always wanted but never realized I could have, never knew was possible for me. I will not lose it, and I will spend my life protecting it." He finally kissed me, as if that sealed his promise, like swearing on a Bible.

My knees weakened, my head spinning. While I knew we had something between us all, I hadn't allowed myself to believe we could ever make it this clear, that we would ever all accept it. Believing that would have been too dangerous, would have set me up for pain if I'd been wrong.

Yet here they were, offering me all I'd ever really wanted.

I broke the kiss because if I didn't, I knew damn well I'd be naked and breathless before I got to get out what I wanted to—what I *needed* to say.

I stepped backward to face the four of them, the men who had changed my world. I drew my hands into fists to force myself to speak. "I hated you *all* so much at first. I blamed you for my dying, for my going to the Chasm, for everything. I thought that if I hadn't met any of you, I could have lived some quiet little life." After a deep breath, I went on. "I was wrong. I never hated you—I hated me. I hated my fear, and my powerlessness, and all the things I'd done. It was easier to blame someone else than to make changes. Sometimes I wonder what would have happened if I hadn't met you, if I'd stayed ignorant of this world, of everything. I'd have stayed in that little corner, struggling and afraid and I wouldn't have learned and done and grown like I have."

I turned to stare out at the desert, at the home I had now, the safe place with the men who meant everything to me.

"You all taught me how strong I am, that I can do things I never thought possible, and that I can have good things in my life. You *are* the good things in my life. I don't think I'll ever be able to thank you for that, but I swear that I'll spend every day I have showing you what you mean to me."

The men didn't move at first, and for a moment, I worried I'd gone too far. I thought maybe I'd been too cheesy, too clingy. Had I scared them off already?

"That was too fucking cute," Hale said. "That's it, come on, I need to fuck her."

Gorrin nodded. "I must agree. You can't say things like that and expect us not to want you."

"It really is your own fault. I hope you have cleared your schedule because I do not plan to let you return to work for at least two days." Tyrus started to loosen his tie.

"Wait," Yazmor said.

"Don't listen to him," Tyrus said. "He doesn't appreciate sex enough to understand how important it is right now."

"But there's one more part of the gift." Yazmor brought his fingers to his lips and whistled loudly. "You all talked about protecting this place, but guess what? I have it handled! I have an old friend taking care of that."

"An old friend?" Hesitation hit me. Yazmor didn't *have* friends, after all, and anything he called a friend seemed like a bad idea.

Noise of running came from the back of the house, and from around the corner came…

Guardian?

My eyes widened at the sight of the spider-tentacle creature we had faced off against in the Path.

"What the fuck?" Hale asked, his mouth hanging open. "Why the hell would you bring *that* here?"

Yazmor went off the porch and crouched down, scratching Guardian on the head—or where the head would have been. "Well, after Hubis was gone, this little guy was all alone. He was a part of Hubis, acted based on his desires, but without that, he really isn't all that bad. I figured he'd be a good guard dog!"

I stared for a moment until the absurdity gave way to laughter. How could I *not* laugh when Yazmor did something so oddly sweet and outlandish at the same time?

"Well, to be fair, I doubt anyone will fuck with this place if they've got to face off against Guardian there," I admitted.

Tyrus shook his head as he pulled his tie off. "I suggest you hurry up," he called over his shoulder as he entered the house. "I will add one spank for each second you make me wait."

"Joke's on you—I'm into that!"

Gorrin snorted and followed Tyrus. "Take your time then, Loch. It's your ass, after all."

Yazmor pressed a kiss on Guardian's head then skipped past me. "I'll grab water! Hydration is important!"

Hale shook his head as he looked out at Guardian once more, then snickered. "Well, if you ever feel we aren't living up to our responsibilities, you have a tentacle monster right there, huh?"

"They were right—you are a pervert."

Hale grabbed me, tossing me over his shoulder. "Yep, sure am, and you fucking love it."

And as he carried me into the house, into the home that they'd made for us, the family we had all needed so desperately, I knew he was right.

They were all violent and dangerous and more than a little crazy and *mine*.

Whether in heaven, hell or on Earth, at the end of the day, these Lords were my whole world, and finding them was proof that I really did have the Devil's Luck.

Want to see more from this author?
Here's a taster for you to enjoy!

Black Heart Auctions:
Selling Innocence
Jayce Carter

Excerpt

Kenz

Someone once told me the only cages that hold us are the ones we make ourselves. The idiot who said that clearly hadn't ever found himself locked up in an actual cage like *this*.

People walked past, glancing in as if I were some exhibit in a zoo instead of a flesh-and-blood woman. Some paused, leering or looking on with pity, but none stopped long enough to make me think they'd help.

A gag in my mouth kept me silent, and the cuffs on my wrists hooked together behind me, which meant escape on my own didn't seem all that probable.

Nem would have found a way…

I cursed myself yet again for not being my older sister, for not being as tough or as smart as the others in my life. They would have never let themselves get abducted, but I wasn't them.

I never lived up to the people around me, did I?

Whispers drifted to me, from the faceless people who walked by. Due to the light at the far wall, shadow bathed their faces and kept me from recognizing anyone.

She's so pretty.

A little old for my taste.

Might be worth some fun if she doesn't go for too much.

I wanted to shake my head, to tell them to screw off, but instead, I only trembled. Their words hit home, reminding me of *exactly* where I was, of how I'd gotten here.

I was at some sort of auction, and I was nothing more than merchandise here. The people who walked by were customers, people who had come to buy whatever illegal goods were put up for sale.

In addition to myself, I'd spotted paintings, jewelry, even a white tiger with the prettiest black stripes I'd ever seen. This was a place where people could buy anything — including me.

I sighed and rested against the bars at the back of the cage, trying to drown out the noise that surrounded me. How had everything changed so fast? How had I ended up here when my life had been so predictable just yesterday?

I just want to go back to yesterday...

* * * *

Yesterday

"Yes, Colton, I know!" The phone rested between my ear and my shoulder as I rushed through my room.

"You say you know, but the last time I visited, you weren't using your window locks." Colton's voice held the same annoyance it usually did. It was the sound that would send most smart people running, but I'd grown up with that voice.

"You don't understand. This is *Florida*, and it gets hot and muggy! I have to crack the windows."

"We'll have a better air conditioner set up, then."

"I don't need that. I just need to open the windows at night to let the cool air in."

"And when you let in perverts along with the cool air?"

"Well, at least I'll have a man over then." I let out a little squeak of happiness when I spotted my sketchbook, tucked under a sweater. I really needed to learn to organize better, but I'd never been good at it. Now that I didn't have people hired to do the job, I'd had to recognize how bad I was at it.

"You are more than welcome to have men over," Colton said. "Of course, I hope they aren't men you care about, since dead men don't make it to second dates."

I rolled my eyes, glad he remained safely on the other side of the country so he couldn't see it.

"Don't roll your eyes."

This time I stuck my tongue out, wondering just how I had lived so long with such overprotective worriers in my life.

"Now, if you don't listen and keep the windows closed and locked, I'll have cameras put in."

"You will not," I argued for what had to have been the millionth time. Having them see how I came and left was bad enough, but the idea of them actually *watching* me every moment I was home went way too far.

A scuffle on the other side of the phone happened before a smoother voice spoke, one who could convince almost anyone to do almost anything. "Do you have a boyfriend, Kenz?"

"No, Dane, I don't."

He let out a long sigh as if relieved. "Good. Now, have you gone to the doctor recently? Aren't you due for a checkup?"

"I had a checkup two months ago!"

"Her red blood cells were low," Bray called from behind, telling me Dane had put me on speaker. "She should go back to see if the iron pills resolved it."

I nearly asked how Bray knew that but shut my mouth before I did. Bray was a tech genius. He could find *anything* if he wanted to. My medical records and test results would have proven no challenge for him.

It drew my gaze to the pill bottle on the counter, the one that had gotten delivered to me the day after my appointment, the proof that they'd been involved from that point.

"I set up an appointment for her to see her diabetic specialist," Bray added on. "It will be in three weeks."

"She won't answer our calls anymore if you do this," Rune muttered, and I could almost see him shaking his head at the others. "Leave her be."

"She's leaving her windows open!" Colten argued back. "And there have been break-ins around there. She's in a nice apartment, but that doesn't mean she should ignore her own safety."

"Enough." Nem's voice cut through the chatter of the others, and again I found myself jealous. It took only one word from my sister for her to take control, even of men like those four. The noise on the phone changed again, making me suspect she'd taken the cell and turned off speakerphone. "I'm sorry," she said softly. "You know how they are."

"Yeah, I know." I tossed my sketchbook into my bag, checking to ensure my insulin pen was safely tucked inside, then surveyed the room once more for anything else I might need. "Look, I've got to get to class."

"Okay, Kenz. Have a good day. I'll call again in a few days." Just when I'd thought I might get off easy, Nem's voice floated back through the line. "Make sure you bring your pepper spray."

I glanced at the pink pepper pray that hung beside my front door, one of the ten that I had because each time any of them visited me, they always brought more.

And it wasn't *just* the pepper spray. I also had stun guns, tasers, blades of all sorts and a 9mm in a safe in my closet. Normal people brought candles or sweet treats as gifts, but not my family. They brought weapons with them each time.

"Got it. I'll talk to you later." I hung up the call and tossed my phone into my bag with the rest of my things. At the door, I glanced at the pepper spray, then shook my head.

I didn't need it, and I refused to live in fear just because my family was paranoid. I locked the door behind me, then rushed off for school.

* * * *

I sipped my coffee, the elevator taking *forever* to get where it was headed. Then again, I had a feeling that was less about the speed of the elevator and more about just how my day had been thrown off by the call earlier.

The light over the doors lit up at floor three, and I let out a loud sigh. Of course, the time I was busy, someone else had to get on. The elevator slowed then stopped at that floor. The doors slid open, and a man got on along with me.

I had a moment of wishing I'd brought my pepper spray.

The man was tall and lean, but he had a physique I knew well. After growing up surrounded by killers and fighters, I could tell the difference between a body crafted in a gym versus one built by hard work and violence.

He had short black hair, long on the top but shaved tight on the sides and stunningly golden eyes. He said nothing as he got on but placed himself in the back corner of the elevator. Again, it set off warning bells in my head—it was something I'd seen the Quad do enough times to prevent anyone from sneaking up on them.

He didn't look my way, but I still felt as if he studied me. He wore a pair of slacks and a dark gray button-up shirt, the sleeves undone and rolled up to his forearms. He certainly didn't look like a student here.

I narrowed my eyes, wondering for a moment if Nem had lost her mind and hired a bodyguard for me. She'd threatened it enough times, but maybe she'd finally gone ahead?

If she had, she had another think coming. This man didn't come close to blending in anywhere.

The elevator shuddered to a hard stop, causing me to lose my footing. I stumbled forward, sure I would end up face first against the floor.

Before I hit the ground, however, someone strong and hard caught me. I jerked my gaze up to find the man there, having moved so quickly and silently that it startled me, reminding me that I had no idea who he was beyond identifying him as dangerous.

"Thanks," I whispered before pulling myself back together and stranding straight.

The man nodded and took a step backward.

"These elevators are always stopping." A nervous little laugh escaped me. "When I first got here, I never took the elevator because it scared me, but now? I guess dying in a fiery crash is better than walking up all those flights of stairs."

I cringed at my own words, the ones that escaped me in a rambling mess.

Worse, the man didn't even *try* to respond. He turned his golden eyes to me, as if to acknowledge that he'd heard me, but he said nothing back.

I pressed my lips together instead of saying anything else and digging myself any deeper. Thankfully, the elevator shuddered to life again and started its crawl toward my floor. When it reached there, I hurried off with one more soft *thanks* to the mystery man before I escaped the humiliation.

Attendants packed the room by the time I arrived, but at least all the people meant I didn't have to worry about anyone noticing how late I'd gotten there.

Of course, the full room confused me. The art department at my college hosted many artist meet-and-greets like this. They said that speaking to working artists was the best way to learn and gather information, so they'd host such events a few times a month. My professors always offered extra credit to go, and I sure needed that, so I always came.

However, it was usually just a few people and one artist questioning their decisions in life as they spoke to a mostly empty room.

This time, though, we had standing room only.

"Ms. Fox." Grisham Oreando, my student-advisor, said as he walked up to me.

"It's still weird that you call me that while not letting me call you Mr. Oreando," I pointed out and took a sip of my coffee.

"I dislike that name. It feels too distant. However, it's a matter of basic manners to call a girl by her last name." He offered me a familiar smile, the one that made us almost feel like friends rather than him just being my advisor.

"Why's it so busy? Did Professor Calling offer extra credit or something?" She had made her lectures nearly impossible to pass, and she rarely offered extra credit. It was the only reason I could think that so many students would show, especially because I swore I spotted a few who never bothered coming to classes.

"You didn't hear? Vance Moore is here."

I twisted to cast a look of pure disbelief toward him. "Vance Moore? Are you kidding?"

"I am not. He rarely does these things, but I hear he was in town and contacted the school at the last minute to see if they might want him to speak."

"I guess that explains all the girls here. They probably just want to get a glimpse of that playboy. I mean, is there a model he hasn't bedded?"

Grisham chuckled softly. "I don't disagree. However, if you want your extra credit, you should go sign in officially."

"Fine," I muttered. "I'll go sign in then leave before I end up squished by the hordes of girls." I offered a wave to Grisham before heading toward the back, where the table with the sign-in sheet sat. I didn't expect to learn anything from some playboy artist who cared more about getting his paintbrush wet than actually drawing, but the day would be a waste if I didn't at least sign in.

I set my coffee down beside the clipboard and exchanged it for a pen on a chain connected to the clipboard. Once I'd scrawled my name there and checked the professors whose classes I was taking, I picked my cup back up again and turned.

Only to find a wide chest before me, so close that I nearly ran right into him. I jerked backward, avoiding touching him, but I didn't come out unscathed. The lid to my drink popped off and coffee spilled over the rim.

I hissed as the hot liquid touched my hand. More splashed onto my shirt, but that had more time to cool.

"Sorry," the man muttered in a clipped tone as though *I'd* been at fault, then turned and walked off.

It left me staring at his back, glaring at the idiot. He'd stood close enough to me that he could have played the part of a train molester, but he acted as if it had been *my* fault?

He was tall and broad, with dark, neatly cut hair, which was the extent of what I could identify from the back. *Well, he has a nice ass, too.*

I grabbed a napkin and patted it against my shirt — not that it helped. It was like trying to soak up ocean waves with a handkerchief.

"Are you okay?" The masculine voice was almost lyrical. It sounded far too pretty for someone male and drew me to turn.

The face that stared back at me made me freeze in place.

Why was it that seeing celebrities in person felt so weird? I'd seen Vance Moore on TV plenty of times, in magazines and on internet sites. I could pick him out of a lineup with ease.

However, having him staring down at me with those familiar bright blue eyes rooted my feet in place, making me suddenly understand why so many women had come.

He pulled his lips into a smile, one that hinted at mischief. It reminded me that he'd asked if I was okay, and I had entirely missed that.

"Yeah," I said, rushing the answer out as if to cover up my previous distraction. "No use in crying over spilled coffee, huh?"

His gaze dropped down my front as he lifted one of his blond eyebrows. He lowered his voice so it didn't carry. "You know, you should consider changing."

At that, I finally looked down to realize that, yeah, the coffee had managed to turn my previously cute white shirt entirely see through. It showed off the lace bra I had on, like the world's worst wet T-shirt contest. "Just great," I muttered, wishing I'd brought a jacket or something.

Vance slid off his jacket and draped it over my shoulders, the action smooth enough to tell me he'd done it plenty of times before. "Come on. I always bring some extra items when I'm speaking. They gave me a ready room just down the hallway."

"No, it's fine." I tried to remove the coat, afraid to get it dirty. A man as rich as Vance no doubt had clothing worth a small fortune. I didn't want to risk ruining the nice coat. "I'll just go back to my apartment."

"I insist." Vance placed his arm around me to halt my objections and guided me back, toward the exit at the far end of the room. "I couldn't in good conscious let a girl wander around with her shirt see-through. If someone attacked you, I'd never forgive myself. Please?"

It was the please that got me. No one asked me anything in my life. Instead, people dictated to me, told me where I would go, what I would do. Sure, he was being pushy, but the please made it impossible to resist.

"Fine," I muttered, giving in. I'd just have to keep my wits about me, because Vance was the exact sort of man I didn't need interfering my life.

* * * *

"Here." Vance dug a shirt out of a black rolling suitcase. The cotton was so soft in my hands that I struggled to not rub my cheek against it when he tossed it to me.

"I really can't take this.". The idea of being indebted to anyone didn't sit well, but the thought of getting any closer to Vance was beyond a bad idea. A relationship with anyone wasn't smart for me, but someone with as much money and fame as Vance would only end up putting me in danger.

Him, too.

Still, Vance flashed me a smile I'd seen so many times from him in interviews. There it was, the face that had made the world fall in love with him. It made my stomach shift, that old cliched feelings of butterflies I knew better than to trust. He'd used that smile, that face to get him a place in the world.

Despite the fact he hadn't released any new art in five years, as far as I knew, he'd managed to stay the It-Boy of the art world because of his charm, his money and his good looks. He wore a long-sleeve black turtleneck along with a pair of gloves that covered his hands. I thought back to the interviews I'd watched.

Did he always wear them? I couldn't recall a time when he hadn't. Maybe it was some weird artist quirk?

"I insist," he pressed. "This is just a T-shirt. It's no big deal and it's the least I can do. Come on, change. There are wipes on the table over there in case you need to clean off the coffee. Take them into the dressing room right there, and I'll keep an eye on the door since there's no lock."

My ability to say no had dwindled to nothing, so, defeated, I grabbed the wipes and went into the dressing room at the back. It had a curtain for privacy, and I pulled that closed. Red skin showed where the coffee had hit me, and I used the wipes to clean the sticky area. Once I'd done the best job possible at that moment, I pulled on the shirt he'd handed me.

It was baggy on me, of course, but something about the soft cotton made me want to snuggle up in front of a fireplace and drink hot cocoa. It was like a piece of comfort sewn into the form of clothing. A faded image sat on the front, so old that I couldn't make sense of it beyond strips of colors.

Was this shirt important to him? If so, why would he let me use it? If it wasn't, why would he have had it for so long?

Or maybe it was one of those things that was made to appear old while actually just being trendy.

I bundled my old shirt and stepped out, finding Vance there with a sketchbook open and in his arm. He seemed fully focused on whatever he held, a seriousness in his expression I hadn't seen from him before.

It drew me in, made my feet pause as I just watched.

At least, it did until I realized that he didn't hold just any sketchbook. That was *my* sketchbook.

"Hey!" I rushed over to snatch the book away, indignation swelling inside my chest at the fact he would go into my bag and take my private things.

Vance didn't hand the book back, instead twisting and holding it out of my reach. "You're not bad," he said, his tone different from it had been before.

"Give that back! It's not yours."

"What year are you?" He flipped through my book, effortlessly avoiding my attempts to swipe it back each time I tried.

"First year." I crossed my arms, giving up. I wasn't getting that back until he decided. Trying to fight him over it wouldn't get me what I wanted, so why try? I'd only end up looking foolish.

"So you're smart? Good to know. Dumb, vapid girls are fun for a while, but they get boring fast." He shut the book, then handed it over. "You have nice lines, but make sure you focus on your perspective. You forward fill your pictures too much and ignore the background—it's a pretty common shortcoming of newer artists."

I stormed over to my bag, then shoved my book back inside with enough force that a tiny ripping sound suggested I'd torn the lining. *Just great.* "I didn't ask you for your opinion."

"Smart people accept good advice whether it's asked for or not." He smirked, his expression losing the luster it had before. Out there, he'd played the part of gentleman, but here?

He reminded me of a lion, lazy and arrogant and so sure of his own superiority. His blond hair appeared more yellow because of the florescent lights, and his blue eyes were almost shockingly bright. A five-o'clock shadow covered his cheeks, the presence of it enough to make him look a little less boyish than he would otherwise. One of his eyebrows was slightly higher than the other, as though he always had that one cocked up just a bit.

"Polite people don't go through another's things."

"Polite?" Vance waved that off as though unimportant. "Politeness is something for boring people. It's a set of rules I have no intention of following—and I'd suggest you do the same. So, I've given you advice and my favorite shirt. I think that earns me your name at least, doesn't it?"

I gave him the sort of look I'd learned from Rune, one meant to encourage him in no uncertain terms to back the hell off. I'd never really mastered the look, but I could only hope it gave him some pause. "That feels like another one of those politeness things, and since you don't believe in them, I think I'll follow your lead. I'll have the shirt cleaned and left with the receptionist for the art department tomorrow."

"No need."

"I thought you said it was your favorite?"

"It is, but why don't you keep it until I come get it back from you?"

"I don't plan to see you again."

"We'll see," Vance said with a laugh, the sound far too confident for my liking.

Instead of arguing any more—it didn't seem that would get me anywhere—I left the room, slamming the door behind me.

This day was just getting weirder and weirder, wasn't it?

About the Author

Jayce Carter lives in Southern California with her husband and two spawns. She originally wanted to take over the world but realized that would require wearing pants. This led her to choosing writing, a completely pants-free occupation. She has a fear of heights yet rock climbs for fun and enjoys making up excuses for not going out and socializing.

Jayce loves to hear from readers. You can find her contact information, website details and author profile page at https://www.totallybound.com

Home of Erotic Romance

Sign up for our newsletter and find out about all our romance book releases, eBook sales and promotions, sneak peeks and FREE romance books!

www.ingramcontent.com/pod-product-compliance
Lightning Source LLC
Chambersburg PA
CBHW022145010726
47493CB00002B/346

9 7 8 1 8 0 2 5 0 5 5 6 6